BRINKS IN TIME:

A MAGE'S ODYSSEY

TOM ROGAL

1

ACKNOWLEDGMENTS

One thing I have learned as an author, is that it takes more than oneself to not only write a book, but to also get it published, self-published or conventionally. Although writing is very much an individual sport, it was with those closest to me that I can say are the reason that I kept it going, even in moments when things got tough. And believe me, during the publishing of this book, things got very rough. *A Mage's Odyssey* is one of my favorite stories of the series, so I am thrilled to present this next story in the Brinks in Time Saga. I wanted to thank all my friends and family for all the support and patience while finishing this book. For me, they are the true heroes of my story. Once again, thanks to Indie Designz for working on the cover art. Simply amazing work! Thanks to Therese Arkenberg for copy editing my work. Also, thanks to John Rogal for drawing the Order of Battle in Appendix E.

BRINKS IN TIME
TIMELINE

1 BU

THE LEGEND OF VALENDRI'S RELIC

1 AU

THE UNIFICATION
A MAGE'S ODYSSEY

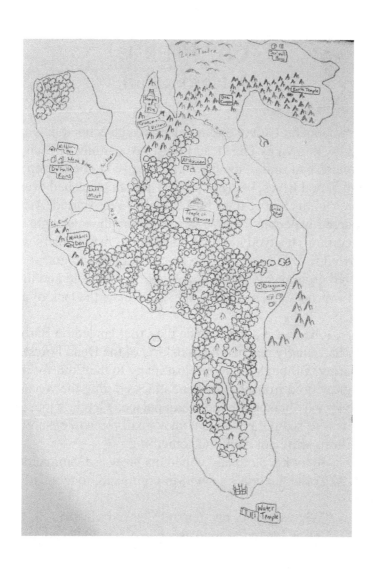

DRAGONIA

CHAPTER 1
A Hero's Fall

General Gelvia Sudin's deep cough echoed in what was now known as The Dead Forest. According to what Thamalos had said in the briefing, this used to be the territory of the Wood Elves, beings that very few humans had ever seen. Months before the Third Elf-Ettui War started, Arionn prepared his people for evacuation, seeing the onslaught that was coming. It saved not only his clan but many others who followed suit. Years later, the beautiful trees and grass-covered ground stood bare. Now, the air was cold and the wind was heavy. He did, though, appreciate the lack of any Ettui.

It had been a week since they first landed on Barbata. They had finally reached the outskirts of the Dead Forest. The army, although it had not lost many to the Ettui forces, still grew tired from the constant attacks during the week since they had taken the mountain palace. Gelvia's job, in fact, was to scout the woods with a small force to ensure that the Ettuiis were not planning something.

He took a cloth and wiped his brow as Commander Marrva Triola, Gelvia's second-in-command, rode next to him.

"What say you, my general?" asked Marrva.

Gelvia looked around as a heavy wind blasted him in the face.

"I don't like this. The winds speak of great dangers."

Marrva exclaimed, "There you go listening to Elvish tales again! It's all folk lore. The wind says nothing."

Gelvia put his head down. Perhaps his commander was right. Marrva was a very intellectual man and had graduated with one of the highest grades in his class. But

Gelvia's own beliefs in Elvish lore gave him a better understanding of life. The elves were the only ones who seemed to pursue peace while the other races sought out war.

Both men had started this mission as privates. After the battle outside of the Thorii Palace and the skirmish that happened inside it, Eraddor promoted them because of their valor and competent decision-making. They were certain this would be temporary, but it was nice to see someone in charge paid attention to the actions of their men. That caused many of the soldiers to side with Eraddor, including Dakarius, who had vocally discussed his doubts against the drifter in the beginning. Gelvia knew that Dakarius was initially bitter too that Thamalos demoted him so Eraddor could take his place. Both knew what it meant to graduate from the Cordcan Academy for Officers, so for the elf leader to promote his friend was unpopular. After the battle, with Eraddor's decisions saving many lives, their entire demeanor changed. They ended up respecting the man, but that didn't mean everyone did. The deposed commanders, all chosen by Cordca's king, would never accept him as their commanding officer.

Gelvia responded, "Perhaps it is and perhaps it isn't. All I know is that we need to be careful. Something is bound to happen."

Nearly right after he said this, one of the soldiers ran up to them with surprising urgency.

"General! In the distance!"

Both gazed in the direction the soldier pointed. He was right. In the distance, a small cloud of dust flew in the air. It was so heavy that Gelvia couldn't see the cause.

Not knowing what Ettui force might be headed their way, it was better safe than sorry. He signaled to the other troops. "Prepare your weapons! Archers ready!"

Gelvia watched with fear. Something was not right here. From the looks of it, there were not many of whatever it was. In fact, it seemed like there was only one. Perhaps this, too, was a scout.

A figure appeared through the dust, a rider on a black horse, and Gelvia examined it more closely. It wore a robe with a hood covering the head. He was confident he saw a mask covering the face.

Marrva asked, "What do you think?"

Gelvia shook his head a little. "I don't know. But it must be an Ettui. Tell the men to fire when they have a clear shot. If it's a scout, it won't live long enough to report our location."

Marrva nodded and shouted the general's command. Gelvia couldn't take his eyes off this approaching figure.

Marrva returned to the general's side, "The archers are ready to fire when in range . . . sir?"

Gelvia almost didn't hear him, all his attention on whatever was traveling closer to them. There was something in one of its hands. It was white. *A surrender flag?* Gelvia couldn't believe it. There was always a chance this was a trick. He reminded himself that if this creature knew what that flag meant, then it also knew what ramifications of breaking the code. Under a flag of surrender, Gelvia would have to abide by the rules of war. He only hoped he was right about this. His knowledge of the Ettui was very limited.

"Tell the men to hold their fire."

Marrva looked at Gelvia, very confused. What was he thinking? Any Ettui scout had to be eliminated, as it could report their position. Worse, it could report where they weren't, opening an attack on an exposed flank. Nothing about this seemed right, yet their commander was telling them to hold.

Gelvia glared at Marrva. "That's an order!"

Though hesitant, Marrva still gave the order. This was not wise. If he was in command, taking the creature out would have been the first priority. When they examined the body later, they could ask questions.

The creature was almost at the human and elf scouting band. Gelvia became a little nervous at his decision. If it was an Ettui, it would be hard to trust it. Then again, what could one do to their hundred? There were no archers present, as the Dead Forest provided enough hiding spots for anything.

Marrva and the others waited in anticipation as the creature stopped in front of Gelvia. The horse was dark black and had deep red eyes; its coat seemed soaked with some liquid.

Gelvia still couldn't get a good look at the rider, as a mask covered his face, but he could see a large pointy ear vaguely under the hood. It was definitely an Ettui, that much was clear. The figure stared back at Gelvia. A long pause formed between the two.

Finally, the creature spoke in a scratchy voice that seemed to echo through the dead trees and landscape: "Levus."

From underneath the rider's cloak, it pulled out a large, yellowish envelope. The rider held it out to Gelvia, who very hesitantly accepted it. Even through his gloves, he could feel the roughness of the paper. It also had a stench that made him believe it was very old.

As he grabbed it, the creature repeated, "Levus."

The Ettui turned around and began to ride back. Gelvia's eyes followed the cloud of dust until it was out of view before returning to the letter. On the envelope, all that was written on it, crudely, was one name:

LEVUS

*   *   *   *

At the base camp of the alliance forces, Levus sat on a fallen log. He carried a book that was open to the middle, thinking hard while fiddling with his pen. One of the soldiers on the ship had shown him a journal on the journey to Barbata, telling him he planned on telling his adventures to his wife and kids after his term of service ended. He fell during the battle, never even getting to write in it once. Since then, Levus resolved to chronicle the events as they happened in his memory. The sad thing was, he never even knew the fallen man's name.

He was trying to get inspired to write today's entry. Levus looked around at the camp. He first noticed Eraddor and Dakarius standing beside a table. He assumed they were going over strategy for the next phase of attack. They would not spend much more time here. They were even prepared to leave this night if they could not make significant territorial gains in the Dead Forest. Besieging the capital turned into regrouping, finally becoming a possible retreat. The troops were losing the desire to fight. Levus felt happy not to be in Eraddor's position. The army were supposed to be within a few miles of the capital by now. They were nowhere near that.

Levus looked further to his right. There, Thamalos and Thetalis spoke together and watched the Dead Forest. He did not know what they were talking about, but he was sure he probably would not understand it. They spoke in such a strange language. When they did speak in the common tongue, they would just tell of tales and folklore.

Levus finally began to write: *Our stay here seems short. The opening attack, which surprised Thamalos and Thetalis because of its ease, was nothing more than a farce. Perhaps Thamalos was right. Perhaps the Ettuiis knew we were coming. Since then has been a struggle. Setting up garrisons was impossible.*

Levus glanced up once more. This time he noticed Tasi and Divi walking with each other, discussing something. Levus began writing again.

No two people have fascinated me more than Tasi and Divi. Tasi seems to be a good man in the short time that I have known him. But Divi has been the one that I've gotten to know very well. In fact, sometimes she is the only thing I think about. I don't know whether I should trust these feelings. What would Leeta think? I am so confused. Just now was the first time Leeta came up in my thoughts since Divi almost died facing that dragon. Was it really . . .

When Levus next looked their way, Tasi apparently was giving Divi a few last words before going into a tent. Divi faced Levus with a big smile. He returned it and went back to his journal.

For now, this will be all. I will probably not write again until our return to Fort Za.

With a small sigh, Levus slammed the book shut and turned to enter his tent.

Divi watched as he did. She was a little concerned about him. She sensed a great confusion in his mind. It was ever since the attack with the dragon, she had felt a change in Levus. It was almost like he was fighting two wars: the one on Barbata and the one controlling his feelings. Both he seemed to be losing.

11

Divi was about to enter her tent when a thunder of hooves hitting the ground echoed the camp. Eraddor and Dakarius drew their swords as they rushed toward the entrance, getting archers into key positions behind them. Eraddor was not going to take any chances while on the Ettui lands. He was not going to make the same mistakes made at the Battle of the Four Forks.

As their visitors rode hard into camp, Eraddor almost breathed a sigh of relief. Their saddles and armor bore the insignia of the Cordcan Cavalry. What troubled him was that they weren't expected to be back so soon. To keep the troops fresh, he had them go on six-hour shifts. They had to have been only a couple hours in.

Gelvia Sudin led most of his forces. Eraddor, not seeing Marvva Triola, assumed he left him on the perimeter to continue guarding it. The men in his unit continued to ride into camp while Gelvia stopped and climbed off his horse in front of Eraddor. They saluted each other.

Eraddor asked, "Is there something to report? You are back early from your post."

"Possibly, Eraddor. The Ettui know we are watching. The only one we saw came to us and gave us this envelope. It can't contain much more than a piece of paper."

General Gelvia handed Eraddor a thin, battered envelope. Eraddor didn't say anything about his current title, which the general had not used when he addressed him. Once they got back to Fort Za, he was certain he would just be plain, old Eraddor again. King Valsuvis Aldaran would never agree to his title as Legion General when they returned.

Gelvia continued, "The Ettui scout said to deliver this to Levus."

Levus' name was on the envelope as well, Eraddor saw as he examined it. It seemed normal, but he was not willing to take any chances.

12

"Thamalos! Can you come here?"

At once, the elf prince ended his conversation with Thetalis and walked over to Eraddor.

Divi now stepped fully outdoors. She wondered what was going on. When Thamalos reached Eraddor, they began to discuss something. She wished she could hear what was being said. Eraddor then handed Thamalos what appeared to be some type of paper. After a few seconds, the elf returned it to Eraddor, who, in turn, gave the envelope back to Gelvia.

Tasi, who stepped out of the tent, started saying something to Divi before he noticed her gazing forward. "This place is murder on one's skin. Everything is so dry here. And with our robes . . . Divi, are you listening?"

She barely heard Tasi's question, more interested in what Gelvia was holding as he walked past them. Who would be sending a letter to Levus here on Barbata? Gelvia disappeared into Levus' tent. Divi sent a quick glance over toward Eraddor, who was watching Dakarius plot points on the map.

"What's on your mind?"

Divi jumped as Tasi spoke. She took a deep breath as she wiped the sweat off her face. "Nothing . . . it's just nothing."

Tasi knew she wouldn't tell him what was bothering her. She was never really open with anyone about her true feelings . . . except with Levus. Tasi could feel it in her. He didn't want to believe it. Yet, to deny what he was sensing would have meant he doubted his own abilities.

"Levus! Wait! What's wrong?" asked Gelvia.

Both mages turned to Levus' tent just in time to see him running out. Divi left Tasi's side and tried to keep up with the boy's pace.

"Levus, what's wrong? What's the matter?"

13

Levus said nothing. Divi thought she could see a tear roll down his cheek as he headed to a horse. She had to find out what was bothering him, whether it was what that note said or something else.

"Levus! Where are you going?"

He jumped into the saddle and turned the horse's head toward the entrance of camp. By now, everyone was alerted to his actions. Some of the men rushed toward Levus, attempted to block him knowing something was out of place. Not used to be surrounded by so many, the horse reared, forcing the soldier to back off. A crumbled piece of paper fell out of Levus' pouch, landing on the dry ground. From Levus' tent, Gelvia ran out.

"Wait! That's my horse!"

Without answering him, Levus finally rode toward the Dead Forest.

Eraddor tried to get his attention. "Levus, what's the matter?"

The boy again replied with silence, not even looking his way as he began to ride out. Gelvia walked up to Divi and Tasi, who still were stunned. Divi's mind was full of the expression she'd seen on Levus' face: a mixture of anger, sadness, and pain. Eraddor and Thamalos soon joined them.

Eraddor asked, "General Gelvia, what happened?"

"I don't know. I gave him that envelope, he read its contents, and he just stormed out. I would have followed sooner, but he pushed his blanket near a lantern, so I tried to prevent it from catching aflame."

Thamalos asked, "What did the letter contain? Did you see it?"

Gelvia shook his head. "I tried, but he put it in his pouch right away."

Divi remembered the paper that fell from Levus' pocket. *Where is it?* There it was, still resting where it

14

landed, not even affected by the wind. She began to inch her way over to it. The closer she got, the more the commanders' words faded, replaced by fragmented voices. She couldn't understand what they were saying no matter how hard she tried.

The others watched Divi with great interest.

Tasi asked her, "What do you see?"

Divi stopped in front of the crumbled paper. She was almost afraid to see what it contained, but she had no choice. If she wanted to know what made Levus go crazy like that, she had to read it. She bent down and picked it up. As she smoothed out the paper, the voices seemed to get louder. When she completed the task, the voices stopped for some reason. Divi was very confused. The paper was blank.

Thamalos asked, "Divi, what have you found?"

Divi paid no attention. For some odd reason, she couldn't take her eyes off the page. Something was drawing her gaze, but what? What could Levus had read from this that caused him to act that way?

"*SILIANTII COLLUNAR!*"

Divi's eyes opened wide. The voice returned with such force that it nearly knocked her to the ground. Her hands began to shake as the voice spoke to her in a more common tongue.

"*Levus! Come to capital . . . or she dies!*"

Suddenly, Divi heard a female voice screaming. Even though she had only met her once, it was a voice she recognized all too well.

Leeta screamed, "*Levus! Help me!*"

The voice echoed in her mind until Divi tossed the paper back on the ground. It landed with, to her ears, a loud thud. She was breathing very heavily. How did they find Leeta? How could they know that Levus was close to her?

15

As Divi turned back to her friends, her expression alarmed them. Eraddor, as the appointed commander of the operation, walked up to her. From the corner of his eye, he saw Dakarius joining the group that watched them.

"Eraddor, do you plan on leaving Barbata?" Divi asked.

That was a topic still up for debate, and he knew she knew that. It was hard to keep some things secret when shouting was involved, especially in a cloth tent. If he had it his way, they would stay until the job was complete. Some of the others, a majority, sadly, believed they have done all they could. After many hours of long 'discussion', a compromise was made. Not one Eraddor or Thamalos liked, but they were left little choice.

"We were planning to leave if we couldn't reach Culvaii's Pond at the middle of the Dead Forest, possibly by dawn tomorrow. Thamalos says we are about a quarter of the way through them. Why?" asked Eraddor.

"Have the ships come now. The army can do no more good here. I need to get to the capital and help Levus."

Dakarius looked at Eraddor, exchanging the same confused expression. She had to be mad, trying to give orders to the both of them. Eraddor was a good man and one Dakarius started to respect, but he was too light on his close friends at times, in his opinion. Dakarius was never seen as general material, but he knew he was excellent at what he did. He was a military man. Divi was a mage, and one who didn't know magic, of all things. Why give her a say in what happened?

"Are you out of your mind? It is more than a day's journey from here!" Dakarius exclaimed. "With all the Ettuiis lurking around, you'll never make it!"

16

Divi said, "Yes, I will. That is where Levus is going. They are leading him there. My passage will be safe unless we waste time arguing here."

Eraddor began to think. He looked over toward Dakarius and then at Thamalos, who gave a slight nod. He didn't know if that meant he should agree with Divi or not. This was a decision his heart would have to make. After a minute, Eraddor took a deep breath and faced Divi.

"All right. We'll begin the retreat to the ships. I'll send an escape craft over to the capital's docks. With the mines, I cannot risk anything larger. It will arrive there at dusk tomorrow and will leave two hours later . . . with or without you. Please understand, I cannot place the men in that type of danger. Dakarius, prepare the troops. We leave."

Divi gave a small smile as she headed for the nearest horse.

Dakarius stepped in front of Eraddor as he tried to get to his tent. They stared at each other for a few seconds. He knew his second-in-command supported the original plan to stay. Beside Thamalos, he was the only one who stood up for him in the discussions. Neither man liked the compromise. He was certain Dakarius liked this decision even less. In the short time he's known him, he'd learned Dakarius was a passionate man and truly cared for the men serving under him, even the ones that died in action.

"Very well. I do this under duress, because leaving here now means those lives lost at the coast were lost for nothing."

As Dakarius stormed off to follow his orders, Eraddor put his head down. Thamalos walked over and put his hand on his shoulder.

"Worry not. This is the right thing to do. In another couple of days, the Ettui would've gone for the killing blow.

17

Our time here was not spent unwisely. I feel the answer will fall to us soon enough concerning the Ettuiis involvement."

Thamalos walked away and Eraddor closed his eyes. In his heart, he felt the elf prince was right. But he knew that Dakarius would report his actions to General Medkar once they arrived back at Fort Za. He also knew that General Medkar and King Aldaran were very close. His situation did not improve any.

Divi checked the horse's reins. She estimated that it would take at least the rest of the day and most of another to get through the Dead Forest and across the Black Plains of Arltraii to the capital's gates. As a lone mage not having to wait for troops and equipment, her journey would be faster and draw less attention to any Ettui garrisons. She would have to hurry if she wanted to find Levus and make the trip back.

"Where do you think you're going without me?"

Divi turned around to see Tasi riding another steed.

"Now is not the time to act as my protector, Tasi."

Tasi smiled and said, "You should know me better. Just accept it. I'm coming with you and that is that."

She didn't want anyone else to go. Mainly, she didn't want to put any lives at risk other than her own . . . especially because it was her heart telling her to do this. Yet, she knew that Tasi's magic would be important if the Ettui did attack.

Divi smiled at her best friend. "Let's go!"

Levus pushed his horse to a gallop as he reached the summit of another hill on the Black Plains. He knew that it would be a long ride from their camp to the capital. He would have tried to make the entire trip without stopping, but his horse needed rest and fresh water. And in truth, he saw very little of the latter. There were no lakes or ponds anywhere. A couple bridges he crossed had once gone over rivers, those they had long since dried up. The one lake he did pass held water that looked dirty and unsuitable for drinking. Living plant life was few and far between. Was this whole continent dead? What did the Ettui do to survive?

The horse slowed down to a sluggish trot. Whether he liked it or not, they were not going much further today. Probably all for the better. He was a wreck. He needed time to think. Was this really happening?

At the top of the next hill, Levus dismounted. He probably could have gotten a couple more hills out of his horse, but he didn't want to push it to its limit. He was still barely in the Black Plains, though he was taking the route by the ocean, which in maps he saw was the shortest. If he left early enough tomorrow, he suspected he would be at the capital by midday.

Levus shared what rations and water he had with the horse, though there wasn't much. He was lucky to grab even that on his way out of his hut. He'd need to find a good water source. Without one, he wasn't sure his horse would make it.

He made a small fire with the wood he found, which, given he was on the plains, was shockingly plentiful. Levus supposed the Ettui could have cut trees down from the forest and drag them north, losing many pieces along the way. It didn't matter too much to him. They were here and now. The flame was barely large enough to give any warmth, but he didn't want to risk being seen by the Ettui. He camped near the top of the hill so he could see in any direction, though the way his journey had gone so far, he wasn't even sure he needed too. He hadn't seen one Ettui. If it wasn't for a few small animals he had seen, he would have thought this place deserted.

As he nibbled on some dry rations, his mind became focused once again on the letter. No, not a letter. There was not even a word written on the page. But it was a message. And was it telling the truth? How could it? Never once when Ulcinar was in Arnis had Leeta made any moves or suggestions to show they were close. Was Ulcinar that good? Regardless of the circumstances, he needed to find out. If she was in the capital, he was her only hope.

He was so nervous that he couldn't even finish the jerky, throwing the rest of it on the ground. He had to get some sleep himself. He was driving himself crazy just thinking about this. A couple of hours. That was all he would need. When he woke up and arrived at the capital, then he would see what he was walking into: A rescue mission or a trap. *By the gods, please let it just be a trap . . .*

"Are we sure this is a safe place to rest?"

Tasi was not convinced. He didn't like the idea of the two of them alone with potential Ettui in the area. He wanted to push on even though the clouds covered the moons and stars. Divi compromised with a couple-hour stop so they could see if the sky cleared up to give them light. That way Tasi's spells to provide illumination wouldn't stand out.

"As long as we are not too far from Levus, we should be safe," Divi said.

She knew they were within ten miles from him. She could feel him. She could also feel the worry. She could understand why, knowing whose voice had spoken in that letter.

She wanted to push on so they could go together. Levus would stand more of a chance against Ulcinar with two mages at his side, even though she couldn't cast magic.

20

However, their horses could only be pushed so far. The only water around was what remained in their canteens. Thamalos told her that Mother Terra had let her waters dry up to punish the Ettui. It seemed more a punishment for them now.

Tasi asked once more, "So, what was on that letter?"

She wanted to answer him. But how would Tasi understand? He hadn't been in Arnis. He never met Leeta or knew how she and Levus felt for each other. Divi recalled the silent hatred she'd sensed from Leeta when preparing to leave Arnis with Levus. Divi wasn't doing this for her. She was doing this to protect Levus.

Her main question was, how did Ulcinar know? Was he that good at reading into people's minds? Certainly, as she discovered in Arnis, he had been feeding on hers for years, but he had never used their link to find things out. He had used it to terrify her, and he was successful. Did he have the same power she did to feel other people's emotions?

Whether or not Leeta was in the capital, she had to make sure Levus had some help. If it was a trap to force Levus to join him, Ulcinar would find out that wouldn't be as easy a task as he hoped.

"Divi? Why won't you answer?"

"Just get some rest. If I know Levus, he'll be back on the move soon. When he does, we need to be ready."

Tasi didn't like this. Divi had changed. He'd noticed it back when she first returned to Myyril. She was more impulsive☐no, that wasn't the right word. More reckless. For her, a magic-less mage who was also the future heir to the Myyrilian throne, that was a dangerous way to be. He went with her because she was going to need protecting. He took pride in being able to read people's thoughts at times, a skill he had to learn to become Divi's teacher. Yet Divi

21

found a way to block that occasionally, and now more than ever.

Even more worryingly, he suspected she was beginning to develop feelings for the human. Since Thamalos' analysis of Divi possibly being the fabled Unifier of the Lands, Tasi had tried to remain by her side. Not only to protect her from the Ettui, but also from Levus. There was something about him Tasi just didn't like, and he considered himself a good judge of character. How he was going to convince Divi was another story, one that could wait until they were back on the mainland.

Divi, meanwhile, lay down to sleep. Though she closed her eyes and tried to drift off in dreams, her senses remained too alert. She was anxious about the situation, impatient to reach Levus, and didn't want to settle down. She wanted to be sure Levus never left her telekinetic range. Just like Levus, she was battling internal questions. If Leeta was here, would she help her? She just couldn't help this feeling of jealousy. She had never felt it this strongly before and never about a boy. She didn't know if she liked these thoughts and feelings. They weren't like her.

Maybe all she needed was a little rest to make things right. In a few hours, they would be riding again, arrive at the capital, and discover it was a big farce. *I hope.*

Levus had barely slept, leaving before it was even light. The horse wasn't happy about the early wake up, but it was necessary they leave before first light. The clouds cleared up, allowing both of Gyyerlith's moons to spread their light across the landscape. This caused shadowy reflections of the dead trees that scared him plenty, but he moved forward. He had been riding all morning, encouraged a few hours ago when he saw the outline of a city. It had to be the capital. He didn't listen to many of Thamalos' history lessons, but he did recall him mentioning that there were no towns between the Dead Forest and the capital because of the Wood Elves. The reason for that, Levus never found out because he had lost interest, choosing to write in the journal.

His horse struggled up the latest hill. The northwesterly winds made it hard to travel as they were in their faces the whole time. Though he realized it could have always been a lot worse.

"Kuipoii hardallii."

Levus shook his head. Not now, voice. He had much too important business to attend to. He didn't care how he was beginning to like its empowering effect.

He still hadn't run into any Ettui along the way. After the last few days, their absence was a nice relief. He hoped after this was over that he never saw another Ettui again.

Levus finally reached the top of the largest hill, where he stopped the horse. There it was: the former elf capital of Barbata. To Levus' eyes, it resembled a deserted Tartus, remarkably similar, actually. The buildings were tall, but looked to be in poor shape. Towers stabbed like spikes into the sky, but mostly near the outskirts. They must have served some defensive purpose. The more he thought about it, the more he remembered noticing these structures in the Dead Forest, amid the trees. They must have been perfect for housing archers. He also spotted smokestacks further in, something he was used to seeing in Tartus. A huge dock jutting out into Sjvernii's Bay could be seen in the far distance, but it looked unkept. The skeletons of numerous vessels were moored next to it, partially sunken. He couldn't tell from here, but many of them looked to have fire damage.

He scanned further east. A large group of smaller rundown buildings with smoke still rising from extinguished fires were easily seen through the holes in the walls. The Ettui were here not long ago. He would have to be careful. Levus continued east until his view reached the northeastern part of the city. A large palace lay silently in the shadow of darkness.

"Come to me."

Levus couldn't take his eyes off the palace. That must be where she was . . . where Leeta was. He gripped the horse with his legs and pushed his hips forward, encouraging it to go hard down the hill. He had to get there before it was too late.

Dirt flew with every high step the horse made. The wall surrounding most of the city was forty feet high, twice as large as it had appeared from atop the hill. Yet the gates stood open. As he entered them, he slowed the horse down to a trot by pulling on the reins. The city was silent . . . a little too silent knowing that the Ettui leader never left. He was expecting the place to be littered with troops. Ettui footprints marked the dust on the ground. Something was up.

Maybe this was a trap and Leeta wasn't here. It was too late to turn back now. Levus rode through the twisting streets. He struggled to believe that the elves once lived here. Lozela was so beautiful. Had Barbata once been like it?

Levus dismounted when he reached a long bridge where a bustling river must once have flowed. On the other bank, the palace stood.

Levus untied the reins, rubbing the horse gently. He said, "Ride free. Find your way back to the camp. You have been a good companion."

The horse was hesitant to go, but strange echoes spooked it enough to canter back toward the city entrance.

Levus started walking over the dark bridge of Barbata. It made a sickening sound with every step. He looked over the edge. The bottom of the dry river, now a canyon, was very deep. He could almost imagine what it used to look like in its golden age, filled with water flowing, trees blooming . . . life.

With every step he took, he felt like he was being watched. For the whole trip he had known he was being monitored. Perhaps this was to make sure that he came alone. He was all alone, especially in this place.

"Earittii feraman"

Levus tried to silence the voice, but the deeper he got into the city, the louder it was getting. He had to keep his mind occupied on other things. Maybe that would quiet it.

Levus looked once more to the palace. He could definitely see the similarity between the architecture of Lozela and Barbata. They were just as vast in scale, many having Elvish tales on them. The main difference was the impressions seemed to exhibit much happier times. The ones in Lozela illustrated more violence and sadness. The wars fought between the Elves and the Ettui left a nasty scar on the elves of today. The doorway was huge and carved with Elvish symbols and stories. He had no idea why it would be so large, but there was no one to answer his queries. As he made his way up the steps, the palace doors slowly opened. Levus froze until they opened fully, then moved cautiously forward. He kept his hand tight on the Moonsaber's hilt.

As he went farther inside, the air grew stuffy and his labored breathing echoed. It had a tall ceiling with much of the original art still intact. Paintings of what looked to be their gods and goddesses as they were depicted taller and vividly perfect. The works were crackling, but mainly maintained their true nature. Odd, since the Ettui seemed to destroy everything else associated with their old Elven brethren.

He was getting close . . . he could feel it.

Suddenly, a soft cry reverberated in the hall. It was a woman's voice, and one he knew!

Levus yelled, "Leeta!"

He listened, trying to follow it as he went through the grand hall. He walked slowly between the large pillars holding the great structure up. The windows offered very little light from the outside. He heard her cry again! Levus started to run. He had to find her, and when he did Ulcinar was a dead man.

Divi and Tasi rode to the top of the high hill overlooking Barbata's capital. It was a rough journey, and Divi feared the horses wouldn't make it. She was sure glad they at least had their canteens. With no water on the land, that little water they carried with them was vital to keep them and their horses quenched just enough.

Corking her canteen, Divi stared at the destroyed city. She couldn't believe how destructive the Ettui really were.

"Well, here we are," Tasi said. "Barbata."

Divi looked toward the sea in the east. "We don't have much time. The ship will be here soon."

As she said this, a loud chant was repeating behind them. Both turned around. In the distance, they could see a mass of Ettui making their way. The mages were far enough that they couldn't' be seen by this approaching group, but the gap was shrinking.

"The Ettui are closing in," Tasi said as he and Divi exchanged glances. "Look! Over there!"

He pointed to the city. A large Ettui force was making its way toward the western entrance. Their grunting and yells chilled Divi's bones. She couldn't believe it. There had to be at least two thousand Ettui soldiers coming from the west and who knows how many were behind them from the south.

"This was a trap, and we fell for it. They are converging on the city. If we don't get out of here soon . . ." continued Tasi.

"I'm not leaving here without Levus!" Divi pulled the reins of her horse. "They haven't got us yet. Let's find Levus and get out of here!"

Tasi and Divi both pushed their horses down the hill toward the open gates of Barbata.

Levus readied the unsheathed Moonsaber. He was now deep into the body of the palace. The young woman's cries grew louder with each step. Levus was impressed at how much of the palace remained intact. It was almost as if the Ettui haven't set foot in the place. All the art and tapestries were still in great condition. Age had been the only thing that touched them. It drew his eyes to a large fountain, barren and dead. Sticks were all that remained of once living foliage that surrounded the thirty-foot sculpture of two naked elves climbing up a tree. This, too, appeared to be in pristine condition.

Levus thought he could hear male and female voices coming from all around him. It wasn't Leeta's, which temporarily went silent. Were they ghosts? Perhaps they were just in his head. He still wasn't sure if he could believe all the "spirits speaking" lore that Thamalos preached back when they first met as well as in the Forbidden Forest of the Wood Elves.

The female scream pierced his ears once again. It appeared to be coming from up a set of stairs past the fountain. A row of lifeless trees, one that fell a long time ago across the path, led to them. Levus wasn't sure exactly where he was in the former Elven palace. He had a good intuition that Ulcinar would be at the top, though. He started up them, wanting to run but cautious. Part of Levus wondered why he just didn't charge up there. Ulcinar certainly had to know that he was coming. The Dark Lord seemed to have a knack for that sort of thing.

A dry cough rattled in his throat. The air was very musty now. Torchlight was all that filled the circular stone staircase. The cries sounded almost constantly now. He was very close. Levus moved with haste up the staircase, closer to his destiny.

Divi and Tasi ran past a couple of old elven statues as she searched the area. She was certain the Ettui patrolling the city didn't see them. If they had, sneaking around wouldn't have been necessary. Based off how fast they moved on Dyyros, outrunning an Ettui wasn't an option they could afford. Tasi wasn't as comfortable as she was.

She peeked around the corner. There Ettui group stayed in formation, heading away from them. There had been one close call when they first entered the city, but thankfully they were able to hide long enough for the Ettui to believe they already moved forward. It would only get more difficult the closer they came to the palace.

Divi ducked back behind the statue.

She reported, "There's only that one regiment. They didn't see us."

"This is crazy! Even if we do find Levus, it will be impossible to get to the docks. I swear, Divi, one day your childish antics are going to be the death of me."

28

She turned to face Tasi, a little offended by his comment. "What do you mean? You didn't *have* to come!"

Divi watched and waited for a chance to run to the next statue.

"That's easy for you to say. Being your teacher means that I'm responsible for what you do."

"You're not my teacher! You're my friend. Unless I decide to learn magic one day, please don't be bound by that silly Myyrilian rule. You hardly brought that up until now. What's wrong, Tasi? I've never seen you panic like this."

Divi glanced around the statue again. The Ettui regiment on the far side of the square was just passing out of view. In between two buildings, Divi could see the Great Bridge leading to the palace. She used her feelings to track Levus. Levus' emotions were so strong that it made it easy with her special power. It wasn't exact, but she could sense he was almost to the top floor of the palace. It was time to move.

Divi turned back to face her friend. "Tasi, it's time to . . . Tasi?"

Where did he go? Divi looked toward the main road. There he was, kneeling on the ground . . . in the open. Her eyes opened wide.

Using her telepathic powers, she yelled, "Tasi! What are you doing?"

"Come here, quickly!" Tasi replied in the same manner.

She made a rapid survey of the area. There were no Ettui present, much to her relief, so she ran to where Tasi was and knelt next to him.

"What is your problem? After just lecturing me☐"

"Divi, do you know what this is?"

She looked down at the item Tasi was examining. It appeared to be a blue cloth with a distinct pattern on it, though the whole design didn't fit on the scrap. Circles were partially torn, suggesting they advanced further past a central oval. It looked quite new and the cloth was still soft, so that it didn't seem to fit in an ancient place like this.

"What is it?"

"Look at the style. Notice how the little loops come out of that central one? That was part of the design that your father and I agreed on to have on the mage councilman's robes. It changes every year and these were handed out nearly six months ago. Divi, we are not the first mages to step on this soil recently."

This bit of news was disturbing. Tasi continued to examine the cloth, hoping to uncover some hidden clue as to the identity of its wearer. Who could it be? Sadly, he probably never would find the answer. Most of the old council was killed on Dyyros, most likely disposed of by Ulcinar. Sydis was the only surviving member, but when could he have gone to Barbata without anyone noticing, especially during the year? He always was either in Myyril or traveling with Neeza. This was truly a mystery Tasi would have to solve. He slowly placed the piece of robe in his pouch.

"Come on, Tasi. Let's get back in hiding before we're spotted."

As Divi said this, an arrow slammed the ground next to Tasi. Both mages fell flat from their crouched positions. They crawled behind the statue. Under its shelter, Divi got up and looked at Tasi.

"Well, so much for sneaking in."

Divi and Tasi sprinted toward the Great Bridge. More arrows whistled behind them, all harmlessly hitting the stone. Divi knew time was short. Once they found Levus, they would have to make haste to the docks. If she was correct, the ship would arrive in less than an hour. She wished Thamalos had come with. She had no idea of where to look in the palace. She could track Levus, but she didn't know the layout of the building. She'd have to figure it out quickly. They continued across the bridge as arrows whizzed past their heads.

* * * * *

Levus finally reached the top of the stairs. The air seemed to bleed with the woman's cries. He walked slowly down the hallway, trying to observe some type of caution. The torches flickered as a gust of wind entered through a small hole in the ceiling. He must have reached the highest floor.

"*You are almost there.*"

His breathing got a little easier because of the circulating air. The bones of a fallen Ettui lay on the ground, an elven sword still implanted in its skull. This must have been from that last war Thamalos mentioned where the Ettui successfully displaced the elves from this continent. He believed the elf said it happened over a thousand years ago.

"*I'm waiting . . . We're waiting.*"

"Levus!"

He shook his head. The female voice was screaming. Levus ran as hard as he could to the room it came from, surprised he had this much energy left after climbing all those steps. The door at the hall's end led to a large room. The ceiling was low compared to the rest of the rooms, only about ten feet high with a large circular hole in the middle. It was much darker too. He couldn't see past the center as no torches were lit beyond the entrance. The tiles were also laid out in a circular pattern, and the floor was tiered around a lower middle space. Symbols had been carved on each

31

individual tile. They were probably in some type of Elvish, as he didn't understand any of it.

"Levus?"

He turned his head to the left, toward a familiar voice. His worst dream became a reality.

"Leeta!"

He ran toward her. Despite the cage of chained-wrapped wood she was locked in, a large smile grew on her face. Tears of frightened joy formed in both of their eyes.

Leeta said, "I'm so glad you came. I was so worried."

Levus tried his hardest to break the metal chains keeping the cell together, but they just wouldn't budge.

"Stand back."

Leeta did as she was told as Levus raised the Moonsaber. So far there had been almost nothing his sword couldn't cut through. He saw no reason why it wouldn't slice into this. He swung with all his might.

To his surprise, the sword's progress was halted by the chain's lock. He tried again . . . with the same result. He tried hacking the wood, but even that stopped the seemingly unstoppable weapon. *Why is this happening?* After a couple more tries, he lowered the Moonsaber, defeated.

He said, "I don't get it. I don't know why the sword won't cut through it. I'm trying to think of another way. How did they get you?"

"A man . . . a man who I was very close to told me he had a surprise for me. I followed because I trusted him."

Levus stopped examining the cage for a weakness. He didn't like the tone of her voice. He'd heard it before and it was not used to tell of happy news. Leeta noticed this.

"We can talk about it when we get out of here."

He agreed. He wanted to leave this place as fast as possible. Getting out would not be as easy as getting in, he

32

figured. He hadn't run into a single Ettui on the trip up. He couldn't possibly have that same luck on the way out. There was another factor he had to consider too. Somewhere, the cronies of Dyyros were here. He felt it. He wanted to avoid them as well if all possible.

Levus asked, "Where are Ulcinar and Kile?"

"Closer than you think."

A familiar laugh encompassed the room. The torches in the dark portion of the room lit up brightly to reveal the two villains. Ulcinar was lounged in an ancient throne that must have once held many Elvish kings. Kile stood next to him with a cocky smile on his face.

Levus stepped away from Leeta's cell. He did notice a strange torch was on the opposite side of the throne Kile stood on. It wasn't like the others and almost appeared to hover. The flame even seemed to dance like it was alive.

"Didn't I tell you finding this girl would bring him?"

"You were quite right, Kile."

Both men guffawed, angering Levus. His hand clenched around the handle of the Moonsaber. Ulcinar noticed this and smiled.

Levus said, "If you wanted me, all you had to do was ask. Now that you have me, let the girl go."

With another deep laugh, Ulcinar said, "I am rather sorry I had to drag her into our little business, but you gave me very limited choices. You have something I want. When Kile told me one of my trusted captains was courting this young girl, especially after I saw how she fancied you in Arnis, I simply couldn't resist."

"You lie! Leeta wouldn't betray me. She promised!"

"Mmm . . . this is quite interesting," Kile said. "You didn't know about Captain Corweig? He told me how excited he was to finally meet a girl that cared for him from Arnis. Said her name was Leeta. The details he gave of her

33

beauty and the way she dressed bore a remarkable resemblance that only this girl matched. I ordered Corweig to bring her to me so I could meet her, confirming we had the right person."

Levus turned to face Leeta and asked, "They speak lies, don't they? Corweig is one of them!"

Leeta looked down, tears forming in her eyes. Levus couldn't believe this. He didn't want to. Sure, they had their disagreements. What couple didn't? One thing he'd felt confident of, though, was the idea that despite their troubles, they would remain faithful. Leeta had broken that.

She finally said, "About a couple years ago, when we had that fight, I met Corweig. He was in the engineering class of mine. He and I had so much fun. When you and I resolved our differences, I continued to see him. It was never meant to get so serious, I swear. I didn't tell you because I . . . I didn't want to hurt you."

Leeta was ashamed that she had to tell Levus this, but that did nothing to ease his own confusion. Why would she do this to him? He even felt angry. Of all the years he was faithful to her, and his reward was this?

Ulcinar said, "I would not be so angry at the girl. Besides, you are not as innocent as you think. I've seen how you look at that mage, Divi. You are torn between your feelings. Your love for Leeta is real, but your love for Divi is growing stronger by the day. Perhaps even surpassing it."

Levus yelled, "Shut up!"

"Based on this, I present you a choice."

As Ulcinar spoke, a black ice spear formed in front of his opened palm. The tip pointed at Leeta. When she tried to flinch away from it, it followed.

"Give the sword to me, and I shall spare both your lives. If not, she dies first, and then you. I'm growing tired of this game."

Levus looked between Ulcinar and Leeta. What was he to do? Learning that Leeta was cheating on him didn't sit well with him. If he gave up the sword, maybe he and Leeta could figure something out. Yet this sword was all that he had of his father. Could he just give it up that easily? His emotions were torn.

"I don't have all day, Levus. What is your choice?"

Levus saw Leeta gripping the bars of the cage desperately trying to loosen them while Ulcinar stood firm with a slight satisfactory grin. He wished there was someone who could help him. Anyone.

* * * * *

"*Rapidom Icsara!*"

A ball of ice crashed into the incoming Ettui warriors, freezing them. Divi, using her telekinetic powers, wielded a broken piece of a column to shatter the frozen creatures into pieces. She watched as three more took the positions of the ones they crushed. Tasi met up with her in the middle of the Great Hall behind a fallen column.

He commented, "This is quite the mess we are in."

Tasi shot a fireball at two more Ettui as they came through the doorway. The wake of the attack knocked over two Ettui in hiding near where the fireball connected. He didn't even know they were there. This only provided further proof that they couldn't hold this position for long. They were trying to surround them and eventually would succeed.

Divi asked, "What can I do to help?"

"Just go get Levus! I can hold them!"

She was befuddled by his request, knowing there was no way that Tasi would be able to hold off an entire army on his own.

35

"Are you sure?"

"Just go!"

Divi didn't want to, but if they tried to fight off all the Ettui they would miss the boat. She sprinted toward the staircase. Tasi took one glance to watch her enter the stairwell before shooting another fireball at the incoming Ettui.

* * * * *

"I'm losing my patience, boy."

Sweat poured heavily from Levus' brow. His hand began to shake.

Kile scoffed, "The boy is weak like you thought, my lord. His courage shrinks when given a choice between his friends and his past."

Leeta watched with mixed emotions. Learning that Levus was really in love with Divi broke her heart, as it manifested her worst fear when she first met the mage. Yet how could she be angry at him? They had just been delaying the inevitable, not being true to themselves. That fight they had tore them far apart. Both wanted to look past the true damage it caused because their relationship meant so much for their two families. Both tried to put it behind them, but she at least could not. The boy that she was attracted to years before had changed, much like she had. As they changed, the distance between them had grown.

Leeta closed her eyes. Many thoughts came to her mind. She felt responsible for getting herself and Levus involved in this. If she had not been weak that one time, this might not have happened. She was the one who started it when Levus caught her cheating on him the first time. It should be her that ended this. That was a very difficult decision for her to make, especially because Corweig was not going to be here to comfort or save her this time.

She finally opened her eyes.

Leeta said, "Levus, forget me. Don't give him the sword."

All three turned toward her with great surprise.

"Leeta."

She continued as she walked up to the cage bars, "My hatred for Ulcinar is far greater than what I felt when I learned about you and that mage. Don't give him the sword."

Levus approached Leeta. Kile faced Ulcinar with a concerned look and the Dark Lord shook his head. *So much for our insurance policy.* Kile had hoped the girl would be enough to convince the boy to voluntarily hand over the sword. He seemed to have underestimated the feelings Levus and Leeta shared. *Oh, well.*

His master was tired of showing mercy to one who didn't appreciate it.

"So, you have made your choice."

As Levus reached the cage, Leeta said "Levus, he must not get that sword. Defend it with your life."

He reached out and touched her hand, wet with perspiration. He could feel her shaking, knowing this decision could cost her life. He held it tight, letting her know that whatever happened, he wouldn't desert her. Even though by now he understood that no matter how hard he tried, they wouldn't budge, it still didn't stop him from trying to pry the bars open with his other hand, dropping the Moonsaber to get a better grip.

Leeta said, "Don't give it to him. Your father wouldn't."

"Your choice," Ulcinar exclaimed in frustration, "— was death!"

Ulcinar unleashed the spike toward Leeta. It happened so fast that Levus wouldn't have been able to stop it even if he wanted to. He could do nothing but watch as the spike pierced clean through Leeta. Her hand left his grasp. His eyes opened wide as he watched her fall to the floor.

This couldn't be happening. This was all a bad dream. Just a dream. Levus turned to face Ulcinar, who already had another spike floating in the air, pointed directly at him.

"If you are not willing to give me the sword, then we will have to take it from you."

Levus stepped down to the lower tier and fell to his knees. He wanted to scream for help, but there was no one to hear him. He had left them all back at the camp. He was alone. No one would come to save him. This was how it was going to end. He'd been so foolish. He should have told his friends.

A strange feeling began to engulf Levus. His body went numb and could hear nothing unless it was a couple feet from him. The emblem and the sword began to glow a bright white. Ulcinar and Kile watched with great concern as the white light surrounded Levus.

Suddenly, Divi came through the doorway.
"Levus!"

She stopped instantly when she saw the scene. In the cage, Leeta was on the ground lifeless, her open eyes looking at nothing. In front of her, Levus knelt with Kile and Ulcinar standing over him in shock. What was Levus doing? It couldn't be magic. Was it another one of those techniques? It couldn't be. The Moonsaber rested on the ground.

The bright light crept ever closer to Kile and Ulcinar. Kile unsheathed his weapon, showing no fear. He couldn't in front of his master. Ulcinar, however, responded with more rational consideration. This was not a battle they would win.

"Levus?" Divi asked.

Suddenly, Levus gave a blood-curling scream. "No!"

The white light grew so bright that Divi couldn't see Ulcinar and Kile anymore. She couldn't move, frozen by the foreign illumination's gaze.

From behind Divi, several Ettui crept forward, only to be likewise frozen with horror. In seconds, the light swept over them. All she could do was scream as the mysterious light overtook her.

CHAPTER 2
Divi's Odyssey

Divi quickly pulled herself up, her breathing heavy. Had it all been a dream? It certainly felt real. Divi wiped the sweat from her brow. As she did, a realization came to her. She was in a bed. Where? The last thing she remembered was running up to Levus; he did some type of technique, and that was all.

She examined her surroundings. The walls were aged stone bricks. The only decoration was a banner, ragged at the edges. There were also a table, a chair, and a bowl with some fruit in it.

A slight chill entered the room from an unseen crack. Divi quickly covered the exposed parts of her legs with the thick blanket. She really wanted to know what happened to Levus. That bright light had been so strange! *How did he do that?* It couldn't have been because of the sword, as he wasn't even holding it when the light appeared. That light had a strange feeling in it, almost like it was something . . .

Her thoughts once again strayed to wondering where she was. A sudden realization came to her that perhaps they were captured and still in Barbata. She had no idea what happened to Ulcinar and Kile after that light engulfed her. The room offered no clues as to where she was. If her fears were correct, what had been Tasi's fate? He was a gifted mage, but it would be impossible for him to fight an Ettui army on his own.

Divi looked toward the door. Through the crack at the bottom, she could see a shadow walking past. It kept pacing back and forth the whole time Divi watched. She was about to stand up when a voice came from the other side of the door. She listened carefully. It sounded like Elvish. She wasn't sure if this was bad or not because the enemy spoke Elvish, too. After the voice finished speaking, the shadow stopped and went out of view. Divi found herself silently praying that she wasn't in the hands of the enemy. She shivered as the handle began to shake and the door slowly creaked open.

From the hallway, a tall figure stepped inside. So far so good. It couldn't be Ettui because whatever it was, it was too tall. It couldn't be Ulcinar because she could never forget what she felt when they met Ulcinar back in Arnis.

The figure stopped and stared at her. The light from the hallway cast it in silhouette, so Divi still couldn't tell who it was.

The figure finally said, "*Erritii maginiia cuhronti.*" (*What courage for a mage.*)

She recognized that voice. A second figure entered from the hallway as well, this one with a candelabra. The emerging light revealed Thamalos and Tasi. That was a relief. At least it meant that they were off Barbata.

Divi replied in Elvish, "*Uiitar.*" (*One tries.*)

She began to rub her forehead. A sharp pain caused her to wince. She didn't think she'd fallen that hard, but she couldn't remember anything after the light consumed her.

"What happened? Where are we?"

Tasi scolded, "You are lucky to be alive, Ms. Divi!"

Thamalos pushed his way in front of Tasi and began to explain. "You are in Fort Za, the human and elf stronghold. We sailed here after we rescued you. Tasi found you passed out on a floor in that tower. With his telekinetic powers, he was able to carry you and Levus to the boat before any of the Ettui knew where we were docked."

Divi's eyes grew wide as she asked, "Where is Levus?"

Thamalos turned to face Tasi, concerned as to how they were going to explain this.

Tasi said, "Why should that matter? As long as you're safe. . ."

"What happened to Levus?" asked Divi forcefully.

41

"I think you better see for yourself," said Thamalos.

She was now extremely concerned. She already had been worried about what happened to Levus because of that light. What did it do to him? Divi slowly stood up and followed Thamalos and Tasi. The hallway was bright with candlelight. The walls were very well made, with banners being the only decoration. A couple human soldiers carrying pikes stood motionless in front of a stairway. Their armor looked Cordcan in design, but there were small differences. A silver strip outlined a golden center with an emblem made from some weird ore. The guards didn't even flinch when Divi and the others walked past them.

As they moved up, a slight chill entered the stone stairwell. She found the source, a large window. The sky was gray with a few dark clouds. Was it night? How long had she been knocked out? She could smell moisture in the air. It must have rained not long ago.

They reached the top of the stairs and moved into another hallway. She smiled as she noticed Eraddor pacing in front of a door. He stopped when he saw his friends arriving.

Thamalos asked, "How is he?"

Eraddor glanced at Divi before answering Thamalos. "His condition has not changed."

"Condition?" asked Divi.

Eraddor looked at her and then at the ground. She pushed Thamalos to the side and entered the room. She froze with disbelief. On a bed by a window, Levus lay motionless covered by a white sheet. Three guards stood over him, as if he was a prisoner.

Divi's vision blurred with tears as she stared at him.

Divi asked, "Is he . . ."

Eraddor, who entered with Thamalos, replied, "No. He breathes, but does not answer when we speak to him."

Thamalos added, "He was like this when Tasi found him."

Divi knelt next to Levus' bed. She began to brush back the hair covering his eyes. Tears fell from hers onto his shoulder. She started feeling his forehead, but the chill was almost too cold for her to bear touching.

"What happened to him?"

Tasi said, "I was on my way up the stairs when a bright light consumed the area. I have no clue what happened."

"What about Ulcinar and Kile? I saw them briefly before the light overtook me, too."

"You and Levus were the only living things in that room. There was a girl in a secured cage, so I couldn't reach her. She was . . ."

Divi stood up and walked away from Levus. "Dead. That was Leeta. She and Levus were . . . She was like that when I arrived."

Tasi looked at Divi, showing a hint of skepticism. Although he didn't believe Divi was the kind of person to kill out of jealousy, he couldn't eliminate it as a possibility. The feelings that Divi confessed for Levus caused people to do . . . strange things.

Thamalos asked, "Divi, is there anything that might have caused that light?"

Divi didn't hear the question. Her eyes were fixed on a table in the corner of the room. The Moonsaber and the emblem from Levus' breastplate sat silently on the wooden surface. She could not take her eyes off them. A voice began to fill her head.

"*Suntoya eiionyiup deiiama.*"

She had heard this voice before. Was the sword speaking to her? It was as it sought a new master now that its old one was incapacitated.

"*Guinta friientian kilaniia.*"

Divi reached toward the sword. A desire grew inside of her. What was this feeling?

Her hand was five feet away from it. A large shadow with a purple light illuminated her mind. A dark figure could be seen, but it was not Ulcinar. What was going on? Divi closed her eyes. As she quickly pulled her hand away and fell to her knees, Thamalos covered the sword with a cloth. He and Eraddor looked at each other while Tasi rushed to her aid.

She was able to stand up on her own accord. Her legs felt weak.

"Are you all right? What happened?" asked Thamalos.

Divi wiped sweat off her face. Without saying a word, she ran out of the room. Tasi wanted to follow, but Thamalos stopped him.

"Let me talk to her."

It took Thamalos a couple minutes before he found Divi standing on a balcony overlooking the vast courtyard of Fort Za. One thing about Fort Za that had fascinated her when they first arrived several weeks ago was how deceptively large this place was. Below, many troops were running their drills or standing in formation. Past the courtyard was a large wall from which a tower rose that must rise around seventy-five feet. It was the tallest point of the fort from what Divi could see, with a stone staircase coiling around the tower to the top.

Divi jumped when she felt someone touch her shoulder. She eased her body and wiped more sweat from her brow, seeing it was only Thamalos.

"Divi, what did you feel when you were near the sword?"

She didn't know what to say. Thamalos took hold of her softly with both hands.

"Divi, you must tell me what you felt. It is very important."

It was hard to meet Thamalos' eyes. "It was . . . It was like it was calling me. The voice . . . it was almost as if it was . . . It was horrible."

Thamalos frowned in concern. His suspicions about that weapon Levus used were getting more and more concrete. The elf prince turned to face the door back into the fort. "That sword is dangerous."

Divi watched Thamalos suspiciously. She felt that he was hiding something. Why would he hide anything from her? "You know what has happened to Levus. Don't you?"

Thamalos looked to the ground before facing Divi and answering, "Levus is in what the humans call a coma. Most get them from hard hits to the head or when their heart has trouble, but Levus' is unique. My first thoughts pointed to the Moonsaber being the cause, but Tasi said the boy didn't even carry it at the time. There is only one other explanation for his condition that my elf brethren believe and agree as the true reason for it."

Thamalos paused for a few seconds before continuing. "Levus is lost in time."

"What do you mean, lost in time? He's still living and with us!"

Thamalos explained, "Levus is re-living a moment in his mind. Perhaps it was when Leeta was killed. A few people can fix their memory and return to the real world. Those who cannot get consumed by their memories . . . and so they never wake up."

Divi couldn't believe Thamalos' story. She had never heard of this condition, even with all the notes her mother left. Then again, most mages never fought in close enough in battle to feel the blunt edge of a weapon to their head. She also led a sheltered life, so there was much she didn't know.

"There must be a way to help, though. I cannot simply sit here with Levus like this!"

"There is one way. The Isle of Time."

Divi remembered Levus telling her about the Isle of Time on their way back to Porsita, en route to their second encounter with Kile. It was when these feelings for Levus had started to become stronger. Back then, she would already have done anything for him. Those feelings hadn't changed.

Divi asked, "But isn't it impossible to get past the heavy storms surrounding it?"

"Time is something not be taken lightly," Thamalos said. "It needs that natural defense. If you want to quell the storms, you must gather the four elemental stones located on Dragonia. It is also known as 'the continent of the dragons'."

Divi had heard of that place before, a long time ago. Her mother told her stories about a large landmass that housed only dragons. She had always thought of them as myths, wondering why a flying beast would stay in one place and not try and travel to other parts of the world. The Shadow Dragon on Barbata had convinced her that dragons were not beasts of lore. The scar she had as a result of its nail would remind her of that for the rest of her life.

Thamalos continued, "The Elves and the Dragonians once shared a great friendship. Yet, things changed when the Ettui took over Barbata. The Dragonians used to give us dragons in exchange for fruits and equipment. The dragons would help us with chores and defense against the Eratuu. We both understood the importance of stopping the Eratuu, yet we failed all the same."

Thamalos suddenly stopped and began to stare at the floor. He finally faced Divi once again.

"It will be very dangerous for you to go. Many knights of strong character who have heard of the legend went there failed to return. I do not wish you go. We can always just wait to see if Levus wakes up on his own . . ."

Divi countered, "Nothing you can say will prevent me from going. If you say this is the only thing that will wake him up short of blind luck, then I will do it."

46

Thamalos wanted to try to stop her, but he knew better. He wished he had not said anything about the Isle of Time. Divi was, if anything, a good listener. By telling her this was their only option, he backed himself into a corner. He also didn't want to send her because of the cost attached, and he didn't mean in terms of money.

"All right. I will try and crew a ship with elves willing to make the trip. The Dragonians dislike humans and will do their best to prevent them from gaining the power of Time."

Divi lowered her head and looked at the ground.

She finally said, "Thank you, Thamalos."

* * * * *

A few hours had passed since Divi had convinced Thamalos to send her to Dragonia. She walked to the port of Fort Za. Its built made mainly of blackened wood caused by the construction process with some metal at the edges.

The dock only large enough to hold one ship, General Medkar was grateful that Divi would sail it out. They needed the space to receive the delegates' ships arriving for an important meeting occurring soon at Fort Za. If Divi had not needed it, General Medkar was going to send the ship back to Formia, the northern most town on the mainland. It had three sails and was skinny when compared to the vessels that took them to Barbata, but it would suit Divi's purpose. The hull didn't look as thick as the *Cordcan*-class ships, so she assumed it would not last long in a battle.

The crew had been bringing barrels on board all morning, so it was a busy scene. Not one greeted her, though, as they went back and forth bringing goods to the ship. Were they mad at her for dragging them away from their restful routine? Did they just not want to be disturbed?

47

She was so focused on the ship that she didn't realize Thamalos and Eraddor had come up next to her.

Thamalos stated, "It is not the strongest, but it should get you to Dragonia swiftly. Ten elves have volunteered to take you. Listen to them without question and you will arrive safely."

Divi turned to her two friends and smiled. "Well, I guess I'll be off."

Eraddor extended his hand and grabbed Divi's arm. Divi accepted the Elvish handshake, "Have a safe journey, young mage. May the sea bring you to your destination quickly."

"Thank you, Eraddor."

Eraddor let go of her and Thamalos made the same gesture. "May the winds bring you swiftly to Dragonia. You will have to row once you get near. The captain will know when to let you off. The boat will not make the full trip."

Divi nodded as Thamalos stepped back. He could tell her nod was a nervous one and patted her shoulder in an effort to comfort her. At least that was how he'd observed the humans doing it.

"Good luck, my young mage. I will pray to our gods for your success in reaching the Isle of Time and for your safe return."

She didn't say anything as she followed one of the elf crew members. Thamalos and Eraddor watched her walk away uneasily.

Eraddor leaned over to Thamalos and asked, "Do you think she will be all right?"

"Her path is different from ours. Though she goes with thought of going alone, I feel that she will not be without a friend."

"I hope so. Come. When the mage representatives arrive, General Medkar will want to start the meetings."

Thamalos slowly went with Eraddor toward the interior of the fort.

Divi made her slow walk up the ramp. She was not even sure if what she was doing was the most sensible answer. Her emotions decided for her, but were they going to be enough to survive what Thamalos had warned her about? She could only hope. All the same, she couldn't hide from herself that she was a mage who still didn't know magic. If great warriors had failed to retrieve the stones, what could she possibly do?

She would find a way. If this saved Levus, nothing was going to stop her.

"Divi! Wait!"

She turned around in shock. From the port entrance, Tasi was running as fast as he could. What was he thinking? He pushed a few soldiers out of the way before reaching the loading ramp where she stood.

"Tasi! What are you doing?"

It took Tasi a few minutes to answer because he was trying to catch his breath.

"I'm not letting you go alone. I heard from one of the elves what you planned."

"I don't want anyone else to put their life in danger for something that I alone must do."

Tasi snapped, "Even though I don't agree with why you are doing this, I am not going to let you die because of it. Your father gave me the mission of being your teacher, your protector. It is something I take very seriously."

She almost went into tears at Tasi's dedication. A few escaped as she put her hand on his shoulder. He slowly lifted his head, wiping the tears that welled in his own eyes.

Divi said, "Of all the things I may say to you, I am very grateful for your friendship."

Both mages smiled and they shared a soft hug. Physical contact was frowned upon with other mages unless married, so Tasi held on for as long as he could. As they separated, Divi looked up at the ship. It appeared that the elf

49

crew was ready to depart. She looked once more toward Tasi.

"It is time."

Tasi nodded. "Let another adventure begin."

Still smiling, they walked together up the ramp toward the deck.

The hot sun beat on the deck of the elven ship. Divi was the only person aboard who had not gone below deck. Tasi had retreated there because his mage body temperature grew too high. She didn't understand what was happening to her. Her temperature hadn't changed despite the hot weather. She even began to feel cooler the longer they sailed. Perhaps the overheating incident at Rudann was good for her.

It had been at least six hours since they left Fort Za. A particularly fast time for the trip, or so the elf captain said. He said they would only get another hundred miles closer before Divi and Tasi were on their own.

She walked toward the bow of the ship. Ahead of them was the open sea. To the west, though, a large landmass with high cliffs was visible through the haze. The sky appeared menacing in that direction, the clouds as dark as the blackness of night. One other thing caught Divi's attention. Also in the west, a small mountain range seemed to sprout from the ocean, connected to no landmass. She had never seen that before. Then again, other than the path they followed through Sardon and the Thorii Palace on Barbata, she had little knowledge or experience with mountains in her lifetime.

Her train of thought was disturbed by Tasi, who came to stand beside her.

He exclaimed, "What an unbelievable trip! I never sailed in such hot conditions. You should get inside soon. Your body must be near the breaking point."

Without looking at Tasi, Divi replied, "I'm fine."

A short silence came between them as Tasi joined her looking west.

She suddenly asked, "Did you ever have a feeling that you were meant for something special? I mean . . . really special?"

"I think that is a feeling we all have at one point in our lives. I guess it is a question of when and not how. For my part, yes, I've had that feeling. I still think that I haven't met my purpose. Why do you ask?"

Divi didn't know how to answer his question. It was just . . . a feeling. Tasi grabbed her shoulder and began to lead her to the middle of the deck.

He continued, "We all have different paths. Our choices are what makes each life unique. This journey we are on now has come because of the choices you made."

"And how am I doing?"

"In the end, I cannot be judge of that, but I think you are making everyone proud."

Divi gave a small smile as they continued to walk together. She could feel the ship making a slight change in direction toward the northwest.

"I sometimes wonder how my father would think of my choices."

"For someone who hated their father, you sure think of him a lot."

She laughed faintly. "I guess it's not that I hated him. After all, he was the only one who took care of me after my mother died. That is a truer testament of love, isn't it?"

"Perhaps one day you will be able to ask him that question."

They were both smiling again when suddenly a horn trumpeted overhead, blown by the elf on the mast. Divi and Tasi looked around. The elven crew moved rapidly to the sails. She had hardly noticed that the waters were getting rougher. The dark clouds had moved over them.

Tasi pulled one of the sailors aside.

"What's going on?"

The elf replied, "Grab onto something sturdy and get out of our way!"

He said no more as he rushed over to the bowlines holding the shroud sails up. Tasi and Divi ran to one of the sides and looked overboard. Water slammed into the ship, much of it flowing on the deck. The winds picked up. Another hard wave hit the ship. An elf close to the side fell overboard into the violent sea. Divi and Tasi, disrupted by the chaos, could do nothing to help the poor sailor. They moved away from the edge quickly.

Tasi said, "How is this happening? I've never seen such a fast transition from nice weather to this! And it is only in the few miles around us!"

He had a point. Toward the horizon in every direction from them, sunlight shone down brightly. This was not acting like any normal storm she ever saw. Divi would know, being outside nearly this entire time.

Divi and Tasi fell to the deck as the ship shook violently from another hit. More water crashed over the rails, soaking everyone. She wiped the water from her eyes. As the next collision happened, the mages met each other's gaze. That was not the waves.

The hull began to creak, and the entire crew listened with fear. Another hard blow rocked them. Divi struggled to stand up as an eerie silence filled the surroundings. Then the snapping of wood was heard all around the ship. She rushed over to the edge to see if she could spot anything. Divi noticed something very strange. Only the waters around them were violent, while everything else was calm. She glimpsed a shape moving in the water, something huge, with a glitter like scales. That was no fish. She couldn't really tell, as another deafening smack knocked her down to the deck. A hard rain began to fall.

Suddenly, to their left, the creature erupted from the sea. Divi and Tasi couldn't believe their eyes. The monster stood erect at least two hundred feet tall above the water. The elf captain, amazingly, kept his composure. He began yelling orders out to his crew, yet it was to no good use. The crew were too petrified to do anything. The monster unleashed a loud, shrieking roar that made all the people on the ship cover their ears.

The elf captain, trying to maintain calm, tried to turn the vessel around. He was able to get the bow to face southwest before the monster shrieked. As it did, it came down toward the deck—and directly toward Divi and Tasi. Both mages jumped out of the way as the monster crashed through the middle of the deck, and the hull below it, splitting the ship in two. Pieces of wood flew in the air as water began filling the exposed halves. Divi screamed as she grabbed onto the railing as a few elf crewmen fell into the ocean. She looked toward the other half of the ship, which was sinking the opposite way.

"Tasi!"

He spotted her, though he could only see her vaguely. "Divi!"

This couldn't be happening! She yelled once more, "Tasi, help!"

Just as she said this, her half of the ship began to tip backwards. The monster was trying to capsize them. Tasi could only watch in horror as the creature wrapped its body around their section, helping tip the ship on its port side. More water rushed inside.

She screamed again, "Tasi! Please help me!"

The monster succeeded and the boat began to overturn. Divi screamed as she slammed into the water.

He tried concentrating to hold her with his telekinesis, but the chaos of the sinking ship made it impossible as he lost her among the wood and waves. Tasi didn't know what he could do.

"Divi!"

CHAPTER 3
City of the Dragon

Divi coughed roughly. She tried to open her eyes, but they felt heavy. A rush of cool water brushed across her nose as she coughed again. Feeling every aching muscles, she tried to move her arms and legs. She finally opened her eyes. She appeared to be in a series of tide pools, the high tide slowly receding. Where was she? Last thing she remembered was falling off the boat after that sea monster attacked. Divi began to crawl across the shallow water. As she did, she grabbed onto a slick rock. It wouldn't be much help if the creature attacked again, yet she couldn't stand being completely unprepared. When she looked southeast, she saw the mountains in the sea that she had seen from the boat, shadows in the distance. She'd made it to the continent . . . but how? They still had to be hundreds of miles away from here when they were attacked.

It was then that she noticed there was no one else near her.

Divi yelled, "Tasi!"

The only answer was the slosh of water around her ankles. She continued to scan the area.

She yelled again, only louder, "Tasi!"

This was not good. In the distance, she saw something floating. Her heart lifted up with hope. Divi quickly waded through the water, as close to running as she could, in the hopes that someone had survived the wretched attack. As she got close to the figure, her hope turned to sorrow as it was the lifeless body of one of the elf crewmen. A few tears escaped from her eyes. Was she it? Was she the only one to survive? That would mean that Tasi . . . it was all her fault. It was because of her that all those elves and her truest friend had died.

Divi's thoughts escaped her lips: "I'm all alone."

She tried to hold back the tears, but the more she thought about it the harder it got. She put her hand over her forehead. Divi felt a sting as she touched a wound there, but it didn't last long. A few more shards of wood from the hull and a ragged scrap of sail floated by her. She had to get away from this place . . . wherever she was.

Divi ran out of the water and began to walk up a steep slope to the right. Climbing it was easy because the rocks offered many hand- and footholds. It was almost as if they were set this way by someone. As she made it to the top, she sat on the largest boulder. Divi stared at the water. This is not how things were supposed to happen. The elves weren't even supposed to land and here she was all that remained. She lowered her gaze to the ground.

Depression flooded her mind. She wished there was something she could've done to save the ship. Maybe if she had known magic . . . No, there was nothing she could have done. Perhaps this was meant to be. But why did they have to die? She even began to wonder if it was worth all this suffering. An image of Levus entered her thoughts. A tear rolled down her cheek at just the memory of him in the condition he was in. If what she was doing would save him, she would do it.

Suddenly, Divi heard a small laugh from behind her. She looked around for the source of the sound. There it was again! It seemed to echo in the woods behind her.

She spotted a small child dressed in white garbs and cheap sandals on her feet crouched among huge, ancient roots. The child had a frilled nose with a tiny horn at the tip. The skin was smooth and a crème color.

Divi wiped her tears away and asked, "Who are you?"

The child didn't seem to pay attention to her question. All the youngling did was skip around in a circle a couple of times before sitting down on the grass.

Divi asked, "What do you want?"

The child just stared at Divi and gave another laugh. Judging by the laugh, Divi assumed this was a girl. She finally stood up and advanced toward her. Divi was amazed by this little girl's courage. Here, a stranger was approaching her, and she just watched playfully.

She bent down so she was at the girl's level. "Hi there. What's a little girl like you doing all by yourself?"

Once again, the girl seemed more interested in something else than in hearing what Divi had to say. Divi was beginning to wonder if she even understood anything she was saying. She stood up, thinking. Was this little girl a survivor from an attacked ship like her? Was there a village nearby? Whatever it was, she had to find out. Divi tried to move closer.

"Don't be alarmed. I'm not here to hurt you."

The girl finally faced Divi. She stared at her, but still did not look scared. Divi inched closer with her hand extended.

Suddenly, the girl stood up and ran into the forest. This was what Divi had wanted to avoid.

"Wait! Hold up!"

She ran as fast as she could after the young girl. Divi had a hard time not only because of the brush and low branches, but also because the child was fast. She almost seemed to glide with every step she took. Divi was quickly running out of breath. As she tried to jump over a log, her back leg caught on it and she fell face first to the ground. She lifted her head to see the little girl go through a thick cover from the brush about twenty-five feet ahead of her. Divi slowly stood, grimacing from her latest fall. If she was on Dyyros at this moment, the Night Predators—or Ettui, as Thamalos called them—would have easily caught her. After regaining her breath, she slowly walked over to the brush and passed through it.

All Divi could say was, "Wow!"

As she stepped out on the other side, a large town came into her view. It was a town unlike any other Divi had seen. All of the buildings were the same height, though each one looked exquisitely made. A large arch at the entrance of the town was covered in a golden substance. In the middle of the town stood a statue of what looked like a dragon.

Divi was so amazed that she almost didn't notice the little girl she had been chasing standing at the foot of the steep slope. She began signaling for Divi to follow her, gliding down the last few steps to enter the town, which made the mage feel a little hesitant. From what the girl did, it seemed almost like they were expecting her. How could they know? Divi finally determined that there was one way to find out. She slowly walked down the slope and entered into the town through the arch.

The town was very spaced out, with lots of empty areas separating each building. There was very little grass as much of the ground was stone. What disturbed Divi the most was that everyone was standing outside staring at her. It made her feel very uncomfortable, like being back home in Myyril. Divi continued slowly toward the town center.

As she reached it, she saw the little girl sitting on the ground next to a small group of older men and women. There were others in the plaza, but these were the only ones standing near the dragon statue. When Divi made her way over, one of the men and woman left off what they were talking about to see their new visitor. She stopped in front of the two as a moment of silence was shared.

The male finally said, "Hello, Divi. I'm so glad you made it. We expected you sooner, but it took you longer to awaken then we thought."

Divi asked, "Who are you? How did you know my name?"

"How rude of me. My name is Gionti. This woman next to me is Tetoliis. We are the co-rulers of Dragonia. We know your name because we were expecting your arrival."

It was a little hard to understand what he was saying because he pronounced his r's with an accented rolling sound.

"Then you know why I'm here?" asked Divi. She still didn't understand *how* they knew.

Gionti took a couple of steps to his right, like he was looking around her. "That is correct. You seek to recover the four elemental stones so that you may access the Isle of Time."

"I do it in the interest of helping a friend," Divi reassured him.

"As do many," Tetoliis said. "Dragonia is no longer a safe place to explore. Not like in the olden days."

"How long have you been here?" Divi asked.

"We have been here since the beginning of time," Gionti explained. "It is why we were entrusted with its protection. You see, unlike the other races, we cannot reproduce. In time, we will die. Yet, because of our important duty, our lives are granted near immortality."

Gionti pointed to the little girl, who was playing on the stone. "My daughter, Hiiminta. She is the last of our kind to be spawned. Once she passes on, we will exist no more. Our purpose is to grant those that we see as fitting enough the ability to access the power of time, by first providing the opportunity to prove their worth. Many a hero has come here, yet all fell as men and not heroes."

Divi stepped closer to Gionti, which seemed to surprise him. They had to give her the chance to help Levus. She didn't come all this way just to be denied. "I don't care what the dangers are. I need those stones."

Hiiminta suddenly said, "I sense great fear, yet a great emotion conflicting with this fear."

Gionti and Tetoliis both smiled at their daughter's comment.

"She is very young, but already she surpasses some of her brothers and sisters," Tetoliis said. "It is good that you show confidence. Confidence can lead to both weaknesses and strengths. Perhaps passing the first test was not blind luck."

Divi asked, "What test?"

Gionti answered, "Why, the sinking of your craft, of course. The first test of strength is in making it to our lands. You must understand, Time is a very dangerous tool. One who possesses the power to change time has a significant weapon. We must make sure that only the strongest are allowed to compete for the power of Time. Those with a pure heart will succeed. Leviadon judged you worthy to try, or else he would not have carried you to our lands safely. He is one of the best, so his opinion is rarely questioned."

Divi was shocked. These people had that dragon attack their ship just so they could see who was strong enough to survive? That was no excuse for mass murder. Those elves didn't want to be there. They were completely innocent.

She countered, "But there were elves on the ship, and you let them die! I thought Thamalos said you and elves had a relationship of mutual respect."

Gionti walked up to Divi and put his hands on her shoulders. "We still do. Thamalos understands our actions. He would have most likely told the captain it would be a one-way trip. Why else would they give you a minimally crewed vessel? It is also why he likely resisted your going, knowing that by doing so he would lose some of his own. Leviadon has retrieved their bodies. They will have honored burials."

Divi's shock turned to guilt. *So, Thamalos knew this but he sent them anyway*. That would explain the uneasiness the elves displayed the whole trip before the attack. If she had known that the journey would cost lives, she might have re-thought her options. Then again, maybe that was why Thamalos didn't tell her. He knew that was what she would do, so he decided against letting her know. She couldn't decide if she should have been angry or grateful.

59

Divi asked, "Did he recover another like me?"

"Leviadon made no mention of another," said Gionti.

That filled her with even more sorrow. Tasi didn't make it. He must not have. Why would they lie to her? Nor could they have been mistaken. Aside from herself, Tasi was the only other non-elf on board. She held back her tears. They could be shed later. She had to show them she was strong. Strength seemed to be important to these people in deciding who proceeded with the challenge and who did not. She didn't want to get this far only to be turned down.

Gionti continued, "The test is for our security as well. Years ago, a dangerous creature tried, and almost succeeded in landing on our home. If he had made it, we might not have beaten him. We stopped him, losing many brethren in the process, which forced the dragons who guard our lands to extend their boundaries. The Island Wars between the Elves and Ettui also caused this necessary change. We have the only suitable lands on which to raise a dragon. If a large army came and seized them, it would be just as dangerous as controlling time."

Divi wondered who this creature was that was strong enough to defeat a dragon by himself. Initially she thought it could be Ulcinar. He was the only person she could think of who could take one down without help. But if that was true, it meant he would have been here since before the Ettui Island Wars, which were nearly a thousand years ago. Was it possible that the Dark Lord could have lived that long? Maybe someone else had tried to retrieve the stones. The mages had many tales about the powerful creatures that used to roam the land before The Silence happened and they went into hiding.

She knew about the Ettui Island Wars because of Thamalos. Before she left, he'd told her that the Ettui tried to seize the islands near Dragonia to act as a midway point from which to attack northern elf installations. The dragons sank their vessels, feeling themselves threatened after losing some

60

of their kin to Ettui in the takeover of Barbata. After hearing Gionti explain it, she began to understand why they were on edge about approaching ships. That didn't mean it was right to attack every craft, even friendly ones. The elves lost many on their trip up. She lost something, too. *Tasi* . . .

Gionti and the other Dragonians in the town center suddenly began to walk toward the buildings around them. The wind had picked up slightly, but she couldn't see anything else to warrant the immediate departure.

"What's going on?" Divi asked in confusion.

Gionti explained as his wife and daughter walked past him, "Night is falling. It is a very dangerous time here on Dragonia. Many frightening beasts roam our lands taking advantage of the dark—none more terrifying, though, than the creatures called the nitklarii. Their name is Elvish for 'night killer.' They will only attack living creatures in the open. The time of their awakening is near. It will be something you must be wary of on your quest. We shall grant you access to our continent, but we will wait until morning. I will have Minat guide you to the border then. Please, you may stay with us for the night."

Divi really didn't care anymore whether she traveled by day or night. Being on Dyyros and Barbata had quelled her fear of the dark. These people had no idea of what fear was. The nitklarii couldn't be any worse than the Ettui on Dyyros were. She knew, though, that all she could do was wait. If she didn't cooperate with them, perhaps they wouldn't let her find the stones. She followed Gionti toward their home.

* * * * *

Thamalos sat on a stone bench looking out a window. Not looking out, actually, but trying to scry. He had been trying to see anything involving the ship's fate the past twenty minutes, but still could learn nothing. It should have been near the Dragon's Teeth by now, where Divi was to be sent on her journey. Yet, he felt the disturbance of panic from his elven brethren much sooner than that. Elves, due to their close bond with each other, would occasionally feel when something happens to a large enough group. He could feel their fear and almost hear their screams carried by the wind.

Eraddor came near him and sat down. "Any luck?"

"None."

Both sat in silence for a minute before Eraddor said, "The opening meeting is about to commence. Give it a rest for right now."

Eraddor stood up and entered the meeting room just down the hall. He didn't have the heart to tell his human friend that he knew the ship's destruction was nearly inevitable. The captain only went because he was older and had family to carry on his name, and the crew had their reasons. Some simply did it because their future ruler asked them to. Others did it because they knew Divi from her trips to Lozela and sensed something special with her. The rest he wasn't sure other than they wanted to go with their captain. Regardless their reasons, he was appreciative for their sacrifice.

What was odd was how soon it had happened. It was part of the deal the Dragonians defined after the Ettui Island Wars. The elves had little choice on that stipulation. He'd expected the group here at Fort Za would get through the first day's meeting before feeling the disruption. His concern for Divi's welfare was genuine, as he knew mages weren't great swimmers, and the ship must still have been several hundred miles from land. Were the dragons wilder now than he remembered? He silently prayed to their gods that she and Tasi were safe. He knew the dangers of the trip, to the point that he almost regretted mentioning it to her during such an emotional time. There was nothing he could do about it now, though. He would just have to continue his attempts to find out if they made it safely.

Perhaps Eraddor was right. He did feel exhausted, as this was the most extreme effort he had ever made to use his powers of great sight at one time. Thamalos finally stood up and walked toward the meeting room.

He hoped that something would come of this. He knew how volatile things could become when you put all the races in one room. Thamalos almost wished that they started the meeting earlier, though it was customary for every race to make a sacrifice, prayer, or homage before such gatherings. The elves normally mediated for an hour to clear their minds and pray for success. More times than not, though, the meetings usually failed.

The assembly taking place here was known as the Summit of the Six. It was attended by representatives of all the major races and cities: the mages, elves, half-elves, and the three kingdoms of men. These assemblies were designed as an outlet for the major kingdoms to gather in the hopes of finding peaceful solutions to problems ranging from serious to the mundane. They took place twice every decade in Fort Za because it was a neutral site, despite being a joint elf/human fortress. On an island, the meetings were devoid of the ears that might usually try to overhear had these taken place in Cordca or some other location. Plus, it was the safest location on Gyyerlith as its walls had never been penetrated by an invading force. The elves considered it their new Mount Hrithgorn, their former crown jewel island fortress.

When Thamalos entered, he was one of the last to be seated. The room contained only a few stone chairs and a pedestal covered by an expensive pillow in the lower-tiered center, all lit by candles. At the head of the circle sat General Seth Medkar, the acting commander of Fort Za. Even though he had the least amount of power among the individuals in the room, since the meeting was on his grounds, he would lead the proceedings. Seth was an aged man, nearing his late sixties. His beard went down to his shoulders and was a dark gray. He wore his Cordcan-style breastplate, obviously old but showing little in terms of battle scars.

Thamalos sat down next to Eraddor and another elf who wore similar clothes, who he knew as his eldest son, Lascedis. He was happy that he even showed. Lascedis gave up his right to be the heir after himself years ago, a fact known by little. Still, the elf prince wanted his son to be an active member of his family and his people. His lifestyle kept trying to diverge from that path, something Thamalos didn't want. He was certain his mother was the reason he ended up coming, but he was happy nonetheless just to see him. It had been at least a year. There would be time to catch up during their tenure here.

When the last man entered the room, he left the door ajar behind him. There were no windows in the room except the hole in the ceiling, which did little to provide light, but it supplied some air circulation while providing secrecy. Even the hole would be covered until the meeting ended.

Once everyone took their places, Seth stood up and opened his arms.

"Good day, everyone. I would like to thank all the representatives of each kingdom for showing up for this. We run these meetings every five years here, so for some of us this is nothing new. Still, we are not without different faces this year compared to the last. Before we start, I would just like all representatives to state their name and those whom they accompany."

The first gentlemen to Medkar's left stood up. "From the kingdom of Rudann, I am Servion. With me is my squire, Cyp."

The following two gentlemen stood up. "From the kingdom of Garlock, I am Hirronisse. My son, Herippi, sits with me."

Sydis and Bironn both stood up. The representatives from Garlock and Rudann looked away in disgust. "From the great kingdom of Myyril, I am the Honorable Sydis with my assistant, Bironn."

Both sat down, Sydis doing so majestically. Thetalis stood up next.

"From Desris, I am Thetalis. The guard at the door is Girjinii, my personal guard."

Thetalis sat down as Thamalos and the other elf stood up.

"From Lozela, I am Prince Thamalos accompanied with my eldest son, Lascedis."

General Medkar nodded as all eyes switched to Eraddor. Thamalos was curious what Eraddor would say here. He led no kingdom and called no land his home, the normal requirement to attend this meeting. As he had lead the last expedition on Barbata, Seth saw that as enough.

He cleared his throat before standing up. "My name is Eraddor. I will be representing Dyyros."

Thamalos could hear a few snickers from the council. He himself gave a smile. Seth looked at Eraddor doubtfully, knowing full well he wasn't from there. Then again, he enjoyed the ingenuity of his reply, which made him chuckle.

"Really? I was unaware that Dyyros would be sending any to this council. Unless we were renamed the Summit of Seven and didn't know it. Well, no matter. I will be representing the kingdom of Cordca and my name is General Seth Medkar. Very good, shall we begin?"

Seth sat down. The others started gathering papers and materials they brought with them. Thamalos tried to get as comfortable as he could. It was going to be a long day. He knew usually the first day would mainly consist of listing the problems to be discussed while on the rest of the days the representatives would argue each point in specific. How many days that took usually depended on the willingness of the races to cooperate . . . so, in simpler terms, a long, long time. Thamalos remembered the last meeting had taken nearly three weeks and no real conflicts were resolved. He hoped this would be different.

Seth continued, "Here are some of the issues on my plate. As you know, the attack launched on Barbata did not go as planned. The Ettui apparently were aware of the attack and defended against it well. This, in my opinion, means one of two things: Their intelligence found out about the plan . . . or we have a traitor. We will discuss this at a later time. Another matter to be discussed is the apparent army that Thamalos reported in Sardon. We here at Fort Za are sending scouts to find out more, but until then we can only speculate. One of the final matters, though, that we will touch upon today . . ."

Seth gave a signal to a Za guard, who opened the side door. There entered a young man in exquisite robes, carrying something completely covered in a dark cloth. Everyone, except Thamalos and Eraddor, watched with great curiosity. The man put the object on the pedestal and stepped away. He waited until Seth nodded before unfurling the cloth with a snap. All the representatives began talking amongst themselves. On the satin pillow, the Moonsaber and Levus' breastplate medallion sat mute. Thamalos looked at Eraddor before facing the group again.

Seth continued, "Upon this pillowed lecturn are the sword and medallion which were carried by one of the men in the party, Levus Sintar. Although they look innocent, Thamalos tells me that when Levus wielded the sword, he spoke in the language of the Eratuu. It nearly cost the party twice on Barbata as he seemed be possessed by the weapon. It has a fearful power."

Hirronisse commented, "Perhaps it is not in the hands of the right person. Let a member of Garlock take it and wield it against the enemy. We, along with Rudann, have fought off the likes of Sardon, protecting the mainland from their armies. You all bask in the pleasures of antiquity while our people continue to struggle."

Thamalos interrupted, "It is dangerous enough that Levus is succumbing to its evil. Besides, some of us are unable to even wield it."

"Let us take a test, then," Sydis said. "Let all the races attempt to grasp this supposedly cursed weapon. This will prove whom the sword is trying to manipulate."

Everyone began talking to their companions. Seth nodded as he thought about it.

At last he said, "That idea seems just. Since you brought it to the council's attention, you may go first."

Sydis signaled to Bironn, who seemed very hesitant to pick the sword up. All this talk about this weapon being evil made him leery. He finally mustered enough courage to approach the Moonsaber.

The council watched earnestly. Thamalos had an idea of how Bironn would react, because Divi had previously gone to grasp the sword.

His hand was near the handle of the blade. Suddenly, a strange language entered Bironn's mind. His hand began to shudder uncontrollably. The council watched the mage's reaction in amazement. The shaking moved through Bironn's entire body. After what felt like an eternity, he ripped his hand away from the blade, falling to the floor. Bironn grasped his wrist as he tried to catch his breath. Thamalos and Eraddor both rushed to help the fallen mage.

Seth asked, "Is he all right?"

Thamalos looked at Bironn, who finally was able to settle down. "What did you see?"

Bironn looked at Thamalos, almost terrified. He took a large gulp before answering. "I saw darkness. A blacker darkness than the night without her moons and stars to light her. Then, flames came and a strange language began speaking to me. The longer I listened, the more I felt a burning inside of me. I have never been that afraid."

Sydis stood up. "I'm glad that a mage could not be responsible for this matter."

Eraddor said, "It isn't always about race, Sydis."

Sydis was offended at his comment. "Well then, Eraddor, representative of Dyyros . . . why do you not try and take the sword? We've seen that it affects mages, and Thamalos, an elf, has already given us an account of the evil sensations he has felt when near it. Let us see what happens when a representative of man tries to take it."

Eraddor looked at Thamalos, who could tell he didn't want to do it, though it was necessary now. Thamalos nodded as he helped Bironn back to his seat. He knew that like Levus, Eraddor would be able to grab the weapon with no issues. This *likely* would do nothing but prove Sydis right and add more fuel to the inferno. But he had no choice now.

Eraddor turned to face the blade. It stared at him coldly as he walked closer to it. Sydis, along with the other council members, watched with great interest. Eraddor reached his hand slowly toward the blade. He closed his hand around the hilt and lifted the Moonsaber from its pillow.

The council burst into talk. A large smile grew on Sydis' face. Seth yelled to quiet everyone, but it was to no use. Eraddor finally let go of the sword. As it fell on the pillow, it somehow released a metallic clang. A hush fell over the council. How it could do that when landing on the softness of the pillow?

Sydis commented, "Well, I see it is clear now. Obviously, the race of Man is the most oblivious to the sword's dark power! He did not even flinch when grasping it!"

Eraddor fired back, "I felt nothing when I touched the blade, this is true. That does not mean that the race of Man should be vilified. Levus has been able to wield the sword to take out more foes than even a mage's spell. He's able to utilize that power while most men could not. That dark energy has only been apparent a few times. Yes, it is of great concern that we determine how it works. Yet to make an assumption like this so early is preposterous!"

"I agree with Eraddor," Seth said. "This sword is something that no one in our world has ever seen. That is why I have brought in someone who might know more about this blade."

From the same door the young man brought the sword through, a familiar figure limped in. Using a cane, Cerrapies walked over to Seth and nodded.

"Master Cerrapies, you are a blacksmith from the Dyyros continent and have previous knowledge of this sword. If you would please share what you know with the council, it would be appreciated."

Cerrapies nodded again and turned to face the council. He moved haltingly to the blade.

"It is because of the metal used to create it that this blade is special. Nearly twenty-five years ago, Jared Sintar, who resided on the mainland before moving to Arnis on Dyyros, found the metal on a mission to recover stolen goods from a rich business owner in Cordca by some thieves. The metal was part of that cache robbed. Customary at the time, the Cordcan Guard could keep a small percentage of the recovered items if the bounty left the city walls. Jared chose it instead of any jewels and precious stones. He came to me and wished me to make a weapon of it."

Cerrapies took up the sword and began to look at it. Sydis and Bironn watched curiously. The rest of the council, however, was focused on another aspect of the blacksmith's explanation.

Hirronisse stood up and asked, "Jared Sintar? The same one who won the last Elf Games? I was there at the final event of his victory. Just a boy myself, entering my manhood."

Thamalos answered before Cerrapies could. "The same. Who else could produce a child as resistant to the

69

sword's powers? The more time I have spent with Levus, the more I begin to think I'm with a young Jared."

Cerrapies continued, "The Elf Games were when I first met Jared. He was always an unexpected and clever man. To win the games and disappear is no easy task. Enough about that for now, though. When the government fell to Ulcinar, Jared soon disappeared. He left the sword and this medallion, but hoped to hide them from his son, Levus. He was acting strangely before he vanished. Kept saying voices were telling him to do things that he didn't want to do."

Servion asked, "What happened to Jared?"

"The details are not exact, but this is what I heard. Jared wanted to destroy the sword, but as normal fire didn't affect it, he tried to get to the Isle of Time. He was hoping to get answers from its supposed sole resident. No one knows his or her name, but the idea it was a one-way trip must've crossed his mind. Taking a crude 'flying' device someone in Tartus invented, he went to the highest point in Dyyros and jumped off as sort of a trial run. I have no clue about his fate. He entrusted the sword to his wife, who did her best to mask it from her son. Levus is just as resourceful as his old man was, though."

The council sat in silence, trying to figure out what course of action should be taken. Thamalos and Eraddor were very intrigued by this news. The whole time they knew him, Levus never had mentioned the history of his sword. Had he kept silent on purpose, or did he just not know?

Seth played with his beard. "This is very interesting. This sword has more to it than meets the eye."

Cerrapies said, "With the approval of the council, I would like to take the medallion, melt it down, and add its metal to the sword. My reasoning is that back on Dyyros, Ulcinar knows that Levus has a sword and a medallion. By taking the medallion and adding it to the sword, we can mislead the enemy as to its location, being the only ones who know what truly happened to it."

The council looked at each other, more shocked than anything. It certainly was an odd request. Yet this man did seem to be able to block the sword's power long enough during his work as a smith.

Seth finally stated, "I can find no objection to this. Unless there are others present who think otherwise, you have the council's permission."

The room was silent. Thamalos wanted to say something, because he believed that combining the two objects might make the dark power of the sword stronger. Yet, if the council came together on something this early, it might lead to future agreements with similar ease. Cerrapies nodded as he grabbed the sword and medallion.

As the smith headed out, Seth said, "Not that I don't trust you, but I will have five guards watching over you the entire time you have the sword in your possession."

Cerrapies replied, "A reasonable precaution. I'll even return the sword to that pillow once it is completed."

When Cerrapies left, three guards followed him. Eraddor glimpsed two others waiting outside join them as the door slammed shut. When everything quieted down again, Seth cleared his throat.

"Well, until Master Cerrapies returns with the sword, that matter will have to wait. Let us move on. Those are my main points. I'll let everyone list their top five grievances, starting with Thetalis. Then we'll take to lunch and return."

* * * * *

In an outpost tower near the Ettui city of Corelitii, Ulcinar and Kile stood in the strategy room. On a stone table, a miniature model of the island of Fort Za sat, surrounded by large cylindrical stones in the part representing the ocean.

71

"I have varying thoughts about this plan, Lord Ulcinar."

"What seems to be the problem? The attack is brilliant. With the situation as it is, now is the time to begin my plan. In the end, the mainland will be no threat to us."

Kile walked to another table, staring up at a light. He drew his sword out and pointed the tip of his blade toward the southern tip of a more detailed Fort Za model.

He explained, "The basics of the attack are very standard and under normal conditions would work. Yet Fort Za is no normal fort. It is defended by an island-long wall which no army has ever penetrated. It is then guarded by a second wall, which holds the gate to the fort. Both walls are heavily defended by archers. The fort itself has nearly 30,000 troops in it."

Ulcinar gave a confident laugh. "What of their leader?"

Kile slowly followed as Ulcinar left the room.

"They are led by General Seth Medkar, a rapid yet controlled man. He hasn't seen major combat in years and when he did, the victory did not have pleasing results."

"Then we agree that if we can penetrate the walls, Fort Za will fall."

"Yes, it should. But it would take an army of thousands to topple it."

As Kile said this, he followed Ulcinar outside to a balcony overlooking the plains past Corelitii. Kile's eyes grew wide as he reached the railing. A deafening chant arose from what seemed to be a countless amount of Ettui soldiers.

"Will this suffice?"

A sick smile grew on Kile's face. With this army, it would be impossible for Fort Za's to be victorious . . . or anyone's army for that matter. Kile gave a vile laugh.

"I want you to lead this army into Fort Za, and to not let up the attack until the sword is in our possession. The vessels will be completed at the Barbatan shipyards in a few weeks. I must return to Dyyros to ensure that my power there does not slip. When you take the fort, join me there. Can I trust you with this?"

"Yes, Lord Ulcinar."

Ulcinar walked back into the tower leaving Kile to bask in the sight of what would be the most dominant army the world had ever known.

CHAPTER 4
The New Ally

Divi and her Dragonian guide, Minat, followed a stone path leading into the woods. Minat was a taller individual then the rest of the Dragonians she had met. He wore a special white robe with gold trimming. What she'd heard about Minat awakened Divi's curiosity. From what Gionti had described to her, Minat was the only Dragonian to ever fight in a war: the legendary Great War between the barbarians. He was also the one whom the dragons of the continent trusted most. That was why he had been chosen to lead her.

"You are very brave, young mage."

The statement took her aback. This was the first time he had spoken in the whole hour they were walking. Divi looked down at the ground.

"It's something I have to do."

Minat responded, "People do not do things because the things are necessary to do. Wars don't have to be fought, but people still die in them because it is something superiors tell their soldiers they must do. You don't have to bury a loved one, yet you do because others tell you to or you care for the deceased enough to do it. Then again, we believe in cleansing by fire rather than burying. We only do that in respect to our elven friends. Who is it that drives you to come here?"

Divi didn't know how to respond. Could she tell him that she, a mage, was in love with a human? How would he understand?

"There's a man . . . a man I care for very much. So much that . . . I'm willing to die for him."

With a smile, Minat looked ahead. "Self-sacrifice. A tell-tale sign of love. I always wondered how one person can influence the feelings of another so that they would be willing to kill . . . or be killed to defend or save them. People throw 'love' around foolishly, yet I see it as something different for you."

Divi replied, "It is hard to describe. It just . . . happens. My mom would always say that I would find love after experiencing the darkest of nights, heading into the light of the dawn. In a way, she ended up being right. I never saw it coming. But now that I have, I don't want to lose it, so will fight for it with everything I have."

Minat stopped as they finally reached the end of the pathway. The road was flanked by two large monuments. Beyond that was nothing but forest. Divi turned to face Minat as he took a couple more steps.

"This is it. This is where I will leave you. Beyond this point, you will be on your own. I cannot interfere or help you. I am certain Gionti told you why."

Divi adjusted the bag the Dragonians had given her. He did mention that since she was seeking the elemental stones, that none of the townsfolk could assist her. If she wanted to get them, she'd have to fight through their dragon protectors. Facing a dragon without magic scared her, but if that is what had to be done, she'd find a way. Minat put his hand on her shoulder.

He continued, "I wish you much luck, Divi. Your intentions are pure and that is the essence of success. Be careful of the dragons, though. Most of them have no masters anymore and do what they please, taking orders only from their appointed king. Yet you still may find a friend on this continent if you seek hard enough."

Divi nodded that she understood the dangers as she walked past Minat and into the forest. She didn't know what she would run into, but Minat was right. She had a feeling that she wouldn't be alone in the woods. That thought carried her along until her guide was no longer in sight.

* * * * *

Hours had passed since Divi left Minat at the end of the path. She had run into nothing but a few small animals and some birds. She even thought that perhaps the whole dragon thing was just to scare visitors. No, it couldn't be. Thamalos had often mentioned Dragonian dragons to her and their usefulness when the elves controlled Barbata.

Divi sat on a rock near a stream. The heat was almost unbearable. She was so determined to find whatever it was she was looking for that the humidity didn't faze her until now. She opened her pouch and rummaged through it. No water. This was what she feared. Divi threw the pouch on the ground near her. It befuddled her that the Dragonians didn't give her water. Instead, they gave her a bunch of tools that she didn't even know how to use. She gave a deep sigh, but then she heard a distant noise. It sounded like a running stream. Divi jumped off the rock and ran toward the sound, heading up a small hill. Water! The stream was small, but it would suit her purpose.

Divi took a smoother way down and dove her face into the stream. How good it felt to have the cold water on her face. She pulled her head out and cupped some water to her mouth. The water was refreshingly good as it passed between her lips. Divi splashed her face again. She though that nothing could ruin the moment.

A sound like the crack of thunder carried from the distance. Divi quickly lifted her face from the water. After a short silence, the same sound reverberated through the forest, appearing closer than the previous one.

This was not good. She stood up and searched the area. From what she could see, nothing was even close to her. A vibration suddenly rocked the ground beneath her. Divi at first thought she was feeling things, but there was the vibration again! She knew it this time because a puddle of water on the ground began to ripple.

Roar!

Whatever it was, it was getting closer. Divi climbed back up the hill and grabbed the pouch she had thrown. The vibrations were getting larger now. She began to sprint in the opposite direction of the roar . . . or so she hoped. Yet with the vibrations growing, Divi saw no other option but to face whatever it was that pursued her. In a quick motion, she grabbed her staff and readied it for battle.

Nothing was behind her. Everything got eerily quiet as she scanned the area. Something wasn't right here. She moved a couple steps to her right.

Suddenly, a huge white dragon using the thick foliage of the treetops for cover, landed in front of Divi. Her eyes opened wide as it instantly began to hover.

The dragon had a narrow face with orange whiskers. Its red eyes burned deep into Divi's. She slowly backed away as the dragon grunted in her direction. It never took its eyes off her as she backed into a tree.

It gave a loud roar when it settled on the ground, causing the earth to shake. Divi could smell its breath despite being at least fifty feet away. She had to do something because she knew it was only a matter of time before the dragon charged at her. If only she was camouflaged, like the lizards that blended into the rocks around them when they stood still!

Divi dashed away from the dragon, who with another deafening roar gave chase. She tried everything she could think of to lose the creature. She started by weaving in between trees and rocks, but the dragon seemed to still be able to track her. She quickly tried to change direction, but it was not fooled. A gust of wind slammed against her as she changed direction again. She knew she wouldn't be able to keep this up for too much longer.

Divi decided to take on the dragon, and hope that she would get lucky . . . very lucky. She turned around, and the dragon stopped as well. Divi drew her staff and held it in attack position. The dragon slowly advanced toward her until she backed into a tree. As the dragon snorted, hot air ejected from its nostrils. Despite the fear she felt inside, she stood her ground. The dragon moved its head forward until it was nearly nose-to-nose with Divi. It breathed more hot air on her.

Suddenly, from the tree she was standing under, a woman with a vine tied to her ankles dropped and stopped at Divi's eyeline. The dragon seemed just as surprised as Divi was.

The woman said, "Boo."

The dragon roared while the woman twisted on the vine to free herself. As she did, she kicked the dragon in the face, which caused it to fall back a few steps. Divi couldn't believe the courage this woman showed. She had no fear as she unsheathed her sword. Feet now planted on the ground, the woman took a couple of swipes, but none hit the dragon. Divi was confused that the creature was so easily frightened by someone just swinging a weapon at it.

It attempted to bite the woman, but she moved out of the way and apparently slashed at the dragon's side. The creature cried and quickly fled. The woman watched until it was out of sight before turning to face her.

Divi gave a sigh of relief as she examined the woman. She wore armguards that went up to her elbow, lightweight body armor, and a skirt that reached just above her knees. Her boots went up just below her knees. Her brown hair reached to her shoulders and her blue eyes twinkled in the declining sun. The woman sheathed her sword and took a deep breath.

"Are you okay?"

Divi replied, "Yes. That was amazing! How could you fight a dragon off like that? It was like it feared you."

The woman was about to answer when a male scream sounded in the distance. Both of them looked in the direction it came from. A loud roar followed. The woman looked at Divi.

"Come on."

Divi and the woman sprinted toward the sound. Divi was running her fastest, but her new companion was much too quick and surprisingly agile with the armor she wore. As they reached the source, Divi tripped over her own feet in shock. It was Tasi! He was alive!

The dragon roared again. She realized that if nothing was done soon, Tasi wouldn't be alive for much longer. She faced the woman, who was shockingly doing nothing.

"Tasi!" Divi yelled.

The woman looked at him and then back at Divi. "Do you know this person?"

"Yes! You must help him!"

The woman breathed a sigh and shouted, "Gerritonnee! Huriop freii triya!" *Gerritonnee! Let him go!*

Why did she speak Elvish to the dragon? Baffled, Divi watched as the dragon moved slowly away from Tasi, who was stiff with fear. He dropped to his knees when the dragon left. He was breathing heavily, but otherwise appeared fine. Divi sprinted over to him and helped him up.

"I'm so glad you're alive! I thought you had perished!"

Tasi finally shook off the shock from the dragon attack and replied, "You're glad? I though you died!"

"What a lovely reunion."

Both Divi and Tasi faced the woman, who was petting the dragon.

"Sorry about Gerritonnee. She was just doing her job."

Tasi asked, "You and this dragon . . . know each other?

"Who are you?"

The woman halted her interactions with the dragon to face them, adjusting her wristbands as she walked up to them.

"We can talk about this over supper. Though it would be appropriate for me to introduce myself."

She extended her hand and Divi cautiously accepted it. "My name is Amber."

"My name is Divi and my companion's name is Tasi."

"Well, Divi and Tasi, follow me."

Nighttime came shortly after they arrived at one of Amber's camps. From what she described, she had a number of these bases set up, made so she could travel anywhere in the south forest and have some haven to call her own. It had been helpful as well when bad weather was on the horizon; she knew she wasn't far from having a dry place. "Also, this way I can . . ." she trailed off and did not continue.

When they arrived, Tasi gaped at the vast, multi-room construction of sticks and leaves. Divi gave a low whistle at the hearth Amber had built for her campfire, partially surrounded by a screen made of wood and some netting. A line made from hard tree roots served as a clothesline, and from it a couple of brown cloths were hanging. In one corner of the camp, Divi saw many bones and animal furs. Amber must have been a very good hunter, though Divi realized that she had two mouths to feed in her dragon companion.

Amber prepared dinner, positioning their cooking meals for their final minute over the open flame. She wasn't used to having to feed so many, but she admitted the company was welcome. After being and seeing what Amber had been and seen the past couple years, she was relieved to see anyone friendly.

The wind was cool, but very light. Despite this, Divi still covered herself with a nearby animal fur. She didn't know what it was, but when she was someplace she hadn't been before, she felt cold. It had been the same way on

Dyyros. She didn't think it was because she was afraid. Perhaps it was because each time, lives were lost, yet here she was still alive to talk about it. What made her so special, to survive while others fell? Not knowing magic didn't make her unique. In the eyes of nearly everyone, it made her seem weak. Time would tell.

Tasi was warming his hands close to the hot flame as Amber returned with some plates. After confirming their meals were well-cooked, Amber dropped two pieces of meat in front of Divi and Tasi, who responded by gaping at them. Tasi looked at Amber, who now sat across from them, ripping large chunks of meat off the animal thigh with her teeth. As she reached for her drink, she noticed both mages staring at her.

Amber asked, "Not hungry? If I were you, I would eat while I could. You never know when your last meal will be in this place. Plus, it's just rude to not eat something your hostess provided. This animal is hard to catch."

She took another chunk out and began to chew. For some reason, Amber seemed very familiar to Tasi, like he had briefly seen her before.

Divi sniffed the meat. It looked disgusting, especially because she didn't know what animal it came from. Yet the meat smelled delicious. She nibbled at a small piece. Surprisingly, the meat was just as good as Amber seemed to find it.

"Tell me . . . Amber, what are you doing here?" asked Tasi.

Amber waited until she was done swallowing before she answered.

"I'm on a quest. I'm supposed to bring the four elemental stones from this continent back to the person who gave me the quest. From then on, I'll be free."

Curiously, Tasi watched Amber place her cup down and wipe her mouth with a cloth. A smile of recognition grew on his face. *Well, if the gods aren't watching over us!*

He knew exactly who this woman was. They had never met, but he knew her from reputation and because Neeza could never stop talking about her when he ordained her quest.

Tasi exclaimed, "But of course! Now I remember! You're a half-mage."

Divi looked up with great interest. A half-mage coming to Myyril was very rare indeed. She was only three the last time she remembered an attempt at the Paladin Trials. She wondered how Amber sneaked under the system, as paladin hopefuls returning home was usually a big event and highly publicized. There was even a scribe who kept records of every half-mage that tried, yet she never saw Amber's name in there. The only one who had the authority to keep a Paladin Trial secret was the High Mage . . . at the time, her father. What made Amber's case so special? She figured perhaps if Amber's family had passed on, in which case they might have a small ceremony, but to have none at all? Divi gave a silent sigh. She shouldn't have been surprised. It was just another secret that her father had kept from her. And he wondered why she didn't trust him more.

Her father never even told her exactly what Trials the paladin candidates had to accomplish, but if they succeeded, their families would be able to once again re-enter Myyrilian society. It was Myyrilian rule that all half-mages be taken at birth to an island called Tydos. Their families would be barred from the Myyrilian city unless their half-mage child returned as a paladin. No one had succeeded, at least in Divi's short lifetime. Only seven in the long history of the paladinship, have ever completed their task. This, she supposed, caused some friction between the mages and half-mages.

Amber looked at Tasi suspiciously. "What is it to you?"

Tasi replied, "Divi and I are mages. I was actually there . . . well, more of an accidental observer, the day Neeza appointed this task to you. That was four years ago. Where have you been all this time? And wasn't your quest to acquire the Seven Jewels of Arr'Rallzeen? They were fabled to be on this continent as well. Why are you chasing after the stones?"

For whatever reason, Amber paused. It appeared the half-mage was analyzing him. She took another bite before tossing the bone behind her.

"What you heard, you will speak nothing of. My real quest was tasked to me before that show with the rest of the council. What was said, I promised not to tell. Neeza met with me. Although I didn't know him well, he seemed like a good, trustworthy man. It's why I agreed to it. Know only that everything Neeza did was so I would end up here."

Tasi was taken aback by her answer. It was highly peculiar that Neeza would assign a Paladin Trial behind the council's backs. Was she lying? If he did put her to acquiring the elemental stones in secret, why would he do that? And what did she mean by saying *she* agreed to it? Paladin Trials were ordered. There were no choices for the hopeful. They performed their tasks or they failed. Whatever the answers were, she wasn't about to divulge them, based on her tone of voice.

Divi didn't seem to care about that, only asking, "Am I the only one who had a different opinion of him?"

Amber stared at Divi, confused at her question.

Tasi clarified, "She is Neeza's daughter, heir to the Myyrilian throne."

He faced Divi to see how she would react to his comment. Her gaze went to the ground, never even meeting his. It wasn't the reaction he hoped for. She would have to be ready to assume the responsibility one day, whether she wanted to or not.

Amber ate a loose piece of meat left on her wooden plate as she looked at Divi and Tasi.

"Well, that is interesting. I thought that the daughter to the High Mage would be stuck up."

"You can't assume everything," Divi said.

"Anyways, to answer your question . . . Tasi? It took me a while to get to this place, but I eventually climbed up the steep cliff on the west."

Divi interrupted, "What about the Dragonians? Didn't they try to stop you?"

"They were more impressed that I was able to sneak onto their land without their knowledge. I told them about my quest and they obliged. I spent the next year setting up camp here and a few other places, then started exploring and mapping each section of the continent. It's amazing just how much the dragons will avoid you until they find out what you're after."

Divi asked, "How about your dragon friend?"

"She and I . . . ran into each other in the northern forest. I was just coming back after scouting the mountains up there. We fought, I won, I spared her life, and she's followed me ever since. So, I have her guard the sacred items I collect. You were getting close to the camp they were currently hidden in, which is why she acted the way she did."

Tasi repeated, "Sacred items?"

Divi said, "We came here also to find four special stones. Will you help us? They may even be the sacred items you seek."

"If you mind me asking, why do you seek the stones?"

"There is a friend in need. Those stones will let us reach the Isle of Time so we can try to correct a wrongful past."

Amber looked at her strangely before she replied, "Well then, you are fortunate to run into me."

She stood up and walked to one of the smaller buildings. When she returned, she was carrying two burlap rice bags. Amber sat down again and dropped both to the ground softly. She reached into the bag to her left and pulled a rock from it large enough that she had to use two hands to hold it. Divi and Tasi both stared in amazement. In the middle of the rock, a green jewel glowed brightly as she took it out. The light, though, died shortly after. In the brief time it was there, Divi did see a strange symbol on it.

"This is the Relic of Wind. I also recovered the one of Earth."

Tasi nodded and said, "Elementals. These stones are representatives of the four elements, each containing the essence of the element inside them."

Levus' explanation of the Isle of Time suddenly entered her mind. 'Only those who hoist the elements may prove themselves worthy of entering the Gates of Time.'. Things about this fable were finally coming together. She only wished Levus was here to see this. Amber put the stone back into the bag and seemed to listen carefully to her surroundings. After a few moments, she walked back to Divi and Tasi. En route, she grabbed a bag of nuts, taking one out. She used her teeth, struggling to break the tough shell as she joined them.

Tasi asked, "You got these yourself?"

"Yes. I didn't say that it was easy. It took me over a year to get those two. I've been recovering from my injuries in between. You two came at a good time. I was going to the Water Temple tomorrow to hopefully get the Water Relic. I guess I could use the help of two mages . . . that is, if it's not against the Myyrilian Code for the Paladinship. I would hate to be denied because of a technicality."

Tasi chuckled at Amber's sarcasm at the end. "I won't say anything if you don't."

Divi said, "We will go with you."

Amber gave a big smile. "Well, I like your courage. You're going to need it."

Getting frustrated about her inability to retrieve the nut's innards, unsheathed her sword and crashed it against the nut. The shell shattered into numerous pieces. Amber victoriously grabbed the nuts and ate them.

"That is a phenomenal sword you have. What is it made of?"

Amber explained, "I searched for some of the best metals that Tydos had to offer. What made my sword unique was this large crystal shard that I found and mixed it with the other metals. Oddly, it not only made my attacks stronger, but it from time to time will sparkle like the sun hitting the water. Because of this, I named it Hiyyan Litarrii."

Tasi asked, "What does that mean?"

"It's elvish for Holy Light."

Tasi said, "Its beautiful."

She said nothing at first. She was still being cautious with her answers toward her new companions. They were mages after all. Granted, these were the nicest mages she had met up to this point, but she couldn't completely trust them after just a few hours. She already said too much when it came to how she got her Paladin Trial.

"Is that how you've been able to beat all these dragons before you met us? Just relying on the power of the sword?"

Amber replied, "Well, sort of. I guess you can say there was one dragon that I didn't take care of, but I got what I wanted and he hasn't found me yet. So, I'm not worrying about him."

A heavy wind suddenly blew across the camp. Amber looked to the sky. Gerritonnee, who was lying down on the far end of camp, even glanced up. Divi and Tasi followed their gazes, but couldn't see anything in the sky themselves. Maybe it was just an ordinary wind, if a bit stronger than usual.

Amber finally said, "We should get some rest now. Be up by first light so we can arrive at the Water Palace by midday."

She signaled to Gerritonnee, who got up and walked over to the fire. In one snort, Gerritonnee extinguished the flames. The entire camp went dim as the moon provided the only light. Divi could see Amber walking toward one of the huts as Gerritonnee returned to her place.

As Divi decided to stand up, she thought she heard a roar in the distance. She really couldn't tell what it was, but it sounded loud. She walked up to the other hut before lying down inside. A cold breeze came as she covered herself with a blanket. Divi listened again for the strange noise, and she heard it one more time before she eventually fell to sleep's whim.

* * * * *

General Seth Medkar paced the halls of Fort Za. The first day of the meetings went by as smoothly as he hoped. Yet he knew that not all the days would go this easily. There was so much to discuss. Seth hoped this council would last no more than a week, but with all the issues that needed to be examined it could take as long as a month. It was nearing the middle of the night, but he couldn't sleep. His soldiers just thought he suffered from insomnia sometimes, but he had an odd intuition. Of course, this wasn't the only reason he was up this night. His medics were examining Levus to see if they could figure out the problem that plagued him.

As he approached, the door to Levus' room opened and the chief medic, Hideon, peeked his head out.

Seth turned to face him. "So, have you determined what is wrong with him?"

The medic cleared his throat and said, "Unfortunately, I have found no visible signs of sickness. It's almost like . . . like he's asleep. Trapped in some sort of dream. Come inside."

Seth gave him a skeptical look as he followed him in the room. Hideon knew the reaction he would get from his superior. Their general was not a believer in the Elvish folklore and ancient legends that usually interested anyone. Too many existed just to try and explain irrationally why something happened. That Levus was trapped in a dream was one of those theories he never ascribed to.

Seth followed the medic into Levus' quarters. The room was fairly well lit with candles. Hideon brought in a few extra. Both men slowly walked to the unconscious patient's bedside. Seth didn't see anything particularly wrong with the boy initially.

The first thing to catch Seth's eye was an amulet around Levus' neck. He began to fiddle with it. It was damaged heavily.

Hideon noticed the general's curiosity and explained, "It is some Elvish medallion. Probably to ward off evil spirits or something like that. The orb is deeply cracked, however. Whatever function it served, it can no longer do it."

Seth released the amulet. It was rather strange that the elves gave gifts to anyone but a sovereign friend. He doubted they would give this to a boy they hardly knew. There was a reason—perhaps to ward off evil spirits. *What is with this boy?*

Hideon continued, "Even without success in my original search, I did notice a few things on him that you might find very interesting. While I was examining the body for marks or discolorations, I checked to see if his eyes showed any signs."

Hideon slowly pulled up his eyelid so Levus' green right eye could be seen. Seth didn't look very impressed so far. Hideon let go of his brow, closing Levus' eye.

Seth stated, "He has green eyes. What is the big deal about this? I know many with this eye color."

"Not like this."

Hideon next lifted Levus' left eyelid. Seth couldn't believe it. This one was blue! This was truly odd, indeed.

He had never seen that in his lifetime. The medic let the boy's eye close again.

"Have you ever seen that before? A person with two eye colors?" asked Seth.

Hideon shook his head and replied, "No, not many cases like this have ever been seen. Actually, I could find none. In this fort's existance, nearly a million soldiers have come here, and all the records show no one had this. I even asked the half-elf doctors. They too have never seen it, almost shocked it doesn't happen more. But that is not the only thing. I saw this."

The medic switched his attention to Levus' right arm. When he turned it over, the veins near the elbow and wrist had a black and blue color. Seth, again, was unimpressed in the beginning. It appeared to be just a bruise. It took a few seconds, but the closer he looked, the more he could see a pattern of some sort. It looked almost like a large eye peering at them from Levus' skin. *What is going on?*

Hideon explained, "It has been like this since we took the sword away from Levus' room. This mark wasn't there when he was first brought in. It's not a bruise, nor is it a burn. I summoned Bironn, since he's had some training in the Divination School, to see if it was some type of black magic or curse, but he sensed nothing."

Seth walked over to the window overlooking the interior garden of Fort Za. The mostly cloudy sky covered the moons of Gyyerlith like a blanket.

He finally asked, "Hideon. Is this boy evil?"

"I don't think so, but certainly something is hiding inside him and doesn't want to be found. These 'bruises' are a manifestation of whatever it is. I know that sounds crazy."

With a narrow smile, Seth faced Hideon.

"Perhaps. It is late, so the lighting might be playing tricks on our thoughts. Re-evaluate him in the morning. If conditions remain the same, return the sword to the room and check him at night. If the sword has an effect, I want to know."

Hideon nodded as he turned to gather his things. As he moved to leave, he suddenly stopped. "General, where is the sword?"

Seth replied, "That blacksmith, Cerrapies, was supposed to forge the medallion into the blade."

The council room lay silently in the darkness of night. As usual when nothing was going on inside, a stone slab covering the gap in the ceiling had been removed to provide natural light and airflow. The clouds covering the moons had departed, bathing it with a beautiful bluish tint.

One of the doors slowly creaked open. The noise echoed throughout the hall and the meeting room. Cerrapies sneaked in and looked around. Just as he thought. No one was around this part of the fort, not even a couple of guards. The five guards who were supposed to watch him had been tricked out of their duties. He hated playing by anyone's rules. He was surprised by the success of his guile on the elf guards. He thought they would be not so easily fooled, but now he knew they were no different than the Dyyros soldiers. How disappointing. Cerrapies closed the door and walked down the two steps to the next tier.

He was very pleased of his work on the Moonsaber. Welding the medallion to it had gone much faster than expected. This sword was truly amazing with its ease to manipulate and its astonishing beauty. Cerrapies slowly unsheathed the Moonsaber to marvel at his improved weapon of death. The sword appeared the same, but by melting the medallion, he made it an inch longer and added another coating around the blade. Small traces of gold remained on the hilt, the only clue to indicate what it used to be. It seemed even sharper than before, yet what surprised Cerrapies the most was how it still felt the same weight.

When he finished, he expected the sword to be heavier. He had to make a new sheath for it, but that was not an issue. For an island with no wildlife or trees, they certainly were well supplied with fresh leathers, furs, and wood.

Cerrapies grasped the handle tighter. He had always been curious why Jared never gave him the sword instead of Levus. The boy was a great hunter, but no one could match the master of swords, Cerrapies. He held the blade high up in the air as he neared the pedestal in the middle of the room. The sword felt as if he had held it all his life. A deep smile grew on his face.

"Vuituii opii hui."

Cerrapies quickly dropped the sword and it landed with a crash. What just happened? What was that voice? It was the first time he had ever experience that sensation, and he was frightened of it. *Nothing can frighten the mighty Cerrapies*, he told himself.

He took one more glance at the Moonsaber. It sat silently staring at him with its red eye at the base of the hilt. Cerrapies couldn't take it anymore. He ran out of the room and slammed the door shut. As he did this, a cloud covered the moon, blanketing the night in complete darkness.

CHAPTER 5
The Temple of Water

The next morning was a breezy one on the Dragonian continent. Amber had them wake up early so they could get a jump on the other creatures of the island. From the stories Amber told en route to the Water Temple, there were other dangerous creatures on the continent besides the dragons. One of which were the suikans, wolf-like beasts that stood on their hind legs and were ruthless hunters. Suikans, Amber said, were surprisingly nimble and extremely strong. They feared no creature but the mighty dragons that populated the continent. Amber had fought and killed one of these creatures and even showed the scar that went across her back. Most of their trip passed with conversation between Tasi and Amber. He seemed to have an unheralded curiosity about Amber.

Tasi commented, "That is a very interesting story. May I ask you something?"

"Go right ahead. I have nothing to hide."

"What type of path did you choose on Tydos? From the stories you describe, I can't tell if you mastered in healing spells, attack spells, or a combination of both."

Amber gave a deep smile. "Neither. I chose the battlemage route."

Tasi suddenly stopped dead in his tracks. Amber and Divi continued to walk until they noticed that he wasn't following them. Amber doubled back toward him and put her arms to her hips.

"What's up?" she asked. "I don't mind talking, but we can't stay stationary for too long in this place."

Tasi finally asked, "You're a battlemage?"

Amber nodded while giving him a strange look. Was he deaf?

"That is the rarest of the classes ever trained in on Tydos."

Amber said, "That's right. Keep walking and I'll explain."

Tasi rejoined them as they walked uphill through the ever-weakening woods.

"You see, most half-mages, when given the choice for which class they will master, like the option to be able to heal themselves if injured. As you probably know, if you train for both attacker and healer, those skills are weaker. Those who are strictly healer class never do well in the Paladin training. Yet most fear the route I took because they fear getting hurt. I don't. So, I took the battlemage class. There were only four of us."

Divi, who was quiet throughout most of the trip, asked, "What is the battlemage route?"

"It means we only know how to use attack spells. We can't heal ourselves, but our spells do double the damage. As a battlemage, I use all my spells through my weapon. Whether it's my sword, an axe, whatever."

Divi couldn't believe how much her father hadn't told her about the half-mages. But she smiled, remembering how Levus was when she told him about the elves. When she realized that she was acting the same way, all she could do was grin. She hoped against hope that she would be able to have more experiences like that with Levus. Her greatest fear was that she had made the wrong choice. What if there was something simpler than fighting dragons and going back in Time to help him?

Divi's thoughts were interrupted by Amber running up the last incline of the hill. She seemed to be laughing as she did.

Tasi commented, "Well, she certainly likes what she does."

Both mages joined Amber, who stood at the treeless summit of the hill. At the base of its steep slope stood a medium-sized building made of stone, surrounded by water. A short bridge led to the door, which was flanked by low pillars. The cloudless sky and the waves gently hitting the shore was calming and serene.

"There it is," Amber said. "Let's go."

Tasi asked, "That's the temple? I was expecting . . . something larger."

Amber was already running down the hill, the large sack carried over her shoulder bouncing uncontrollably. Tasi and Divi proceeded down the hill carefully. By the time the two mages made it to the bottom, Amber had already entered.

Divi couldn't believe what she was seeing when she stepped inside. The small interior was dominated by a statue against the back wall. The statue looked like a dragon with human legs and arms and it was sitting presumably in meditation. The floor had many strange grooves all leading in different directions, some difficult to see because of the moss and water fungi. On the walls, had waterfalls ended either in pools on the floor or in various elevated bowls five to seven feet high attached to the wall. One waterfall in the center of the room coming from a skylight landed in a very large pool.

"What is this place?" Tasi asked.

Amber stepped forward with her hand on her sword hilt. As she moved around the central waterfall, Divi and Tasi followed. Amber stopped in front of the large statue and sighed.

"I hate this part."

Tasi asked once again, "What *is* this place?"

"This is the Temple Gate. In order to enter the temple, a puzzle needs to be solved. It took me days to figure out the Wind puzzle. The Earth puzzle was easier, but still took me a day. That's why we left early."

"Great," Tasi commented

Divi asked, "What does that slate say?"

94

Amber examined it carefully before pulling a small book from her pouch. She flipped through the pages. From time to time, she looked up, back to the words, before returning to her book. After a few minutes, Amber closed the book and returned it to her pouch.

"So, what does this mean? What is that?" asked Tasi.

"The riddle. Every temple gives you a riddle to help you decipher the puzzle. This one reads: *From the sea to the sky, the driest river or lake may hold the key to life rather than the most plentiful. Celebrate the greatness of the gods, for they reward those who are humble in their presence.*"

"Rather vague, isn't it?"

Divi asked, "What do we do now?"

Amber gave a small chuckle at Divi's question. "We do what it says, so what are you waiting for? Start looking."

She began to walk around the room, touching the walls around the waterfalls and pressing flagstones with her feet. She noticed some strange cylindrical curves that melded with the steps by the entrance, almost as if someone built the stairs over them. It was dry, but she couldn't see anything referring to a river like the clue stated.

Tasi looked around aimlessly. He had no clue what to look for. Although he was considered one of the brightest mages, puzzle-solving was never deemed necessary on Myyril. He began to put his hands in the pools of water, hoping to find a key of some sort.

Divi walked slowly along the edges of the chamber. She was trying to figure out what could possibly solve this thing. Just by how the place was constructed, Divi assumed that it was going to take the entire room to solve it. On the walls, there was an intricate design of lines like the ones on the floor, but when Divi compared them the wall design had nothing to do with the floor. As she moved closer to the statue in the back, she suddenly felt a vibration coming from her chest. Divi reached under her top and pulled out the gift from Arionn. While on Barbata, one of the female elf soldiers made it into a necklace for her, which she was thankful for. Now, the orb was glowing. At first Divi didn't know what do. Finally, Arionn's words came to her about using it to find the answers you might seek. She decided to try something. Closing her palm around the orb, she shut her eyes and focused.

In Divi's mind, she saw the room, empty until a sole traveler entered it. The traveler placed his bag down and reached for one of the deep bowls. From the bowl, a small piece of rock slid down, forming a downward channel that routed the water to spill out and into the floor rock grooves. It was the last thing she saw before Divi awoke from her trance. She dropped the orb back to her chest when it ceased to glow anymore.

"That's it!"

Amber and Tasi, who were still clueless as to how to solve the puzzle, watched with great curiosity as Divi ran to a bowl near the floor and examined it. They joined her.

Amber asked, "So . . .what's on your mind?"

Divi explained, "These bowls . . . this room is all important to this puzzle."

Neither Amber nor Tasi understood what she meant. Divi began to blow some dust and dirt near the exterior of the bowl. She certainly hoped that the vision she had was reality. If it wasn't, then she would just look like a fool. As she began to clear some of the dirt layers off, she uncovered a small crevice. The vision had been right! Divi worked her nail in the crevice to pull out the stone channel. It took her a couple minutes, but she finally slid the rock piece out. As she did, water flowed from the pipe and a small stream formed on the floor . . . right in the grooves!

All eyes followed as the water flowed toward the statue before turning left. Divi looked at the floor, particularly near the bottom of the statue. It was here that she made an amazing discovery. Two of the grooves went underneath the statue while the rest went around it. So that's how the puzzle was answered.

Divi ordered, "Try and find all the rock channels on the bowls and open them. Quickly!"

She ran toward the next bowl to her right, while Amber and Tasi ran to separate one's opposite of her. All three had a hard time finding the stone ducts. Some bowls had complex ones. There were some that had two, some that turned, and some that needed to stay closed in order for it to work.

A couple hours had passed since Divi discovered the secret of the temple gate. All three were getting very frustrated. She knew this had to be the way to unlocking the gate, but what more could they do?

Amber threw her sword to the ground and yelled. "I can't believe this! We've tried every well and every single combination possible. Why is it not working?"

Divi replied, "We must be missing something."

"Then again, we may not be doing what is necessary to unlock it," added Tasi.

She thought hard. The vision she'd had told them what to do, but it hadn't told her the right way it was supposed to be done.

"All right. We know what these grooves and bowls are for, but none of them went to the correct outlet. Amber, what was that message on the statue?"

Amber slowly began to recite it again. *"From the sea to the sky, the driest river or lake may hold the key to life rather than the most plentiful. Celebrate the greatness of the gods, for they reward those who are humble in their presence."*

Divi continued her rambling "From the sea to the sky . . . they must . . . They must represent the location of the bowls on the wall with this waterfall in the middle being the sea. Umm. . . celebrate the greatness of the gods . . . Humble in their presence."

Divi studied the two grooves that went underneath the statue. Those must be what that part meant.

"Humbleness to the gods . . . usually refers to kneeling . . . usually in the center is preferred since that is where most statues representing them are. Makes the one praying feel closer to what they're worshiping. That part must describe those grooves. Okay, the driest river or lake may hold the key . . . driest river or lake may hold the key," continued Divi.

Tasi and Amber joined her in looking around the area for what that could mean. Divi wasn't sure if there was anything dry in the temple gate. Most of the floor was saturated with green moss or water fungi, and the walls had the waterfalls coming from them. The air had so much moisture in it as well. Nothing on the statue seemed out of place. Divi was baffled.

Amber was also getting frustrated. She picked up a jar she just noticed filled with water near the west wall. She thought something may have been underneath or behind it, but no such luck. There were a few other pots lined against the wall on both sides, hard to see since they blended in.

"I can't believe they make this so difficult!"

The statue stared silently at Amber as if it was mocking her. A sudden fire grew in her eyes.

"You! You get a thrill out of this! Take this!"

Amber threw the pot at the statue's dragon head. Divi went to her knees, ducking to avoid the shards. Throwing the pot gave Amber a little pleasure and relieved some of the stress she felt, but Divi was about to get up and yell at her until she noticed something happening to the pool near the statue. On the ceiling, the skylight opening seemed to close very slightly. Divi stood up and examined it.

Tasi said, "Hey! I don't know if this is good."

Amber and Divi looked where Tasi was pointing. Water dripped above the entrance to the temple. Divi once again looked at the statue. The pot Amber threw had

98

knocked out several of the dragon's teeth, and water that had spilled out of it now dripped from the crack in its mouth. *That's it!*

Divi yelled, "Amber! Tasi! Get me all the pots with the water in them! Quickly!"

Curious, both did what Divi requested. Divi poured the pots contents into the dragon's mouth. With every pot used, Amber noticed the waterfall in the center shrank a bit while a new waterfall was forming in front of the entrance. When all the pots had been used, the waterfall in the center ceased, while the one at the entrance began filling an area surrounding the stairs. The group watched in amazement. When the bowl was filled, the water spewed from two breaks in the pot. When that led the water to a pair of grooves on the floor, Divi finally understood what the riddle meant. The dry area was a bowl that blended in with the stairs. Not even the sharpest eyes would be able to see its true purpose without the water filling it up. Even the grooves were difficult to see because of the wear and weather damage.

All watched in anticipation as the water traveled past the center pool and headed for the gap below the statue's middle. The water finally flowed underneath the statue. For a couple of minutes, nothing happened. Amber grunted.

"Well, I'm thoroughly disappointed."

Just as she said this, the ground began to shake violently. All three dropped to the floor as stones from the ceiling began to fall all around them. It seemed too late to hope that they hadn't triggered a trap set by the ancients who made this. All Divi could hope for was that when the shaking stopped, they would be alive to tell about it.

* * * * *

At Fort Za, the entire council rushed out of the meeting room and out to the balcony. Thamalos stood next to Eraddor and Seth Medkar. When the quake started, Seth considered continuing during it. He didn't believe it was strong enough to cause structural damage, but with so many important dignitaries, he figured best to play it safe. The shaking had stopped nearly a minute ago, but everyone was still alarmed.

Seth said, "This is odd. Fort Za hasn't had a shake like this since we were first established."

Thamalos, despite knowing the history of the area, was still surprised. He knew this used to be a larger island almost connected with the southern tip of the mainland, separated by about thirty miles of water. Years ago, the ice at the northern most tip of the world began to melt, raising the oceans enough to engulf the doomed island. Fort Za's location was actually the top of a large hill.

After a few minutes, the group filed back into the meeting room. Thamalos and Eraddor were the last ones to re-enter. The elf prince had a weird feeling that this quake was not caused by a natural disturbance from terra. He felt Divi had a part in this, but what part he didn't know. A positive thought, because that meant she was alive and well. He was hoping to be able to sense her like earlier, but he failed. After another minute, he and Eraddor finally returned to the meeting room, a guard closing the door behind them.

* * * * *

Divi lay motionless on the ground. It had been about five minutes since the shaking had stopped, but she remained unsure whether it was safe to move. Amber was the first one to get to her knees and look around. With the exception of a few bricks that dropped from the ceiling, the structure maintained its integrity. The waterfalls continued to flow into the bowls, causing the only sound. Amber stood up just as Tasi and Divi decided to do the same.

Tasi asked, "What was that?"

Amber replied, "Don't know. That never happened in the other temples. Let's see what it looks like outside."

She headed for the exit. Tasi was about to follow, but he realized that Divi was getting up slowly and rushed to her side.

"Are you okay?" he asked.

"It's just a bruise. I'll be fine."

Tasi didn't believe her, so he kept by her side as they headed for the exit. Divi was glad he did. When the quake struck, the corner of a fallen brick hit her shoulder and it was very sore.

In the distance, Amber yelled, "Hey! Come quick!"

Tasi and Divi walked through the waterfall in front of the exit. The water felt surprisingly good. It seemed to have a healing effect on her. As they stepped out, they searched for where Amber went.

"Over here!"

Amber stood on a rock behind the temple gate, looking south. She obviously saw something of interest. They had to go up a slight incline, which blocked their view. When she and Tasi joined her, Divi forgot her pain at once. The waters of the ocean had parted to reveal a short bridge leading toward a large building entrance. The structure was not very deep, reminding Divi of the shrines back home to the Myyrilian gods which were only one room. If they were supposed to fight a dragon inside, there had to be more to it than what was in view. The ancient white bricks still dripped after being exposed from its extensive, watery veil. Gigantic pillars stood erect on each side of the door, and between them statues of dragons towered with their mouths open wide and their claws out. Divi shivered at the craftsmanship, as if every one was a stone breath away from being a real dragon.

Amber jumped off the rock and headed toward the bridge. She said, "What you two are about to experience will be the most terrifying fight of your lives. You had better be prepared."

Tasi asked, "What will we face inside?"

"The stone will be at the very end. When we reach it, we must prove our worth and defeat the Dragon Guardian. Each Guardian uses the power of the element it stands over, so I hope you know a lightning spell or two or we might be in for a short fight."

Divi gulped, flooded with terror as they first stepped on the bridge leading to the Water Temple. If what Amber said was true, what good would she be in this fight? She didn't know any lightning spells. She didn't know any magic at all. Divi tried to scare her fears away by looking up at the clear blue sky, but all she saw was the menacing gazes of the stone monsters.

As they entered through the doorway, a cool breeze struck their faces. Ahead of them sat a stairway leading down into the ocean's depths. It was evident water filled this entire room, drained upon its exposure. Divi and Tasi were starting to regret agreeing to this. Both had let their desire to help cloud the fact that mages are not good swimmers. On the contrary, Amber was fearless, storming down the stairs.

Tasi wondered how she could be that way. They were possibly about to fight a dragon. Granted, she had already fought two and survived, but this was something he and Divi never trained for. In Divi's case, she'd never trained at all. He was certain mage shield spells could block dragon's fire, but for how long? All things considered, he would rather fight a sacred-blood mage than go up against one of those mythical beasts.

A mysterious bluish light was the only illumination, dimming the area just enough to see the steps ahead of them. Tasi wasn't even sure where it came from. The sounds of water hitting the sides of the stairway startled him every time, unable to locate the source. After a few minutes of walking down the seemingly endless stairs, he could see the end of them, and a strange white light glowing there. What was that?

As they neared it, anticipation filled Divi's stomach. She could hear the powerful waterfalls in the distance. She wondered how those could still be pouring so deep under the water.

At the bottom of the staircase, the group stared in awe as they entered a long room. The floor was made of exquisite white tiles, matching the white walls on which vast, colorful pictures of dragons which must have been painted in ancient times. Waterfalls flowed from the ceiling into pools that went the length of the room along both sides. It reminded Divi of some of the wall fountains Cordca had, only much grander in scale. In some spots, the waterfalls completely engulfed the walls, hiding whatever story their pictures were trying to tell. The room shone with a bright white light, which befuddled Divi because like the one on the stairway, she could see no source for it.

Amber stopped and faced the two mages. "Ready?"

Tasi replied, "Whether we like it or not."

Divi felt the fear in him and could tell he was against the idea, but what choice did he have? He was doing this because she wanted to. They followed Amber slowly up the long room. The further they moved along, the more the waterfalls covered the walls. As deep underwater they must have been, how was the room not flooded? She really didn't like the way things were situated.

After a few minutes, they finally reached the end of the corridor, down which three large waterfalls poured. The central waterfall was much darker than the others. And there it was! The Relic of Water! It sat on a pedestal that jutted out of the corridor's end pool. One wouldn't even need to wade in to grasp it.

Tasi said, "Well, let's get this thing and get out of here quickly."

Amber quickly stopped his advance. She knew better.

After staring Tasi down, she moved forward a couple steps☐before she, too, stopped.

Divi was confused by her actions until she saw what Amber looked at. From the central waterfall, a man in a dark blue robe stepped out. His feet never fell below the water, as he stepped on it as if it were baked earth—soil made dry and crusty by the sun beating down on it. In appearance, he resembled the inhabitants of the town Divi had visited when she came ashore. Did some of them serve as temple defenders? Amber unsheathed her sword and held it before the stranger.

This was the first time Divi noticed the peculiarity of Amber's blade. Perfectly straight, it seemed to sparkle as if embedded with glass shards from the sharp tip to the beautiful hilt, in the shape of an angel holding an aquamarine jewel. The rest was made of silver, gold, and a strange metal that Divi had never seen before. She would have to ask her about that later.

She watched Amber wait until the man was in front of her before she lowered her weapon and held it before the stranger, as if displaying it for inspection. The man never took his eyes off of her. To Divi, he seemed middle-aged, though she knew he was probably centuries old. Noticing deep, red scars on his face and on his hands, she wondered how he received those.

He said, "I congratulate you all for solving my puzzle. Not many have had the privilege of seeing me. All who have, unfortunately, have not been able to tell their tales of bravery and valor."

Amber replied, "Don't try and frighten us, Guardian. I have taken two of you on and see no reason why I'll not succeed now."

This was the Guardian! Divi thought Amber told them they would be facing some type of water dragon. What was going on?

The Guardian turned his attention to Divi and Tasi.

Wearing a confident smirk, he observed, "I see you bring friends with you. They smell ripe with fear."

"Who says we're afraid?" asked Tasi.

The Guardian's booming laughter disturbed Divi. "I felt it when you entered my temple and still do now. Those who show fear will never win."

"Look," Amber interrupted. "I didn't come here to talk. Let's get this over with so I can get back to camp by nightfall."

"Confident, I see. Very well. You will fall like all the others. Leviadon will gladly take your lives."

Divi's eyes opened wide. They were going to fight Leviadon, the dragon that sunk their ship? How were they supposed to do that? She couldn't imagine how it would even fit into this chamber. She would never forget staring high in the sky before the creature, marveled and terrified by its size, dived into their vessel. Its attack had shown an unmatchable brutality then.

Then again, it was also the same dragon that carried her and presumedly Tasi to safety. Perhaps it could be an ally. Still, was this what it would take to save Levus?

After he said that, the Guardian turned and walked back toward the dark waterfall. The Water Relic disappeared behind him. *Just as I thought. An illusion.* Amber knew full well that the relics never came easy. The Earth Relic hadn't even appeared until Titarin, the Earth Dragon, submitted. The Wind Relic, she'd been able to acquire by fortune. She had a feeling Leviadon would be more cautious. Amber raised her weapon and prepared for an attack, while Divi and Tasi raised their staves in defense. The area remained very quiet.

Much to their surprise, nothing emerged. The waterfall parted like a curtain, although Divi couldn't see far over the threshold behind it, as everything there was completely dark. Amber took a cautious step closer.

"I think it wants us to enter. Come on."

Tasi and Divi followed Amber cautiously. He was terrified about this place. Not just for the fact it housed a dragon. He didn't like water unless it was in a glass for drinking purposes. The place where the Guardian stood was thankfully shallow, despite how deep it had appeared from their perspective. The walk wasn't very long, though at the end all three looked on in amazement.

Amber commented, "Woah."

They were in a gigantic cavern, lit with some sort of magical white fire that glowed against the walls. The ceiling had to be hundreds of feet high. Except for some rocky islands, the floor submerged in water. Amber couldn't tell how deep it was, but she imagined it was deep enough to drown in if they took a wrong step.

Divi understood why this chamber was so huge. It had to fit the monster, longer than seven of the ships they traveled to get her, ferocious in a way she didn't think she could match.

"You two stay here a minute. I don't want you falling in on me until I know where Leviadon is."

Tasi didn't have a problem with that. The rocks looked very slippery. One false move could be the end for him and Divi here. He really wished mages could swim better. He often wondered if there was ever an event in the Elf Games that required swimming. None of the ones he was alive for had one, but he was certain that they had at some point.

Amber reached the bottom of the path that led to the water. The first island was reachable if one leapt. What she didn't like was that the rest of the islands were laid out in a line, each within jumping distance for the average athletic person, but none were closer, and from each island you could only reach the one ahead or the one behind you. It meant escape routes from attacks would be predictable. Sure, one could swim instead. But who would want to do that when Leviadon could pop up at any time?

106

She jumped onto the first island. The rocks were slick and jagged. That meant moving around was going to be tough and landings from a fall would be painful. They were at least a large enough size that one could fight on them if necessary. A waterfall thundering in the back of the cavern was the only other sound besides her echoing footsteps.

She paused a few minutes. *What was Leviadon waiting for?* Maybe the Guardian lied to her and he wasn't even here. Wishful thinking. Maybe there was another cavern. Although she had never seen him, she had heard Leviadon was the longest dragon, only beaten by Tiiamite.

Amber waved the mages over as she headed for the next island. Divi and Tasi proceeded carefully, so as not to slip on the path. She was having an easier time, as Tasi's robe kept getting caught on the rocks. Divi was uneasy about the entire situation. It was too quiet. She would have expected the dragon to be on them the moment they entered its lair. Her recent experiences showed her how aggressive they could be.

As they neared the first island, Divi took notice of all the boulders and loose slabs of stone cluttered against the walls of the monstrous cavern. As she didn't know magic, she had to know and use her surroundings. Those would be her weapons. She examined to see if there was any way to get to the perimeter of the cavern, but swimming was the only way. None of the islands were in leaping distance. All those unstable stones would make it unsafe to navigate anyway. Sizable, broken pillars stood as shadows of their former selves. They must have been a couple hundred feet high at least. Now the ones still standing barely stood at fifty. The fallen sections rested on the perimeter floor.

The two mages cautiously leapt onto the first island while Amber observed. She was on the third island, closer to the center. Occasionally, she checked the water to see if she could gauge its depth. The lighting was not the best in here, though, so she could only peer a couple feet down.

107

Divi, halfway across the first island, nearly slipped but was caught by Tasi, "Take it slow. Seems like falling in the water is the biggest danger in here."

Just as Divi stood up, a sinuous, scaled shape, as long as a lightning bolt itself, shot out of the water beside them. The mages fell to the ground as the dragon held its head erect. The lighting on the walls grew bright enough now to illuminate the entire cavern. As the light blue monster roared, Divi nearly cried. Its huge size was even more obvious now that it towered directly in front of them. It had a long, thick face with short, scaley whiskers nears its nose, its mouth close enough to see these intricate features. The dragon wrapped its body around numerous boulders on the cavern's edges, crushing some with ease. With about twelve visible sets of webbed-legs, it had to be fast. Its roar echoed so loudly that Divi and Tasi had to cover their ears.

Even Amber wanted to take those words back about wanting Leviadon to reveal himself, wondering what kept him from attacking the moment they entered his lair. The dragon sniffed around, then roared again, cocking its head back. She could tell Tasi realized the same thing. Leviadon speared down back into the water, causing a wave to engulf them.

Tasi yelled, "Brace yourself!"

Their staves slammed in the ground, giving them the anchor needed to stay on their current island. The wave was powerful despite not being large.

Amber looked around furiously for the dragon's location. "Keep your eyes sharp! He can come out of anywhere there's water!"

As she yelled this, the Leviadon exposed part of its body, seeming to circle the central islands. Divi was shaking very noticeably. She didn't care if that Guardian felt it, she couldn't hold in the fear this time.

Amber held her sword with both hands, waiting for the perfect moment to strike. She exchanged a quick look with Tasi, who was getting a ball of lightning ready, just waiting to carry out the enchantment. *Almost.* She wanted it to expose its head before they attacked.

Leviadon emerged behind Amber, bringing with it a blanket of water. Not where she expected it to be. Amber yelled a warlike scream as she let loose the ball of lightning from the tip of her sword. The dragon dodged Amber's attack. The water crashed over her, sending her to the floor. The liquid dropping on her wasn't normal water. It seemed heavier. She slowly got up, her arm stinging where it had been cut on the rocks.

Tasi knew it was his chance and yelled, "*Liuto Dopia!*"

The ball of lightning released from his hand headed for the dragon's body. The creature didn't see it coming and was hit. It cried in pain, but not for long. It focused its attention on Tasi, much to his dismay. He started backing away. The dragon roared again as Tasi lifted his arm to cast another spell. Before he could, a jet of water sprouted from the waterfall and connected with his hand, causing a sharp pain. *How did that hurt so much?*

Another jet hit Tasi in the legs, knocking him down. The dragon raised its head so that it was looking up at the ceiling. Tasi followed its eyes to a waterspout forming above. This was not good. As the dragon's head lowered, the spout came down as well. Tasi quickly moved out of the way as the spout crashed into the natural stone, leaving a dent in its wake. His body was already sore just from rolling on the rough rocks.

Amber charged and stabbed the dragon near the tail, again using a lightning charge from her sword. The dragon screamed for as long as Amber held her sword in it. It finally threw her off with a lashing from its tail, and she slammed into the water near the east wall, able to grab a hold of her sword again as it thankfully fell right next to her. She quickly attacked the beast again. Leviadon directed its tail into the waterfalls, perhaps hoping the rushing water would loosen her, but she held on strong. It succeeded only when it threatened to plunge her into the pool and hold her there. She pulled the Holy Light out and began swimming toward the surface. An underwater blast of water kicked her in the air before she could surface on her own.

She landed hard on the ground, knocking the wind out of her. Fresh blood poured from gashes the fall had given her. When she stood up, she saw Leviadon jutting toward her, preparing to bite. She jumped into the water, barely missed by its strong jaws. Amber hid underneath a part of the west wall's rock face that jutted over the water when the dragon submerged itself and began searching. Seeing it approaching fast even with her limited vision, Amber quickly swam to the edge of the nearest island. A couple bubbles came near her. Just as she flipped out of the water, the dragon sprouted out. Amber turned on her back to see a sheet of water collapse on her. Like the previous wave, this felt heavier than normal water.

The dragon stared straight down at her. Amber tried to move, but couldn't. *What is going on?* Leviadon's roar sounded confident, if such a human emotion could be ascribed to the beast.

Before the dragon could attack, Divi telekinetically threw a loose boulder at Leviadon's head. It faced Divi as she threw another stone slab at it. She was on the farthest island from the entrance, having used the time it chased Amber to get as far away as possible east. The dragon was at the west wall while Tasi was on the central island, one behind Amber.

Divi yelled, "Stay away from her!"

She was able to lift another large rock to hit it before it began to advance toward her. Divi's courage shrunk as Leviadon came within ten feet from her. Tasi, still recovering from the water jets, saw what was unfolding. He had to do something!

Tasi stood up and yelled, "*Liuto groipnii!*"

Lightning beams were ejected from his hand and hit the dragon as it was about to attack Divi. Leviadon faced Tasi and roared. He suddenly felt his legs go out underneath him. The dragon wrapped its tail around Tasi and pulled him toward its head. He thought for sure he was about to become dragon food and screamed as he passed Leviadon's open mouth. Then Tasi breathed a short sigh of relief as the dragon continued to hold him upside down, not showing a sign of snacking yet, but panicked again when he saw he was headed straight for the water. The dragon drove its tail into it, submerging Tasi.

After a few seconds, the dragon's tail reemerged, only without him.

"Tasi!"

Divi quieted her mind. She could feel him down there. He was struggling to swim up to the surface. If she didn't do something fast, Tasi would drown. Divi searched the surroundings with her mind. To her pleasure, there was a loose stone below Tasi's flailing body. She quickly used to telekinetic powers to jog the stone loose and lifted it from the water, bringing Tasi along with it. He was struggling to breathe, but in a few seconds he should be fine.

Amber finally was able to move again, freed from the dragon's binding technique. She didn't like the way this battle was going. Leviadon was trying to disable them individually. When Amber had fought the other two dragons, they acted very differently. The others were continuously trying to ready what she called their ultimate attacks. With Titarin, he tried to command the stones to make a cage and crush her. Tiiamite tried to weaken her to the center of the room so his beam attack would encompass the entire area they fought in. Leviadon didn't seem concerned with doing that. That was good and bad. Good because it meant she wouldn't have to survive against their most powerful attack. Bad as it meant she had no clue what to expect. She ran around the perimeter of the northern most island as fast as she could without slipping. Her body had begun to feel the exhaustion. By the time she made it within two islands from Divi, Leviadon was heading toward the mage again.

Divi dodged attack after attack as Leviadon did its best to clasp his powerful jaws around her. She lost count how many times she fell. The cuts and bruises on her arms and legs couldn't be counted.

When she staggered again, the dragon went for the kill. Telekinetically, she lifted a large stone in front of her, and Leviadon got the stone instead of her. She took advantage of the dragon's confusion to reach the next island west. Her legs were so tired, she barely made the jump.

Amber pointed her blade to the ground and slammed it in. As she did, a lightning charge traveled from the sword into the roots of the island, then spread through the water. When it reached Leviadon, the bolt stabbed through the dragon to hit the ceiling. Shards of stone fell from the impact, some hitting the writhing beast on the way down. It yelled in pain. Amber was able to pull her sword out of the island before the dragon used its tail to drive her back. She landed on the island Tasi was on, slamming hard on the rocks. She coughed out a little blood, slow to move. She had trouble even sitting up. *Everything just hurts!*

Divi, seeing Tasi and Amber incapacitated at the moment, tried her own offense. If it worked, she would be able to distract the dragon enough to hit it anywhere with her telekinesis without being blocked. Divi concentrated hard on the solid walls of the chamber. As the dragon began to move forward, she was able jog a few pieces of the pillars loose. She struck the dragon's back, head, and legs with them while readying more pieces.

When Amber regained her feet, she stared, amazed the tactic was working. With Divi distracting the dragon, Amber ran over to Tasi, who sat on the central island, catching his breath after his near-death experience in the water.

Divi was able to land a few more blows on the dragon before she felt the hard-scaled skin of the dragon's tail smacked her, skidding her back onto the eastern most island.

Amber and Tasi looked up to see Leviadon staring at them. Divi's tactic ultimately failed. Both were frozen, staring in horror at the dragon's teeth that they barely noticed that the dragon had coiled its body around them in a sphere. This was not good.

Tasi asked, "What's going on?"

"It's preparing its special technique . . . their finishing move."

Leviadon began to move in a circle. As it did this, the water surrounding the islands became attracted to its body. The dragon began spinning so fast that it caused walls of water to rise around it□and them.

Tasi held out his hand and prepared a lightning spell. *"Littari Hittari!"*

The bluish ball, unleashed from his hand, headed for the advancing shield of water. As it hit, the spell reflected and began bouncing from wall to wall within the dome the dragon made over them with its body. It nearly hit him or Amber numerous times so that they had to duck or dodge it.

When the spell dissipated, Amber stood up and punched Tasi's shoulder. She yelled, "Never do that again!"

"I don't see you giving any bright ideas!" he yelled back.

Amber did have one . . . and it was their only chance. "Divi! Can you hear me?"

Divi could, but barely because of the noise of the water and dragon between them. "Yes!"

Amber yelled, "You have to cast a lightning spell and hit it from the outside! We can't hit him in here!"

Tasi looked over at Amber. If this was their only hope, they would not see the light of day again. The water began to eject from the wall, closing in on them.

He yelled, "I don't know if we have that kind of time!"

Divi heard Amber's words, but she only stared at the dragon, who was still luring water from outside it. She couldn't do what Amber requested. She didn't know how to. Fear entered her insides as she stood there, not knowing what to do.

Amber yelled, "Divi! Did you hear me?"

The dome was beginning to fill at the bottom, slowly submerging it. All Amber and Tasi could see was water. The winds were becoming so strong that they could feel themselves being pulled toward the water.

"Damn it, Divi! Can you hear me? Do it now!"

Divi could hear, but what could she do? She could form the illusion of lightning, just like the fire she'd used to fool those thieves on Dyyros, but an illusion wouldn't scare the dragon or cause it pain.

As the winds inside became heavier, Tasi became more frightful of their fate.

"I hate water!"

As he said this, both he and Amber were sucked inside the rotating water gathered by Leviadon. The island they were standing on was fully engulfed and everything inside began filling up with water.

Divi could feel that they were inside. If she didn't do something, both would drown inside this unescapable water wheel.

Fortunately, there were gaps in the water cyclone. Amber and Tasi managed to hold their breath until they got those few seconds of air. Amber couldn't yell, but she hoped Divi would hurry. The holes would fill up with water soon to the top near Leviadon's head. Its constant spinning held them in this whirlpool by its body, not allowing them to swim freely. . . there was no escape.

As Divi stood there, she realized there was only one thing to do. Using her telekinetic powers, she jogged a large piece of stone loose now exposed from the lowering levels of water outside Leviadon and levitated it near where its head would be. This was not going to be easy. She figured in order to stop the dragon, she would have to hit it in the head. With the dragon going faster than anything she had ever seen, she would have to be patient. She would only get one shot at this. Divi closed her eyes and tried to do something foreign to her: use her telekinetic powers on two things at the same time. She had seen her father do something similar, as even mages who could use magic couldn't cast two spells at once. Unsure if she was strong enough, she would have to try.

Levitating the stone, she attempted to see the dragon's head. It moved so fast! Divi concentrated harder. It was useless. She could feel her control of the stone dropping the more she tried to hold it. She opened her eyes and stared at the stone she controlled. She was going to rely on luck to save them.

Tasi was very frightened. The holes were getting further spaced and breathing became almost impossible. This was not how he pictured himself dying. He always thought he would fall as a hero, not to the webbed-claws of a dragon on a whim from a half-mage paladin candidate.

Divi finally gained the courage to jet the stone at the dragon. She prayed as the stone crashed against it. To Divi's surprise and pleasure, she heard a roar of pain. Leviadon slowed down so abruptly that the water crashed to the ground. Amber and Tasi fell with it, and from what she could see, both were still alive. Divi's joy, though, turned to terror when she realized that the dragon's attentions had turned strictly on her. She backed away slowly as Leviadon advanced on her.

Amber, recovering from the water well, noticed that Divi was in trouble. She searched the room as quickly as she could for a way to help. Her search ended when she saw that the dragon's tail was near them. Amber reached for her sword and crawled toward the tail.

She knew she had to do more than just stab it. She needed something that would hold Leviadon in place while she used her attack, otherwise it would just hit her with its tail again. Looking at the wall she found her answer. One of the boulders Divi had tried to grab with her telekinesis earlier in the fight rolled and was halted by a luckily placed group of stones just before it plummeted off the edge of a high western dip. Amber had a couple spells that might be effective that far, and the one she knew would work the best she didn't like. Light spells were very draining on a half-mage. She wasn't sure she'd even have the strength to strike Leviadon after casting it. Considering the circumstances, she had to try.

She aimed the Holy Light carefully at the debris holding the boulder up. She'd only have one chance to get this right. The spell wouldn't have the same force if she tried to cast it again as the first try would physically weaken her enough. She lined the blade up with intense focus. *Please let my aim be true!*

She fired a beam of light toward the rocks. She had to hold tight against the kick-back from the spell. Her arms kept straight and the beam hit the loose stones dead-on. The boulder fell off the edge. So long as she hadn't misjudged where it would drop . . . She breathed a sigh of relief when it landed on top of Leviadon's tail, pinning it in the small crevice it was resting. Just by how deep the boulder dipped in, she knew it jammed up well. It was going to take quite a bit for the Water Dragon to loosen it.

Leviadon, stunned by the sudden burst of pain, roared and took its gaze off Divi. It had no idea Amber was still behind it, thinking that it had taken out two of the three. As she raised her blade, electrical currents formed around it.

Amber said, "This ends now!"

With almost everything she had left, she stabbed the dragon through the tail, using so much force that the blade jammed in the island rock. With the electricity flowing through its body, Leviadon cried in pain. It tried to fight free, but the sensitive tail couldn't jog the boulder loose, much less the sword. Amber held on with all of her might as the electrical currents began to surround the entire dragon.

Because of how close Leviadon got to her before Amber distracted it, Divi fell hard on the far east island from the intense magnitude of the attack, even feeling the heat from the crackling lightning. Tasi shielded himself with his arms and legs, which wasn't enough to entirely prevent stray electric bolts from shocking him. After a few seconds, the dragon was able to free its tail, shaking Amber and the Holy Light off. It sent her flying about forty yards. Still, as quickly as she could, Amber stood up, wobbly on her feet, but ready to fight off the dragon once again.

To her surprise, Leviadon began to cower, sinking back into the dark waters of the cavern. From her distance, it even looked like it might be hurt. It gave one final roar before diving back into the pool of water.

The area became silent except for the waterfalls.

Divi stood up and watched in amazement as the last of the dragon disappeared under the water. Tasi went up to a knee and looked around. The dragon was gone! A smile grew on Divi's face. They did it! They won!

The Guardian returned from behind the large waterfall. He walked out somberly facing the ground in defeat. Divi could feel shame inside of him—this must have been the first time he had been defeated by anyone other than another dragon. She and Tasi joined Amber as the Guardian stopped in front of her.

The Guardian said, "I fear I have underestimated you. You have fought with great courage and have forced Leviadon into submission. But be wary. You may have won my prize, but not all of us have been defeated."

The Guardian turned and approached the large waterfall. Amber was about to say something when a blue glow emerged from the water. As the Guardian entered the waterfall, the relic of water rose from the depths, its blue crystal shining brightly. Amber went to the levitating stone and carefully reached for it. As her hands grasped it, the crystal's light grew brighter before dimming to nothing. A small smile grew on her face.

Amber said softly, "One more."

CHAPTER 6
Divi's Choice

The three walked out of the Water Temple having won a great victory. Amber led the group back across the bridge toward the Temple Gate, carrying the sacred stone in a cloth sack slung over her shoulder. She seemed to be the only one who didn't join in on their jubilee.

Tasi had a big smile on his face. Divi herself was pleased they could defeat the dragon, especially since it caused the deaths of those innocent elves on the ship. It had paid for many a death. In fact, she was so excited that she fell behind on purpose so she could skip to catch up. She exclaimed, "We really showed him!"

"I was never worried at all," replied Tasi.

Divi gave him an amused laugh. She knew he was lying and he didn't try to hide it. Both walked side-by-side as Amber continued to lead in silence. They were still soaking wet from the battle, but it was nothing the hot sun couldn't fix.

Divi said, "I can't wait until we go for the next one. Amber! When are we to fight the last dragon?"

Puzzlingly, Amber did not answer.

She asked again, "When are we to go for the last dragon?"

"You're not going for the last dragon."

Divi looked at Tasi, befuddled by Amber's answer. She could feel discontentment inside the half-mage, but didn't know what it was about. "Why not?"

Amber stopped walking and dropped the sack on the bridge. "Why? Why, you ask?"

She finally turned around. There was a fire in her eyes that frightened even Tasi. She seemed so angry that the water on her wet skin looked like it was boiling.

"I'll tell you why! Because of your insolence, we almost died back there! I have spent far too long to get to this point and I don't want anyone ruining this . . . especially a mage! Is that why you are here? To test me? To make sure I don't succeed in my Paladin Trial?"

"Amber, what are you talking about? We helped in every way that we could."

"Oh, you know very well what I'm talking about, Tasi!"

It took him a couple seconds, but he remembered the moments right before they were sucked into the water during Leviadon's finishing technique.

"But it wasn't Divi's fault!"

"Not her fault? We almost lost that fight because she froze up!"

She faced Divi, who was looking down. The water from her hair dripped onto the bridge.

"Why didn't you cast that lightning spell?"

Tasi yelled, "That's enough, Amber!"

Amber yelled louder, "Why didn't you cast that lightning spell?"

Divi couldn't take it anymore. She had to let it go. She lifted her head to face Amber. "Because I don't know how to cast magic!"

Amber looked at Divi perplexed. An eerie silence grew between the three. Divi lowered her head again, mainly to hide the tears.

She continued in a lighter tone, "I chose not to learn."

Amber was still staring at Divi oddly. Tasi could see this news shocked her. To the surprise of them both, though, Amber began to chuckle.

Divi and Tasi exchanged glances before facing Amber, whose chuckle grew louder. What was the half-mage finding so funny about this?

"Well, a mage who doesn't know how to use magic. Now it all makes sense! I was wrong about you, Divi. I

120

thought that you wouldn't help me much during this. Now I know that you were absolutely worthless to me the entire time."

Those words hurt Divi more than any blows she sustained during the dragon fight. Her bleeding legs and arms were miniscule compared to the knife-gash inflicted by Amber's tone.

Tasi was infuriated. Although he knew Divi wouldn't be helpful if they needed magic, her involvement did save their lives. Amber seemed to have forgotten that.

"How dare you make such an accusation!"

Tasi advanced toward Amber, but she quickly responded by unsheathing her sword and pointing it at his head. Using her powers, she made lightning bolts surround the blade.

Amber shook her head. "Don't tempt me."

Tasi fell back a couple of steps, and she sheathed her sword again.

"You may stay in camp the night we return because I know you have no place else to go. I expect, though, to be rid of you two by the next morning."

Amber grabbed the cloth sack and slung it over her shoulder again. Even as she proceeded along the bridge, Divi and Tasi didn't move. He was more surprised than anything by Amber's behavior. Was she really that ungrateful? If they hadn't been there, she would probably have been killed by this dragon. Half-mages . . . maybe the council was right about them and Neeza was wrong.

Tasi patted Divi lightly on the shoulder. "Come on, Divi."

He walked on, but Divi refused to move. Tasi felt sorry for her. No one deserved to be treated like this. He would most certainly have a few words with the half-mage tonight.

"Divi, I know it hurts, but hurry."

She didn't feel like moving, but began to slowly follow Tasi as they continued their return journey toward camp.

The light of sunset lasted barely long enough to guide them back to camp. It had been a very quiet journey. Amber once and a while talked to herself, while Tasi would say a short Myyrilian prayer occasionally. Divi was the only one who remained completely silent. She did even now as she sat on a small hill near Amber's camp. The sky was cloudless and the two moons glowed brightly, casting silver brilliance on Gyyerlith's surface. Stars added to the night's light show.

Divi usually looked at these objects, observing their eloquent beauty. Yet this night was far different from any other night. Never in her life had so many things been on her mind. The first being, what she was doing here? Had she been too quick in following her own beliefs . . . her own heart? Divi peered further into the distance, toward home. Back in Myyril, whenever she had a question or a problem, she sometimes looked to the sky and prayed to the gods. She wasn't too sure if praying would do any good, yet she had no one else to turn to other than herself. Divi focused on the brightest star in the sky.

She prayed, "To the gods who listen to your children's needs, please hear me in mine. As movers of the seas and breathers of life, let my prayer be as simple to you. I ask not for any fame or glory. I ask not to be as powerful as the ones who made us. I only ask to know whether my journey is just. My heart tells me that what I do is in the right. You know my reasons for my quest and assume you disapprove of them, but I ask . . . is there no stronger prayer than the one made by someone in love? Mages have devoted their lives because of their love for you. Isn't this, my love for Levus, just as worthy? Will it really come to me doing the one thing that I wished never to do just for my love? You know I would give anything to protect Levus. Is this the cruelness of fate?"

Divi's gaze dropped back to the ground. Tears rolled down her cheek. The more she thought of her words, the more she realized she was going to have to do it. Even in this time of denial, she knew it would be the only way she could save Levus.

As she thought this, she felt someone coming from behind. A quick glance revealed it was Amber. Her steps slowed until she stopped in front of Divi. Divi kept her eyes on the ground as Amber knelt to her level, clearing her throat.

"Look. I understand if you are mad at me. Gosh, I'm no good at these . . . um . . . what I'm trying to say is that I was out of line when I yelled at you earlier. It was selfish of me to say those things to you. I . . . I guess I'm trying to say I'm sorry."

Amber looked at Divi, who hadn't moved since she knelt next to her. Amber did feel bad, which was rare for her.

"Divi? Well, I guess you don't want to talk. You and your friend can stay, though we won't leave for at least a fortnight, up to a month for the last dragon. He's . . . he's a special case that I need time to figure out. Plus, I think we all need a little time to heal our wounds from this Leviadon fight. I know it's a long time, but Leviadon proved how close one can come to failing when not truly prepared."

Divi still showed no reaction. Amber had a feeling she would get none from the mage tonight. She stood up and patted Divi on the shoulder.

As Amber turned around, she stopped suddenly and said, "Don't think because I am the way I am, that I don't care about others or how they feel."

She waited a couple seconds to see if there would be any feedback. Seeing there wouldn't, she walked away slowly. Divi gave a small smile. She forgave Amber for her derogatory comments. Although she was hurt by them, they were the truth. What good was she to the group unless she could . . .

Divi heard another person approaching. She didn't even have to look to know it was Tasi. He sat down beside her. Divi, though, continued to stare at the ground.

"It's a lovely night out tonight!"

She could not disagree with Tasi's observation, but she wished the thoughts in her head were half as pleasant as the view of the stars in the sky.

"I passed by Amber on the way here. I don't know if you accepted her apology, but if not, I wouldn't take her earlier words to heart. She spoke while angry, which sometimes causes us to say things we always do not mean."

Divi almost wanted to shake her head. *No, Amber was right. Every word Amber spoke on the stone bridge was right.*

She finally asked, "Tasi, you would do anything I ask of you and support any decision I make, right?"

She had not asked him anything this strange ever since they were kids. Yet, despite his confusion, Tasi said, "Divi, I will stand by you on whatever you wish of me!"

She raised her eyes to the sky. The moon's light reflected off her tears.

She had to ask it. Her mind was made up. If this was what it would take to save Levus, then so be it.

"I want you to teach me to cast magic."

Tasi stared at Divi, his jaw dropped. *Did I just hear what I thought I heard?*

"What?"

She repeated, "I want to learn magic."

Divi turned to Tasi, who still couldn't believe what he heard. Why would she want to do this now? He knew Divi. A few sharp words from someone she barely knew wouldn't overcome a lifetime of stubborn avoidance.

"Why now?"

"I almost cost us a few times already because I didn't know magic. The Shadow Dragon on Barbata. Leviadon. I can't watch my friends fight and die while I sit there and only hope to contribute."

"Divi, your telekinetic powers are a great help, no matter what Amber says."

"It's not just because of Amber."

It finally hit him. Tasi knew where this was going, and he didn't like it.

He asked, "It's because of . . . *him*, isn't it?"

Tasi stood up and took several steps down the hill. Why was he purposely offending her during the most important decision of her life?

"And what is that supposed to mean?"

"I can't let you give this up because of that human! Not learning magic was your strongest resolute belief. I was the only one that supported you on it, if you remember. And if you did, I hoped it would be for a better reason."

"And love is not a good reason?"

"How can you be sure it is 'love'? You don't even know if he loves you! The chances are too risky."

"No, I don't know. All I can go by is how I feel! My promise to never learn magic would one day come to an end. I knew this, though I always denied it. I didn't know how it would end, but I can gratefully say that I don't regret how it will happen."

Tasi exploded, "I will not teach you under these circumstances! I don't care what you say! Mages and humans will never coexist! Trust me, Divi. I have been studying them my entire life! You are wasting your time!"

A fire grew in Divi's eyes, one that Tasi didn't believe he'd ever seen from his friend before in all the time he knew her.

Divi yelled, "You know nothing about them! You claim you know them, but attending a few meetings with human leadership doesn't make you an expert. My feelings for Levus are not going to change, so your opinion better. Besides, what was the one duty given to you by my father?"

Tasi didn't want to admit it and was very hesitant to say so. She knew the answer, just as she knew he did. He could have told her every word Neeza said to him exactly because it was a day he would never forget. However, he knew the part Divi wanted to hear.

"To train you when you finally requested."

"Please, Tasi! Do this . . . if not for my reason, then for me."

Tasi began to pace slowly. This decision before him was not fair. It was his duty to train Divi, but doing so now might have severe consequences in the near future. Yet, what could he do? The responsibility of being a teacher was supposed to surpass even the bonds of friendship. For once, he wished he had a rebellious side like Divi. Yet, he knew himself, and that was not who he was. He had to hide the anger and despair which pained him.

Tasi said, "All right. I will fulfill your request to train you."

A smile grew on Divi's face, and a sigh of relief came from her lips.

Tasi added, "But realize I do this under duress. I still do not agree with your decision, but what I say will not matter. Get some rest. We will begin training tomorrow."

Tasi stormed off down the cliff toward the camp. Divi once again stared at the stars. She hoped that her decision was the right one. Even though in her heart she believed so, being able to cast spells might not matter. It might help them get to the Isle of Time, but would it even be helpful in saving Levus? She hadn't really thought too much of the consequences of her learning magic, either. To her, that was unimportant. She had broken her most solemn oath for Levus, and even though she'd always known she would, doing it hurt her pride and shook her knowledge in herself. And she endured the suffering for Levus' sake, a testament to

126

her feelings. Divi finally stood up and made her way back to her temporary domicile.

CHAPTER 7
Training: Life Particles

Tasi met Divi in a small clearing a mile outside Amber's main camp. It was not as large as he would have preferred, but it would do. Most training yards were double the size in Myyril. He was a little nervous about having it so far away from their base, but Gerritonnee's presence meant the ravenous creatures tended to stay away. The setup was very basic. He had spent most of last night making stick people to serve as targets. Amber helped a little, though her dragon friend did most of the gathering. There would be more work, but it would not need to be done at least until Divi threw her first fireball.

Divi herself looked much more nervous than usual. Had she started to regret her decision? That was probably partially true, but she would not run from this. Her mind was settled.

Although Tasi would have preferred the more traditional setup, he was limited in resources. Some aspects of his teachings would need to wait until they returned to Myyril. He could at least teach her the basics and some of the more complex spells used for close fighting here. Anything that would be beneficial to them now would be most important. Everything else could wait. He also wished she wore the more traditional robe when training. Amber had one for the cold nights, but Divi refused to wear it. He hoped she wouldn't be so defiant with his teachings as she was with her wardrobe.

Seeing she was basically ready, Tasi started. "All right. Normally, we would begin by strengthening your telekinetic powers, as having full control of them is an essential first step. But, seeing as you have shown a good mastery of them, I think we can skip that step.

128

"Now, in order to learn the essential component of casting any spell, we will work on the fireball. At first, it will require heavy focus. As you probably know, when you use your telekinetic powers a lot at one time, you begin to physically feel weaker. That is your limit."

Divi was getting a little impatient because she knew all of this. She figured, though, that this was the moment Tasi had waited for years now. Her dad made Tasi a teacher specifically so he could teach her and now had his chance. She chuckled to herself thinking of him standing in his room rehearsing this very speech to her. The sad thing was that her imagined scene was probably true.

"Pay attention, Divi."

She instantly straightened, more out of surprise than anything. Did he know what she was thinking?

Tasi continued, "I'm going to need you to listen. You may already know most of what I'm saying at this point, but if you fail to listen to me you will not be able to *apply* what I teach. You do want to learn, don't you?"

She knew he already knew her answer. She sighed and said, "Yes."

"All right. And no . . . I didn't rehearse this. Your father and Dinermar, The Illusion School's headmaster, made sure I would be ready when you asked me to train you, so they made sure I could teach you the correct lessons in order so well I could do it sleeping. The first thing they taught was how teachers dealt with young apprentices. Until you can prove to me that you can maintain focus, I will use my telekinetic powers to my fullest so I can hear your thoughts. I hate to do that, but it is common practice by all teachers in the early stages. If you hadn't noticed, it's the reason only mages who score high in telekinetic ability can become teachers. That is why we are so few."

Divi was a little troubled that Tasi would be able read her thoughts. She hated it when Ulcinar had entered her mind, and now her friend was going to be doing it to her too.

When she finally finished her training, she would make sure she learned to shield her thoughts, if one existed.

She replied, "I understand."

Tasi nodded and said, "Good. Now, for starters, although you have great knowledge of using your telekinetic powers, it is now time to take them to the next level."

"What do you mean, the next level?" asked Divi.

"When you use your powers, you use them on physical objects, objects you can see like a rock, a branch, or even a person. The next step is to use your powers on objects you can't see or physically touch."

Tasi could see that he had lost Divi, wearing her confusion as she did nearly every other emotion, doubting the possibility to move something that one couldn't even touch. This also proved that Divi was telling the truth: she never had read any of the special tomes her father gave her. If she had, she would have known about this previously.

He continued, "If you cannot do this, then learning magic will never happen. You must learn to control the life particles if you . . ."

Divi asked, "What are life particles?"

Tasi chuckled, aware he was getting a little ahead of himself. "I am sorry. Life particles are what we call them. The elves have a different name for them and the humans seem to reject the idea that they even exist. But I can assure you, they are the source of a mage's power. They are small particles that exist in everything. You already know how to feel them using your telekinetic powers, but they are much easier to control when you can see them.

"I can tell you are still confused. Let me show you how this works in a visual way."

Tasi reached to the ground and picked up a handful of pebbles. He dropped them on an animal skin he had brought to the clearing, being sure to space them out as much as possible. Divi watched curiously. She had never heard anything about "life particles," not even from her father. She was certain he would have told her about them if he was that determined to get her to learn magic.

Tasi finally looked up, but gestured to the animal skin as he continued, "Let us imagine, then, that those pebbles are life particles. They would be more numerous and invisible, of course, but this representation is adequate for our purposes."

With a flick of his wrist, the pebbles levitated up slowly and randomly in the air. Divi was engulfed in Tasi's explanation. Then again, she always had been a visual learner.

"Now, when enough of these particles bind together, they form a physical object."

Tasi controlled all the pebbles so they merged into a lumpy stone. *That was simple enough*, Divi thought. She knew how to move physical objects with her powers easily.

"For the life particles that remain in the air and all around us, we can control them to follow our command for a short while."

Tasi separated the pebbles once again and had them float in the air for a few seconds. Then, as he brought his hands back, the pebbles gravitated toward them as if they were magnetized. Tasi waited until all the stones were in reach of his palm before he continued, "And then, when you have enough of them under your control, you say the spell's words and . . . *Firammii morza!*"

A small fireball was ejected from Tasi's hands toward one of the targets, destroying it. Divi couldn't see the pebbles anymore, but she figured it was easy to lose them in the glow and force of the fire spell. The concept was clear enough though. She couldn't wait until she could do that!

"Are there any questions so far?"

Divi asked, "Are we similar, then, to the stones that we step or sit on? Life, I mean?"

"Not exactly. Although both living and non-living objects possess life particles, only people have what is called

131

a 'life force'. Animals have something similar, but it is noticeably weaker than a person. I'm not certain what dragons have as I think we're the first mages to see one, but maybe Gerritonnee will allow me to feel them during our stay. Humans refer to it as the soul. When one can no longer feel the life force, then that person dies. When you finally learn to sense these life particles, you too will be able to feel it."

Divi replied, "I can see why life particles are so important. Why do they do it? Help us, I mean?"

Tasi slowly explained, "Because we are all connected. Without us, life particles would not be so plentiful. In turn, they help us live. With every wound we suffer, some life particles escape from it. The life force can replace them, though, if the damage is not too severe. Mortal wounds are where the damage is too much, so that the life particles are all lost from a person's body. They return to the air to bring life to others.

"Now I want you to try and find the life particles in the air. This part will take you the longest, so diligence will be required. Use your powers on physical objects if you need to. It sometimes helps to feel their particles before moving on to the invisible ones."

Divi nodded. It seemed like logical reasoning. She held out her hand and began to focus on a stone.

Tasi interrupted, "Do it without using your hand. You are too advanced to still be using physical gestures as a crutch. The power to sense the particles is in your mind. It will be useful to know how to control life particles with your mind alone because this allows you to surprise your enemies."

Divi sighed heavily. This was going to be a long day. She never had tried moving an object before without utilizing her hand. It never even came to her as a possibility. How hard could it be, though? The hand couldn't make *that* much of a difference. Except for the fact that she kept her hands at her side, she began to focus on the rock just as she would normally, causing it to rise slowly in the air. Tasi nodded with approval.

"Now, make the stone move between those two trees there."

She confidently looked toward the trees and began to move the stone. Tasi shook his head, knowing this was not going to be as smooth as she thought it would be.

To Divi's surprise, the stone moved wildly, going north of the trees. She released the stone and it hit the ground with a loud thud.

"I don't understand. Why didn't it work?"

Tasi explained, "As I said, you've been working with a crutch all these years. Now is the time to grow and expand on what you already know. Mages have a unique ability to use the life particles. Whenever you use your hand to guide something with your telekinetic powers, you are directing the life particles where to go. This is the weakest connection one can have with them. To throw your first fireball, however, will require a strong link to the life particles. The method I am teaching you will strengthen the bond you'll make with them. Instead of guiding them, I want you to tell them where to go, and then have them listen. Hopefully, it will make it easier on you when we move onto feeling the loose particles. Now, try it again."

Night seemed to come fast. Once it fell, the lessons ended. Divi sat alone around a small fire in a makeshift tent. Tasi had Gerritonnee construct a place where she could spend time alone to reflect on his teachings. Of course, he needed Amber's persuasion to convince the white dragon to perform such a task. It was nothing elaborate, made of mostly animal skin and broken tree trunks. It was well camouflaged, though, which Tasi approved of.

133

Divi flipped stones across the low flames. She was still frustrated that she couldn't finish Tasi's exercise. It seemed so simple. How could the gesture of her hand be the difference between making this easy and hard? Regardless, it was the reason for her failure.

She wanted to continue training, but she had felt weaker as the day went on. Divi only lasted two hours this morning, but Tasi told her it was an encouraging sign. The rest of the day was spent resting, but she found it harder to sleep at night now. She couldn't stop thinking about Levus. How helpless he probably was, lying in the bed in Fort Za. She had to learn this . . . and fast.

She quickly stepped out of her tent and searched for a large stone, which didn't take long. It was a little bigger than the one Tasi had her move, but it would do. She closed her eyes, trying to quiet her mind. The rock she concentrated on slowly lifted in the air. That was the easy part. Now she had to control it without assistance from her hands to guide it. *I can do this*, she thought to herself.

She found two trees evenly spaced just to her left. She breathed a heavy sigh as she moved the stone toward the trees. The problem for her wasn't getting the stone to the location, but guiding it. She could feel something tugging at the stone and making it go against her will. Were the life particles doing this? Why would they be resisting her? Did she have to make them trust her?

She moved the stone closer to the trees. The tugging began to get stronger the more she tried to concentrate. *Just a little further*, she thought. *Just a little further . . .*

As she tried to send the stone between the trees, it violently resisted Divi's powers and veered roughly to the right. And she was so close, too! Divi dropped the stone and wiped sweat off her forehead. She felt very weak, probably exerting herself too much. Of course, she was going off of limited rest. She didn't want to kill herself by overexerting her abilities. It had been known to happen with young mages who made the fatal mistake of trying too hard and too often. She sat on a stone to rest up for one more try.

Meanwhile, from a small hill just above the two trees, Amber and Gerritonnee watched the mage with great curiosity. Even though they carried a torch and were easily in view of Divi, she had too much on her mind to pay them any of it. Amber looked toward her dragon friend with her arms crossed across her breast.

"What do you think, Gerritonnee?"

The dragon, speaking in the common tongue, replied, *"She has great potential. It will not be easy for her, but once she discovers how to command the Eirzalif, her limits will be boundless."*

Amber asked, "Eirzalif?"

"It is what the elves refer to as 'life dust'. It is what resides in every living thing. The elves use it differently than mages do. Where as mages use it for their magic, elves use it to refresh the land and keep it growing, allowing life on this planet to reach its full potential. People do not realize how important the elves are in that sense."

Amber really didn't understand, nor did she really care. To learn how something was done was to look too much into the past. She only wanted to care about what was ahead. Besides, she would probably never understand how a mage learned magic. It was different from the way she learned.

"I hope it doesn't take too long for her to learn, especially with you-know-who trying to find me."

Gerritonnee gazed at her before replying, *"You can rest easy, little one. Tiiamite still does not know where you are."*

Amber gave a silent sigh of relief. She knew the only reason she was able to avoid *him* was because of the efforts of her dragon companion. She also knew the risk Gerritonnee was taking for her.

135

"While on that matter, you are sure you're still okay with helping me? If he ever found out . . ."

Gerritonnee responded, *"He suspects nothing, trust me. It is not uncommon for dragons my age to stay within the boundaries of the forest. Food is ample for us here. As I get older, I will be expected to hunt outside these woods. You will most likely not be here for that day."*

"Just as long as your helping me doesn't jeopardize you," added Amber.

"It will be fine. The kindness you have shown me will never be forgotten."

Amber nodded as she looked toward Divi, who appeared to be trying to do that spell again. Her whole body gave the impression like it wanted to tip over from exhaustion, but that didn't seem to faze her. Divi had not been very open with her since they first met, but from what Tasi had explained, something was driving her. She was a very strong, person of conviction. If Amber were in Divi's shoes, it'd have to be a pretty big deal to get her to make the effort. She once again glanced at Gerritonnee.

"So, you think this mage is something special?" she asked Gerritonnee.

"I don't think it was a coincidence that we ran into them. I believe you and the mages were meant to help each other."

Amber observed as Divi began to move the stone toward the trees again.

"I wish I had your faith. I'm just worried that once we get the final stone, they will betray me."

Gerritonnee stared at Amber with some concern. She had only known her for a little over a year, but she knew her very well. Amber, seeing the white dragon's interest, looked back toward Divi.

"Why would they do that? What have you said to them?"

Amber faced the white dragon, a little surprised by her question.

"What do you mean, what did *I* do?"

Gerritonnee eyed Amber in a disconcerting manner. Her dragon friend obviously knew her better that she had thought. She sighed.

"All right. I may have been . . . a little stern with them. I got angry and said some things I'm not proud of. And I . . . kinda told them they had to leave the camp."

"That would explain why you were practicing an apology the other night. I can see why you think that now. You are very impulsive, Amber. It is both a strength and weakness for you. You must practice your judgment, then you will never doubt your decisions."

A silence came between the half-mage and Gerritonnee before the dragon finally asked, *"When are you going to tell them about Tiiamite?"*

"I'll tell them when they need to know. As long as Tiiamite stays in the dark on where we are, what's the point?" said Amber.

"Thanks for proving my *point."*

Amber laughed as she leaned against Gerritonnee's scales. She could already feel them beginning to harden. When they first met, her scales were still soft, which was primarily why Amber was able to beat her back then. Soon, her scales would become hard enough that no normal sword would be able to pierce them.

Amber commented, "It's moments like this which makes me sad that I'll have to leave here when this is done. I'm sure the Dragonians will try to keep me away in the future. We may never see each other again. I'd love to take you home with me."

Gerritonnee gave the best equivalent to a laugh that a dragon could give before saying, *"Regardless of what happens, before you breathe your last breath of life, we will see each other again. I promise."*

Amber gave her dragon a couple pats on her scales and said, "I hope that won't be anytime soon. I like living. Anyway, I'm going to sleep. It's been a long day. It appears our mage friend is thinking the same thing. Until tomorrow."

Amber walked past Gerritonnee toward the main camp. The dragon stayed, though. As she continued to watch Divi, she considered the promise she made. Although a young dragon, she had a keen sense of the future. She didn't know yet exactly when her friend's death would be, but she did know that when it came, it would be a warrior's death. One very fitting for her and that she would even be proud of. But since very little could be seen as to when it would happen, she focused her attention back on the mage.

Divi had given up for the night, retiring to her tent. Gerritonnee knew there was something special about her. She could feel powers radiating from her, even though she was just learning magic. Once she had learned, she saw her becoming the most powerful mage to ever live. It would come at a price, though. Only time would tell if Divi would be strong enough to accept the fate she was avoiding.

Gerritonnee looked up at the sky in alarm as a flock of creatures flew from their peaceful positions. Was it possible that Tiiamite had resumed hunting Amber even during the night? She hoped that wasn't the case. Dragons could go without sleep for days, but it was just inconvenient.

She waited a few more minutes listening to the surrounding forest. Silent. It must have been something else that startled those birds. If it were him, Tiiamite would have made his presence known already. The white dragon slowly turned around and headed for the camp.

"All right, let's try again."

Tasi folded his arms, waiting for Divi to once again try to move the stone through the trees. This was the third day she had been attempting the exercise, though it only

138

seemed like she was making little progress. Due to her looking worn out and exhausted after just an hour the last couple days, she was probably practicing at night. It was the only time she wasn't under his supervision. He would have to talk to her about that.

Divi grunted in frustration as once again the stone veered way off its mark. She began to wonder if it would have been easier to just throw the stone between the trees. Tasi obviously read her thoughts, as he scolded her for even thinking of taking the easy route. Divi closed her eyes to try again, but suddenly opened them.

Tasi asked, "What's wrong?"

"Why is this not working? No matter how much I try to change how I do this, I still can't get the stone where I want it to go. What am I doing wrong?"

"You are allowing the life particles to control the path of the stone. The farther you are from an item, the less control you will have over the life particles inside it. That is the resistance you are feeling. In the early days, you will need to maintain a strict focus."

"But why resist me? Do they think I'm a bad person? Do they think I will abuse them?"

Tasi sat down and crossed his legs, motioning with his hand for Divi to do the same. As she looked into his eyes, she knew that he wanted to make a point clearly.

"Life particles do not distinguish between good or bad. A mage who learns the forbidden Dark Magic uses life particles just like every honest mage. How could they make the distinction of which is good and which is evil? The spells we cast are not evil. It is the intent of them that make them that way. Life particles do not sense intent. Our actions are what determine what kind of person we are. You can be a good person, but still have some evil in you. As long as the good wins out, then that is primarily what you are."

Divi nodded. She understood a little of what Tasi was saying. Levus was a good person, but that sword perhaps brought out the evil side of whoever possessed it. As she thought about it, it appeared even Ulcinar had a good side, albeit a very minimal one. The way he spared Levus and Cerrapies' lives in Arnis sort of proved that. She was certain that he had his own dark reasoning for doing so, but she at least couldn't see it.

She closed her eyes once again. She wanted to try something new. Instead of instantly lifting the rock, she would try to get that strict focus Tasi was talking about. For the time being, Levus would need to be in the back of her mind. She began to roll the rock on the ground, first in random directions, but then in deliberate circles. Tasi smiled when he saw what she was doing.

Divi maintained her focus until all she could see in her mind was that stone. It was a weird sensation, despite her eyes still being closed, to see the rock move when it felt like she was doing nothing. With her normal powers and using her hand, it was like grabbing the item from afar. Right now, she believed the only way to move it was to sense every ounce of that rock's being. After a few minutes, she finally lifted the stone. Even though she could see the trees, her entire concentration remained on the rock. It began to move slowly toward the trees. She could feel the resistance as she neared her target. Somehow, though, it seemed lighter than before. Odd.

She was very close to the trees now. The trembling of the stone became heavier, causing Divi to focus even harder. The stone tried to resist, but she wasn't letting it as it began to pass between the trees.

"Congratulations!"

Divi dropped the stone and opened her eyes. The rock had landed five feet past the two trees. She did it! She grinned at Tasi, who was clapping his hands.

"Great work, Divi. You have just taken your first step into a larger world."

"I'm so happy! I could feel the difference!"

140

"I know. You did what I hoped you would do. Instead of going straight for the target, you got the feeling of the stone, moved it around a little. Becoming familiar with the object you move is a major step to controlling it. Let's not stop now. Let's do it again."

Divi closed her eyes again and focused on another stone . . .

Night came that day sooner than usual, mainly due to the storm. They had to cut the lessons short because of it. Tasi thought that it was good they did, though. Divi had a very good day. She was able to control an object without use of her hands much more quickly than most students. It was, however, just the first major step. Once he considered her a master at it, then he would go on to the next phase, by far the most difficult.

Divi entered the tent, wet from the downpour outside. Tasi had actually encouraged her to sit in the rain for a few minutes, as it had been proven to have a massaging feel to mages learning magic, easing the muscles and resettling the mind. Training was physically taxing on the body, so it was only fitting that Mother Terra's natural water would be a relaxing catalyst. It was discovered completely by accident hundreds of year ago by a training mage group stalled by a storm. When they got home, they were recovered to full strength. He suspected that it helped rejuvenate the life particles, but he couldn't prove it and most likely he never would. One thing was true, though, Divi did appear much more refreshed after taking his suggestion.

She wrung the water from her hair, trying to dry off. Amber had warned them that storms could be very strong here. They never had violent weather like this on Myyril. Of course, if a strong one did come, the leader would set a barrier over the city to limit the rainfall. It usually caused flooding once the shield went down after the storm passed as water would collect on the ground and travel the slight downhill toward the capital. Neeza had brought the issue to the council many times, but seemed disinterested since there was no public outcry. Most mage valuables were on shelves, not on the floor.

Divi felt like a new person after standing in the rain. Tasi had worked her very hard today once she proved she could control the life particles without the use of her hand. She was almost thankful the rains had come as she was physically exhausted. Despite hearing from other mages how strenuous training could be, she never had believed them. Learning the simple telekinetic abilities were very easy, so the thought the rest would be hard she never grasped until now.

"You aren't complaining about the results, are you?"

She forgot Tasi was reading her thoughts this whole time. She really hoped he would stop doing that soon. She found it rather annoying.

Divi replied, "No, it was just a little harder than I thought."

Tasi laughed and said, "Well, you are doing very good so far. We will continue this exercise for the next couple days. Even though you had done well, you are still using more power than necessary. We will refine your technique until you can do it as easily as breathing."

That answer made her a little nervous. They didn't have that kind of time. Levus needed her as quickly as possible. She now understood that learning magic was not going to be as easy as she thought, but she had to learn it fast. This was her choice. If there were another way that would save Levus faster, she would do it. But . . . there was no other way.

Tasi sat silently. He knew that she was thinking of Levus again, and her choice to learn magic to save him. He could already tell this was going to make the rest of her training difficult . . . especially when casting her first fireball.

If she could not control her emotions, she would never succeed. In fact, the first time she successfully moved the stone between the trees was when she put Levus in the back of her mind. As much as she didn't want to admit it, his presence in her thoughts was going to be a distraction, one that could extend her training, not shorten it. But would she listen to him on this matter? He knew the answer. *Not a chance.*

"Do you think Ulcinar uses life particles? His magic is not like a mage's or an elf's. Now that I'm able to feel the life particles, I can see he uses something different."

Divi's question took Tasi by surprise. How would he know the answer to such a question? He had never seen Ulcinar fight, or even heard about him other than through Levus.

Tasi answered, "I can't imagine what he would be using. Life particles are what give most magic users power. It is possible another source exists that we are not aware of. You should not concern yourself with Ulcinar. He will, like all other would-be conquerors, fail."

"What if Ulcinar is not doing this to conquer land to rule? What if he is just doing this . . . just to do it? What if he has no reason for his actions other than fun? And why is the Moonsaber so important to him?"

Tasi explained, "Power. It is a characteristic that corrupts humans. That sword represents an unearthly power he is trying to harness. If you ask me, we should just toss the weapon into the ocean and let Gyyerlith swallow it into her fiery belly."

Easier said than done, Divi thought to herself. The sword was a tool that controlled its bearer. Those strange techniques one could do while holding it made them arrogant and feel invincible. It may give that power to humans who so desired, but not her Levus. He had no need for such power and would never seek it or demand it.

143

Tasi finally said, "It is getting late. You should rest. Tomorrow we will resume your training if the weather cooperates."

He stood up and headed to his sleeping area. Divi sat for just a while longer. Her unanswered questions continued to swirl in her mind. She knew that against mage magic, elven magic was stronger, and certain Dark Magic was strong or weak. What if Ulcinar's spells were stronger than even an elf's? What could stop him? One thing she knew for certain: Tasi was wrong. She shouldn't forget about Ulcinar. He was no normal human—in fact, she believed he wasn't human at all. One day she felt she would once again stand before the Dark Lord like she had back in Arnis. Only now, there was so much more at stake . . . so much more.

CHAPTER 8
It Comes at Night

"Why did you want me to come with you?"

Divi had been a little surprised by Amber's request. Since she started her training, Amber kept her distance, only really seeing them when it was supper time. Even then, sometimes it was just Tasi and her as Amber would eat earlier.

Amber replied, "Three reasons. Firstly, I thought that you could use a few hours away from your teacher."

Divi gave a short chuckle. She didn't want to admit it, and she hoped it wasn't revealed through a mental slip earlier since Tasi kept tabs on her thoughts, but she was getting a little fatigued. Training was a lot harder than she suspected it would be. She thought she would already have thrown her first fireball by now. How difficult could it be? She was finding out it wasn't going to be that simple.

"Secondly, since I now have more mouths to feed, I've had to place more traps to feed us. Since Tasi keeps boasting you have the strongest telekinetic powers of any mage he knows, you could help me carry back the kills."

Divi asked, "And what is the third reason?"

Amber smiled and said, "Thirdly, I just figured us girls can talk. I think ever since we've met it seems all I do is yell at you, but we can learn more about each other given we're going to be fighting the last dragon together."

She was happy that Amber was willing to accept them and their help. She had been certain that she and Tasi would have to face the Fire Dragon themselves after how the half-mage talked to her. Even though she didn't show it initially, it warmed her heart that Amber had a change in hers.

The night was clear and the temperature was nice. Not even one cloud littered the sky. Even the wind was gentle and refreshing. It was almost too perfect. In all the days they had been here, there had always been some kind of weather that slowed them or halted them completely, whether it was training or traveling. The night they beat Leviadon they were met with a horrible thunderstorm. Divi was sure she had been in worse storms, but to be out in the open with no roof to protect them made things scary.

Even though Amber seemingly wanted to talk, she remained mum. Divi guessed the half-mage wasn't used to company. If what she said about the battlemage route was true, then she must have led one of the loneliest lives she had ever known.

Divi finally asked, "So, why didn't you want to have a large ceremony for your Paladin Trials? The pomp and circumstance that it brings is quite the event in Myyril. Encouraged, actually."

"Well, believe it or not, it was your father's idea to keep it quiet. Not that I didn't agree with him. He sent someone named . . . I can't remember her name, but she didn't speak much. Anyway, she met me at the dock when the ship arrived at night. The council met with me and Neeza gave me my quest. The captain of the vessel made the trip entertaining at least. His name was Mimerck."

Divi knew that name. The mage captain had taken her and her father to Porsita that fateful night. She heard his instructions had been drop them off, sail to Tartus with a manifest, then come back to Porsita to pick them up five days later. She was certain he heard the commotion after dropping them off. Did he still continue on to Tartus? Did he just return home?

She even began to wonder why her Dad would keep Amber's trials shrouded in secrecy. Paladin candidates loved the celebrity of just being selected to attempt the task brought them. The mage community usually came out and gave a parade to the hopeful as they departed. Mages were always welcoming when a half-mage was that close to cleansing the sins of their parents. Unfortunately, in the Trials' long history, not many came back.

Amber continued, "Tasi tells me that you and your Dad didn't get along before his passing. I am not going to ask you why, but I will say that at least you have memories of your parents, good or bad. It is something often taken for granted."

"You've never met your parents? Not even through letter or pictures?" asked Divi.

"It is illegal to have any contact with the mainland on Tydos. Not to say that it doesn't happen. I only know what races my parents were. I do know my mother's name, but not what family I hailed from. Quite honestly, I am convinced they are both dead. The letter I got a couple years before I earned the Right pretty much said the same."

That would certainly lead to a private meeting instead of the parade. If everything was lost at home, what did the Paladin candidate have to gain? Still, it was very odd for the Council to agree and meet at night just for a Paladin. She would have to ask Dinermar more about that whenever she returned home.

Amber asked, "So, just out of curiosity, what makes a mage not want to learn magic? I haven't talked to many, but the ones I have talked to made it seem like it was the proudest moment of their lives."

Divi answered, "It was mostly because of my mom. When I was a little girl, she told me how hard it was for her to learn magic and how the Kittara were very rough on her during her military time. She would always tell me that mages don't understand how lucky we are to have the gifts we have and that if we waited to train until a much older age, we would appreciate it more. That was what started me on that path."

Amber could certainly relate when it came to the Kittara. When she arrived in Myyril for her Paladin Quest, she could almost feel their presence. She was glad they stayed hidden, though. If any had come out of the shadows, she was pretty certain that she would have killed them and been sent back to Tydos a corpse.

"So, did your mom not learn magic?"

Divi replied, "No, she was a fully accomplished mage when she had me."

"If I'm driving you crazy with the questions, I am sorry. I just don't see why she would want you not to learn. The Kittara are cold-hearted bastards, I agree, but like all police or security teams, they can be bought. I'm surprised it hasn't happened more often. They can also be blocked too, but I understand doing so can be difficult. There has to be some other reason for her not wanting you to do it. Something she wasn't telling you."

Divi hoped not. She had to go years with her dad hiding stuff from her. She didn't even want to think that her mom had also. There may have been some small things. In the later years, the Gerrun's disease made her less talkative before it took her voice from her fully. But□

"She wouldn't have hidden anything from me. I just know she wouldn't. She . . ."

"Shhhh."

Divi stopped talking as Amber went to her knees behind a bush. She was going to ask what she saw, but it looked like Amber was trying to figure that out. The focus of her eyes became something Divi got more used to the more she hung out with the half-mage.

Amber stared forward for a long time before searching in every direction, including straight up. The entire area was quiet. Even the wind seemed to have died to nothing. She slowly drew her sword.

"Stay here and stay silent. I'll signal you if it's safe."

Divi nodded, curious what was troubling Amber. The half-mage crept slowly to a clearing in the leaves and branches. It was amazing how stealthily she moved across the landscape. She had the same hunting prowess as Levus.

Amber stopped at the edge of the clearing and seemingly just stared at it. After a few minutes, just as Divi was beginning to feel uncomfortable, Amber waved her to come. Divi tried to move as quietly as Amber, but anyone would have heard her from a mile away.

Divi asked, "So what is all the . . . what is that?"

In the center of the clearing was a metal object with a red and brownish mess attached to it. Blood was everywhere. Even in the night, the sound of flies echoed throughout the clearing as they stepped closer.

Amber said, "That used to be a gillantis deet. Think of it as a large deer. It got caught in my trap."

"So another animal grabbed your kill. Maybe it was one of the dragons."

"No, I have seen Gerritonnee eat. If it was a dragon, it would have eaten everything, including the trap. Or the dragon would have noticed the trap and shaken the prey until it tore from the force. In other words, the trap would be somewhere else, far away from where I planted it. Whatever did this ripped the leg off the deet, crushing the bone below the hip socket," Amber analyzed.

The thought that there was something that could do this to a huge deer was frightening. From the size of what remained of the leg, a deet must have been about ten feet high. The only other wildlife she remembered seeing since she got here was a large, slow-moving beast that Amber called a sloof. They were harmless, though, eating only the higher leaves from the trees. Other predator animals stayed north to avoid getting hunted by dragons, so some species thrived in the south because of it despite them.

Divi asked, "What could possibly have done it, then?"

Amber tried to think of the wildlife that Gerritonnee told her about. The only one animal that seemed capable of this were the ulkitmores, large cats that roamed the land. Their speed and agility made them tough. They killed quickly too, because they could open their jaws wide for a strong bite. But they never traveled south of the Temple of Elements, as they were on a dragon's food chain. There was another possibility . . . but it couldn't be one of them. It just couldn't be.

Divi pointed, "Look! There is a blood trail."

The mage was right. A trail of blood headed north. Consequently, it led toward some of her other traps. Amber knew the smart thing to do was cut her losses, make new traps tomorrow, and try again. Whatever had scavenged her kills was larger than them. Then again, her food supply was getting very low because of her two guests. If she could secure a meal from just one of the traps, then she would call it a win and go back.

Amber said, "Follow me. Hopefully we can avoid the creature who did this. The first animal we find in my traps we grab and bring back."

Divi couldn't have agreed more. What was supposed to be a quick and easy trip to collect food was becoming potentially dangerous. She hadn't been able to learn to throw a fireball yet, meaning all she had were her telekinetic abilities at the moment.

The blood trail turned west. No matter how far they went, all they ran into was carnage. They found four more of Amber's traps. Of the four, three held kills, but the prey vanished except for whatever parts were caught fast in the metal teeth of the traps. The one that had caught nothing was mangled beyond the point of fixing.

What alarmed Amber were the footprints they saw along the trail. Whatever it was, it stood on its hind legs . . . or at least walked on them. Bits and pieces of animal flesh and bone were scattered to the sides of the path. The bones showed obvious tooth marks, and some were entirely crushed. Now she had more reason to find a kill and return to camp.

Divi commented, "Another trap destroyed. You know, we should head back. Whatever is out here wants the food more than we do. Tomorrow is another day."

"Yeah . . . yeah, that's a good idea. I don't like this at all. Let's get out of here."

Just as they turned around, they heard thunderous sounds coming from the north and the south from the air. Amber knew it could only be one thing.

"Head for the trees! Hide!"

They ran as fast as they could for the edge of the clearing, not more than a hundred feet away. Caution had to be tossed to the wayside temporarily. Amber didn't want to meet the creature destroying her traps, but she didn't want to be found by the dragons either. She knew it wasn't her Gerritonnee, as she traveled alone.

They arrived at the trees and hid just as four shadows hovered over them. They peeked around the trunk to see a yellowish-red dragon landed in the clearing they had just stood in. It started sniffing at the ground, the animal bits, and the path of blood. As it moved, following its nose, the earth trembled with each step. It sniffed until its attention was aimed at the woods ahead of it . . . exactly where Divi and Amber were hiding. It began to beat its wings, hovering over the ground.

Divi was too scared to move, while Amber kept her cool. Her breathing was rapid, but controlled. She had been confident...but the sounds...told her otherwise. She closed her eyes, her hand clenched on her sword hilt.

With a soft roar, the dragon flew north, just above the treetops. Hundreds of leaves fell to the ground wherever its body made contact. More fell from the south heading north from another of the dragons. The beating of their wings grew more distant. Amber and Divi sat silently until they felt assured that the dragons had moved on.

Divi commented, "That was close. How did they know we were here?"

Amber replied, "They weren't looking for us. I think they are looking for whatever has been decimating my traps. It's just odd. I have never seen this coordination between the dragons before. They normally stay to themselves. Whatever they're hunting, I'm not even sure one dragon can defeat it on its own."

That thought chilled Divi to her core. What creature could possibly live here that even the dragons feared? She guessed that was the nature of things. Sometimes the hunter became the hunted. Then again, every dragon on Dragonia was tied spiritually to one of its residents according to Minat. He mentioned it briefly, not thinking of it much at the time, saying it was why his people rarely fought in wars. Looking at it that way, Divi felt compelled to help the dragons, as they were technically people as well.

Amber wanted to do nothing but get up and run back to camp. Unfortunately, that was out of the question. The beating of dragon wings still sounded close and she couldn't risk getting seen, especially if Tiiamite was among them. They might not be looking for her at the moment, but if she was discovered, she was certain they would make time to take care of her.

In the woods on the other side of the clearing they heard a dragon land as the earth shook. It wasn't as strong, but close enough to feel. There must have been another clearing there. The northern reaches of the forest were still not familiar to the half-mage. Amber set her traps more to the east, away from the dragon lairs.

Again, the dragon softly roared and its wings beat like drums. Amber didn't want to wait much longer. Even though it might be a risk, she had to get herself and Divi out of here. So long as they stayed, they were in terrible danger. If not from the dragons, then from what they were hunting. The kill in the last trap they ran into looked very fresh. For their flying friends to be hanging around this area meant that whatever did it was close. If one dragon couldn't kill it alone, they stood little chance of doing it either.

Amber said, "Let's go."

As soon as they stood up, two loud roars were heard . . . and the first one was not a dragon. It was much deeper than any beast she encountered on Dragonia thus far. The exchange lasted only a few seconds; the roars of the dragon became cries before a resounding snap like a tree broke in half and then silence. Divi and Amber froze. What just happened? They couldn't even hear the beating of the dragon's wings.

Divi said, "What in the hells was that?"

They were in quite a situation. In the air, dragons patrolled like they never had before. On the ground, a killer was hunting and slaying everything that got in its way. Of all the nights that this could happen, why did it have to happen now? Amber wasn't afraid of much, but the creature causing this carnage had made her list.

"We should go see if it is okay."

Amber glanced at Divi in shock. "See if what is okay?"

"The dragon, of course. It might need our help."

"I think I'm going to have Tasi give you a day of rest, as you are suffering from delusions right now. Do you even hear yourself? Even if the dragon is mortally wounded, what are we supposed to do? You're still learning magic and I don't know any healing magic. And what if it is hurt and the creature that did this is still there, using it as bait?"

Divi retorted, "Our alternative is run back to camp, praying that another dragon or the creature doesn't find us on the way while we are in no position to fight. Once the beast is done with that dragon, who do you think it will come after next? Let's at least see what the situation is and if we can't do anything, then so be it."

This was not a good idea. Yet, the mage had a point. Wherever this creature came from, it was in the southern part of the continent, where all of her camps were located. Its path of carnage began here judging by how the fresher kills were more northeast, meaning it had to have a den or cave nearby. With all the dragons flying overhead, there would be no way for this predator to make it this far from the more plains dominated north. It was using the forest for cover. If it was still there, they might be able to delay it long enough for the other dragons to located and kill it.

Amber finally said, "Okay, I thought it was this way. Come on!"

They ran as fast as they could, though because it was hard to see the ground beneath the fallen leaves and tree roots, they did so cautiously. About three miles ahead, they came to another clearing. Here, their eyes opened wide.

A dragon lay on the ground, and it wasn't moving. The left wing looked broken and torn. Its back faced them, so they couldn't see what the possible mortal wound looked like. Amber didn't want to know who, either.

A tear rolled down Divi's cheek. It looked like the dragon was dead. Did that mean that one of the members of Dragonia had also died? She couldn't imagine feeling fine one moment and then the next moment falling dead because the dragon she was tied to had been killed.

"See?" Amber said. "There was nothing we could have done. Let's get out of here before the dragons come back and think we did this."

Divi suddenly yelled, "Wait! Look! I think it's moving."

When Amber looked closely, she too saw the dragon's body jerk slightly. Maybe it was alive, just terribly wounded. Still, what could they do? The only one who knew healing magic between the three of them was Tasi, and he was sleeping nice and sound back at camp. She didn't want to be here when the other dragons found the body. Knowing her luck, Tiiamite would blame her for this. She didn't need that right now.

The dragon's body jerked a little more. For whatever reason, Divi and Amber moved closer. She understood that there was nothing they could do to help it, but perhaps they could help the other dragons find it so they could help.

Divi suggested, "Amber, light some wood so the other dragons can see this location."

Amber did so without question. If this was what it took to convince Divi to return to camp, then she was on board.

Divi walked up to the dragon and placed her hand on its back. The scales felt cool to the touch and hard to the touch.

She said, "Stay strong. We are getting help for you."

Something grunted loudly. Strangest thing. It didn't sound like it was coming from the dragon, whose head was to her left. It sounded like it was coming straight in front of her, but that would be in the direction of the dragon's belly.

Amber, returning with the wood, glanced up and froze. Her mouth opened wide as the wood fell to the ground. Divi followed her gaze and saw the source of the grunts. Standing on the other side of the dragon was a creature standing nearly thirty feet tall. Its fur was a deep black, allowing it to nearly blend in with its dark surroundings. Two horns protruded out of its cheeks. Its entire face was dripping blood, some flesh impaled on its horns. That grunting sound wasn't from the fallen dragon at all, but this creature feasting on its innards. With a loud roar, it revealed very large teeth.

Divi slowly backed away.

"It's real," Amber whispered.

Divi asked, "What is it?"

"A nitklarii."

She remembered Gionti mentioning that name when she first got here. When he described it to her then, it hadn't scare her. About thirty-five feet away, it terrified her now. And just their luck, none of the other dragons who'd been

155

searching were in sight. They had to fight this beast on their own.

Amber said, "I knew this was a bad idea. Why did I not listen to myself?"

"I think I want to go back now."

"No time. We have to fight. Kind of wish Tasi had joined us."

Divi did too. She was still working on the basics for strengthening her telekinesis. If only she had started sooner she might have been able to throw fireballs.

Amber, knowing they had to do something, pointed her weapon at the nitklarii's heart, or where she thought it was, and fired a sword projectile at it that she called Steelbreaker. She was the only battlemage who could do, not even sure how she learned to do it. The attack looked like a beam of light when she fired it, but reflecting the top part of her sword when it hit something physical. It was her most effective attack spell because it could even go through chain mail and, like an arrow, had to be removed for the injury to heal. She hoped that she could injure it and it would go away, but she had her doubts. She'd heard its skin was very tough. As her projectile bounced harmlessly off its chest, she was disheartened to learn the rumors were true.

"Okay, we're in trouble."

The nitklarii's roar caused the forest to tremble around them. She had a bad feeling it would not accomplish anything, but Amber raised her weapon and surrounded the blade with a fire spell. She toyed with the idea of using a wind spell, but she didn't think it would be strong enough to slow the beast down. It had done little against the three dragons she had faced thus far.

Just when the nitklarii started to climb over the dragon carcass, two logs came from both sides, sandwiching its head. Amber looked at Divi, who was concentrating. She wasn't using her hands anymore like she did when Amber first met her. The mage girl was getting stronger.

156

Amber commented, "Nicely done."

After a few seconds, though, the creature shook its head and roared louder than before. If anything, the logs did damage to one of its horns, bending it inward. At this point, something was better than nothing. More importantly, it seemed they located perhaps its only weakness.

"Okay, Divi, that works. Keep aiming for the head!"

Divi nodded as Amber tried to figure out what she could use that might hurt the nitklarii. Divi could feel many fallen trees, which she assumed had been knocked down by the same beast they were fighting. How ironic the trees would be returning the favor.

Using her telekinetic powers, she began tossing the downed trunks. The first one hit its target, stunning it slightly. The nitklarii was confused, as it had obviously never had this happen to it before. Trunk after trunk hit the beast, but their effectiveness lessened as it swatted at the logs, sending splinters and chips of bark flying.

Amber, meanwhile, was looking for a way to contribute. *Funny, here I was the one who knew magic and now I'm the one trying to find ways to help while Divi does all the work.* She finally found something she could do. As she ran, she froze a bunch of rocks with her ice spells. When they were frozen solid, she stabbed her blade into them. She was hoping the smooth rocks, now slightly jagged because of how her freezing spell worked, would do some damage to it. When she had an opening, she used a wind spell to blast the stones toward the nitklarii's head. Her accuracy was unmatched, hitting it every single time.

Unfortunately, the rocks were too small to do any significant damage. Even though they were hitting hard, it was still the equivalent of throwing a pebble at it. She would be exhausted before she could throw enough stones to kill it. She ran back toward Divi, who had begun to wear a worried expression.

Divi asked, "I like your idea, but might need something bigger. I'm running out of logs!"

She glanced up to see the nitklarii easily swatting at the trunks. Its massive paws shattered the wood like it was glass. *What in the world can we do that will defeat this thing?* Its size and power they could not match, and outrunning it was out of the question. She leaned on a nearby boulder.

That's it!

Taking her sword, she froze the boulder, again giving its smoother surface a more serrated one. It took a minute due to its colossal size. She was convinced her idea was sound with the frozen rocks, but they were too small to damage the monster. *Let's see how it handles this.*

Amber yelled, "Divi! Use this stone! I'll use a wind spell to give it more speed!"

Divi nodded, throwing the last trunk she was telekinetically controlling. The nitklarii caught it in its mouth, snapping it in half with its powerful jaws. It seemed to make sure that no more logs were heading its way before focusing on its attackers. It roared as it placed its claws on the dragon's body.

Amber asked, "What are you waiting for? Let's hit it!"

Divi calmly replied, "Wait for it."

The nitklarii snarled as it sized up its prey. Much smaller than it was used to. But it was not going to discriminate. Food was food, large or small. After the pain they caused, it would be satisfying.

"Wait," Divi said again. "Almost there."

To the nitklarii, it looked like they were not going to run, which meant it didn't need urgency either. It moved its paw reaching near the dragon's wings.

Amber grew very nervous. What was Divi waiting for? She hoped she wasn't going through flashbacks of the Leviadon fight, when she hadn't been able to cast magic. A stressful moment like that sometimes stuck in a person's mind.

Divi, on the other hand, smiled. She was hoping it would do that: climb over where the wings were, which was the biggest part of the dragon. If they ran, it might leap over the body or move to a small part such as the neck so it could pursue them. Staying put, the nitklarii believed it could take its time and that they were just accepting their fate. And in order to climb over the body, it needed its paws. If they were busy, they would not be free to block her and Amber's surprise.

She waited until the nitklarii got one leg over, nearly straddling the carcass, before she yelled, "Now!"

Using her telekinesis, she lifted the frozen boulder and gave it a slight spin. Amber activated one of her wind spells just as Divi tossed the stone with all her might. Amber's spell sent it toward its destination that much faster. The nitklarii had no time to react. The rock hit its head with such force that it was driven back at least two hundred feet. Amber smiled. That had to have killed it. Any normal being would have had a shattered skull from the boulder alone. She walked up to Divi as they listened. The area was silent. She thought she heard the thundering sound of dragon wings in the distance, but couldn't be sure.

Divi finally sighed in relief. "We did it!"

Amber replied, "Wait until I tell Gerritonnee about this. She's not going to believe me. I'd take a trophy, but I don't think I can pierce that thing's skin."

Would anyone believe them? She was certain once the dragons found the nitklarii's body, they would either decimate it beyond recognition after what it did to one of their kind or put it on their menu. They would know who had killed it, though. That was all she needed.

Her thought was broken when a paw clamped on the dead dragon's back, followed by the other. Soon after that, the head followed. The damage their boulder did was evident. Blood rushed from its nose. The tip of one horn dangled by a thread, nearly broken off. The other horn was bent out more, but still firmly attached. Other than that, the only other thing the stone did was make it angrier at them.

Amber said, "Okay, now we run!"

Both women turned and started sprinting toward the woods. The nitklarii roared louder than they had ever heard. It jumped over the dragon carcass and pursued them. It brushed the ancient trees aside like they were nothing. Amber glanced back only once. It had almost caught up with them. It didn't stride quickly, but the strides were long. Its steps caused the earth to shake, making it tougher to keep on her feet as she fled.

The nitklarii pounded the ground with its fist, sending a shockwave that brought them both down. Divi's legs were beginning to cramp up, a symptom she had when she used her telekinetic powers too much in a day. That was the way a mage's body warned them to stop and rest or else. It started at the legs and feet since they were the farthest from the heart. Even if she wanted to fight more, she wouldn't last much longer. The nitklarii was nearly above them, its paw raised, ready to strike.

Suddenly, a white beam pierced the nitklarii from the back and came out through its belly. The contents of that belly spewed out, covering Divi and Amber with the beast's blood, flesh and remains of its nightly kills. After a few seconds, the beam died and the nitklarii dropped to its knees lifeless in front of them.

Amber abruptly forgot her disgust at having the creature's guts all over her when she realized there was only one being on this continent that could have caused that beam. She'd never wanted to see it again after the first time. He was here! If he found her, they were going to be in a whole lot of trouble.

Amber quietly said, "Divi . . . do not . . . move . . . a muscle!"

Divi's focus was wiping the blood off her lips and face when she heard Amber saying something. She was about to ask what she said, but the blotting out of the moon caught her attention. They both froze as a large group of dragons flew overhead. She couldn't believe it. There were so many. Instead of roaring though, it almost sounded like they were . . . crying. They all circled the dead dragon.

Above them, a large dragon flew higher than the rest. Amber knew which one this was just by the beating of its wings. Thankfully they were still partially covered by the trees, as well as covered in the nitklarii's innards, which masked their scent.

When the largest dragon arrived, the others in the circle let out cries that brought tears to Divi's eyes. They knew their brother had fallen. It made her realize that dragons were not much different from any of the other races. They experienced loss and were just as hurt by it as mages, humans, or elves were. In Dragonia, a similar ceremony must have been happening.

The large dragon fired four white fireballs, one after the next, straight in the air. At this signal, the other dragons cocked their heads back and breathed flames at the dead dragon. They lit the entire area as if the sun were shining in just this one spot.

Amber, as afraid as she was to be this close to nearly all the dragons onto the continent, watched curiously. She was certain she was not meant to see this, which made it much more interesting to watch. She tried to find Gerritonnee, but couldn't from her vantage point.

Seconds later, the fireballs that the large dragon shot in the air fell directly on the dead dragon's body. They caused the red flames to turn a dark blue. Divi could feel the heat even from their position a hundred fifty yards away. A few seconds later, the dragons stopped shooting their flames. The blue flame died, revealing nothing but the dragon's bones. The grass in the clearing around it was also burned to ash. Amber wondered if anything would grow in that spot for years. Dragon fire was known to be hotter than any kind of fire on Gyyerlith. The blue flame had to have burned the seeds along with the rest of it.

A few minutes later, the largest dragon flew away to the north. The remaining dragons cried out again for their fallen comrade before also dispersing. Once more, there was silence. The sounds of the insects, which had gone quiet when the flames were lit, returned.

Amber stood up and walked to the nitklarii. Using her sword, she hacked at the dangling horn. It took some time, but she eventually succeeded in removing it. Unfortunately, they were going to come up empty in terms of food. Nitklarii meat was supposed to be so tough that only dragons had jaws strong enough to tear it. If that was the case, they had zero chance of even chewing it.

Divi eventually stood, but with sorrow filling her heart. She wondered which member of Dragonia might have fallen as a result of this dragon's death. She hoped it wasn't Hiiminta. She was but a child.

Amber patted her on the shoulder, startling her. "Come on. We should get back. I've had enough excitement for one night. I'll construct and set new traps tomorrow; we'll just have to ration what meat I have left until then."

Divi nodded as they slowly made their way back in the direction of the camp. She took one more glance at the dragon bones they were leaving behind. *I'm sorry we couldn't help you. But at least we were able to help bring down your killer, brave dragon.*

"You look a little . . . tired. How late were you out?"

Tasi had no clue what they experienced last night. Thankfully, he had also been tired, so tired that he stopped spying on her mind in order to get some rest himself. That

162

meant he saw and heard nothing about the activities of their hunt.

Divi replied, "Pretty late. Amber's traps were a little farther than anticipated. She was convinced that something moved them. Sadly, no catches."

She wanted to avoid telling him what really happened, and in fact she and Amber made a pact last night to keep it secret. Tasi worried about too many things. Adding the fight with the nitklarii and the dragons would only have caused him to be stricter than he already was.

Divi felt that the little altercation with the nitklarii brought her and the half-mage closer together. Amber, in the little time that she had known her, had not seemed one to show her feelings too often. Yet, they fought well together, taking their current strengths and combining them to survive and defeat their foe. She was really glad that she forgave her. Amber could be rash at times, but she had a good heart, albeit a focused one.

Tasi commented, "Seeing as you might not be at your fullest strength, we will keep training light today. I wouldn't mind a light load myself. I will talk with Amber about returning you sooner next time. I should have stressed the importance of rest for a training mage. I'm glad she invited you, but she'll need to be more understanding."

Divi smiled and said, "Yes, teacher."

"Very well. Let's get back to practicing on rocks again, shall we?"

As Divi started her training for the day, Amber watched on a hill alongside Gerritonnee. She had a feeling her dragon friend would be coming to visit her after last night. Amber was uncertain if Gerritonnee had known she was in the forest near the fallen dragon, but the haste of her visit suggested otherwise to her. Perhaps they were just that close that she knew Amber was involved somehow.

"It is amazing you survived an attack from a nitklarii."

"How did you know I fought one?" Amber asked.

"*I noticed the piece of its horn that you've made into a necklace around your neck. That and you still reek of its innards. I smell them on Divi as well. It will take more than what you have done to wash the stench off completely. I also noticed footprints. Tiiamite had me investigate and dispose of the nitklarii body since I am the smallest of the dragons and still fit in the tight forests.*"

She couldn't hide anything from Gerritonnee, not anymore. The dragon was growing just as much as she felt Amber was. Amber was convinced that they met for a reason, although she was not one to believe in fate. Never had been.

"Is that why there were so many dragons around? Because of the nitklarii?"

"*Nitklarii are ancient predators and some of the only ones that have ever fed on dragon flesh. They are usually drawn to fluctuations in the Eirzalif, but it was also near time for one or two to rise from their long slumber. Haven't had more than that in years so I'm told. When they do, we must hunt them together or we will be torn apart separately.*"

That made a lot of sense. Amber never really saw dragons as pack hunters, but if these nitklarii came in greater numbers, dragons would need to gather to survive. Last night they lost one dragon to one nitklarii. What would it have been like if there were more?

"Did you know the dragon that died very well?" asked Amber.

Gerritonnee lowered her head before answering. "*He was called Borrifrit. He was separated from our pack, looking at the clearings as he noticed many dead animal carcasses in previous ones. Convinced it would show itself in one, he went more east. He was a good friend. He will be missed.*"

Amber was going to ask her if someone from Dragonia had perished in consequence to the dragon's passing, but opted not to. She could tell her dragon friend was hurt by the loss of Borrifrit. She didn't want to remind her too much more of it.

"At least the nitklarii is dead. Borrifrit's death was not in vain."

"We killed that one, yes. More will come. They always do. Yet you speak truth. Among the dragons, Borrifrit's death was a meaningful one. I wish I could thank you officially as well because without you and Divi interfering, it may have taken us longer to find the beast."

It saddened her that more of those blasted creatures would come back. If she had any say, she would find their lairs and kill every last one of them to keeping Gerritonnee safe. She was just glad she could help. Those things were a hard foe to face, one she hoped to never fight again. Amber wanted to tell her that it was Divi's idea to stay and help, so she deserved the credit, but Tasi had a knack of hearing his student's name even from afar.

Amber asked, "Was that what a dragon funeral looks like?"

"One of many ways. When a dragon dies in combat, it is our custom to burn the body to the bones and leave them there where they fell. This is so its spirit can always find where it was reborn to the Eirzalif. Dragons are born of fire, so must they return to it. You witnessed a rare event last night. Not many not from here have seen one. For your sakes, I am glad the others couldn't sense you or Divi. They would have been insulted that prying eyes were observing a private moment."

It wasn't like they had a choice. As soon as the nitklarii was killed, the dragons had arrived to pay tribute to and burn their fallen brother. She wanted out of there sooner than that, but Divi made her stay. Amber wasn't mad at her. It ended up being the right decision.

Gerritonnee commented, *"The girl mage is growing on you."*

165

Amber smiled. "I don't know. She has an undying spirit that wants to do whatever she can to help. Reminds me of myself a little, I guess. Plus, she is growing stronger. When she finishes learning magic . . . it is going to be scary what she can accomplish."

Chuckling, the white dragon said, "*You are going soft on me, Amber. I must go. Tiiamite is calling all the dragons together. I am curious what he wants. I will visit you again as soon as I can.*"

Gerritonnee turned around. Flapping her wings, she hovered into the air and was soon out of sight, thanks to the treetops. Amber watched Divi move rocks where Tasi directed. Her dragon friend was right. The perky little mage was growing on her. Plus, she saw it as only beneficial to befriend the future ruler of Myyril. Maybe she could end the mage's policies on half-mages.

Amber was looking too far ahead. *I had better return to making new traps as our food supply shortage is still very real.* If she wanted to succeed, staying well fed was important. She was only one elemental stone away from completing her Paladin Quest. Just one. Then she would be unshackled from Myyrilian tyranny against half-mages. Divi, though, wanted a different kind of independence. On the surface, she appeared to desire free will and to not be restricted by her family bloodline. As she was learning, there was more to Divi than met the eye. She had something else driving her on this dangerous quest. She'd find out eventually. All she knew was that her and Divi were willing to risk their lives to gain these rights being taken from them.

She looked one last time at Divi and said, "Learn fast. We both need that last stone. It represents freedom for both of us in different ways."

CHAPTER 9
Training: Trials and Tribulations

Three days had passed, everyday Divi showing more improvement. She was really learning quickly in her exercises. When the rains subsided, Tasi had her lift more rocks. The next day, he moved on to fallen tree trunks. Yesterday, he had her move onto large stones. He would have continued down the path had she not begun to feel the invisible life particles. That was the biggest step to being able to use magic, and she was able to do it sooner than most. He was almost against accelerating her through more telekinetic exercises, but he felt that she was ready for the next step, though it would be a hard one.

At least Divi seemed excited about it. She was out in the training grounds even before he was. However, she also took his advice about not starting before he got there. In the early going, she would practice before Tasi arrived, so by the time training began she was already tired. It was a tough balance she tried to achieve. Not to say she couldn't do it, but they would need to train here longer or shorter depending on how well she handled the constant strain she was placing on her body.

"Good morning, teacher."

Tasi chuckled to himself. He had joked yesterday that he wanted her to call him "teacher" whenever they were training. He didn't think she would take him seriously, but then again, Divi was not your average mage. It was one of the attractive qualities he found in her. Mage women seemed to fall into a pattern that inevitably led them all down the same path. Divi dared to veer off that path and fight the system. He figured she was lucky, though, to be noble. Had she been a commoner, her family would have disowned her for not wanting to learn magic. Fate had strange ways of revealing itself, however.

Tasi returned from his thoughts to the wide-eyed Divi, who looked very eager to move forward. He cleared his throat.

"Before I continue, I again want to say how well you've done. Because your progress has been tremendous, I've decided to begin showing you how to throw your first fireball. Fire, being the first thing that Kazcum-hi stole from the gods to give to us, is also the easiest spell to cast. Be wary, however. Although the easiest, until you actually do it, it will be very frustrating. It can also be very dangerous. Many a mage apprentice has perished for not concentrating, burning themselves alive or drowning themselves because of lack of discipline. There is no room for ego here."

Divi instantly flattened her smile. Tasi was happy that she knew what he meant. He could tell she was overconfident when he told her his plan. Overconfidence when learning your first fireball could get you killed. He knew it all too well.

Tasi continued, "If we are ready, I will start. Now, in your exercises yesterday, I could see you were able to locate some of the invisible life particles. Although you didn't control them, at least you were able to recognize them. In order to cast magic, you must be able to control these particles so that they can give you the power you desire. Most magic originates from a mage's hand, which is what makes our staves important. A stave strengthens our spells without using any extra energy to do so. Grab your staff."

Divi took the staff off her back. It encouraged Tasi that she knew the proper way to hold it. Mages didn't need a staff when they were only using telekinetics, but back in Myyril he had seen Divi using hers to fool other children into thinking she was learning.

"Now, I want you to feel the invisible particles. Focusing on them is more difficult than on a solid object. Your recognizing them yesterday tells me that you can do it, but your focus must be even stricter than before."

168

Divi didn't know how that was even possible. There were times this past week she felt her head would explode because of it. There must be a way, though, if every other mage before her was able to do so. She extended both arms forward, holding the staff at a forty-five-degree angle.

Tasi was pleased so far. She definitely looked the part of an experienced mage. Most of it she probably picked up from Neeza, who he remembered being strict with posture and form. He believed that a mage could maintain clearer control of their powers by having perfect posture, but it was never proven—or really even studied. Neeza had strong beliefs and was widely considered a maverick when he took over Myyrilian rule from the former leader, the honorable Bynaris. He was unable, however, to convince the teachers of many of his beliefs, and probably forced them onto his daughter to make up for his failure. Another reason now that he could see why Divi despised her late father so much.

Divi continued to focus as hard as she could, trying to recreate what happened yesterday. It was hard to describe what the life particles were like, although Tasi said he had known it right away in his own training. The best description she could come up with was that it was like seeing and feeling a ghost, which was supposed to be cold. Tasi explained to her that ghosts were life particles recreating a being they used to be a part of, and that coldness she felt was common in mage apprentices. The particles were supposed to feel warmer when she learned to use them. She would see.

After a few minutes of trying, Divi broke her concentration and gave a heavy sigh and lowered her arms. This was going to be a little harder than she thought.

Tasi said, "Try again. Remember, feel them first. Do what you did with the stone, only with the particles. Then control them toward your hand and speak the words: Firammii morza."

Divi closed her eyes and again positioned her arms. She wanted to try something different, hoping it would do the trick. She lifted a medium-sized stone and moved it around in every direction. At least she no longer felt a great strain on herself when she moved solid objects around. Yes, she had her arms extended, but she wasn't using them anymore for her telekinetic powers. Even though it had only been a week ago, she almost couldn't believe she had been so reliant on her hands for her powers.

There it was . . . that feeling. Now came the hard part. She dropped the rock and concentrated hard. The fact that she could feel the invisible particles was one thing, but to control them was not going to be as easy as controlling the rock. Unlike the rock, she couldn't "grab" them. Again, she tried her hardest to get them to do what she wanted, but it was like they didn't listen to her on purpose. She broke her concentration again.

Tasi could feel she was having difficulty, but he expected that. All mages fell short the first time, even ones like Neeza. As long as Divi did not break in her determination, she would learn. It was the mages who failed to control themselves, —and their emotions, who took the longest to learn. He hoped Divi would do neither.

He once again looked at Divi and said, "Try again."

* * * * *

It was a cool night on the Dragonian continent. Divi was relieved to sit in front of the warm flame that Amber made. It had been a long, exhausting day. She was unable to use the invisible particles like she hoped. Detecting them was becoming easier, but it did little good in casting magic if she couldn't control them.

"Want a drink?"

Divi was startled as Amber handed her a cup carved of wood, but she sipped from it. She didn't know how she made it, but Amber's concoction was refreshing.

"Thank you."

"Where did Tasi go?" asked Amber.

"To the training site. He apparently didn't expect me to cast my fireball today, so he never set it up properly. He's supposed to be doing that now."

She wished Tasi would have told her that, though. She was confident, albeit only slightly, that she would be able to do it. She would show him.

Amber replied, "I'm glad he's finally giving you some space. I feel sorry for you. Is he always this suffocating?"

Divi chuckled. *He can when he wants to be,* she wanted to answer. Somehow, though, she suspected Amber already knew the answer. If Tasi was reading her thoughts at this moment, so did he.

Amber took a sip of her drink, silent. Not because she didn't want to talk, but there was something on her mind . . . something she needed to get off her chest.

"Amber, I'm sorry I didn't answer you days ago after the Water Temple. It was rude of me, even though you were being a self-righteous, selfish, and overall just a cold-hearted *trilannta.*"

Trilannta was the elvish version of a Myyrilian swear word. It compared the target to the backside of a horse, as she knew Amber would know.

She continued, "However, it did not give me the right to purposely avoid answering you even though I was angry at you. I just wanted to let you know that I accept your apology."

Amber nodded. "Thank you. Was I really being a *trilannta?* That's kind of harsh, isn't it?"

Both women laughed as they drank. Divi was already starting to feel the effects of Amber's beverage, which she could only compare to the experiences she had at the festival in Lozela. Amber must have made it with some of the native berries from this land. Whatever it was, it made Divi forget about whatever was troubling her. Amber smiled when Divi began to giggle lightly. She was such a lightweight.

"Tell me, Amber, how did you learn magic? Was . . . was it anything like the way I was learning it?"

Amber grinned. This was only the third time that she had given Divi her special blend, but every time she did, she always gained new insights about Divi . . . and life too. Plus, she found it a little cute.

"No. We learn very differently. We never do any of this floating telekinesis stuff. We are aware of the powers we contain and when we choose, we train. Battlemages' training is more difficult than the others, but I've always been different. Want more?"

"Yes!"

Amber poured more of her mixed drink into Divi's cup, which she was already having a little trouble holding on to. She did admit she made it a little stronger than usual today, but she was certain both she and Divi needed it. Tasi was not exactly a forgiving teacher. If he knew that Amber was getting his pupil slightly intoxicated, he would probably throw a tantrum. Oh well, what he didn't know couldn't hurt him.

As soon as Divi sat somewhat stable again, Amber continued, "Because battlemages can't cast healing magic, we focus just as much time in combat training as we do in magic training. I've become very flexible and have gained a lot of endurance from the path I chose. Most of the magic we learn comes from books and tomes."

Divi commented, "I know those books. I never read them."

Amber laughed. "It would seem that way. Let me ask you something. Why are you doing this? Why are you here?"

"Levus."

Amber repeated as Divi nodded, "Levus. Well, tell me. What is a Levus?"

Divi explained, "Levus is a he. He's a great man. He saved me numerous times already. Now it's my turn. I'm going to save him. I care so much for him. I will do anything. I wouldn't be learning magic if Levus didn't need me to. I will save him . . . I will save him."

Amber could see clearly now why she was doing this. She was in love. The target of her affection was the boy named Levus. She was a little curious what Levus had done for her, but Divi's diminishing alertness made it obvious that Amber would need to wait another night to ask that question.

"Sleep tight, brave little mage."

Divi was already lightly snoring as Amber spoke. With a small smile, she began to douse the fire. The moonlight instantly became the dominant light. Amber began to feel the light chill that the fire protected them from. She covered Divi with a nearby blanket before heading toward her camp.

As she walked past the fire pit toward her tent, a shadow passed over the moon. Amber quickly hid behind a rock, remaining still. She could see that it was a dragon, that much was for sure. But was it her Gerritonnee? Her dragon friend tended to keep watch at night and return closer to morning. Just by the wings structure and the number of heads on the flying beast, she was certain it wasn't Tiiamite. What a relief. But the question of if it was Gerritonnee kept her remaining still. The dragon, after a few moments, flew off to the south. Amber waited until it had gone completely out of sight before standing up. She really hoped Divi would learn fast and they could soon retrieve the final stone. Every day they avoided detection was a gift, and she didn't want to be around the day their luck would run out.

* * * * *

"For our next order, I would like to discuss the supposed army gathering in Sardon."

The council had been meeting for about two weeks and a half. In that time, today was the first they were first getting to this issue, much to Thamalos' dismay. He had hoped they could convince Cordca to take action, but how do you convince a nation to help that has no desire to assist her allies?

The weeks prior had dealt with miniscule items, although the three days spent on trading were very heated. The kingdoms of Rudann and Garlock had been vocal on the issue, mainly due to Cordca's strict trade restrictions on the other realms of men. Sydis threw more wood on the fire by commenting on how Cordca did trade with them. Thamalos knew he probably referred to the trade between the border towns of Artis and Nesseis, but he was certain that the mage capital and Cordca had not traded in quite some time.

Seth continued, "Now as you know, these reports have come from Prince Thamalos and Eraddor as they recently passed through the kingdom of Tyranis."

"And why were they there?" Sydis asked. "It is my understanding that the Sardonians are enemies of men. Why not come by Cordca's route?"

"Why not letting me finish first, Sydis, before you make any inquiries?"

When Sydis sat down again, Seth resumed. "I myself heard the news from King Feradis who was in Fort Corrka the day they arrived there, and from many in the village, who were eyewitnesses to a chase between their crew and a Lamiadon. This army, they say, is not only composed of Sardonians. It also includes Ettui soldiers. That is the reason we are bringing this issue up. Anything involving the Ettui, especially at this possible scale, must be discussed. Now, I open the floor to those who have questions."

174

Seth gave Sydis a glare, almost expecting the mage to stand before he finished his sentence. Surprisingly, he remained seated while Servion stood up.

"People of the council, Rudann is the closest neighbor to Sardon, and despite our failed requests for help, we have defeated the Sardonians at every turn. However, if what they say is true, that there are Ettui aligned with Sardon, that might be the straw that breaks Rudann's back. I think Cyp and I agree all nations should send at least a token force to assist Rudann defend her borders against this new threat."

Seth asked, "What makes you so sure that they will attack Rudann? Garlock is just as close, if only a couple hundred miles further."

Herippi stood up. "The nation of Garlock agrees with Rudann. If the Sardonians have aligned themselves with the Ettui, they have most likely told them about the Harlrem. They have seen more attacks than we have and we assist when we can, but the forces at Fort Corrka must be reinforced."

Thamalos felt quite pleased at how well this was going so far. Granted, Garlock and Rudann were the main contributors, allies by their own situation, but positive nonetheless. Eraddor was the only one who remained silent for most of the meetings. Although he claimed himself the representative of Dyyros, he knew he was in these meetings at the grace of General Seth Medkar. As he had no allegiance to any nation, Eraddor could have been thrown out if Medkar wanted. Because of that, he tried to remain as much a ghost in this room as he was when he lived on the elvish frontier.

"A charming theory, indeed."

Thamalos sighed, quite certain that everyone else in the council thought the same thing when Sydis' voice once again commanded the room. And just when matters were starting to go smoothly.

175

Sydis continued, "Now, you would have us believe that this supposed army is going to attack the realm of men. Yet why would they do so? Why not attack the elves? If they have employed the Ettui, the Sardonians have the perfect weapon to counter the elves' advantages. Or worse, how do we know they wouldn't make their way to attack the mages?"

Seth interrupted, "What is your point?"

"My point is that we must wait for confirmation before we even discuss where we send any troops. We would appear to them as fools if we guess wrong. We must wait for them to make the first move. If, of course, this army even exists."

Sydis' comments obviously angered the representatives of Garlock and Rudann. It annoyed Thamalos was somewhat annoyed as well. *Here we go again.*

"It is easy for you to say," Herippi pointed out. "You have not had to worry whether an army was going to attack your city. To live every day wondering if your friend, brother, or neighbor would be around on the next or if you'd be digging their grave . . ."

Sydis muttered under his breath, but still loud enough to hear clearly, "Then do something about it."

Bironn was as surprised as everyone else when Sydis made the comment. What was he trying to do? He had been acting like this ever since they started these meetings, and he realized Sydis didn't want to be here, but he had never seen him so offensive. The Garlock representative had to hold Herippi back as he tried to make a move toward Sydis, though the mage never even flinched.

Seth, tired of the way things were unfolding, yelled, "Herippi! Sit down! Sydis, I have warned you about using this provoking language! We are here to discuss and resolve, not instigate. I am warning you one last time to change your attitude. You have a closed mind while we are keeping ours open. We need cooperation, not dissent."

Sydis stared hard at Seth. He obviously didn't like being told what to do. Yet, Bironn was sure none of the other men liked it, either. With the exception of Eraddor, every member here was a highly ranked person or soon to be. Sydis, however, was the only one who would not leave his ego out of this.

The tension in the room eased when Sydis finally began to sit down, but that soon changed as the mage muttered, "And you say I am the close-minded one, cattle herder."

Bironn glanced over at Sydis, befuddled. *What was he doing?* He knew what it meant to call a higher official a "cattle herder", a job occupied by lower-class individuals. He was sure Sydis meant it in its other meaning, describing how Seth wanted everyone to cooperate like good cattle would. Either way, it was very offensive to call someone that . . . and Sydis said loud enough for Seth to hear. Bironn had never seen such fire in a man's eyes. He was even more surprised when Fort Za's general sat down, apparently calm.

"You will go to my quarters after the meetings today, Sydis," Seth ordered. "This is neither the time nor the place."

A small smile grew on Thamalos' face. He was impressed with how Seth handled himself just now. To find that control amongst the ranks of the human race was very rare indeed. Eraddor had been able to develop it only because he spent years living with them. Perhaps there was hope for mankind.

Seth said, "Now, back to this Sardonian army."

* * * * *

"Sit down, Sydis."

177

The mage sat on the old chair in front of General Seth Medkar's desk. Despite how angry he appeared at the meetings today, he honestly thought that the general was bluffing when he told him to come to his office. It was a small room lit only with candlelight. Drips from an earlier rain fell through cracks in the ceiling and landed on nearly everything. If this was Sydis' office, its condition would be unacceptable.

"I assume you know why I have asked you here, but I want to hear it come from you so I know you understand."

Sydis moved uneasily in the chair. He didn't want to spend a lot of time here. He had other, more important things to do. He only had to tell Seth what he wanted to hear and things could go on like normal.

He replied, "If my answer was anything but my conduct in the meetings, I assume I would be wrong."

Seth looked at him indifferently. Sydis, for whatever reason, was having a difficult time reading his intentions. He knew the human wouldn't hurt him lest the backlash move swiftly across the mainland. This was why he felt the mage and human races would never get along. Humans were so unpredictable.

Seth finally replied, "You are correct about your conduct, indeed. I just want to know why?"

"Why, what?"

"You know very well what I am asking, Sydis. Why are you, instead of contributing like the other nations are, choosing to instigate division? If this is about the silly mages versus humans argument, then save your tongue because I don't want to hear excuses. You have an agenda, unlike the others. I want to know what it is or else I will make a motion to bar you from the meetings and have your assistant take your place."

Sydis didn't like the sound of that. Bironn was not ready to shoulder responsibility like this yet. Even at two hundred and thirty-five years old, he was but a child in the ways of politics. The humans and elves would eat him alive and perhaps convince him to do things as they deemed fit, not what was in the best interest of the mages. They wanted a puppet, that was clear to him. He wasn't going to give them that satisfaction.

"I can assure you, General Seth Medkar, that my intentions are strictly honorable. This . . . so-called agenda you say I have, it is nothing more than over-cautiousness. I have been alive much longer than you have and this is not the first meeting of this kind I have attended. I have seen their inadequacies firsthand. If the Honorable Neeza was still alive, he would support me in this claim."

Seth replied, "You are correct that I haven't, nor could I ever, be alive as long as you have. That is an incomparable difference between our races. However, that is why we record these discussions. We can go back to previous meetings, see what mistakes were made and correct them."

"I wish it were that simple. The fact is that despite these records, humans have continuously made the same mistakes. It has not changed in my lifetime, and never will, most likely. That is why I am so skeptical and act the way I do."

Sydis half-hoped Seth would refute his claim, as he was willing to argue his point to the death, but the general remained silent. He looked again at the mage with that stare Sydis was beginning to loathe.

Seth finally replied, "I want you to think about what we discussed tonight, and come tomorrow, I want to see a change in attitude. This is your final warning from me. Go to bed."

Sydis wanted to retort, but it was obvious that Seth had finished listening as he was already exiting his study for his quarters. Once Sydis stood up, the guards guided him back into the main hallway. Walking down the darkened hall, he chuckled to himself. *Think about what we discussed tonight*, he had said. Sydis had forgotten most of it already. Seth was just too ignorant to see that in the end, what was discussed here would not matter. Things never changed and Seth would soon enough learn the hard way. Sydis was not going to sacrifice the mages to his stupidity. He would soon learn.

* * * * *

Frey sat comfortably in a cushioned chair at Diera's house. For as long as Levus and Leeta had been seeing each other, she had never been in their home. Then again, it wasn't too common for the parents to visit each other's homes until a couple was officially engaged. There were exceptions, but not many. Today, however, was one of those rare exceptions.

Though Frey didn't care for most of her son's company, at least she knew who he was with. Diera had not heard from Leeta for weeks now. It was not like her to leave for this long without telling her mother where she had gone. All Diera knew was that she supposedly went to meet one of her school friends in Porsita.

Following Diera with her eyes as the woman paced the floor allowed Frey to examine more intricate details of the room. Apart from everything being of better quality than in her own home, everything was shorter. Diera was not much taller than her, so access to cabinets and such was much better. That was the disadvantage of marrying a tall person, Frey figured. Diera's late husband, Sipher, was not much taller than she was. Jared, on the other hand, rose above Frey by over a foot.

Any further observations were disrupted by Diera's crying. Frey really did feel bad for her. She had gone through the same troubled emotions weeks earlier when Levus went missing during his hunt. The thought of losing

your only child was frightening. Despite that, Frey almost
hadn't come to Diera's aid. She'd made the same invitation
to Diera when Levus didn't return, and she never came.
Frey, however, was brought up to help others in need, even if
they wouldn't return it.

"Why? Where is my Leeta?"

Frey answered, trying to be encouraging, "Leeta will
return home soon. We were concerned when Levus
disappeared. He came back all right."

"It is not the same. Levus is a fighter. This is a cruel
world we live in. You're only as good as the weapon you
wield. Leeta is no fighter."

"Leeta is one of the strongest women I know. She is
probably just delayed by one of the checkpoints Ulcinar has
set up. She will come back."

Frey was hoping she would. Not only for Diera's
sake, but also for her own. If Leeta was alive, then Levus
would marry her instead of continuing to see that mage.
Diera was not aware of Levus' relationship with Divi. Frey
had considered telling her, but she decided against it,
believing Leeta was the appropriate person to deliver that
news. It was obvious that she hadn't.

Diera said, "Leeta is my only child. If I lose her,
there is no one else alive in my family."

"Don't talk like that."

"I will . . . I must. Sipher never made a will because
he believed things would get better. If I die, there will be no
one to carry our possessions . . . our name."

Frey asked, "What are you saying?"

Diera breathed heavily. This was a difficult time for
her. Frey understood that. But what was she going to say?

She finally answered, "If anything should happen to
Leeta or myself, I am giving you and Levus everything I
own. This house . . . everything."

Frey nearly dropped her tea upon hearing Diera's
decision. Did she really feel that strongly that something had

happened to Leeta? Every woman in the village had claimed to have moments of "women's intuition" concerning the safety of their child. The horrible deaths they came up with for their children could be frightening, but were always proven wrong as they came back fine and happy. She herself was confident Leeta would come back, and Diera had never been known as a pessimistic person.

Diera continued, "I see you are surprised. You shouldn't be. If Leeta feels that Levus is the one, then all this would become theirs anyway."

Frey, still shocked, replied, "Your request is generous, but I can't accept all this."

"It was never a choice for you to make. I have already filed the will to the mayor's quarters. Mayor Vullner understood why I'm doing it and has approved. It is done."

Frey said, "I really don't know what to say."

"Just tell me it is going to be okay. Even if you know it's a lie. I need that."

Frey stood up and walked to Diera's side. She truly *didn't* know what to say. Even though she had been in the same situation when Levus was missing, she never even considered what the future would hold if he never returned. Perhaps it was because she never worried he wouldn't come back. Levus was tough, just like his father. That alone eased her in her time of trouble. That was something Diera could not lean on.

Frey softly put her hand on Diera's shoulder and whispered, "It will be all right. She will be safe."

* * * * *

Divi woke up from a restless sleep. Tasi had ended their training early today. She seemed stuck in the mud with her progress, so he thought it best to stop and reflect on the mistakes made. She had noticed him getting shorter with her the past few sessions. Her friend was always very patient, yet that had started to change rapidly.

As she exited her quarters, the visible moon shined bright in the new night sky. This was when she normally went to bed. Although the attitude of her friend troubled her, it wasn't what awakened her. Her growling stomach was the responsible party. Amber tended to have a meal ready for her and Tasi before the sun set, but she hadn't felt like eating after how today went. Now, she was paying the price. Luckily, she could see a small fire in the camp. It meant Amber was still up and most likely had some food.

Nearing the fire, she heard something she never thought she would hear coming from a warrior like Amber: a song. Whatever tune she began, it had just finished. Almost immediately, though, she began humming another, one that was slow and melodic. Divi, instead of stepping into the light of the flame, remained still and listened as Amber started singing:

The days went by as the sun rose high,
Came Merrah to the garden of Ghrove.
She wept and she prayed, for the ones who were gone,
The ones she cared for the most.

The winds whispered of voices passed on,
All now ghosts in her mind.
Flower florets instead of stones
To ease the sorrow and pain.

Shadows born from the setting sun,
Gone when the moons shine above.
Unlike memories that come and go,
The pain never went away,
The pain never went away.

The dust settled cold, bodies lay like logs,
Is this the cost to be free?
War, anger, hate, in the end what did it mean?
You only lose those that you love.

Shadows born from the setting sun,
Gone when the moons shine above.
Unlike memories that come and go,
The pain never went away,
The pain never went away.

The sun rose high, on the garden of Ghrove,
Only souls to fill the void.
The silence stayed, Merrah's heart fell like rain,
The pain never went away.

Divi couldn't believe how beautiful a voice she had.
Amber didn't seem to be the type of person that would sing.
Most of the mages who went into the military after their
required service term weren't great with their voices. That
was left to the more musically inclined, who normally came
from the Schools of Illusions or Divination.

"I know you're back there, Divi."

Darn. Amber was so good at noticing when she was
around. Divi stepped into the light to join her. Just as she
had hoped, the remains of an animal remained spitted over
the fire. She quickly grabbed a chunk of meat and placed it
on a wooden plate.

Amber laughed. "Well, I thought it strange when you
and Tasi left your meals untouched. He's been pushing you
harder, I hear."

Divi sat down next to Amber and began chewing the
tough but delicious meat. That was ever the truth. A couple
times Tasi had resorted to yelling. She was not used to that
from him. He always controlled himself shortly after, not

letting the anger linger. Or did he and she just couldn't sense it?

"Yes, the days and the tribulations seem to grow. Not sure what his issue is. I'm doing my best. I wish he would just let me know what was on his mind. Something is bothering him, but I can't sense it. Wish he'd just talk to me."

Amber smiled, reminded a little of her training when she started the battlemage route. Their trainers were hard in the beginning. They told her that a warrior must feel the brunt of pain early so that it wouldn't bother them on the battlefield. They would beat the students if they failed. She was sure she still had some bruises. Those rough lessons hardened her, made her more efficient, though. She knew one thing: she'd never have had the courage to fight dragons if it wasn't for her training.

"What was that song you were singing?"

The question threw Amber off guard. *Darn, she was there long enough to hear that. I didn't want anyone to hear that.*

"It's called 'Memories of Merrah.' Based off the story of Merrah, the widow of the leader of the first and only Tydosian rebellion, Firtarr, many years ago. It ended when a traitor divulged their meeting spot in the Garden of Ghrove. Those not killed during the battle were executed. This song shared Merrah's grief for the events of that day. Although the mages spared Merrah's life, she disappeared after returning many times to the site of the massacre. Some say she took her own life; others think she somehow left Tydos, living in secret under a different name."

"Sounds like a sad tale. Why sing it, though?"

Divi was such an inquisitive mage. Amber shouldn't have been surprised at her intuition. The young mage was getting stronger, and even though she had yet to throw fire, Amber could feel her strength growing.

Amber explained, "The song is interpreted many ways. Battlemages believe that Merrah, along with all the men and women who died during the ambush, are martyrs. We use it to show that one day our suffering will end and that no matter how many of us Tydosians fall, our freedom is worth it. I guess that nitklarii fight shook me a little, too, that it had me feel the slightest fear . . . and regret. Do you have any regrets, Divi?"

She thought about Amber's question. She had never been asked that. As privileged a life as she had led, she didn't know if she had any. But like a rainbow after a powerful storm, one did enter her mind.

Divi said, "I guess the only thing I can think of is not getting resolution with my father."

"Interesting, especially after how much you told me you two didn't get along."

"My father did some terrible things to me. Things that made me so mad that I was convinced I hated him for it. He would always apologize, but I eventually turned a blind eye to those apologies as I didn't think he meant them. Yet deep down I know he cared for me. If I was in trouble, despite our issues, he would still be there for me. My mom always tried to teach me that no matter what race, we all make mistakes and we shouldn't judge someone off them. Looking back, I wonder if I was doing that to my dad all along."

"In Tydos we have a saying, 'Hate should only be skin deep, because if it reaches your heart and your mind, it will drive you mad.' Do half-mages hate the mages for what they have done in the past? Absolutely! But if the mages came and offered a just peace agreement, we would take it in a heartbeat. What I'm saying is, don't let your father's transgressions be how you see him in totality. Ten years is not a large sampling for a mage."

Amber had a great point. Divi truly didn't hate her father. She was only mad at him for what he had done the past few years. Instead of talking it out, she just let the hatred get deeper into her heart, being blinded by it.

"If I could give you some advice before I head to bed. I know it is too late for your father, but in the future, when given the options of hate or forgiveness, always try and choose forgiveness. Never assume the way a person is feeling from the outside. Although you may be angry because you think they don't care, the other person might be dying in a private hell. And think hard about it. Did everything your father do to you deserve the punishment he suffered? Skin deep, Divi. Skin deep. The bucket next to you has water to put out the fire when you are done."

Amber walked to her hut as Divi stared at the ground and her half-eaten meal. The half-mage gave her a lot to think about. She knew Neeza changed after her mom died. Was that the real version of her father, or was it the man whom her mom always called a loving husband and father? Maybe she was judging him too harshly. But as Amber said, it was too late for her to even say goodbye. That chance disappeared in Porsita.

Divi yawned. She finished a few more bites of her meat before grabbing the bucket. She had a long day ahead of her and knew getting more rest would only benefit her.

Skin deep, Divi. Skin deep. It sounded so simple, but could she do that after everything that had happened? It would hopefully be an answer time would tell.

* * * * *

"Concentrate, Divi!"

Divi lowered her arms, nearly slamming her staff to the ground. It had been nearly a week since she first started learning to throw a fireball. Her progress had gone very well until this point. She just didn't understand. She could feel the life particles almost every time now, but no matter how often she said the spell, the fire never came.

187

She was so obsessed with her failure that she began to practice on her own again, something Tasi picked up on rather quickly. Since then, he became even more determined, working her harder in practice while waiting until she went to sleep before he would. He scolded her every day about her limits and how she had to be careful not to cross them. It led to more than one shouting match between the two, though Tasi would always win. He had to. He was her teacher. Still, it frustrated her even more. She would go to sleep so angry sometimes, that even Amber had to make sure everything was okay. She seemed to know what to say to calm her down, but lately, not even those were helping Divi.

She had to learn this quickly. She had no time to waste. Levus was relying on her. The sooner she threw a fireball, the sooner she would get to hold him again.

"Are you listening, Divi?"

Tasi knew she wasn't. In fact, he knew exactly what Divi was thinking about. She didn't understand why she couldn't cast her magic, but he had already told her weeks ago what was stopping her. He was hoping she would have figured it out on her own. She was actually extremely close to throwing her first fireball. One thing prevented her: focus. How could she ever maintain the strict focus needed in the beginning when the first thing to enter her mind was that human?

Divi shook her head and replied, "I was not. I was . . . clearing my head."

Good choice of words. That was what Tasi wanted to hear, but he somehow saw them *only* as words this time. Divi was not a great liar. Most mages weren't, as a matter of fact. The politicians were the best at it, and even so, Neeza was not a great liar either. He preferred to remain silent rather than fabricate the truth. Lying was just not in Divi's known history.

Tasi commented, "Good. With your head clear now, you should be able to do this without any trouble. Try again."

Divi was offended by Tasi's sarcasm. She didn't understand why, but Tasi's annoyance with her the past few days reached unforeseen levels. Instead of suggestions, he offered insults. After lessons, they hadn't had their fireside chats like normal. Something was on his mind, and she would need to find out for her own sanity.

"Well?" Tasi asked impatiently.

Divi flashed him a look before closing her eyes. Tasi sighed nearly as soon as she shut them. There that human boy was again. Dancing around in her mind as if it were his own. It was sad to see how someone so simple could cause such complex problems. He wasn't even someone with any power. He owned no land. All he owned was that evil weapon . . . and Divi's heart.

When Divi lowered her arms again in frustration, Tasi was not surprised. He could tell she was almost in tears at her inability to do it. He refused to say anything aloud, however. *Go ahead and ask why you failed*, he asked her in his mind. He was getting tired of her making the same mistake, just as much as she was getting tired of failing. *I dare you, Divi. Just ask it.*

Divi stood erect once more, this time noticing Tasi's posture. She had seen it before. It was the 'I know what you're doing wrong' look. Her friend was not too hard to figure out if you knew him for a long time. He tended to wear his heart on his sleeve, which in turn made him a poor liar. Not that mages were any good at it anyway.

She finally asked, "All right, Tasi. What am I doing wrong?"

If only she realized the box she had just opened up. He supposed he set her up by the way he was standing, as he knew that Divi read him very well. It had to be said, though. He had to get it off his chest now before it drove him crazy.

189

Even though he didn't want to be so blunt with Divi, there was no other way around it.

Tasi said, "You are failing because you are not focused."

"What do you mean? I am focused just like—"

Tasi interrupted, "No. No, you are not. When we started you were, but with each passing failure, your thoughts turn to people who only hinder your concentration, not help it. It clouds your mind. A clouded mind will never be able to control the life particles."

He still avoided telling her. He continued hoping that she would finally get what he was talking about. Based on her answers, however, it looked like he would have to do the dirty work himself.

"Look. I have done everything you have said, so . . ."

Tasi suddenly erupted. "Don't treat me like I'm an idiot, Divi! Remember, I can read your thoughts while you train. You are failing because you can't get *him* out of your mind!"

So that was it. She seriously thought that Tasi was past this. The entire time they trained, he had said nothing to her about it. And now, at a time she needed encouragement more than ever, this was how he spoke to her.

"Tasi, you knew why I am doing this. It is all for him."

"But that is the problem. In order to learn magic, complete focus is needed. Levus' face is like a virus on your mind. By the gods, it's no wonder they make children learn at an early age before love and other emotions complicate things!"

Divi yelled, "So what? You're just going to give up on me because I'm too difficult? I thought you were above all this, Tasi! I thought you would understand."

"Me understand? Me, understand? Divi, you are the one who doesn't understand! If you are not going to listen to

190

me then we might as well stop now and forget this! Without focus, you are just wasting your time."

Divi was shocked. In all the years they had been friends, she had never seen Tasi this angry. He was always calm and relaxed, not letting even the most difficult thing bother him. Tasi's anger, however, was like an earthquake, releasing in small doses until the big one was finally unleashed.

She yelled, "I am listening. You should know since you've been invading my mind this whole time. It is clear that you don't understand what I'm going through. You don't understand love!"

A shouting match continued between the two, more heated than any they had in the past few days. Divi, who had done her best to suppress her disgust, began to flash signs of anger. She didn't understand why, but she suddenly felt a burning inside her body. The more they argued, the stronger it became. She wanted it to stop, yet it felt so good. It made her feel alive.

"Listen, Tasi! It is my feelings for Levus that are driving me to learn magic. He is my muse."

"He is no muse! He is nothing but an arrogant, ungrateful excuse for a human! You will forget him, Divi! If you are not going to forget him, then you will be a failure as a mage. Your father was right about you. He warned me you'd be difficult, but I told him otherwise. But now I see he was right. You are too damned stubborn and I will no longer train you as long as you continue to do it for that bastard human, Levus!"

Divi didn't know right away what happened after Tasi's comment. Her mind seemed to go numb. Her vision became increasingly narrow. She was a little scared by this feeling, yet also excited. That burning inside her was growing stronger. With every second her enraged desire fed off her. It was like a piece of her very soul was being used. Is this how it felt to cast magic?

191

Her vision soon became so focused that she could only see what was directly in front of her. That included a slightly worried expression on her friend. His lips moved, apparently trying to tell her something, but it was inaudible. Probably just telling her she was a failure. *Now is the time you see, Tasi. I am no failure!*

"*Firammii morza!*"

The air around Divi and Tasi went ablaze. Tasi jumped back as quickly as he could, but it was not fast enough, and parts of his robe caught flame. He quickly patted out the fires, but he had no time to waste. Divi was screaming and crying as her skin and clothes continued to burn.

Tasi reached back and yelled, "*Wutari bullzon!*"

A large ball of water fell on top of Divi, extinguishing the magic fires immediately. Through the smoke left in their wake, Tasi could see the damage they left. Divi was on the ground with some serious burns on her arms and legs. As they were magic-inflicted wounds, his limited knowledge of healing spells would do nothing. All he could do was yell for help, unnecessary since both Amber and Gerritonnee were almost there.

"What the hell is going on?" Amber demanded.

"She needs medical attention! Quickly!"

Amber was no doctor, but she could see that her burns were severe. Gerritonnee sniffed at the wounds before looking at Amber.

"*I can help cure these. We must go quickly before infections set in.*"

Amber grabbed Divi, shutting out her cries of pain as she did so. She wanted to know what happened, but now was not the time to ask questions. Divi needed help and Tasi looked like he saw a ghost. After Gerritonnee thought Divi was okay, Amber would seek out her teacher and get the truth from him. *If he did this to her . . .*

Tasi remained kneeling, trembling as he tried to comprehend what had just happened. She did it. No . . . she did *something* that resembled the magic a normal mage cast. With his heightened senses, he should have been able to feel the life particles do whatever it was Divi commanded of them. Yet, he felt nothing. How did she do it, then? Was it possible that she didn't need life particles to perform her spells? It would be a first, but Divi had proven to be anything but a normal mage.

There was, however, another way she might have done what she did. That was a thought he didn't even want to consider. Did she use not outer life particles, but rather inner life particles to cast her spell?

A shiver ran down his spine as he said to himself, "By the gods, Divi. Please tell me it isn't so. What have I done?"

* * * * *

"Tasi!"

Amber was puzzled. It was unlike him to not be by the fire or training area. She knew that both mages had a very stressful day, but she had to find out what happened. Divi was in no condition to speak, so Tasi was the only one who could help her now.

She told Divi to stay in bed to give her wounds time to heal, but she should have known better. Gerritonnee reported she left minutes after, promising to keep an eye on her. Amber wished the mage would have listened this time. She suffered some harsh burns to her arms and legs. Amber's first intuition was that Tasi did it to her. After thinking about it more, however, she dismissed the thought. The randomness of the burns was much too sloppy for a seasoned mage like Tasi. Plus, Tasi knew what Amber would do to him if she found out he hurt Divi in any way. No. Those were the wounds of an apprentice mage whose spell went terribly wrong.

193

"Tasi!"

Amber tried to keep her shouting to a minimum. Gerritonnee had informed her that the night was becoming increasingly unsafe. Tiiamite had started recruiting other dragons on the continent to look for her. Some refused, so fortunately, Gerritonnee's own refusal was not out of place, but many agreed to help the king of the dragons in his search. Amber's friend remained confident that it would take some time before the camp was found, but they were going to need to finish this last stone, the faster, the better.

She was about to yell again, but stopped herself after seeing a small fire in a clearing. There was one of her mage friends. Tasi certainly didn't pick a very good spot. Amber chose her campsite because the landscape made it difficult for adult dragons to reach it. With very few young dragons left on Dragonia, it was a relatively safe spot. Tasi's fire was small, but she was going to make sure it was doused before she left. No need to give the dragons a clue where they were.

As she reached the small clearing, Tasi had himself cuddled into a ball like he was trying to warm up, rocking back and forth slightly from his crouched position. It wasn't cold at all, so she wasn't sure what he was doing. Only one way to find out, she figured.

"You okay?" After a short pause, she continued, "Divi will be fine. We used dragon saliva. It sounds worse than it is. Dragon saliva has the most remarkable ability to cool down inflammation."

Tasi didn't acknowledge her question nor her report on Divi. He just continued rocking. *C'mon Tasi. Don't make me yell louder than I have to.*

"Hey! I'm talking to you!"

Tasi finally turned his face. He looked spooked! His eyes stared blankly at her and his face was pale. She had never seen anyone like that before.

"I'm sorry," he replied before staring again at his ever-dying flame, back to his rocking routine.

Amber stood for a couple seconds. Normally very composed and confident, Tasi didn't even look her way as she situated herself next to him.

"So, are you going to tell me what happened or am I gonna have to beat it out of you?"

Even though Tasi knew it was an idle threat, he also knew she would find out sooner or later. Better it was by him.

"Divi and I . . . are going to have to halt training for a few days."

Not the words she wanted to hear, especially since she had been labeled as the primary target by the dragons on this continent. Every day they had without interruptions was a gift now. Sooner or later, and she knew it would be the former, the dragons would search the woods more thoroughly. At that point, whether Divi was ready or not, they would need to leave and fast.

Amber said, "You know I've tried to stay out of what you two are doing, but this decision of yours impacts me as well. What happened today?"

Tasi didn't really believe she would understand. How could she? Half-mages trained differently than mages. Ideologies that one followed, the other didn't. Their two races would always have this separation, regardless of any peace agreements.

He answered, "She made fire."

Amber commented, "Well, that's a good thing. Why the hell are you stopping?"

Just as he thought, she didn't understand. He also, for the first time, heard a surge of urgency in her voice. It would be something to ask her about soon.

"It's not the fact she made fire. It's *how* she made fire. She . . . she made it strictly with anger . . . resentment."

"Well, anger is a powerful emotion. Why should it matter? If that's what helps her do magic, then I'm all for it."

Spoken like a true half-mage. They were immune to learning the forbidden arts because they lacked the magic power to do it. Divi was a different story. If she turned . . .

Tasi explained, "If we continue down this path, she will begin using Dark Magic. You do know what Dark Magic is, don't you?"

From the blank expression on Amber's face, he knew she had no idea what he was talking about.

"Dark Magic is cast using internal life particles. It was introduced by the mage God of Death, Kremmos. It originally was a school of magic, but was quickly condemned because students would die from overuse. It didn't take long. The art had no books and very few teachers."

"How did they learn without books?"

"When your anger reached a certain level, Kremmos would come to you for your allegiance to him. Once down that path, there is no turning back. You are literally giving him your soul."

Amber spoke, hoping she was following Tasi's logic. "So, in connection with Divi☐if she continues to use spells with anger, Kremmos will take her as an apprentice?"

Tasi nodded and added, "A very powerful apprentice. At that point, everything she loves would mean nothing. That which is important to her now would lose all meaning. That is why I am taking a couple of days. We both could use time to reflect. Even though all mages take time to do this, and Divi's nowhere near the slowest to progress, it's still troubling. Neither Divi or myself must rush what happens next"

Although Amber had more questions, Tasi was already standing and heading for camp. Amber truly hoped they 'sorted it out' with great haste. She considered telling him about Tiiamite. It would perhaps relay her urgency much more clearly. However, after what she learned, she decided it was best to wait. Both mages obviously had their own problems to deal with. Why add this burden?

Amber raised her sword and lowered it toward the fire, which was almost dead already. The water caused by her spell instantly killed whatever remained of the flame Tasi brought to life. *Divi had better be a quick learner*, she thought to herself as she headed back toward their camp.

About a hundred yards from the camp, in a cleft in the rock, Divi cried. She wanted nothing but to be alone after Amber treated her wounds the best she could. Although she'd noticed Gerritonnee had followed and was watching over her, the young dragon seemed to understand this was a time to remain invisible.

She knew she should have been happy. She actually cast fire! But she also knew what fueled that spell. She didn't want to learn that way. She would lose everything if she did. That was why Divi wept. She worked so hard to get here, and now the road was split. One lead to learning magic the right way. The other would only lead to sorrow . . . and she knew she was on the wrong path at the moment.

Divi turned, grimacing as she rolled on one of her burns. Gerritonnee gave a soft grunt, trying to be comforting in her dark time, but still keeping her distance. Although Divi appreciated her efforts, it still did not stop the pain. It also didn't stop the harsh reality that she was facing.

"Levus . . . I'm failing you."

CHAPTER 10
First Fireball

Two days had passed since the fateful night that Divi cast fire. Tasi was most glad to see her stroll slowly from the camp toward the training area. Although they didn't speak to each other for those two days, he kept coming here as if they did. Instead of teaching Divi, he used the time to reflect. For years, he had dreamed of how it would be like to be a teacher. Divi denied him that until now, but every time he pictured it in his mind, everything happened perfectly. No problems. Only success.

Because of his fantasies, he was puzzled that his method was not working. It all seemed so simple in his head. He was following protocol that countless other mages used to train. He read their books and tomes daily when he was training. The reality of it all was that these books were missing an important element: dealing with the student's personality.

Although he knew he was right about what was causing Divi's inability to take the next step, the books never pointed out how to deal with these problems. They, too, assumed that everything would go perfectly. He even began to wonder if these were issues that his own teacher had with him. Jazeell was a wise man and Tasi felt very appreciative toward him. He was well-known, though, for his short temper. Many a student went home crying because they didn't do it his way. Tasi never had this anger directed toward him, though, because he did what he was told. Did it by the book. *That's the way it has to be done*, he'd been told by Jazeell as a young mage. He believed it back then, but now . . .

Divi eventually made it to where Tasi was standing. She did look very resolved. The burns on her arms and legs had already begun to heal. They would possibly leave scars, but at least she was alive. He would have to thank Gerritonnee later for her help in assisting his student's return to health. Dragons were truly miraculous creatures!

Divi looked forward, not even looking at Tasi. Although she was still upset at him for saying what he said, it didn't stop him from being right. The anger she felt was her own denial that she knew exactly how to reach her goal. After thinking about it, Tasi did have a point. She needed to keep Levus in her heart only, if only for a couple days. That was really where her love should be, anyway.

Tasi began to pace back and forth as he spoke. "I will keep this short. Before we start again, I do want to say that I am sorry. My words were unforgivable, said out of personal frustration. Being your teacher, I am supposed to be an example. Two days ago, I failed in doing so. I have reflected these past days, and hope that you can forgive me for my actions. Things will be different now."

A couple tears escaped Divi's eyes. She knew he meant every word. He was right, though, in that things were going to be different. She could guarantee that.

Tasi concluded by saying, "We have a job here to do, and I for one want to see you do it. I will once again be entering your mind, so let us begin."

* * * * *

Divi suddenly awoke . . . at least she thought she was awake. She was still in the camp in front of a blazing fire, but something didn't feel real. There was no wind and the sky was naked, totally devoid of stars or moons.

"Divi."

She recognized the voice. But he couldn't be here. He was still at Fort Za waiting for her to rescue him. She quickly scanned for Tasi or Amber, but they were nowhere to be seen.

"Divi."

His voice seemed to be getting closer, but she couldn't see anything. Maybe she was just hearing things. Today's training took a lot out of her. Although she was still unsuccessful in casting her first fireball, not once did Tasi complain about thinking of Levus. He told her she was just a little rusty and he had a good feeling that the next couple days would be special. Exhaustion . . . yeah, that was it.

"Divi, I'm here."

She spun around. Standing before her was Levus. She had a hard time making out many of his features, but she knew it was him . . . no, it couldn't be him. He stared at her with still eyes.

"Levus . . . is that really you? Are you really here?"

A long pause ensued. This had to be a dream. This man was her everything, making her feel warm whenever he was near. She felt nothing but cold and fear at the moment.

"Why are you forgetting me, Divi? Don't you love me anymore?"

The question came as a surprise. Of course, she did. He would never ask that question of her.

"You know I do. You are in my heart, always."

"If you cared, you'd always be thinking of me. I helped you in learning this far. Now you abandon me?"

"I'm not abandoning you. And although I am doing this for you, you are not the one helping me in this. I have done this by myself and have allowed my emotions to cloud my accomplishment. I will save you, but for now, you must stay in my heart."

The vision of Levus began to fade, replacing itself with a cloaked figure. She couldn't see any features at all. It was almost as if it was a shadow.

The voice, no longer sounding like Levus anymore and very raspy, said, "Then you are too weak to join my students' ranks. After your performance a couple days ago, I hoped to enroll you early. But now, I see, you would never succeed in learning to wield the greater power I possess. It is a shame. You could have been a Master of Dark Magic, maybe the best of all time."

Kin the depths of the cloak, the figure's eyes began to glow red as he turned. The wind blew heavier. The God of Death slowly hovered away from Divi. It took her some time, but she realized the encounter was no dream . . . nor was she awake. What was most horrifying of all was that it was real. She remembered her father telling her that when the God of Darkness and Death visited, he tempted you with people you were familiar with. Was she so important that even Kremmos would try and recruit her after one incident, when it normally took many?

Kremmos suddenly stopped and, without looking back at her, said, "Divi, watch out for what's behind you."

Behind her was the largest black dragon she had ever seen. Although she could not count how many heads it had, the glowing eyes from them seemed countless. Its mouth opened wide and an orange glow formed in the back of its throat. She had no time to react before a plume of flame blasted from its mouth. All she could do was scream . . .

* * * * *

Divi quickly sat up. Sweat poured from her brow. She was relieved to see she was in her hut. She had been able to resist the temptation of Kremmos, but what was the meaning of the dragon? At first, she thought it was Zazzarat, Kremmos' mount and the bodyguard to the Underworld. Yet it had more heads than even Zazzarat was fabled to have. And why would the God of Death warn someone about something unless . . .

Thunder rumbled. *Must be a storm coming through again.* She had never experienced storms in Myyril like she did here. Then again, in Myyril, she was in a palace. In this place, she had to rely on animal hides and the trees to keep her dry.

The thunder sounded again . . . and again . . . and again . . .

As Divi listened more carefully, the sounds seemed to follow a repetitive pattern. She glanced outside the doorway of her hut. The sky was clear of clouds. The stars and moons all shone perfectly clear. What was causing that noise?

Her answer came as a shadow was cast over the camp. It was not thunder she heard. It was the beating of dragon wings. Her first thought was that they belonged to Gerritonnee, but Amber's friend didn't make that sound when she flew. Whatever owned these wings belonged to something much larger than Gerritonnee.

The creature flew by without incident, not even roaring. Did it not want to be seen? It could have merely been hunting for food. Gerritonnee did most of her hunting during the night or early morning. Yet Kremmos' visit convinced Divi otherwise. Were they the ones being hunted? She didn't know why. Sure, they had defeated Leviadon, but they hadn't disturbed any of the other dragon natives.

Whatever the reason, she was sure they would find out soon enough. Any secrets would be exposed soon. One thing Divi knew for certain, however, was that she must keep this meeting with Kremmos secret. Mages said it was bad luck to talk about one's conversation with the God of Death during your lifetime. What made it different from other superstitions was that bad things *did* happen to those who failed to heed the warning.

Divi waited a while longer to make sure the dragon wasn't coming back before she went to sleep.

The next day was nearly perfect. Clouds, partially hiding the sun, kept the temperature from rising too high.

Perfect conditions for a young mage to learn, Tasi confirmed. These days were few and far between in Myyril as it could get hot, hence why most of the training was done inside. That was a not a luxury they had here, though. They had to deal with whatever Mother Terra threw at them.

Divi was out early again, even before he arrived. He showed her some warm-up exercises to rejuvenate her powers, but now it was time for the hard work. He knew she was close. If she hadn't become exhausted yesterday, with a couple more hours she would have done it. It wouldn't have been wise, however, to push her too hard on her first day back. They already had one too many accidents.

He said, "Now, let us focus on the fireball, shall we? You know what needs to be done, I've told you how to do it. So, let me see it."

Divi nodded and faced the training dummy. Tasi could sense something going on in her mind, but she was blocking him. It couldn't be Levus, because that emotion she wouldn't be able to block from him. It was something different. Although he was curious, he said nothing. As long as it wasn't Levus, it wouldn't matter, because he could feel her focus grow stronger now. Definitely a good sign.

Divi closed her eyes and began focusing on the invisible life particles. She felt them almost as easily now as she could in lifting a rock. She could even move them with ease, but the time had come for her to take the next step. In her heart she wanted to think of Levus at this moment, but if she was going to save him, he needed to stay there just a little while longer. Divi slowly stretched her arms back, feeling some of the life particles following her motion.

Tasi stepped back. The life particles around her hands began to glow. What had been hidden now could be seen. He sensed the life particles around Divi no longer rejected her, but desired her. The glow became brighter. *Come on, Divi! Almost there . . .*

Divi couldn't see what she was doing, but she could feel everything. Her telepathic powers, which had been her only magical resource for years, drew whatever life particles were close toward her open palms. Although they never touched her hands, she could feel their chill. Now she understood what Tasi meant. The life particles no longer feared, but embraced her. They were now one instead of separate. They were waiting for a command, and it was time for her to give it.

Divi yelled, in a voice which echoed slightly in the Dragonian forest, *"Firammii morza!"*

She extended her hands forward. The life particles became a heated ball of flame that flew through the air. It only took a couple of seconds to hit Tasi's homemade target, instantly destroying it. Just like that, it was over.

Tasi's smile was so large he was certain the gods could see it from their homes in the heavens. After all the hard work, after all the trials and difficulties, she did it! He was so proud of her. With the hard part over, he could begin teaching her some of the fun stuff . . . along with more advanced spells.

Divi finally opened her eyes, releasing a small tear. She knew what she just accomplished. She just gotten over the biggest challenge for a young mage faster than any other living mage could attest to. It was not an easy road, but she felt like she had grown more mature. Tasi walked slowly over to her and put a hand on her shoulder.

Tasi said, "You have just entered a brand new world. You should be very proud of yourself."

Divi was, and she showed it by hugging Tasi hard. He smiled, but his body froze as if unsure what he should do. Perhaps it was because mages rarely had such close contact unless they were dating or married. Even as a young boy, Tasi hardly ever remembered doing any activities that involved physically touching any of his schoolmates. With an emphasis on training at a young age, telekinesis was preferred when the children played. Then again, there was another reason . . .

"Thank you so much," Divi said, still hugging Tasi.

She finally released him as they looked at each other. Tasi, from the moment she threw the fireball, had stopped entering her mind. He'd no longer see what she was thinking, but you didn't need to be a mage to know that Divi meant every word.

Tasi replied, "I appreciate it, but it was all you. To learn as fast as you have is proof of your determination. We must now apply what you have learned so you can perform other types of magic. As I said, you have entered an exciting new world. Before we begin, throw your fireball once more."

Divi nodded and looked at the second test dummy. As she reached back, she couldn't believe how smoothly the life particles followed her thoughts. It was if she had been doing this her entire life since birth.

She yelled just before her fireball made the second dummy a smoldering pile of sticks and dry grass, "*Firammii morza!*"

*   *   *   *   *

"Okay, Divi. Now we will learn to use your spells in close combat. Mages, as you know, are much better fighters when given space to cast our magic. Our opponents will try to exploit that by coming in close. Your main objective is to drive your enemy back so as to regain some distance. This spell I will show you requires little effort, as there is no incantation you need to say to use it. You can call it our self-defense spell."

From Tasi's stance, she knew that he wanted her to follow suit, and they faced each other with staves poised.

Tasi continued, "Now I want you to attack me. When you feel there is an opening, use the spell. To cast it, think the same way you do with your fireball, but instead of gathering the life particles for destruction, use them to push me away. It will cause a low-powered energy to be thrown whose strict purpose is to stun: an important spell in a mage's arsenal. There are other versions for longer distances, but this is the best way to start. I will be trying to do the same to you, so remain focused."

Divi nodded as both mages began circling each other. She was not so worried about the combat part, but more about getting an opportunity to use the spell. Tasi was the toughest mage in the schools to hit with this spell. He fought very defensively, making it difficult for the other students to ever find an opening. These first few attempts were not going to end well, she thought.

Tasi, surprisingly, made the first move, with Divi blocking it with her staff. At once she went on the offensive, trying to create an opening. It didn't last for long, as the next moment, she found herself lying on the ground feeling dazed. Tasi stood at ease, allowing Divi to stand up again. How did he do it so fast?

Tasi explained, "I know you take pride in your ability to fight. Your father taught you well. You fight like a true warrior. However, now that you know magic, I need you to start fighting like a mage. Warriors put their faith in their weapons, hoping to overpower their opponent. Mages put faith in their faith: their magic. Instead of overpowering your opponent, you must outthink them. Put them in a position that will allow you to stun them. Now, again."

* * * * *

"It is now time to show you how to defend yourself using strictly magic. This will come in handy against non-mages, but especially other mages. Certain magic can nullify other magic, which makes shield spells very important. The basic shield spell alone can block nearly 65% of a mage's spells as well as any arrows or swords. Masters of magic, like your father, could block nearly 90%. That is our goal.

"For starters, stand in fight position, positioning your staff in front of you at about a 45-degree angle. The top of your staff should be just above your shoulder height-wise, and then hold your left hand out."

Divi did as Tasi instructed, wondering what the point of this was. *Just tell me the words of the spell so I can work on it.* Tasi was meticulous in terms of positioning and body language. She wondered if one had time to get into position in the heat of battle.

Tasi continued after a short pause, "Seeing as you doubt my teaching about positioning, with your slouching and silent sighs, I will prove it to you. Divi, on this first attempt I want you to cast a shield around yourself by holding your staff horizontally. The words of the spell are *Sheildiia suarra*. This is the most basic of shield spells, and the smallest due to the *suarra* part. However, this spell can deflect more than half of the known spells if positioned correctly. I will throw the fireball I taught you, and you must block it."

Divi understood and held the staff horizontally. Tasi ended up standing a good fifty feet away from her, more than enough room to stop a spell. Her teacher was trying to make a point, however, so she assumed this seemingly easy task was not going to go in her favor.

Tasi nodded before shouting, "*Firammii morza!*"

The fireball hurtled toward her. Divi, even though she knew she had plenty of time, instantly cast the shield spell.

"*Sheildiia suarra!*"

A small purple-ish object appeared in front of her. Despite its tint, it was transparent so that Divi could see Tasi's projectile, which almost had reached her. She focused harder in hopes of making the shield stronger. She was determined to prove her teacher wrong.

That would not happen on this day, though. The fireball passed straight through the shield. Divi's eyes widened as the spell hit her, knocking her back about fifteen yards. This was the first time that she was actually hit with another mage's fireball. She didn't like the feeling at all— dizzy, like she got hit in the head with a heavy tree branch. By the time she recovered, Tasi was already over her with his hand extended out.

"Nice try."

He helped Divi up and walked back to the position he had been in before while she returned to hers. She was still a little shaken up by the spell, but she faced Tasi.

"Okay, my great student. Now hold the staff like you normally would, with a slight angle."

Divi did as she was told. This position felt more natural anyway. She hoped this blocked the fireball. She had no desire to be struck with another one. If she knew Tasi, though, she had nothing to fear about that. And the only thing she could do wrong was mess up saying the spell.

Tasi suddenly yelled, "*Firammii morza!*"

At almost the same time she cast the shield spell like last time, enchanting the words, "*Sheildiia Suarra!*"

The transparent purple shield once again formed in front of Divi. As the fireball reached her, she knew the result would be different. Confidently, she held her ground. The fireball struck the shield, which dissipated it almost instantly. Her shield remained, leaving only slightly visible life particles in the wake of the fireball.

She let her shield down as soon as she heard Tasi clapping. He walked toward her.

"Very good, Divi. Your command of the life particles is improving. You barely have to focus on them anymore. You are one with them. The time it's taking you to do this is phenomenal. Pretty soon we'll be able to start on

the advanced stuff. But for now, let's continue to . . .
Firammii morza!"

From only ten feet away from her, Tasi unexpectantly tossed a fireball in Divi's direction. She almost instinctively, shouted the shield spell. The shield came up just in time, stopping Tasi's fireball.

A smile grew on his face. The time was getting near. She was almost ready.

* * * * *

Tasi spent nearly a week on combat training, working on incorporating the new shield spells into her technique. It took her a few days to get the hang of it. Divi had been reliant on her telekinetic powers for so long that the concept of any other fighting style was difficult for her to grasp. By day five, she was almost an old professional. She even surpassed him in some areas, a scary, enlightening moment for any mage teacher.

He was very happy for Divi, though. She worked so hard to learn. Although there had been some sticky moments between them during the training process, any teachers would have killed to have the chance to train her. It wasn't often that you had a mage go through years of training in less than a month. He only wished her cause was better . . . that damn boy could never fully appreciate the sacrifice she made for him. He could only hope Divi would realize this in time and come to her senses. But enough of his personal feelings at the moment. He had to get his mind back on her training.

Despite all the new things he was teaching her, at least one day a week, he liked to go back to the fireball. Not only because he was going to start teaching her how to use the same technique with other elements. He wanted her never to forget the spell that got her to this point. Of all the other spells a mage could learn, many were very situational and hardly ever used in a real-life scenario. The fireball, however, was used in war and peace. It was used to hunt, but also to start a fire to cook your meals. One would be hard-pressed to not use it at least once a day.

When Tasi arrived at the training area, Divi was already there. From the looks of it, she had been there a while, despite it being early in the morning. Destroyed training dummies were littered on the ground, at least seven to his count. He had only made five, so he knew Divi made the others, and she was actually in the process of making an eighth.

He was amazed by how long Divi could go before needing rest. Gone was the mage apprentice who became exhausted after a couple hours. She was becoming an accomplished mage, and soon she would only require real-world experience to further her learning. Experience that, he knew and feared, would come very quickly. He only hoped she would be strong enough when it did.

"You might want to tie that tighter, Miss Divi. Tie it too loose and I might think the wind destroyed the dummy and not your spells."

Startled, Divi nearly dropped the unfinished practice dummy. Was it that time already? She had hoped to be able to replace the dummies she destroyed before he joined her, but she probably should have known better. Tasi was always an early riser, even back home in Myyril. It was a valiant effort.

Divi said, "Sorry. Wanted to test a few things before the lesson this morning."

Tasi took one more glance at the fallen targets before looking back at her and asking, "Just from the carnage on the grounds here, I assume your test was successful?"

Divi smiled confidently. "Watch."

She gave the dummy one last tug to tighten the head on before staking the target to the ground. Then she walked back to where Tasi was standing, some seventy yards away.

The positioning of the targets roused his curiosity. Although the targets were close, five feet was still too much distance for a single fireball to burst across and destroy both. At most a normal mage would take out the arms and knock them down with the fireball's wake. Firing at the ground in front of the dummies would, but he saw no evidence of it from her previous attempts. Could she cast two fireballs at once? Tasi quickly shrugged the notion away. He knew it was impossible for a mage to cast two spells at the same time . . . well, and live to tell about it.

Divi quickly got into position to throw a fireball. By her motions alone, he could see it was all coming naturally to her now. He remembered how uneasy she had felt in the beginning. What a difference a few weeks made.

Divi started to gather the life particles around her hand, but Tasi noticed something different. The aura had grown to nearly to the size of her entire upper body. In the center of this aura rested one of the largest balls of flame he had ever seen. Rather than the usual reddish tint, this one was bluish silver.

Divi's voice echoed as she finally called. *"Firammii morza!"*

Tasi's jaw nearly dropped. The fireball, nearly Divi's size, emitted from her hand and toward the targets. He watched as it approached the dummies, apparently aimed in the gap between them. The air around the fireball seemed to pulsate with energy. No, it wasn't the air. It was the life particles. Her fireball engulfed random life particles in its path, becoming faster and stronger. He assured himself that she had most likely stumbled on this ability by accident. It was a very advanced technique, one normally taught only to students who had studied for years, and one only sacred-bloods were supposed to be able to do. Not even Tasi knew the proper way to perform it, not being in that special class.

The fireball struck the dummies with a phenomenal impact. Despite being thrown between them, the spell dismantled both with relative ease. Even the stakes were driven from their resting place in the earth. Just as quickly as the event occurred, it was over. Even the life particles that were used for destruction returned peacefully to their invisible state as if nothing happened. Nothing remained of the two targets Divi constructed except the stakes, now lying humbly about forty feet from where they had started.

Tasi was very impressed . . . almost frightfully impressed. Divi's determination had led her to do great things in such a short period of time. Tasi's fear was that she was learning certain things by chance and would not use them correctly. Once the fireball is learned, the world of magic opens wide. That unfortunately also left an opening for mages to do something more advanced than they were prepared for. She seemed okay for the moment, but upon their return to Myyril, he would talk with the head teachers about a course of action.

Divi turned to Tasi and smiled, knowing again that he was astonished by her progress, though hiding it. She could see it in his expression. She really didn't fully understand how she did it yet, but the more she practiced, the more comfortable she became. Being one with the life particles almost felt like she gained a new friend.

Tasi finally broke his silence by commenting, "Don't bask in your glory. The true test of knowledge is repetition. Try it again."

He was eager to see if Divi could in fact do it with as much ease as before. She was like-wise much obliged to show her teacher she could. A familiar voice, though, halted their test.

"Tasi! Divi!"

Amber came sprinting from the main camp at full speed. Divi had never seen her run like this, even when she was hunting, trying to catch an animal before finishing the kill.

Tasi asked, "What's the matter? You seem . . ."

212

"No time for questions! Hide! Quickly! Do it now!"

Amber ran past them, heading toward a pond near the training area. Divi was spooked. For the first time, she saw terror in Amber's eyes. Something was coming. She turned to Tasi, who showed an equally worried look.

"We should take her advice," Divi said. "Cover yourself by the trees. Stay as far away from this clearing as possible. Not sure what's coming, but we'll be easy targets out here."

Tasi nodded and ran for a small rock alcove near the training area. Divi also searched for a hiding spot, but there were not many available. Desperate, she grabbed a leather skin that Amber recently cleaned and covered herself with it by the trees on the outskirts. For now, all was silent.

Amber, meanwhile, continued to sprint toward the pond. Using one of her sword abilities, she fired a projectile, slicing one of the strong bamboo stems nearby. She had practiced this many times in the event she was ever found. The only real danger she ever faced in her practices was when a deadly spider made a home inside one of the bamboo shafts. This was not a test, though, and she had no time to check if there were any surprises in the piece she cut. This was the real thing. All she could do was pray as she sheathed her sword and grabbed the bamboo with her open hand.

Amber put her mouth over one end of the bamboo as she jumped into the pond. The cool water felt good on her body, especially after the far run she had. Sadly, she couldn't enjoy it. She had to get as deep as she could. Her armor caused her to sink a little quicker than normal as she grabbed on to rocks jutting out of the natural sediment.

She took care to breathe her first breath through the bamboo. Good. She was deep enough, but not so deep that water was coming from the top end. Now all she could do was wait. She was thankful this pond was relatively clear of marine creatures because of the current that flowed near the bottom, creating a river underwater. Carnivorous creatures on land used to drink from this spot often. Gerritonnee all but ensured they no longer enjoyed that option, so their presence was rare now. When Amber had settled firmly on the edge of the pond's upper bed, she waited nervously.

Meanwhile, at the camp, Divi and Tasi remained just as quiet. Except for the many buzzing insects, some leaves rustling in the light breeze was the only sound. Divi used her powers to see if she could feel anything strange, but she couldn't. Then again, she was still refining her abilities. Her telekinetic powers hadn't heightened as Tasi had told her they would once she learned magic. At least, not yet.

Boom.

Divi looked around from her hiding spot, trying to make as little movement as possible. The sky was clear and sunny, once again eliminating the possibility that the noise came from a storm.

Boom. Boom.

The noises were getting closer and happening more often. Divi had heard something like them not too many nights ago. It was no storm. It was a dragon. A dragon that scared even Amber.

As this thought entered Divi's mind, a shadow engulfed the camp. The echo of the beating wings caused her to cover her ears. The beast did not roar, though. She didn't know why it held back. Its wings had already made them aware of its presence.

The shadow briefly lifted as it headed in the direction of the main camp where their huts lay, but it quickly returned. The wind had died down.

Divi suddenly felt something. About a month ago she wouldn't have recognized it, but since she learned magic, she knew the life particles around them had begun to gravitate upwards. That was when it first hit.

The ground trembled from a powerful bright beam as it smashed on the ground, hitting some of the dead trunks and logs. Dust and tree bark were flying everywhere. Divi felt more life particles leaving them . . . then more. The bombardment of the training area was heavy.

Tasi backed up as far as he could, but it wasn't much. One of the beams landed just a few feet away. He covered his eyes. Although he didn't really like any dragons, he found this one instance where he wished Gerritonnee was here.

The beam attacks stopped for a few moments, and they could hear more striking to the east . . . the main camp. The assault there was brief, as the dragon soon returned his attention back to the training area. Divi wasn't sure how long it went on. It seemed like hours. One more beam landed about twenty feet from her, almost making her lose her grip on the animal skin.

The barrage suddenly stopped, and the shadow headed north.

Even from her underwater sanctuary, Amber could hear the attack from above. She hoped that Divi and Tasi were all right. She would have felt guilty if they died because she didn't want to tell them about her one mistake since coming to this place. She felt confident that at least Divi was okay. Her reason for being here and doing this was too strong. So strong that Amber didn't think even *he* could stop her.

The sun was suddenly blotted from Amber's view. She did her best not to allow any bubbles to float to the top. She wasn't sure if it knew she was down here or if it was just frustrated that it couldn't find her. All she knew was she saw something bright from above her and it wasn't the sun. She braced herself to the rocks.

The beam's impact in the middle of the pond caused a maelstrom. Amber lost her grip not only on the rocks, but also on her sword as it sucked her to the center of the pond. She no longer had the luxury of her bamboo breathing tool, which floated near the surface. Amber swam as hard as she could away from the center, but the maelstrom was too

215

strong. Seeing her sword sinking fast, Amber knew she had to go deeper.

She changed directions. The power of the whirlpool lessened as it seemed to go as deep as the beam went, approximately fifty feet. Amber still had to hurry. Her sword was nearing the underwater river. If it got sucked though that, her weapon might be lost forever. She swam harder than she ever had. She retrieved the sword only a few yards from the current. She instantly swam back up. It didn't matter if her friend was still flying up there. She needed air before she drowned. The good news was the shadow was no longer over her. Amber started to feel dizzy as she neared the pond's surface.

Her emergence disrupted the once again peaceful pond. She struggled to get herself onto a stone next to the edge and, gasping for breath, she lay on her back. The sun was shining bright again. The thundering sound that she'd heard clearly even underwater was also long gone. Amber tried to voice a confident laugh, but a cough exited instead.

That was a little too close for comfort, but he still hadn't found her yet.

Amber waited until she could breathe normally again before slowly standing up. She didn't bother wringing out her wet clothes. It was a hot day, so the sun would dry them. She was more concerned about her two companions than her clothes, anyway. She didn't want to admit it, but the two mages were growing on her a little. She tried running toward the last place she had seen them, but the wet boots and overall exhaustion from swimming kept her to a fast walk.

"Amber!"

She sighed in relief. Tasi's voice joined in, yelling her name. Both were safe. Thank goodness.

Divi and Tasi didn't wait for Amber, opting to run and meet her halfway.

Divi asked, "Are you okay?"

"I'm fine. What about you two?"

"We're okay. Scared, but okay. What was that?" asked Tasi.

The question set Amber at war with herself. Did she finally tell them about Tiiamite? Should she wait until they got the final stone before she told them? Did Tiiamite truly know they were here? Just glancing at the training area damage, he only hit a few select areas, appearing more at random than trying to specifically hit something. She'd had numerous other camps before staying at this one. She wondered if Tiiamite had hit those as well.

Amber smiled and patted Tasi on the shoulder. "So, how long until you think Divi is going to be ready?"

Tasi looked at Divi, clearly confused about the change in subject. "Well, I don't know. It's just hard to . . ."

"Well, we're leaving the day after tomorrow for the Fire Dragon's lair. Wherever you are with Divi, that will have to do."

When she began walking away, Tasi called, "You still didn't answer my question!"

Amber sighed as she hushed him. Of course she didn't. If they left when she said they were going to leave, hopefully they would never have to be concerned about receiving that answer.

"I wouldn't worry about it. Just get whatever training needs to be done before we go. Trust me."

Both mages really wanted to. It was hard, though, when she refused to tell them about this. Divi didn't want to make more of it because she knew Amber wouldn't answer her straight anyway. Tasi didn't push because he was flat-out scared of her, although he would never tell anyone that, especially her. One thing was true: they needed to finish Divi's training for now.

* * * * *

217

"Very interesting."

Gerritonnee and Amber walked across the camp, though she had to move carefully to avoid the craters created by Tiiamite. He'd certainly made a punishing assault on the training area. Divi and Tasi were very fortunate to be alive. She didn't think they could even re-use the area, it was so heavily damaged. The main camp had been hit a few times, but all of the shelters survived. She was still unsure if Tiiamite had known she was in the pond or if the beam blasted into it was just a final statement of his attack, but it was too close for her.

"How did he find us? I didn't see any other dragons. I've been extra careful to keep my eyes open for them."

"That is sometimes when our eyes are the weariest," commented Gerritonnee. *"It is true that it would be difficult for a dragon to sneak up on someone on the forest grounds. From the air, my brethren could find it easier. Divi's latest learning of magic probably helped. Dragons are sensitive to major disruptions of the Eirzalif."*

An unfortunate occurrence. Amber never even considered what effect Divi's magic would have on the dragons. She would have told Gerritonnee about it, but she knew what the dragon's answer would be . . . and she would be right.

Amber analyzed, "That explains why he hit the training area so hard. Probably thought it was me being careless with my training. Had he hit the other camps I've been at?"

"He was having the dragons focus on one of them before the disruption occurred and led them to this one. I have been telling the dragons that I saw suspicious movements at the other camps to buy you some time."

That worried Amber even more. Gerritonnee had gotten herself involved beyond just being an advisor and personal protector of the stones she recovered. She lied to the other dragons, especially to Tiiamite. If he found out

218

what she had done, Amber hated to think of what punishment he would inflict on her dragon friend.

Even though she didn't have Gerritonnee's senses, she certainly expected what the dragon told her next.

"What will you do, little one? Now that they have an idea of where you are, I will not be able to come near you without them suspecting."

"Then you must stay away. Regardless of where Divi is in her training, we have to go. I planned to leave the day after tomorrow and head up the outer edge of the northwest forest."

"That is a risk. You'll go dangerously close to the Temple of Elements."

"Yes, but now that Tiiamite knows where my camps are, I doubt he'll be perched on top like you say he has been. My guess is he'll have the dragons start combing this area in a couple days, leading the search. As we're going in the opposite direction, it should be easy sailing."

"It was a shame you were unable to get the Fire relic the first time. Would have made this much easier."

Gerritonnee was right about that. The Fire relic was the second stone she tried to recover, but she either needed some help or she had to come with a new strategy to get that stone. There was more than just a dragon in there.

As they reached the southern end of the camp, Gerritonnee stopped and slowly turned to Amber. *"I should be going. I had to come as soon as I could to make sure you were okay, but now, I must return to my routine before I met you. Is there anything else you wanted to ask me? Until you recover the final relic, I won't be able to see you again. You will be on your own from here."*

Amber didn't reply right away, instead hugging Gerritonnee around the base of her skull. Normally, this would be a simple gesture of gratitude. With Amber doing it, however, Gerritonnee knew it meant that much more. She growled softly, acknowledging the gesture.

Amber said, "I just want to say thank you for everything you have done. Don't know if I'd have gotten as far as I have without your help. I will get this stone if that's what it's going to take to see you again. Be safe."

Amber finally unlocked her embrace. Blood dotted her arms from Gerritonnee's hard scales. It was a bearable pain, however. Her dragon friend licked the wounds so they would heal faster.

"I wish you luck too, little one. With Divi and Tasi by your side, I am certain you will succeed this time."

With that being said, Gerritonnee lifted herself into the clear night sky. Amber waited until the dragon was completely out of view before looking back toward the camp. A sense of excitement and fear entered her. The excitement came because this meant that in a few days she might have the final stone. The fear came because she now didn't know what the future would bring. There was more at stake now for her than ever. *This must be how Divi has been feeling all the time since she came here.*

As she walked back to camp to rejoin the mages, one thing Gerritonnee said rang truer than all the others: Until she recovered the stones, she and the mages were on their own.

CHAPTER 11
The Power of One

Tasi sat near a large fire in the middle of camp, exhausted, but satisfied. Never had he expected to train a mage like Divi before. She responded much better than he predicted to the grueling training. The basic lessons usually took years for a mage, but Divi was close to finishing just a month after they had fought Leviadon and retrieved the Water relic. It was a phenomenal achievement!

He could definitely see remnants of her father in her as she trained, though he would never admit that to her. Her father was one who would not give up on something until he achieved it.

Amber, who just finished preparing some food, sat next to Tasi. She offered him a drink she called Liesserberry. It was made from sweet berries that grew in the south near the Water Temple. The vineyard-like stalks they sprouted from suggested they had at one point been domestically grown. He truly didn't care how she made it. It was delicious! Tasi slowly took it.

"Thank you."

"I see that Divi is really giving you a handful."

Amber wasn't kidding. When Divi set her mind to something, she really pushed it. Getting her to throw her first fireball was very difficult, but she never gave up. For that, Tasi gave her a lot of credit. He still wished that Divi's cause was worthy in his eyes, but he had no say in being her teacher. If she wanted to learn, he was going to have to teach her.

"So, how is she doing?"

Tasi replied, "Very well. In fact, I have never seen a mage learn so fast . . . or be so powerful. Her spells, for some reason, are three times more powerful than any other mage's . . . even more than her father's and he was strong. I have seen other sacred-bloods cast magic and even they pale in comparison."

"What do you think is the reason?"

"I truly don't know. Time will tell." A short pause came between the two. "Forgive me for prying, but I was curious. What is life like for a half-mage?"

The question seemed to surprise Amber. "I thought all you mages knew what it's like?"

"We are only educated on the rule, not the way of life."

Why did he suddenly care so much? Amber grabbed a few berries and began eating them.

"It's hard," she explained. "Right from birth, from the moment you are snatched by the Kittara, you are alone. Fear is the first thing you feel because you experienced it the moment you left the womb. Even though you are with your own kind, you yearn for the outside world. We only have one ship, but it must be kept in good condition so it can survive the trip to Myyril for the paladin hopefuls. Can you imagine an entire life spent trying to please others? Many half-mages have perished trying to become paladins. It made me wonder why we risk our lives for such a cause. I then realized that the rank of paladin represents the freedom to explore. It's for that freedom that we risk our lives."

Tasi didn't know how to answer. It was the first time in the month they had been with Amber that he saw so much passion in her.

"I can only imagine how we mages must appear in the eyes of a Tydosian."

"Despised," Amber replied truthfully. "Some of it out of jealousy, but to be controlled before we are even minutes old has caused much disdain among our people. I trusted you and Divi because I am usually a good judge, and I believed you two had good intentions. Realize that nearly any other half-mage put in my position would have slit your throats while you slept."

Tasi couldn't believe that half-mages nurtured so much resentment of them. If the humans ever got wind of Tydos, it would not be good for the well-being of the mages.

"I truly am sorry," he stated. "Mages can be headstrong in our ways at times. No one should be forced to answer to another people just because we think we are superior. Not much separates us from you, really. It seems Neeza understood that, giving you the quest that he did. I do too, after this time we've shared. I know my apology will do little in fixing general relations, so I hope you take mine to heart."

Amber gave a smile. "Well, you do have a soft side."

She laughed as Tasi took it. "Just don't spread it around."

Tasi grabbed a small berry and ate it before looking at Amber once again. Although he wanted to ask her more, the half-mage didn't give him a chance to continue. "Now it's my turn for questions."

"Ask away. I have nothing to hide."

"What's the deal with you and Divi? Are you her boyfriend or something? I've never seen anyone so protective of a woman."

Tasi slowly replied, "I am her teacher. That is all."

Amber knew, though, that it was not it. His slight hesitation before answering gave him away. Divi's drunken confessions had also given Amber a snippet of the truth.

"You like Divi romantically, don't you? Don't try and hide it."

"Let's just say . . . that if things had been different . . . I mean, if Divi decided to learn magic earlier . . . then things may have been different."

Amber still didn't understand Tasi's reluctance. If it was because he was Divi's teacher, she saw no problems with that. Many of the paladin trainees had romantic relations with their instructors. It was natural that when people trained another of the opposite sex for a long time, they started to have feelings for each other.

"Just tell her how you feel," she commented. "Can't be that hard."

Tasi exclaimed, "The teacher and student relationship is a strict bond. If broken the consequences would be dire."

A short silence came between the two. Tasi couldn't believe he was telling Amber this. What did she care how he really felt? She couldn't possibly understand, being a half-mage who didn't live in the mage society. Then again, she was the only one who would listen.

Tasi said, "I have liked Divi since I was in my youngling days. I was the only one who never made fun of her because she chose not to learn. It was the main reason Neeza selected me in the first place. I will admit . . . the day Neeza chose me to be Divi's teacher, the boy in me died. My original dream of marrying the woman I cared about ended before I was old enough to be able to do anything about it. In that way, I can sort of understand how a half-mage feels."

Amber chuckled and said, "Well, even if it takes one mage at a time, it's a start."

Tasi laughed too. It was going to take much more than that to sway the mages in their opinions of the half-mage race. But he did agree, he was a start.

Amber continued, "I'm assuming, though, that you are not the one who is driving her to do this."

Tasi regretfully answered, "No, she is doing this for a human. His name is . . ."

"Levus," Amber said. "I know, she can't seem to go a day without mentioning his name lately. She speaks proudly of him. I have to say, her feelings are strong to inspire this. Whoever he is, he is a lucky boy to have a girl like her to care for him. Still, you should not be sad that Divi is only your friend. Relationships are hard. Friendships are much more durable. From experience, there are two things that kill friendships: secrets and silence. Secrets, no matter how hard you try to keep them, are found out eventually and will be hurtful to the one left out of it. Silence stings more than a stab wound because it makes one feel they aren't even worth your time for an answer. Don't ever let those get in the way of what you and Divi have right now. Hold it tight."

Tasi eagerly wanted to change the subject. For right now, especially when Levus' name was involved, he didn't want to discuss it. Still, she did bring up some interesting points. Despite how harsh he'd been on her these past few weeks, Divi didn't let that get in the way of their friendship. He guessed that was the true value of a friend. Not when times were good, but when times were hard. The ones who stayed and believed those moments of weakness weren't your true nature were the ones you kept. He had that with Divi. They were open with each other about darn near everything. He couldn't imagine what it would be like if she started hiding things from him. He could accept her desire to only be friends. But could that part of him that loved Divi ever be completely quenched? That he wasn't sure of.

"How about you, Amber? Do you have someone you love or loved?"

Amber chuckled. "Nope. I guess I haven't found someone as crazy as me. I think the whole battlemage route scares some of them away. The men don't want to be overshadowed by the women sometimes. I'm the only female battlemage to train from the current crop."

"How about the others you trained with? They didn't meet your standards?" inquired Tasi.

"We ended up becoming more family than anything. It would just feel weird. Being a small group, we all kind of looked out for each other. I'm sure it's much different in your mage schools."

"You would think that, would you? Mage schools are strict, yes, but you'd be surprised how many secret relationships occur behind their teachers' backs."

225

Amber laughed and said, "It must have been awkward for you, then. Your love interest never even went to one of those schools."

Her response surprised Tasi, but the way she said it convinced him she was only kidding. Still, that didn't rule it out from being the truth. He was different in that way from the other mages. He chuckled to himself, remembering how some called him a servant to his studies because he always seemed so imbedded in his schoolwork to care about a relationship. That was not the case though, even if the girl he liked was forbidden.

"Hey! You'll never going to sway a mage's opinion with that attitude," he told Amber. "Mages are sensitive people."

Both looked at each other and burst out laughing. Amber patted Tasi on the shoulder in a way she seemed to think gentle, though Tasi thought it a little rough.

She said, "Remind me I'll have to get you drunk. I think you would make a fun one."

* * * * *

As Amber and Tasi talked together, Divi was having trouble falling asleep. It was not the first time. Ever since her decision to learn magic, her nights had been restless. Tasi said it was because of her powers and that many mages in training had a difficult time adjusting. It had grown worse the day she threw her first fireball and continued now. She wondered, though, if this was how it was supposed to feel. She at times felt cold and always sensed a chilly hand near her shoulder.

"Divi."

It felt like someone was near her whenever she slept. It was almost like . . . someone was trying to reach her.

"Divi."

226

What was that? Was someone calling her name? Divi slowly opened her eyes. Everything was silent. She had to be dreaming. Who would be calling her this late at night other than Amber or Tasi?

"I'm glad you are awake, Divi. I see Tasi kept to his word."

Tears came to her eyes. She knew that voice, but it couldn't be! She saw him die! Divi's eyes grew wide. Standing before her, surrounded by a blue aura, was her father!

She had to be seeing things. Divi even wiped her eyes to make sure he was not an illusion.

Neeza said, "Fear not. I can assure you I am here. My time, though, is short. My soul cannot return to the Life Force until I pass on the sign of the true successor."

Divi still couldn't believe what she was seeing. "But . . . but you're dead. I saw it in Porsita!"

"That is a fate I can never turn back. You speak truly. But I come to you now, because I see you ready to learn the greatest spells that any mage can ever know. I regret that I cannot be there in person to teach them to you."

Divi stood up and walked slowly to her father's ghost. The tears continued to roll down her cheeks. "You knew I was learning magic?"

"Yes. I also know why you are doing it."

Divi was startled to hear this. How could a ghost know these things? Her fears heightened as she wondered what her father would think of this.

She asked, "Are you not mad at my decision?"

"Divi, in our lives, your mother and I always tried to teach you that the decisions you make are yours alone. What we both believed didn't matter. If it made you happy, we were content. I admit the day that soothsayer came and told us you might fall in love with a human, it scared me. I didn't want you to live with the consequences such a decision would bring upon you. Your mother always told me I was

227

stubborn. She was right. When she died, I began to lose control."

"What do you mean?"

He sat down on the log she had been previously using as a chair. Even though he was a ghost, he still looked as though his legs were tired.

Neeza said, "On the boat I promised you I would tell you everything. As a child, you would get horrible nightmares. You probably don't remember them being that young. Not many, but a few years after the last Elf Games, they became more frequent. Even though she was sick, Mierena was the only one who could bring you back to a peaceful slumber. She never told me how she did it. I'm not even sure she could explain it to me. When the disease made her bed-ridden, I knew I had to save her. Not only for my personal well-being. I wanted to bring her back to help me protect you. That is why I went to Mount Hrithgorn not long before my last journey. Not only for your mother, but for you. Somehow, I lost my focus when I did lose her. I began to let the soothsayer's premonition cloud over my reasoning. In that aspect, I was a horrible father. It took wise words to bring me back on the right track.

"But to answer your question, I am not angry at your decision. In fact, I hope you live a life of happiness with him because that is all I ever wanted you to be: Happy."

Those words from her father meant more to her than anything in the world. She had no idea of the sacrifices her parents had made for her. The resentment she held against Neeza now felt so pitiful. All this time she thought he wanted her to be something she didn't want. Instead it was because he cared, perhaps even a little too much. She had been such a silly little girl the entire time. The tears flowed freely now.

Divi said, "You mean it?"

"Of course."

No words she could say would describe her joy.

228

Neeza then said, "Divi, hold out your hand and silence your mind. I will teach you the spells that will solidify your claim to the throne of Myyril, whenever you decide to claim it. It is your birthright."

Divi slowly held out her hand and Neeza placed his on top of it. Despite his hands' chill, she could feel a strange warmth. A small ball of light suddenly formed in her hand.

Neeza instructed, "Repeat these words using your telepathy: *Viasonta quueserium bottra. Mettia guddarres fussurott una. Futteeva y futteeva.* You will keep saying it until you begin to feel some pain as my energy and knowledge are passed to you. From your staff, your jewel will emerge, signifying you're a full-fledged magic-using mage. You will gain insight into spells that only our bloodline can produce. Take caution to not overuse them. You are ready to learn and cast them, but until you train more, they may still harm you. Are you ready, Divi?"

Divi closed her eyes and followed her father's instructions. After repeating it the first time, Neeza joined Divi in sync repeating, "*Viasonta quueserium bottra. Mettia guddarres fussurott una. Futteeva y futteeva.*"

After saying the phrase a few times, her body started to twitch. She felt something entering her veins and traveling to every aspect of her body. At times, she even had difficulty breathing. The twitching grew stronger.

Neeza closed his eyes. The ball that he formed in his hand started being absorbed through Divi's hand. She screamed. It was not a scream of terror or of pain. She felt none of those. Only the energy was so strong.

Light surrounded her as she hovered a couple feet off the ground. Although her eyes were closed, she could see things clearly. After a few moments, her body relaxed. Her father no longer stood before her, and something had changed. Divi looked down at her vest and skirt. Her old, brown, shabby clothing was now elegant and white. Inside, she felt a new power engulfing her soul. Her staff had even changed to expose a light turquoise jewel at the top. Her jaw dropped. *Turquoise. That is the rarest color a sacred-blood mage could attain.* It meant she was a protector of life and pure of heart.

She may not have gone to school, but she did know what all the colors meant. When a mage first got their staff, the jewel remained hidden and neutral in color. As they continue to learn, it started adapting to their training, only emerging when they earned being of a master in their field, the jewel's color reflecting that.

"Divi, follow your heart and know that even in our last breaths, we support you and love you. Fulfill your destiny. We are so proud of you."

A large smile grew on her face. For the first time on this journey, she no longer felt fear. In a way, she was born anew. Now, without a doubt, she would save Levus. It was in her hands.

"Divi!" yelled Tasi.

He and Amber had heard the scream come from Divi's hut and rushed there as fast as they could. Amber hoped that nothing bad had entered while Divi slept. Even when her dragon companion was around, predators tried to venture into the camp.

As they headed up the small hill to Divi's hut, Tasi stopped her. What did he feel? It was like nothing he ever felt in his life. They watched as a bright light emerged from the door. When the light dulled, Divi stood in its wake.

Tasi couldn't believe it. She now possessed the most powerful spells in Myyrilian history. The turquoise color of her now jeweled staff confirmed it. Knowing these spells was the only thing that would cause such a transformation. He went down to one knee and pointed his staff toward Divi. This was the bow given to the leader of Myyril. Tasi grabbed Amber and forced her to kneel down as well.

Amber asked, "What's going on?"

He explained, "Divi has just learned the spells all mages want to learn, but fear the power of. They have the ability to destroy cities and end ways of life. But how did she learn them? Only the leader of Myyril can teach it, and her father was killed."

Divi walked out of the hut and met them at the bottom of the hill. Tasi and Amber rose slowly.

Amber commented, "I like the new wardrobe."

Divi threw her head back, laughing. This new version of her felt, to Tasi, like she had been reborn from the ashes of her former self. She faced Tasi and put her arm on his shoulder.

"You have many questions. The answers I will discuss on the way."

"On the way to what?"

Amber knew where Divi was going. "On our way for the final stone."

Divi nodded and said, "Let us finish this."

As Amber and Tasi headed back to camp, Divi paused to face the hut. A single tear fell from her cheek.

"Thank you, father."

She turned and walked after her friends. From the door of the hut, Neeza's spirit smiled warmly as he returned to the Eirzalif with the morning's rays.

* * * * *

On the south wall of Fort Za, Eraddor and Thamalos sat watching the sea. It was so quiet and peaceful. About two miles from the fort, a monument of rock jutted into the sea, a vision of breathtaking beauty. Even though Fort Za had many activities for the soldiers, the two friends enjoyed just staring at the water. Thamalos was here for more than sightseeing, though, and he could tell Eraddor was deep in thought.

Eraddor suddenly asked, "Have you ever wondered what life would be like without such beauty? If it was all destroyed?"

Thamalos replied, "I think Barbata is the perfect example. Yet, I feel that no matter how much good evil destroys, some beauty must remain. If all beauty is destroyed, then how can its opposite exist? That was a very deep thought."

"I don't know what it is," Eraddor said. "We've been here for a month already. An elf guard told me the longest of these meetings ever held before lasted two weeks, and that was during the Ettui Island Wars when no one was certain where they would land. This is taking much too long. I am fearful this beauty is about to be threatened."

"I share your concerns. Though I must say, I am more impressed because you don't have elven powers and you can still see this."

Eraddor lowered his head and smiled. "I'll take that as a compliment. Still, it seems like we are being kept here . . . like bait."

Thamalos didn't hear his final words. He saw a small ship coming from the east, and it wasn't a warship.

Eraddor asked, "Is everything all right?"

As he spotted the ship, too, his eyes opened wide. A ship carrying woman and children passed between Fort Za and the rock in the sea.

Thamalos asked, "What is the meaning of this?"

Eraddor hoped this ship was only passing by. That hope ended as the sailors on deck began to drop anchor. He should have known better. There was no reason for a passenger ship to land on the west side of the continent. Wood Elves and Sardonians would be their only greeters, and both hated humans.

"I see they have finally arrived."

They turned to see General Seth Medkar slowly stepping toward them, his eyes never leaving the ship's deck full of passengers. It was obvious Seth had previous knowledge of this.

He continued, "They said the ship would arrive by midday. With the horrible storms that passed through here, we feared the worst."

Eraddor stood up and stormed to the general. "Who are these people?"

"These are some of the soldiers' families. Once every three years, the human soldiers get to see their loved ones. It is sometimes heart-wrenching, seeing wives embrace their spouses after so long. Some miss their children's entire lives," explained Seth.

Eraddor said, "They must leave now."

Seth gave a look of disbelief. "And for what reason?"

Thamalos rose and stood next to Eraddor. "Because we have a strange feeling something bad will happen here soon. Do you not find it odd that we are still here? We are arguing over simple matters that should take no more than a day."

"I know you wouldn't understand, Thamalos," Seth said. "Fort Za, to the elves, is the last defense standing between Barbata and Lozela since Mount Hrithgorn fell. The elves would give their entire lives defending this fort. It's different for humans. The men have been situated here for almost twenty years and nothing ever happens. They are missing the lives of their kin to watch over a stronghold that no enemy will breach. They don't know why they are here. You try and tell them that they can miss the one thing keeping them sane because you two have a hunch."

Thamalos didn't appreciate Seth's answer. If that was all this meant to the human race, why even bother having them situated here? Fort Za was the first major attempt to bring the elf and human worlds closer. Obviously, the elves had more work to do. Seth stormed off, and Eraddor and Thamalos remained silent as the people disembarked onto the fort's dock.

Eraddor finally said, "This is not wise."

Thamalos added, "For everyone's sake, let us hope these feelings of ours remain just that."

He walked away, leaving Eraddor to stare at the new arrivals. He couldn't believe it. Even young children were on the boat as well as the elderly. Just seeing all these innocent people arrive amid an uneasiness he'd never had before made him sick. He felt like he needed to take charge and do something to protect them, but what could he do as a simple loner to prevent them from getting hurt? If only he had some command like General Medkar. Eraddor began repeating Thamalos' words in his head. *These feelings of ours remain just that.* He truly hoped the elf was right. If not, the situation had just gotten worse.

* * * * *

Divi, Amber, and Tasi continued to climb the steeper side of the Northern Mountains. Amber told them that this temple was the most difficult to reach because of its location. Unlike the Earth Dragon's temple, which was in the mountains but underground, this was located up near the lowest clouds. She was ahead of both mages, but Divi was not far behind her. Tasi pondered the strange change in her behavior. It was like the old Divi had died and a more determined one replaced her.

Even after a couple hours of climbing, Divi still found energy to continue, showing more vigor than their half-mage leader. Amber showed signs of exhaustion from the five-day journey. They stayed close to the western coast. When they neared what Amber called the Temple of Elements, they traveled constantly, not resting even to eat. Last night, they stopped about ten miles from the Northern Mountains, which made Amber happy. They left especially early this morning in the hopes of arriving just before midday. Though the journey was hard, the reward would be well worth it.

Divi could see a small space where the slop leveled out. They were finally reaching some flat ground. Although she wanted to move on, she knew the other two would want to rest. For some reason, she didn't even feel tired. She remembered the caves on Dyyros and how depleted she felt. Maybe it was the adrenaline, which Levus explained to her a warrior felt when determined to get something they really wanted. Whatever was driving her, she knew she would need more of it for the next fight. Leviadon proved to be quite a challenge and this one would be no different.

Amber was the first to reach smooth surface. She never liked this part when she was seeking the temples out. The Earth Dragon Temple had been much like this one: in the mountains and a pain to get to. Only the Earth Temple was harder to find, as its entrance looked like a hole in between a group of mountain peaks.

Amber dropped to one knee and stared ahead as Divi finally joined her.

"They certainly make this difficult."

It was then that she noticed what Amber was seeing. She could do nothing but stare as Tasi finally arrived.

He said, "I need to discover a flying spell."

Neither woman paid attention to Tasi's comment. Their focus was on something else.

"What are you looking at?"

He finally glanced at what the girls were staring at and his eyes opened wide. "By the gods!"

On the other side of a canyon stood an elaborate entrance that had to be almost two hundred feet tall. It was like someone cut the stone slab right off the mountain. Its carving showed two dragons on each side, surrounded by flames. Divi couldn't tell what everything else meant. To her the design was a bunch of miscellaneous pictographs and words. The language was one she had never seen. Divi wasn't certain, but she believed she could see a lava flow through the entrance.

At last, Amber said, "This is the Gunimai Volcano, also known as Fafcul's Temple. Unlike the other temples, this one has enemies guarding the entrance of the Fire Dragon, Fafcul. I actually had to turn back because there were too many of them."

Tasi asked, "What are . . . them?"

Amber looked at him and said, "You don't want to know."

She started walking. Her comment frightened Tasi. What were they going to face in there? Apparently, though, he was the only one worried, as Divi was right behind her. Tasi shook his head.

"What was I thinking when I agreed to this?"

He slowly followed Divi and Amber to the canyon floor.

CHAPTER 12
In the Hall of the Fire Dragon

"This is crazy!"

Those were the only words Tasi could exclaim as they neared the entrance of the Temple. The temperature had risen to a point most mages could no longer take. He was especially worried about Divi because she already almost perished because of overheating. Bursts of gasses and heated water spouted out of the ground. Under the hardened stone around them and through cracks, Tasi could see rivers of lava moving. The stench of sulfur eliminated all other smells. Even the canyon walls were steaming because of the heat. They hadn't even made it inside yet.

Tasi continued, "We can't do this. If the sulfur doesn't kill us, the heat will."

Amber, without answering, began to look around the entrance for something.

Divi didn't take much notice of Amber's actions. Was this really the way to the last relic? If so, Tasi had a point. They wouldn't make it out of the Temple with all the heat. The desert was one thing, but to be inside an active volcano was suicidal. There would be no place to escape the extreme temperatures. She didn't want to admit it, but maybe this was how her journey ended. It made her sick just thinking that, but it seemed truer everytime she looked up to see more lava. If she wanted to save Levus, she would have to survive this and defeat the dragon.

"What are you doing?"

Divi turned around to see Amber with three stones and a strange scaly material with thick fibers attached to each end. She positioned the stone so that the widest surface area was facing the sky. With great force, Amber raised her sword and stabbed the middle of the rock. As she did, it suddenly became a block of ice. Amber waited until it was completely frozen before pulling her sword out.

"Divi. Come here."

Divi curiously walked over. Amber now knelt with a small bunch of gray items lying in front of her.

Amber continued, "Turn around."

She slowly did as she was told. What could Amber possibly . . .?

A small, sudden chill on her lower spine made her jump. At first Divi tried to shake it off, but the coldness on her spine made her entire body cool. Divi was so fascinated by this new sensation that she barely noticed Amber tying one of the strips of scales around her waist and another around her shoulders. Although she couldn't see it, the block of ice must have been held on by the scale.

Amber instantly started making another rock into a block of ice.

"What did you do?"

Amber answered, "Made the one thing that will let you two survive the fires in there. Come over here, Tasi."

Tasi walked over to Amber and turned around. He was hesitant to do so because most mages wore little under their robes. In his case, he just had a pair of leather hose that went to his knees.

Frustrated with his delay, she raised his robe for him to reveal his bare back. Amber began to tie the scaly material around his waist and shoulders as well, the ice block firmly pressed to his lower spine by the scale. She glanced to see Divi chuckle at Tasi's embarrassment.

He asked, "How is this going to save us?"

Amber continued as she explained, "You see, when a mage overheats, the main source of that comes from the lower back. This ice block will cool that spot, while this dragon scale helps keep it cold. Because the dragon scale is resistant to heat, the ice won't melt too fast. I say we have about two hours before I need to give you more ice."

238

Tasi and Divi looked at each other. Neither of them had ever heard of this. If true, it would allow a mage to step into the desert near Rudann and travel its length without fear of perishing. Tasi, though, was a little skeptical.

"And how do you know so much about this?" he asked.

Amber explained, "When I was just starting, a paladin candidate was sent out to the great desert near Desris. His mission was to bring back five different flowering plants for their restorative nectar. He failed when he discovered there are only four types growing there. But he did run into a mage who was near to death because of overheating. He asked the candidate to make him a block of ice, as he was too weak to do it on his own, so that he could try something before he died. The paladin candidate agreed and the mage stuck the ice block on his back. To his surprise, he felt completely rejuvenated. The candidate's journal says the mage was fine and helped him on a couple tasks. But, when the ice block melted one hot night, the mage never woke up."

Tasi and Divi couldn't believe her story. How was it that no other mage in their long history had ever discovered this? Even if it did work, Tasi saw another problem.

"But what about the sulfur? Whether human or mage, too much sulfur can poison you."

Amber pulled two plant leaves from her pouch and tossed one to each mage. She took out another and put it over her nose, tying it with a fiber string around the back of her head. Neither mage knew how this would help, but they followed Amber's lead.

She explained, "Those people who live on this continent gave me these. The plant has a waxy material covering its leaves, preventing them from being destroyed by the heat. Their exhalation of oxygen will help us breath, so I'm told. They explained why, but that didn't interest me. Just breathe through your nose."

As she and Tasi finished placing the leaves under their noses, Divi had to ask one more question.

"Amber, how many mages know about this cooling technique you showed us?"

"You are the only two . . . and let's keep it that way. Mages are more imperialistic then they like to think. Ready?"

The mages nodded. Those nods weren't the most confident of actions, but there was no time for them to gain confidence. Soon the residents here would discover they had company. The further along they were, the better. Amber unsheathed her sword and advanced inside the volcanic cavern.

Divi and Tasi followed slowly behind. They still weren't sure whether Amber's remedy would work. The first test would be walking past a lava river, just wide enough that jumping over it posed too much a risk. A narrow stone bridge offered the only passage over it. Amber crossed carefully. Divi could see Amber sweating, but whether it was from heat or fright she didn't know. Tasi was the next to move across, while Divi came last. As she walked on the bridge, she felt the powerful heat coming from the lava. Even though she was sweating on the outside, inside she felt the icy hand of a winter's wraith. *It really did work!*

When Divi jumped off the stone bridge, a burst of geyser erupted through a crack and sent her backwards. She landed hard on the stone, the hard scale protecting the ice block striking edge of the bridge. Amber and Tasi helped her stand up before she got any closer to the lava.

Tasi asked, "Are you okay?"

"I'm fine. Just a little rattled."

Divi walked off the bridge again, ignoring the cracks in the stone under her feet caused by the scale's impact.

With everyone safely across, Divi and Tasi followed Amber to the next room. It was just as big, only without a river. Instead, lava blazed at the bottom of numerous sinkholes, and even spewed from the walls.

Amber warned, "Careful here. Not only is this the most unstable of the rooms, but the shadow salamanders tend to show up now. And I guarantee you they probably know we're here."

"Shadow salamanders?" Tasi asked.

"Well, that's what I call them, anyway. They are quick creatures. They have six legs that resemble spiders' more than lizards'. Their black, rubbery skin makes it hard for swords to penetrate them, so we're going to have to rely on magic. Oh, did I mention there are going to be thousands of them when they show up?"

Tasi shook his head. Now he could see why Amber didn't tell them about these beasts before. He might have changed his mind about coming in here. The three moved slowly through the room. Much like in the other one, vents of steam randomly spouted from the ground, though none as close as the one that almost hit Divi. The lava coming from the walls made a disturbing noise as large splotches dripped on the rocks.

Suddenly, a different noise echoed off the walls. It sounded like falling rocks. Divi certainly hoped it didn't come from the shadow salamanders. Though she figured nothing could be worse than dealing with the Ettui. Not only were they numerous, but they could do nearly everything a man could do . . . including craft their own weapons.

"Divi! Look out!"

She turned to her left to see a large slab of rock coming down on her. Between her thoughts and the noises filling the room, she had no forewarning of it.

Amber rushed underneath the slab and grabbed Divi. They barely made it out of the way before it crashed intact onto the ground, dust flying high into the air. Coughing, they stood up, their vision hazy from the dust and heat.

Tasi ran over to them as they brushed themselves off. "You two okay?"

"Oh yeah, just great."

He disregarded Amber's sarcastic remark and checked on Divi. Amber examined the slab and the wall it fell off of. Something was not right. This stone didn't fall naturally. At the top, she noticed the scratch marks covering every inch. Amber scanned the walls and the ceiling. She could see nothing out of the ordinary. She knew, though, that they had to be close. She hurried back to Tasi and Divi.

"Come on. We have to move now!"

The mages stood still in confusion.

Tasi asked, "Amber, what's the probl—"

"Hold it! I feel something approaching. Whatever they are, there are many of them."

A strange noise came from the distance. It sounded like a large group of fryyups, bat-like creatures that roamed the night skies of Myyril. It echoed, making it seem to come from every direction. Amber furiously searched around the room.

Tasi asked, "What the . . .?"

"Everyone run! They're coming!"

Divi and Tasi followed Amber's lead as she sprinted away. Whatever caused the noises was getting closer. Divi didn't want to look back, though. With any luck they would outrun it.

Amber wove in between the holes on the ground, which grew more plentiful the deeper into the room they advanced. The haze from the steam decreased their visibility. Amber had run into this problem last time, too. It was hard to fight an enemy she could barely spot.

Divi, though, could see a hallway ahead. That must be where they needed to go. Finally, they had passed all the sinkholes, with nothing but a short stretch separating them with the hallway.

Suddenly, from their left, a black beast leapt toward Amber. She swung her sword at it with a lightning effect. The shadow salamander flew across the room and slammed into the rocks, hard.

The creature recovered, its gaze swaying with its body movement before settling on Divi. Amber was right about its appearance. It was about three feet tall and had six legs much like the common spiders on Myyril did, the rarer ones having eight. Its body reminded her of Levus' sword, from its color to the smoothness of it. The head was that of a lizard with red glowing eyes. It growled at Divi before looking at the ceiling and making a strange noise.

Amber observed, "Looks like we've got company."

At least twenty more shadow salamanders showed up ready to attack. Divi realized the first one had been calling them . . . calling its friends to their prey. She readied her staff as Amber raised her sword.

"We can take these, but we must hurry. There will be more of them."

As Amber said this, four of the salamanders lunged forward. Amber drove her sword in the ground and used an earth spell effect, driving pieces of stone into the air and hitting her attacker.

Divi and Tasi disabled more of them with magic. Amber wasn't kidding when she said magic gave them an advantage. Divi could see why she had a difficult time. Amber had to wait for them to come close to her, as she knew only a few projectile sword abilities Divi and Tasi could take out a group of salamanders with a single spell. *Maybe it was fate that I learned magic before this challenge.*

Other salamanders began to creep forward before jumping at them like lightning. These things were so fast! Divi ducked under one, while Tasi hit it with a spell before it could land. That didn't give her any rest, though, because four more replaced it. Based on their speed, she didn't think she would be able to unleash anything but her stun spell. She aimed the top of her staff forward as the four advanced toward her. Divi jabbed to keep them away from her, even causing the jewel in her staff to light up to scare them. The creatures backed off momentarily, but soon continued to force her back. She spotted an area of loose rock in the ceiling and used her telekinetic powers to drop it. The curious creatures followed her gaze upward, and as they did, the stones fell on top of them.

Amber was having her own problems. Most of the salamanders charged after her instead of the mages. She knocked a leaping one away with her sword, but still had at least ten surrounding her. Amber readied her weapon as two shadow salamanders attempted to strike from behind her. When she used a wind spell effect, a green wave emitted from the Holy Light and killed those two. She ducked underneath one and as another leapt toward her, she slammed the creature's face with the hilt. Amber kept using her wind effect because it could take out more than one at a time. The gale force that followed her attacks drove more of them back. One salamander was able to avoid her attacks and leapt toward her. There was no time to use her sword, so Amber high-kicked the creature. It landed in front of her, rattled. Amber spun her weapon so the blade faced behind her. She had to be careful. With its skin, it would be tough to stab it. Amber stepped on the salamander to hold it down and proceeded to drive her blade through its back. The salamander cried out in pain before dying.

When Amber looked up, all twenty had been killed. Tasi, based off his smile, was feeling very confident about their accomplishment.

He commented, "Well, that wasn't so bad."

As he said this, those bat-like sounds returned. Divi and Amber turned around, looking back at the sinkholes. Divi's focus shifted to the wall and ceiling, where it appeared a wave of black slime came toward them. There were so many of them! Amber hadn't been kidding when she said there were thousands.

Amber yelled, "Everybody run!"

She didn't have to repeat herself. They sprinted toward the hallway, followed by a sea of shadow salamanders. Amber and Tasi continued past the opening on the other side of the hallway, but Divi stopped there. She had to buy them some time. She brought her hands back and waited for the salamanders.

Tasi panicked when he saw she, instead waiting at the mouth of the hall. What was she doing?

"Divi! Get over here!"

She didn't pay attention to him. The first wave of salamanders were halfway down the tunnel. Divi closed her eyes.

"Heiromonn Fiyyama Ulltoma!"

Divi brought her hands forward, unleashing a fireball that encompassed the entire tunnel. It left nothing in its path untouched. The salamanders who had entered the hall were cleared away, along with scores of them who'd been awaiting their turn to enter.

Tasi froze. *Where did she learn that? I never taught her that.* He technically never could teach her that, as it was a sacred-blood version of a fireball. But who did she learn it from here?

Divi was pleased at the results of her attack. Apart from teaching her the spells of the gods that solidified her right as ruler, her father's spirit also taught her many incantations that only her kind could cast. As the next wave entered the room, Divi ran to her friends, who stared at the north wall.

"What's the problem?"

Gazing at the wall, though, Divi could see why they stopped. There was literally no place to go. It was a dead end. Was this all a trap?

245

When she turned around, more shadow salamanders had already entered the room. Many climbed the walls and onto the ceiling. They were totally surrounded and had no way to escape. Based on their slower advance, the creatures must have realized this too.

Tasi commented, "Well, it was nice knowing you."

"I'll be damned if I let these things finish me off when I'm this close!" Amber said.

She readied her sword's wind effect. She truly hoped that this wasn't their last stand. All her life she had made sacrifices to get this far. She did not want it to end this way. And, why would Neeza give her a quest that was impossible? Was Divi right about her father?

Divi readied another fireball, but she didn't know what good it would do. She wished it were possible to cast more than one spell at one time, though no mage in history had done that.

A loud roar overshadowed all the screeches that the shadow salamanders made. Many of them hid or scrambled back to the geyser room. At the second roar, all the rest of creatures scattered back into the volcano walls.

Divi commented, "This can't be good."

"Where is it coming from?" asked Tasi.

Looking around, they could see no doorway or anything. Suddenly, a slab of rock shifted left, swallowed by the walls. The gap it left behind lead to another room. Hot air rushed in their faces. They all stared at it.

Tasi finally asked, "What kind of volcano is this?"

Amber laughed before moving forward. As they entered the room, they stopped near the entrance. The floor was nothing but a bridge over a vast pool of lava. The pool was hundreds of feet below them, but that didn't stop the heat. Amber looked up a hole in the middle of the ceiling high above.

Amber said, "We're at the caldera. There is so much pressure from the heat in here that the top collapsed years ago. Only reason there hasn't been a major eruption in centuries as it allowed the heat to vent out instead of build up. Only minor ones, from what the locals tell me. We better pray this thing doesn't decide to erupt."

Amber led the way as usual. To Divi's continuing amazement, the half-mage's cooling tactic worked. She could feel the heat, especially in this room, but it seemed like an aura surrounded them, protecting them. Still, they traveled slowly over the lava pool. Even though the bridge was wide enough, it was a long way down with nothing separating one from the lava.

At the end of the bridge, a doorway led into a winding hall. For some reason, the further they went down it, the cooler the temperature got. Perhaps they were getting away from the lava, but she doubted that. This whole mountain was filled with insurmountable heat. Divi could feel it. She had noticed that her senses had gotten stronger since her father's spirit taught her all those spells.

At the end of the hall, a large room awaited. It was just like the second room they had been in, but much shorter. At the end, a small, open shrine had been set up at the summit of an elevated platform, with four torches lit. A set of crude stairs led to the top. But that wasn't the most important, for in the middle of the shrine was the Fire Relic. Surrounding the back and sides of the shrine appeared to be a large statue of a dragon. Amber's eyes grew wide as she saw it.

"There it is. The final one."

Tasi looked around the room. This couldn't be how they retrieved the final stone. Granted, the shadow salamanders were an inconvenience, but he was more concerned that they hadn't found the thing that scared them off.

For a few minutes, all they did was stare at the Relic. They each had the same insecure feeling about the situation, but who said it wouldn't be as easy as just taking it? Perhaps the volcano and the salamanders were the test.

Divi finally said, "I'm going for it."

When she began moving forward after grabbing a large satchel from Amber, the half-mage said, "Be careful. This is almost too easy compared to the others."

"Where's that guy like in the Water Temple?" Tasi asked. "Where is the dragon, for that matter?"

Amber searched the room. Tasi had a point.

"I don't know. He should've come out by now. Unless the shadow salamanders were considered the Guardian."

Tasi wanted to believe that, but for some reason he couldn't. For their sake, he hoped Amber and not he was right.

Divi did move cautiously. She felt something, but nothing out of the ordinary could be seen. The ground gradually sloped upwards where the platform was located. At the base, she climbed guarded up the stairs leading to the shrine. A strange wind seemed to blow as she approached, but it wasn't strong. Divi proceeded, her eyes focused on the Relic.

Amber and Tasi watched nervously as Divi got closer and closer. She was almost there, but Amber had a sense that Fafcul would show himself soon. She couldn't imagine any scenario where the dragon would just let them walk out with the prize. She commended Divi and this new-born courage she had. Learning magic had made her a new woman.

Amber commented, "She almost seems to want this thing more than I do."

"She's doing it for love," Tasi said.

Both watched as Divi stood in front of the relic. It was within arms' reach. Her sweating hands wrapped around the edges. As she picked it up, the light in the center glowed very brightly. She could feel the strong radiance emitting from the elemental stone.

The light slowly died down and the jewel returned to its darkened state. They'd done it. She had the final stone!

"Divi! Look out!"

She glanced to her right to see a large set of teeth charging toward her. She dropped off the platform, rolling down a couple of steps just before the teeth slammed shut just above her. Divi looked up and her eyes opened wide. The object she thought to be a statue ended up being Fafcul, the Fire Dragon. How did he remain so still? She didn't even notice him breathing. The color of his skin blended in with the surrounding stone. His whiskers almost reached the ground. He had folded wings, but Divi doubted he could fly anymore. *Where could he in a place like this?*

The dragon roared with displeasure.

Amber yelled, "Come on! This room is too small for this fight! Let's go back to the other side of the bridge!"

As she ran, the dragon spat out fire that blasted the floor in front of her. Amber fell backwards, narrowly avoiding being hit. The flames grew into a firewall blanketing everything on the other side of the door.

Tasi commented, "So much for that plan."

Fafcul roared once again. Divi knew they wouldn't get away from the dragon without a fight. She placed the stone in the satchel and ran toward her friends. Fafcul fully stood up on his hind legs, knocking over the pedestal the relic sat on with its wide body, and confronted them. His stance was forbidding.

Amber suggested, "Split up! Try to combo it! Use ice or water magic!"

Divi went to the left while Tasi moved to the right. Amber stayed directly in front the dragon while Fafcul moved its head, trying to keep the three in view. Amber made the first move by charging at it. She readied an effect and fired a ball of ice just past the dragon's head. It ended up hitting a stalagmite, freezing it solid.

Tasi, seeing this, shot a fireball at the top of the frozen stalagmite. Broken off, the stalagmite plummeted and pierced the dragon . . . barely. Fafcul looked at the small wound he sustained and shook off the frozen stone.

That wasn't a good sign. It was going to take a lot of magic to disable it. Maybe even more than they could expend. Although Divi was confident her limits had grown higher since her father taught her all those spells, she had no idea what those limits were. Even sacred-bloods had their breaking points. And would these more powerful spells drain her faster than those Tasi trained her in?

Responding to their attacks, the dragon grasped a couple boulders. Suddenly, the rocks were set ablaze. Amber backed off a little. She didn't like this. It apparently could set anything it touched on fire.

The dragon threw both stones, one toward Amber and the other toward Tasi. Both came in fast, barely missing them. Amber had to dodge twice as the boulder ricocheted off the wall back toward her. The one thrown at Tasi rolled along, and he was able to recuperate faster than Amber.

Divi suddenly had an idea. "Tasi! Fire an ice sheet and make it hover over the dragon!"

Tasi had not used this method since he trained to learn magic. It was one of those "situational" spells that mages rarely used. For that reason, its mastery was never stressed . . . or practiced. He really hoped he remembered how to create the sheet and hold it.

Tasi chanted, "*Icceron Hootony!*"

A ball of ice shot out from his hand and past the creature. Instead of hitting the wall, it hovered over the dragon and flattened to form a thin sheet of ice. Tasi struggled to keep the spell above the dragon, shaking with the strain, but so far so good.

Divi concentrated hard.

She finally chanted, "*Ytomma Storamaa, furrarr badaran!*"

250

A large cloud formed over the ice sheet and unleashed a downpour of rain. As they passed through the ice, the droplets became frozen needles that poured on the dragon's back. The dragon yelled in pain.

Tasi stared, amazed at what he saw. *Most impressive.* Quite an advanced spell, especially for one who just began to truly understand magic a couple weeks ago. Still, the spell did little to physically hurt the dragon, and eventually it dissipated.

It took a while for Fafcul to recuperate, disoriented after having thousands of small needles driven into him. He swung his tail aimlessly, as if hoping to make any contact with its attackers. Amber and Divi both ducked under some very close attempts, but Tasi wasn't so lucky. The tail connected and threw him against the wall.

Divi yelled, "Tasi!"

Because of the magnitude, he was slow to realize what was going on. When he did, he saw that his robe was on fire. He yelled and put it out with a simple water spell, then stared at the damage.

Tasi said to himself, "And people think mages are crazy for wearing these things."

Seeing he was okay, Divi returned her focus to Fafcul, who was recovering from the last attack. She brought her hands back and readied her next spell.

Divi chanted, "*Icceron Spiyyoli!*"

She brought her hands forward, ejecting the blue orb that had formed in them toward the dragon. As she did, the ball broke up into five ice spears. Each stabbed the dragon with haunting accuracy, strong enough to pierce its tough hide and scales. Fafcul yelled in pain, but it was short lived. It violently shook its body, which sent the ice spears flying back toward its attackers. Once again, all three were forced to be on the defensive.

Divi didn't know what else they could do to it. Whenever they penetrated its skin, the dragon just shook it

251

off after a few seconds and continued to attack. She couldn't even tell if it was bleeding because the blood, if there was any, matched the color of its scales.

When Divi recovered, she realized that the dragon raised its head. As it opened its mouth, she could see that it was full of fire. Amber and Tasi were still recovering from the last attack, so it was going to be up to her. The dragon lowered its head forward and spewed fire toward her.

She held her hands out and chanted, "*Shuiellda vetcuum!*"

A purple wall formed in front of her just as the flames were about to reach her. The flames had no chance of penetrating Divi's spell. She gave a small smile, seeing its success. Fafcul, though, suddenly swept his flames to her left—right toward Amber and Tasi!

"No!"

Divi, keeping the wall spell activated, ran to keep up with the flame.

Amber, who was bandaging a cut she received from one of the ice spears, looked up to see the flame approaching. Seeing there was no way to outrun it, she put her arms up in defense, hoping that it would miss. Luckily for Amber, Divi arrived and blocked the head of the flame as she outran it.

Fafcul, seeing that Amber was still fazed by its last attack, directed more fire breath toward her. Divi would not be able to block this attack. Instead, she held her hand out and chanted an icy mist toward Amber, who once more held her arms up in instinctive defense.

She was startled not to feel the heat of the fire. It almost felt . . . cold. Amber opened her eyes to see a bluish mist negating the flame just in front of her. *Boy, am I ever happy that Divi decided to learn magic!*

Seeing his attack had failed once again, the dragon looked toward Divi. He could obviously see that if he wanted to win, he had to take out this powerful magic user. Divi stared at Fafcul, showing no fear, but rather anger.

She said, "That's it. We need to end this now."

Divi brought her hand back and a large ball formed in her it.

Tasi was fascinated. His pupil looked like she had been casting magic her entire life. The confidence she showed took even him aback. Gone was the girl afraid of her choices and the uncertain future. She had a purpose, and although he didn't agree with it, if it helped them survive these dragons, he wouldn't look back. There would be time to lecture her about Levus later.

"Heiromonn Fiyyama Ulltoma!"

Divi unleashed the massive fireball toward the dragon. All it could do was stare, much like deer did at torch fire in the night. The fireball struck with so much force that it knocked Fafcul onto its side. The gaping wound it left near the dragon's belly seeped blood that smoked like lava.

Amber quickly ran over to Divi. "What's your idea?"

Divi yelled, "Freeze a rock and get close to the wound! Then freeze it from the outside in! I'll finish it off!"

Amber liked her idea. Innovative and original. Never once had she considered beating a dragon that way. Not a normal trait of a sword, hers could penetrate stone as easily it could skin. Perhaps that special jewel she used when making the Holy Light allowed her to do these unique skills. She dashes to the left, stabbing a stone along the way. The dragon was slow to get up, roaring with displeasure. Divi thought that it would be difficult to distract it, but she could see that it was already angry at her . . . very angry. Flames burst from its nostrils each time it breathed.

Tasi wanted to run, but Divi stopped him.

"No. If we move, he might see Amber."

He said, "I wish I had your courage."

Fafcul grew ever closer. The walls that it touched became an inferno. Divi could even see the fire in its eyes. The dragon roared louder than ever before, and Tasi shook with fear at every step it took. Divi, though, stood pat. Out of the corner of her eye, she could see Amber closing in on the large wound inflicted by her spell. She hoped Amber would reach it soon. Even though Divi had confidence in her, it waned the closer Fafcul approached.

Amber was within twenty feet from the dragon's wound when, much to her delight, it finally stopped moving. Yet she knew this meant he was in striking range of the two mages. She had to act quickly. Amber froze the stone and charged for her target.

Fafcul roared one more time before cocking its head back and preparing to spit fire at them. Unable to watch, Tasi hid behind Divi, who still stood firm even in this grim situation. She had her eyes closed, but not in fear. She was concentrating. In her mind, she could see and feel everything going around her. She saw how close the dragon was to turning them into charred corpses, but also how close Amber was. She had to show the same faith in Amber that Amber had showed in them.

Fafcul was bringing its head forward to emit its flames when it suddenly cried in pain. The flame in its mouth rushed to the ceiling. He began to spit fire aimlessly. Amber pushed the stone deeper into the wound as she used an ice spell effect. The flesh in and around the wound was already turning noticeably blue. As the dragon tried to shoot fire, nothing but frozen mist ejected from his mouth. He could see his defeat was near, but he wouldn't go down without trying to take someone with him. The dragon brought his head toward Divi and Tasi. Amber grabbed on to Fafcul's scales, which were cooling to the touch, as she kept the ice stone in the wound.

Divi still had her eyes closed. She could see ice grew along the dragon's scales, but would it be enough to stop him from fulfilling his last attack?

Amber could see how slow it was going, so she clenched her sword tighter, strengthening the ice ability's potency. Fafcul's mouth was only twenty feet from Divi and Tasi.

Divi suddenly lost her concentration and everything went black. That might be for the best. If the dragon was about to claim her life, she didn't want to see it.

Amber screamed as she pushed the Holy Light deeper in the dragon and used her powers to her fullest. A wave of blue light emitted from her sword.

Suddenly, everything went silent. Was she dead? A blast of cool breath slammed against her face. Divi slowly opened her eyes. She jumped when she saw the frozen mouth of the dragon inches away from her face.

Tasi finally got up and looked at what transpired. His reaction was more exaggerated, as he backed up to the wall about ten feet behind them.

Amber, who still had the Holy Light embedded in the creature's wound, sat on the cavern floor, obviously exhausted. That was the first time she became this tired using her spells since her first day of training to be a battlemage. She finally got up and pulled her sword out.

Divi walked over to Tasi. "Are you okay?"

"Yeah, I'm fine. I just never want to see another dragon for as long as I live."

Divi chuckled as she turned to face the frozen dragon. It was time to finish it off and get out of here. She brought her hands back and readied her powerful fireball.

Just then Amber stepped in front of her and put her arm on Divi's. What was she doing? Why wasn't she letting her destroy Fafcul?

Amber said, "No, Divi. Our job was to defeat the dragon and in victory, take the relic."

She brought her left arm up to reveal Divi's satchel containing the fire relic. "We have won the prize and the dragon is defeated. I have frozen everything in him except his heart. When he defrosts, he'll just do what he does. Let it go."

Divi relaxed her arms and negated her spell. Amber was right. Leviadon, after he had taken enough hits, rescinded back into hiding. Divi remembered what Amber had said about a Dragonian perishing because the dragon they were associated with died. She didn't want that on her conscience. Maybe Fafcul would return to its slumber when the ice melted. She didn't want to wait around and find out.

Divi said, "Let's get out of here."

Amber and Tasi agreed and they walked out of Fafcul's lair. The rush of heat as they stepped into the caldera room was almost a knockout punch. Tasi tried to wave air in front of his face, but even that was hot.

Divi commented, "It got a lot hotter here."

"Your ice stones must be melting," Amber said. "We need to get out of here fast."

The ground began to shake violently. All three fell, but Tasi nearly rolled off the bridge. Amber grabbed onto his robe in order to stop him. After a few seconds, the earth lay silent again. They stood up and looked around.

Tasi asked, "What was that?"

Amber glanced down to the lava pool. It seemed very active compared to when they first passed over the bridge. Another small tremor caused some rocks to drop into the lava. That wasn't the only thing happening. A slab of stone dropped in front of the hall that lead to Fafcul' lair. If they had forgotten anything in there, it belonged to the Fire Dragon now.

Divi said, "I don't like the sound of this."

"Bloody hell beast!" Amber cursed. "Fafcul must have been the only thing keeping this place from erupting! With him defeated and frozen right now, I think it's ready to blow."

At the far end of the bridge, the slab of rock that opened after the shadow salamanders left them started closing. It was their only way out.

"Run!"

256

Amber and the mages started to sprint as fast as they could. They had to get past that advancing stone before it was too late. The extreme heat Divi and Tasi felt as the ice on the stones melted made it more difficult to move.

Divi was thankful that it took a long time for the hallway to be closed off. Despite the violent shaking, they were able to remain upright. Amber was the first to make it through. By that time, the slab was two-thirds of the way closed. Divi rushed in after her. Both women looked back to see that Tasi was struggling to make it. His long robe posed as much of a challenge as the heat.

Divi yelled, "Come on, Tasi!"

Tasi staggered, trying to see through the increasing haze. The slab had lowered so far that a man would struggle to fit through the crack it left. Tasi screamed, the heat becoming unbearable. He had to do something. He dove toward the shrinking space. The slab slammed shut just as his legs passed through it. Divi and Amber sighed with relief at the close call. Tasi wiped sweat off his brow, knowing full well that he was lucky to make it.

As he tried to get up, something stopped his progress and he fell to the ground again. He saw that while he had made it past the stone, some of his robe hadn't. Fabric had been caught between the slab and the mountain rock of the hallway.

"I'm stuck!"

Divi ran over to him and both mages tried their best to pull it out, but it was useless. The robe was caught too tightly.

Amber had grown tired of this. They had to get moving and she didn't want to die because of some silly robe. She unsheathed the Holy Light and walked to Divi's side.

Divi asked, "Can you help us pull this out?"

Amber didn't answer with words, but with action. She grabbed the robe near where it was stuck, raised her sword, and sliced the fabric free from the stone. Both mages stared at Amber, Divi a little surprised, Tasi remaining on the ground in shock.

She said, "Come on. Let's go."

"I only get one of these a year!" Tasi yelled. "Cutting a robe is a huge insult in Myyril!"

"Who needs the robes anyway?" Divi countered, to further his shock. "They should follow my style. More agile, and no need to worry about what just happened."

Divi walked past him and Amber followed her, smiling.

"I like this new her," the half-mage commented. "Reminds me of myself."

She rushed to catch up with Divi. Tasi didn't know if he liked this new Divi. Though her mother had been very much like this in her early days, from what Neeza told him. She dressed differently and spoke differently than the other mages, so it must not have been difficult for Divi to pick up on her mother's habits.

Tasi went after them into the room that Amber labeled as the most dangerous. Lava was no longer coming from the walls, though the bubbling could still be heard. The geysers, however, now spouted constantly.

Divi stopped her running, much to the confusion of Amber and Tasi. She felt something coming. Some *things*. None were large, but there were many of them.

Amber asked, "What's the matter?"

Before Divi could answer, the ground shook. This time, it didn't stop. Divi did the only thing she could think of doing: run. Amber and Tasi followed her lead. It was at this moment that the shadow salamanders exited their hiding places.

Amber and Tasi both turned to see their new pursuers, cursing. Before, it had been apparent that Fafcul caused fear even among these creatures. With the dragon neutralized for

258

the moment, the salamanders now had complete command of the area.

The uncontrollable shaking wasn't helping matters, either.

Divi nearly fell numerous times into the holes the geysers shot out from as they made their way toward the lava room.

From there, she could see the gate of the temple far ahead, though hazily. As the ground shuddered, lava splashed onto the riverbanks, forming molten puddles.

"No time to wait around," Amber said. "We have to keep moving"

Tasi added, "I think my ice rock is nearly melted. It's getting too hot."

They both had a point. It was getting very hot and if they stayed here any longer, she and Tasi might not make it. Divi looked back down the short hallway from the previous room to see the shadow salamanders coming their way. Despite their speed and adaptation to living in the heat, they were not equipped for the shaking. Many slipped, fell, or crashed into each other. Still, they were closing in on them.

Divi yelled, "Get to the entrance! I'll slow them down!"

Tasi tried to get her to go with them, but Amber grabbed his robe and forced him to run. She knew if she didn't get Tasi out of here, and fast, he wouldn't make it. For all his talk about how good his robe was, it didn't seem helpful in keeping the ice block cold any longer.

Divi stared down the hallway and concentrated, finally chanting, "*Heiromonn Fiyyama Ulltoma!*"

She unleashed another large fireball, taking out every shadow salamander in its path. Amber and Tasi, meanwhile, made it to the small bridge, the only obstacle keeping them from the entrance. The river underneath was flowing rapidly and some splashed on the bridge itself. It gave Tasi second thoughts.

Amber yelled, "Get going!"

"I'm not leaving without Divi!" he said.

"I'll get her! You need to get out now! I don't know how long until your ice stone is completely melted! Divi will be the least of your worries then!"

Amber gave Tasi a helpful nudge as he moved onto the thin bridge, and he sprinted as fast as he could across it while trying to avoid the splashing lava. Once he made it to the other side, he fell to the ground and began to crawl toward the exit. When Amber saw that Tasi had safely passed, she ran to Divi.

"*Heiromonn Fiyyama Ulltoma!*"

Divi unleashed another fireball with the same results. She could see, though, that her attacks were useless. The salamanders just kept coming. Sweat poured from her face. Her stone had to be nearly melted.

Amber made it to her, "Come on!"

Divi realized that there was nothing more she could do, so she pelted all-out toward the entrance. Amber glanced into the next room one last time to see another wave of shadow salamanders advancing. Amazing—with all the surrounding chaos they were still trying to kill them. She'd have thought self-preservation would become their top priority.

As she stepped on the thin bridge, the part of it which Divi fell on during her first trip over it began to crack further. She nearly lost her footing, but kept her balance long enough to make it across.

Amber was slowing down as she headed to the bridge. The extreme heat was finally getting to her, to the point that walking was a difficult chore. With the shadow salamanders getting closer, Amber reached the bridge and, relieved, took a first heavy step.

When she did, the loosened part from Divi's fall finally broke. Amber screamed as she began to plummet toward the lava river.

Divi shouted, "Amber!"

Amber was able to grab the edge of the remaining bridge. Despite Divi's relief, she knew that the weight of Amber with all her armor would weaken the rest quickly. Amber strained to pull herself up. A few salamanders had gathered behind her at the bank of the river, and they looked ready to pounce. Divi fired a few stun spells that Tasi taught her, hitting her targets with haunting accuracy.

Amber continued struggling, grasping whatever outcrop she could to pull herself onto the bridge. She couldn't blame Divi for not stepping on it again. She wasn't even sure if the bridge could support their combined weight. As she flailed her legs, a drip of lava splashed onto her exposed calf. She shrieked. She'd never known what true pain was until now, but screaming was the only thing she could do to acknowledge the wound. She had to get out of this. Amber mustered all the strength she had and was finally able to pull herself up.

Divi fired three more spells as Amber made it onto the bridge. The half-mage was breathing heavily and appeared to be holding her leg as she slowly crawled. Divi felt her pain.

She yelled, "Come on, Amber!"

Amber's leg stung with every movement. She heard the rocks below her crack. She didn't have much time before the stone gave way.

Divi looked at Amber, who displayed a strange mixture of pain and joy. What was she doing? Why wasn't she moving? She wanted to use her telekinetic powers, but she'd exhausted them to drive the shadow salamanders off of Amber. She needed a break, especially since she wasn't sure yet what her limits were.

As the stone began to collapse, Amber threw herself toward Divi. She couldn't believe the pain that shot down her leg. It traveled through her body like she was stabbed.

Divi looked down to see the stone bridge beginning to crumble at her feet. "Jump!"

Amber leapt just as the bridge completely fell into the lava river. She landed inches away from the edge. Both women watched as the melting fragments were carried away.

Amber commented, "I hate this place."

As she said this, both looked at the thousands of shadow salamanders covering the walls, floor, and ceiling. Yet Divi noticed that not one of them passed the lava that Amber just had to cross. They growled and hissed at the them, yet did nothing.

Divi finally said, "Let's get out of here."

She helped Amber, who limped, wincing with every step. As they passed through the temple's vast doors, the salamanders returned to their places of rest, leaving the cave silent once again.

CHAPTER 13
The King of Dragons

From a distance, all three watched the erupting volcano. In all honesty, it could have been more impressive. It wasn't a large eruption, and most of the lava and smoke spewed on the opposite side of the canyon, not reaching them. Some ash had fallen when they first escaped, but hardly enough to cause any breathing problems, only to give them gray faces. Divi and Tasi stood while Amber sat down, tending to her wound. Divi's ice spell helped lessen the inflammation, allowing her to do what she needed to do to heal.

Both mages had removed the dragon scales letting their thawed rocks roll down the side of the mountain. Based on the dry condition of their stones, they were both lucky to still be alive.

A smile grew on Amber's face. "I can't believe it. After all these years, my task is completed!"

Divi glanced in her direction to see a tear fall. She felt sorry for her. As a half-mage, one waited a lifetime for the opportunity to be a paladin. All Amber had to do was bring the pieces back to Myyril. This must be a day she had looked forward to since she was born.

Amber added, "Of course, first we help your friend with them."

Divi nodded and faced Tasi, who was still watching the volcano. He looked exhausted.

Amber patted Divi on the shoulder as she passed her by, heading down the mountain. "Let's get back to camp, get the other stones, and get out of here."

Tasi, finally alone with Divi, had to ask her. He had to find out the truth of how she learned all those spells. There was no such thing as an awakening that would cause a mage to all of a sudden acquire so many new spells. It took

263

practice and years of dedicated studying, and they had neither here on Dragonia.

Divi noticed his staring and asked, "What's wrong, Tasi?"

"How did you do some of those spells? I never taught you any of those."

She didn't know how to answer. Would he believe her if she told him the truth? She supposed not, but what else could she say?

"My father taught me."

She walked past him, touching his shoulder lightly. He was still unconvinced. Her father was dead. There was no way that he could have done what she said.

"No more games. You can tell me the truth. You did read the magic books back home, didn't you?"

"I did no such thing. Those books would have bored me then."

Divi flashed him a smile as she continued to follow Amber down. Tasi wanted to get to the bottom of this. It was a long walk back to the camp, though, and he would have some time to get the answer. He rushed after Divi.

Amber, Divi, and Tasi walked next to each other at the edge of the forest, where it met the plains. The mountains holding the Fire Temple had become a faint image in the distance. These plains seemed hilly compared to the other plains of the continent. Amber opted to stay near but not within the forest because, she claimed, none of the feared monsters of this place went beyond its outskirts. That is why she made most of her camps near the southern edge.

They were just to the north of what looked like a large tower, which they passed on their way up. Amber had seemed most persistent in staying away from it. They had never gone more than five hundred feet away from some type of cover. She never gave them a reason, but her eyes almost never left the skies. Now, however, she didn't seem too worried about it, walking easily with an arm across Divi's shoulder. What was different now that they had the final stone?

Ahead of them lay ruins, so grand and vast they must have once been an ancient city. An archway leading into the old metropolis must have looked beautiful when it had residents due to the intricate designs she could see. Temples and buildings remarkably similar in design to those in the Myyrilian marketplace stuck out amongst the rest. The stone on every structure appeared weathered and cracked, even from their distance. Divi had noticed them on their way to face Fafcul, but she had been so focused on the Fire Stone that nothing else seemed important. Now she wondered if this was where the Dragonians used to call home, and what had happened here. She could have asked Amber, but would she know? This was not her home.

"Hey, Divi. I just wanted to let you know that you were great in there. That magic was awesome! I take back anything negative I said about you."

Divi replied, "As do I with thoughts."

All three laughed. Suddenly, as they passed a large stone, Divi stopped dead in her tracks. Amber and Tasi moved forward on a few paves before noticing that she wasn't with them.

Amber glanced at her with a smile. "Well, come on. We're not going to get to camp with you just standing there."

Divi asked, "Don't you hear something? Listen."

Amber and Tasi turned in every direction. It sounded normal enough. Birds were chirping and the common insects buzzed.

Amber looked at Tasi before returning her gaze to Divi.

"Divi, I don't hear . . ."

"Shhh! Listen."

Amber once again went quiet, trying to hear what Divi heard. To her surprise, another noise *could* be heard, albeit faintly. Amber climbed to the top of a small hill. She could see the entire clearing from her angle. Tasi and Divi joined her.

Tasi asked, "What in the world is that?"

"I don't think that's the question we should be asking," Amber replied. "How many?"

A large group of animals came charging out of the forest. Amber stared in disbelief. Large creatures and small, herbivore and carnivores, and they were all running together.

Divi asked, "What's going on?"

"I don't like this. I'm watching predators running next to their favorite foods. They are afraid of something."

"Umm, I think we should find some cover," Tasi said, "because if you hadn't noticed, they are headed straight for us."

Amber dashed down the hill, both mages at her heels. The rumbling was getting louder as well as the shrieks of Dragonia's wildlife. The thick grass made it hard to keep up any speed. No sooner did they reach the bottom of the hill did the first wave of creatures appear over the top of it.

Amber yelled, "Get some distance!"

A massive, scaly creature known as graysclah, avoided her while she had to squeeze through two elk with long legs. Behind the elk charged three carverinns, ape-like animals that typically were aggressive hunters. Followed close behind and passing were herds of olisers, long-necked omnivore birds, which were twice the size of a human. Normally territorial with other herds, they ran together with panic in their eyes. The rumbling made it very difficult to stand, much less run. Amber weaved left and right so as not to be knocked down by other animals.

Tasi seemed to run with the speed of a god when he saw the creatures. Quite amazing, considering how the robe tended to slow him down. He was the first to make it to the "safety" of a natural niche from an elevated hill edge as his reward.

Divi turned her head to see five large wolves called fenrises moving her way. The first one evaded her, though she had to stop and drop to avoid being hit by its tail. She dived to her left, a wolf's huge paw landing on the ground where she had been a moment before. The ground was rumbling so loud it was almost deafening. She began to lose her bearings.

Amber turned and stopped. Behind Divi was a verritiss, a tall, hind-legged herbivore known for their defensive spiky tails, with a partial tree trunk stuck to its tail. It must have struck it exiting the woods or from the many logs being kicked by other fleeing animals. It had to know something was attached as the trunk had to slow the creature down, but its panic made it not care. Divi was too preoccupied with the remaining fenrises to take notice of it.

Amber yelled, "Look out!"

Divi's eyes grew as she saw the timber coming toward her.

Tasi, from his shelter among the rocks, also noticed Divi's predicament. He tried to cast a spell, but it just wouldn't work. He knew why. . . he was afraid. All the incantations seemed jumbled in his mind. He felt so helpless.

"Divi! Duck!"

For some reason, she couldn't move. Her body froze on her. There was no time to even get a spell off to destroy the log, which, connected to the verritiss' tail, had come within ten feet of Divi.

From out of nowhere, Amber tackled her to the ground. With both flat on their backs, the tree trunk sailed a couple inches from their faces. A large foot coming down toward Amber followed. She quickly rolled opposite of Divi as the animal just missed stepping on her. The trunk disconnected from its tail, continuing to roll toward the fault scarp.

She helped Divi up, and they ran side-by-side with some the most feared hunting creatures on the continent. The half-mage didn't want to know what was coming.

They finally made it underneath the stone where Tasi was waiting.

He exclaimed, "I'm glad you two are safe."

They stayed underneath the rock until the wildlife stopped coming. The rumbling could be heard past them now. Amber got out, then, and ran to the top of the rock. Divi and Tasi joined her, and they watched the animal masses reenter the forest on the other side of the ruined city.

Tasi was going to ask what could cause this, but a loud roar from the north answered his question. The three adventurers turned toward the source of the sound. For a few moments, all was silent.

They couldn't see anything yet, but Divi could feel that whatever was coming was bigger than Fafcul. She had sensed it before, twice. A chill ran down her skin.

A thundering vibration echoed in the clearing, getting closer and closer. Tasi felt like it surrounded them.

Amber could barely even say, "Oh no! I hoped to avoid this."

Tasi asked, "Avoid what?"

Suddenly, from the northern forest, a dragon flew toward them at an incredible speed. Amber forced Divi and Tasi to duck and they barely missed getting run through with its claws. As the dragon lifted straight into the air, Divi and the others stood up and stared. The dragon beat its great black wings as it hovered, every flap sounded like thunder. From what Divi could tell, the dragon had to have at least ten heads. Its underside scales were a dark grey, and its back scales were black, very similar in color to the shadow salamanders'. The tail was very thin for the dragon's size.

Divi asked, "What is that?"

Amber explained, "That is the Wind Dragon, also known as the King of the Dragons. He's called Tiiamite."

"I thought you defeated all the dragons?" Tasi yelled.

"This one was too powerful for me alone. I tricked him, got him tangled in a room full of chains, and took the relic. I've hid from him for nearly a year."

"I can see why he's angry with you!"

Tiiamite turned toward the three of them before charging down at full speed. Its claws were wide open.

Amber yelled, "Brace yourself!"

The dragon was within twenty feet of them when something knocked Tiiamite from its course. Amber, who had her eyes closed, cracked them open to see what was going on. When the dust settled, her eyes opened wide at the sight of a white dragon squaring off against Tiiamite.

"Gerritonnee! Get out of here now!" screamed Amber.

Gerritonnee heard her friend's plea, but she was in too deep to turn back now. Tiiamite was much stronger than herself, but if fighting bought Amber even a few moments, then it would be worth it. Both dragons snapped at each other, but neither got close. Gerritonnee breathed a fireball toward Tiiamite, who blocked it with his large wings. From inside Tiiamite's wings, Amber saw a purple glow.

She fruitlessly yelled, "Gerritonnee! Leave! Please!"

Tiiamite spread its enclosed wing, from which a large purple fireball connected with Gerritonnee. She flew almost a hundred yards before slamming into the forest. Trees that had stood there for ages cracked like twigs as the dragon collided with them. Gerritonnee voiced a cry of pain before losing consciousness.

Anger grew in Amber's eyes as they returned to Tiiamite.

"No!"

Her cry would have caused anyone's spine to shiver and strike fear into anyone's heart. She became a mad-woman, firing any projectile sword spell she knew as she charged toward Tiiamite. Divi and Tasi tried to stop her, but

269

were no match against her strong emotions. Tiiamite's attention shifted toward Amber, and all ten heads roared, as if hoping to intimidate its attacker. He should have known better. It would take more than noise to deter the half-mage after what he did.

Tiiamite hovered off the ground, which his long tail still brushed. Amber was near the edge of the fault scarp when Divi and Tasi caught up to her, struggling to pull her back.

Tiiamite spat a white fireball where Amber once stood, rock shattering from the impact.

Amber yelled, "Let me go!"

"Control yourself!" Divi yelled back. "We need you to settle down if we are going to win!"

Amber looked at her and finally shook the mages off, turning back toward Tiiamite. Through the dust, she stared deeply into the dragon's eyes. The hatred the two felt for each other burned in the air, white-hot as the fireball. Amber readied her sword.

"This ends now," she said. "No one hurts a friend of mine and gets away with it!"

Six of Tiiamite's heads roared. Divi didn't know how they would defeat this dragon. It was three times the size of Fafcul and seemingly ten times more aggressive. He flew slightly higher so his tail was no more than a couple feet off the ground. The wind from his wings pulled at Amber and Divi's hair and Tasi's robes. Their thunderous sound was almost deafening this close to it.

Amber unleashed an ice technique, aiming toward Tiiamite's stomach, before she took cover among some of the branches and tree trunks dragged into the clearing by the wildlife during their escape. Her attack was ineffective against the dragon's tough skin. With a roar, Tiiamite landed and began to snap her sheltering logs with its powerful steps.

Tasi tried to hit it with a light spell of his own, if only to draw it off. His attack was no more successful than

270

Amber's. Tiiamite wasn't even fazed as he uncovered the half-mage.

Amber knew all too well it would give up eight of its ten heads to slay her at this moment for the disgrace she did. What the king of dragons didn't realize was that she would give her life to avenge Gerritonnee if he had mortally wound her.

Amber began weaving through the fallen logs as Tiiamite kept breaking them. Although she was glad these trunks were here, most likely moved by the former residents of the ruins behind them to the top of this fault scarp, her cover wasn't going to last very long. She nearly fell over when one of Tiiamite's heads bit at the tree trunk near her. *Damn! How did he get so close?* She tried her best to get out of view, but the king of dragons saw her. Three of his heads shot white fire. Wood and dirt flew in the air. A fireball landed just in front of her, and she fell in the crater left in its wake. Ears ringing, she tried to recover.

Tiiamite reared above her, ready to shoot another fireball directly into the crater.

A large spell hit from the side, preventing his attack. Tiiamite turned its heads to see Divi near the edge of the fault scarp, another fireball in her hand.

"Heiromonn Fiyyama Ulltoma!"

The second magic spell connected with the dragon's hide. Much to Tasi's surprise, Divi's spells were hurting it! That was a plus in the sea of minuses. The only bad thing was that now Divi would be the prime target. Tiiamite knew how effective her spells were, which meant trouble.

Tasi yelled, "Divi! Move! Hide!"

She didn't need him to tell her. Tiiamite lifted off the broken trunks heading directly toward her. She quickly leapt over the alcove to the ground below. The dragon tried to snatch her when she jumped, barely missing. Divi ran toward the tree trunks and took shelter inside them. Many were hollow, probably thanks to insect infestations. She

271

wasn't complaining. It might be the only thing keeping her alive at the moment.

As she crawled inside the longest hollow trunk, she could feel the vibrations of Tiiamite coming closer. It was haunting hearing the echoes of his footsteps. Just as she was about to escape out the other end of the trunk, it abruptly tilted back. She could see Tiiamite's enormous claws at the bottom, but not for long, as one of his heads began biting at the log. Then another head . . . and then another. Divi ran as fast as she could before it made her dinner.

When she made it to the other end, she leapt out. She had to be at least thirty feet in the air. Tiiamite was right up to her even though he still held the trunk, not even extending his body to do it. She greatly underestimated his enormous size, as it surpassed her wooden shelter.

As one of the heads tried to grab Divi out of the air, she yelled, "*Heiromonn Fiyyama Ulltoma!*"

The fireball connected with four of the heads, causing Tiiamite to retreat briefly into the air. Divi had enough time to land as softly and run back up to the others. When she arrived, Tasi was helping Amber out of the crater. Both looked dazed and spooked.

Tasi exclaimed, "Divi! You're all right!"

"Yeah, but not for long. I fazed it, but it will be back very soon. We can't fight it out in the open like this. He'll kill us for sure."

Amber looked behind them and smiled. *That was the answer!*

"Over there! We can fight it in city! Maybe do to Tiiamite what we did to Fafcul!"

That was a good plan. Sure, the buildings were old and the walls barely standing, but if they could remain hidden long enough to hit Tiiamite with enough powerful spells, then maybe they could beat him. The adventurers sprinted toward the city grounds.

They could hear Tiiamite roar out of sight, but not nearly far enough away. Time was not on their side. As they passed the gates, Divi noticed some writing on them. It read Al'Huriman in the common tongue. That must have been the name of the city before it was deserted. The roars got louder. As Divi passed through the gate, Tiiamite landed on top of the fault scarp they just left. She knew it saw them, or at least her, because it shot a white fireball at the gate. Divi dodged the flames and the falling rubble as it crashed in the building ahead. The dragon roared as he approached the city.

When he arrived in what must have been the town square, he stopped. Everything was silent. Tiiamite scanned the ruins, looking for any clues to the locations of his prey. He knew they were there. The city was vast, but he would decimate these entire ruins if it meant defeating the one who tricked him out of his stone.

With every step the mighty beast took, the ancient stones of the streets were crushed to pebbles. His long, thin tail, which had as much bite as his teeth, whipped around as he hoped to hit them by chance.

Tiiamite finally spoke in a deep voice that echoed though the ruins of Al'Huriman. "Cunamma, cunamma fulasa huwarlii, mii theriiva berranii! Knessi sunnana. Cannaata ceimma ferranii." *(Come out, come out wherever you are, my troubled thieves! I know you're here. You cannot hide forever.)*

The King of Dragons continued to stalk them. Divi, hiding in a nearby house, trembled with fear at its voice. It had the power to shake the stone walls. She had a feeling it would have done so even if they were soundly built yesterday, not left to decay over years of neglect.

Tiiamite spoke again, this time in the common tongue. *"Perhaps I can be better understood to you now. It is no use hiding. I will find you. All I want is the warrior woman. I will even let the rest of you go free. She must pay for her trickery! If you choose to side with her, then you will die with her."*

Amber tried to move into a better position to attack. She was on the third floor of some building, trotting as softly as she could. It was hard because loose stones clattered under each step. She heard the dragon's offer. Although her gut told her she should be worried because her companions were mages, for once, she was going to listen to her heart. They wouldn't desert her.

Divi, from her vantage point, saw Tasi hiding behind a wall on the north side of the city. The streets were all wide enough to accommodate the size of a dragon, which made sense if the Dragonians and the dragons were as close as they were thought to be. Tiiamate passed both mages, walking deeper into the ruins.

Tasi telepathically said to Divi, "Try to come to me. We can coordinate an attack on this thing."

She dashed toward him. It got deathly quiet. They couldn't even hear Tiiamite's footsteps. Maybe he had moved far enough away to be out of earshot.

She wasn't far from Tasi when an explosion suddenly rocked about the area. Disoriented, Tasi crawled, struggling to reach a hiding spot. Divi heard Tiiamite's thunderous wings and saw him hovering with a plaza at least a hundred feet wide between them. She glanced over to be certain Tasi was okay before facing the King of Dragons, who came close enough to sniff at her.

"You are the one who is causing the strange ripples in the Eirzalif. I was close to finding you days ago. You are powerful, little one. But you are nothing when compared to me, the mighty Tiiamite! I have seen many of your kind fall. I know you know where my stone is. Tell me!"

She had to be honest with herself, the ten staring heads intimidated her. As scared as she was, though, this conversation as well as when he spoke entering the city showed one of Tiiamite's hands. She knew which head was the main one now. She would need to focus on that one.

Divi yelled, "I will not! I need the stone to save my friend . . . the one I care about! If you are the only thing standing between me and saving him, then I will defeat you!"

Tiiamite laughed. "*Ah, love! The simplest of mortal emotions next to anger. Your dedication will not be enough. I am not letting you leave with my stone! Not unless you pry my body from the ground!*"

Divi stood confidently, trying to mask her fear. "If that is what it takes, then I am sorry. Your reign as the King of Dragons will end."

"*You reek of fear, little one! If you will not give me my stone, then your fate is death!*"

Tiiamite prepared to breathe a fireball at Divi while she began readying one of her strongest shields.

"Tasi! Now!"

Tiiamite looked behind himself just as a guard tower toppled over the dragon. Using an ice ability, Amber tried to freeze the stones that felt on the mighty King. Tasi began shooting fireballs toward that spots Amber froze, hoping the explosions and the ice shards would be able to at least make it bleed.

Divi took advantage of the situation by telekinetically toppling more buildings onto Tiiamite. With any luck, they could injure it enough to make him admit defeat. Within minutes, every building that had surrounded Tiiamite lay on top of the dragon. There was only faint movement from underneath the rubble.

Amber stopped casting, as did the mages. Everything was once again quiet, apart from the occasional stone or brick that clattered from the top of the pile.

"Did we do it?" Tasi asked.

Divi, who joined him, replied, "I don't know. I wouldn't think so, but the silence tells me otherwise."

Amber was still on the other side of the rubble when Tiiamite emerged, sending stones soaring in every direction. With no place to go, the half-mage fell to the ground and ducked. Divi blocked what she could with a shield spell, while Tasi took one against the leg. And did it hurt! He limped to the wall, hoping to cast a healing spell so he could at least walk normally.

"*It will take more than that! Ah, there you are, warrior woman! I promise your death will be slow and painful for the insult you have done to me. You will beg me to end it all, but I will not. Not until I kill your friends and leave you knowing you have nothing left–then I will take your life.*"

"My name is Amber, you bastard!"

Tiiamite suddenly folded its left wing. Amber slowly stood, still trying to recover from the rainstorm of stone. When she looked up, Tiiamite unfurled his wing, releasing three green, glowing projectiles at her. *What in the heavens are those?* She didn't want to find out. She ran toward a building, never toying with the idea of looking back. With a billowing sound, Tiiamite began opening and closing his wing, sending numerous strange missiles toward her. She could hear and feel the impact of the others behind her.

After the last one landed nearly on her ankles, she knew that next would be spot on. She dropped her sword among the rubble. To get it now risked running into whatever Tiiamite was throwing at her. She grabbed a sturdy piece of shattered wooden beam that had acted as a building support at one time. The first projectile, a spinning green orb, missed her by a good margin, but the second one was dangerously close. Amber was going to use the wood to knock it out of the way, but the angle it came at made such a defense impossible. She fell to her back as it barely missed her. Amber was about to stand up again and ready her temporary weapon when she saw it was now barely the length of a knife. She glanced at the ground to see a gray

276

circular blade sticking out of brick street. So *that* is what
Tiiamite had thrown. It resembled a piece of his scales,
though she doubted he was throwing his actual scales. It
acted much like Amber when she did her Steelbreaker
technique. This was trouble.

"Oh, man!"

She turned around as she heard the dragon's wing
open. Two more projectiles headed toward her. She waited
until they were near before she made her move. The first one
just missed scraping her shoulder. As Amber dropped and
rolled, the second one skimmed the back of her skirt. She
quickly grabbed her sword as Tiiamite once again brought
his wing toward his body.

Seeing the situation, Tasi realized he had to buy
Amber at least a few seconds. They also had to get the
dragon to retreat, if even for a short amount of time, so they
could regroup. Unfortunately, only one of them was capable
of doing this.

"Divi! Get into a safe casting spot! We need to get
this thing off us!"

She nodded and headed west. He quickly shot a
fireball at Tiiamite, who faced him. Annoyed at the
interruption, the dragon unleashed three green ovals toward
the mage. Tasi fired at one, knocking it back toward
Tiiamite. He evaded it, and three of the dragon's heads
watched it slam against the ground behind him. Tasi froze as
two remaining projectiles advanced toward him.

Suddenly, a flat rock floated in front of him. The
green blades slammed into the stone, burying more than half
their length. Tasi looked over to see Divi concentrating hard.
Not what he planned for her to do, but he was grateful.

Divi motioned her hand toward Tiiamite, hurling the
stone with its captured blades in the dragon's direction. This
caught Tiiamite by surprise and barely missed a direct hit.
One of the blades managed to cut Tiiamite, and black blood

trickled from the wound. Divi pumped her fist in excitement as the dragon yelled in pain.

Although she didn't want to act over-confident, especially after causing such a minor wound, Divi knew it was a large step in this battle of wills. In their fights, most of the dragons they'd faced had held back from their full potential. They could have just swooped down and impaled them with their claws or blasted them with fire . . . or even tried to eat them. Instead, they fought using special attacks that were probably rare outside of these battles. All the other dragons they'd fought this way had lost. She had a feeling, though, that Tiiamite wasn't going to stick to this approach for long. The King of Dragons was angry at them. She feared they would need to bring him near death before he would submit.

Tiiamite flew higher into the air and south, past the city. Tasi and Divi let out sighs of relief. *At last! A breather!* Amber began to collect herself, making sure she hadn't been hurt by all those blades. Fatigue was setting in.

"We've got to think of something to bring him down," she said. "We don't want him in the air!"

Her orders surprised both mages. Sure, when he was in the air it made Tiiamite harder to hit, but they were also harder for him to hit. Plus, Divi didn't want to attempt to outrun a dragon. It just couldn't be done.

They tried to regroup, but the thunder of Tiiamite's wings grew closer. Amber couldn't believe how fast he moved. Suddenly from the west, a white beam shot across the ground. It barely missed Amber and forced the mages to retreat. The beam cut through the ground as the dragon turned north.

"I can't figure out why it's attacking like it is," Tasi said.

Divi looked toward Amber, realizing the horrifying truth to Tiiamite's method.

"He's isolating Amber. That beam cut a ten-foot gorge in the ground. He wants her! We have to reach the other side and help!"

"How? That ditch looks to be thirty feet long. We'll never reach her in time!"

Divi looked up at the structure they took cover under, one of the few left erect after they toppled most of the ruins on top of Tiiamite. Was it going to be the easiest option? No, but it was safer than using telekinesis to move each other across it in the open. Although Amber was his prime target, the dragon would probably have little objection to swallowing either of them whole if he had the chance.

Divi ordered, "Follow me!"

She climbed up the stone wall to the second story as it was the only one that still had some floor intact against each wall. Tasi wished he knew what she was thinking. Since she learned all these spells, she had gotten overconfident in herself. Something he might have to talk to her about later . . . if there was a later.

On the other side of the gorge, Amber grabbed the Holy Light, looking around nervously. She wished she had an idea what was coming. The King of Dragons unleashed his full arsenal at her now, something he hadn't done in the Temple of the Elements. *Guess stealing the stone before our fight was finished wasn't the smartest thing to do.* But it kept her alive, something she wouldn't have been if she continued fighting that day. If not for her deception in getting Tiiamite stuck, he would have had her number.

She heard a strange sound. It wasn't the familiar thunder of the dragon's wings beating down toward them. Nor did she hear any of the roaring. The only indicator Amber received that the dragon arrived was when she saw his shadow cast over her. It wasn't swooping or changing course. A strong wind accompanied the dragon as he slowed down above her. She raised her arm to block the sun as its position behind the dragon only gave her his silhouette.

279

A sharp pain seared across her left forearm. She dropped to the ground as Tiiamite passed her. When she looked at her arm, she noticed a wound like one left by a whip. *What in Gyyerlith did he do to me?* Did the wind he carried with him have the power to cut his opponent into submission? From the Wind Dragon, it was possible.

As she stood up, Tiiamite's shadow once again appeared over her, coming from the south this time. As he passed her, she felt the same searing pain against her back, despite her armor. She dropped to her knees, but tried to recover. When she stood up a third time, the shadow appeared again. This time it struck her leg. She dropped harder. This time, though, she finally saw the source of her pain. It was its tail. Because it was so thin at the tip and moved so fast, her only warning was the dust kicked up just before it struck.

Amber again tried to stand, but again, Tiiamite took her down. Blood seeped from her wounds. She wasn't in a good spot. She had to hide. She had to get to Divi.

Both mages saw Tiiamite's attack against Amber. They had to do something or else the dragon would keep doing this until she was dead or too weak to defend herself. Tasi reached the edge of the floor where Tiiamite's beam had broken away the building. A good ten-foot gap separated them from the other side.

"Now what?" he asked. "I won't reach this level past the gap. You might, but not me in these robes."

"That's why you're going to be aiming for the first floor. You should make it easily. I'll look to continue on the second floor. I want to get him on his next pass with a strong fireball. I'll have a better shot on the higher ground."

Tasi wasn't sold on the idea. He thought the dragon was moving too fast for even Divi to make an accurate attack. Then again, she was able to hit Leviadon at the precise spot to free them from his finishing move. Although

280

he saw that more as luck, perhaps her luck would continue here.

"You ready?"

Tasi nodded as Tiiamite made another pass, followed by a scream of pain from Amber. He ran and leapt across the gap. Just as Divi predicted, he landed a good five feet from the scar Tiiamite left on the land. She didn't know what this building used to be, but she was glad its two floors followed along the outer wall. Now it was her turn.

Divi gave herself at least twenty yards of running space. She was one of the best jumpers in Myyril, making a fifteen-foot jump to win a dare just a few months prior to her fateful trip to Porsita. Not wearing a robe had its advantages. Of course, back home she never carried her staff while jumping. Now it might shorten her leap by a couple feet. After taking a deep breath, she sprinted to the edge and leapt toward the other side.

As she was halfway across, Tiiamite's shadow passed over her. Divi felt a sting across her cheek. It interrupted her jump and she barely managed to grab onto the edge of the second floor. The stones she held began to come loose under her weight.

Tasi yelled, "Hold on, Divi!"

She tried her best to climb up, but flagstones would never be able to hold her weight. That combined with the pain on her cheek was making it too difficult. The stones gave way, and she plummeted with them toward the ground.

A hand grabbed her, stopping her fall. It was Tasi. *Thank the gods he has good hands!*

He did his best to bring her up, but he was struggling. Beat up and physically exhausted, he felt almost too tired to even cast a spell. After a minute, he was able to get her up just as Tiiamite's shadow made another pass.

Tasi commented, "I don't know how much more I can take. I think I'm getting close to my limit."

She came to that realization too. From the moment Tiiamite had swooped down on them until this point, they had been at it an hour, if not longer. They were still recovering from the fight with Fafcul earlier that day. Both mages needed to recuperate soon. But they couldn't. Resting now meant they were all dead.

"I know you're tired," Divi said, getting up. "So am I, but we need to keep going! We've got to reach Amber!"

After Tiiamite made another pass, both mages rushed toward their comrade, who was now on her stomach, bleeding from every wound Tiiamite inflicted on her. She looked so weak, not that they could blame her. She had to have been struck at least fifteen times. Divi had just been hit on the cheek and it stung unmercifully. She could only imagine the pain Amber was going through.

Tasi said, "Try and heal her as best you can. We need to take cover. I won't have the strength to carry her, but I'll keep you safe with a shield spell and hold it as long as I can."

Divi rolled Amber onto her back as she began preparing the healing spell order in her mind. She had to be careful. This was her first time healing serious wounds☐well, any type of wound, actually☐something that normally took years in the School of White Magic to perfect. The spells had to be cast in the right sequence and for the right wounds, otherwise they would heal nothing or heal improperly. Right now, she was going off what she remembered from the few tomes she *did* read and the magic her father's spirit had taught her.

Tasi chanted, "*Shielda Circallis!*"

A purplish shield formed around them. This was one of ten spells that had this effect. There were stronger ones, but he didn't think he'd be able to hold those for long. Not in his state. This should be able to block Tiiamite's attack . . . maybe. The length of time he could hold the shield would be determined by how hard or often the dragon hit it. The more power that was blocked by a mage's shield, the more draining it was on the caster. If the attacks had too much force, he might only be able to block a few. *Please be quick, Divi!*

As Divi whispered a series of chants, Amber's body began to glow. Her cries of pain soon ceased as her wounds healed enough to stop bleeding. Divi wasn't sure how much blood she had lost, and thus, even with the wounds healed, how effective she would be.

Tiiamite's tail smashed across Tasi's shield with such force that he thought for sure it should have broken. Yet he was able to keep it up somehow. He didn't know how many of those he'd be able to sustain, but he was going to have to try. Divi needed time. Another attack whipped against the shield and his spell began to flicker. *Damn, this thing hits way too hard!*

As Divi finally finished her spell, the purple glow surrounding Amber dissipating to nothing. She hadn't taken the time to heal the wounds completely, because she could also feel Tasi's strength waning. This would have to do.

Amber slowly sat up. Still dizzy, she put her hand on her forehead. The sting of a wound there made her wince. She had other cuts on her arms, legs, back, stomach, and face, but at least the bleeding had stopped.

"What did I miss?" she asked. "Are we dead?"

Divi said, "Not yet. We will be if we don't think of something fast."

Amber struggled to her feet as Divi joined her. Tasi's shield was failing him. He could probably sustain one more hit before having to negate it. They had to stop this. She quieted her mind, trying to feel where the dragon was. She was going to do the only thing she could think of: nail Tiiamite's main head with a strong fireball.

No matter her best efforts, she couldn't feel the dragons' presence. He was either blocking her ability or she just hadn't refined it enough to sense something that fast.

Divi stood between her friends, her hand gathering the life particles.

She said, "Tasi, lower your shield."

He didn't want to leave them unprotected, but he could barely hold onto it anymore. He negated the spell and fell to his knees. Amber went down to make sure he was okay.

Divi, however, stood waiting with eyes closed. If she could maybe hear him coming first . . .

It was then that she felt a slight wind change to her right. Without verifying if she was right, she turned and opened her eyes. A large fireball was already formed in her hand.

"*Heiromonn Fiyyama Ulltoma!*"

Divi made a direct hit on the main head of Tiiamite. He cried in pain, flying at least a hundred feet in the air. *Please say that this is over now!* Amber and Tasi both stood up, supporting each other; Amber unsteady from loss of blood and Tasi from over-exhaustion.

For whatever the reason, Tiiamite remained hovering there.

Divi asked, "What is he doing?"

Tiiamite soon spoke. "*You have fought well, mortals. But now the time has come for me to end this. Your deaths will be remembered by the people of this place, perhaps told in your home lands. Enjoy your last breaths, little ones!*"

Amber replied, "He's getting ready to finish us off with his ultimate attack. If he does it, everything in a two-mile radius will be dead. We can't let him do it. Fire everything you've got at him! We have to bring him back down!"

All three prepared for their last stand. Divi could barely see Tiiamite as he flew so high in the air after speaking to them. Despite that, a rain of fireballs slammed the earth near them as a reminder that they were trapped. Amber yelled as she fired the first of her projectiles while

Tasi and Divi followed by casting spells. Tiiamite could see the objects coming toward him, though he only seemed concerned about Divi's. She did manage to hit him once, but it wasn't enough to bring him back to the ground. Amber continued to fire spells, but with every wave of her sword she slowed down. Between the wounds and the exhaustion, she was ready to collapse. After three more spells, Amber dropped to her knees. Tasi abandoned his assault to tend to her, exhausted as well.

Divi, too, stopped, seeing it was no use. The middle head cocked back, ready to fire. The other heads began to do the same.

Amber looked up. "This is it. We're finished. Whatever happens, it was an honor fighting by your sides."

The main head unleashed a beam of white light. Amber closed her eyes as Tasi covered her with his robe.

"*Sheildiia Heipara!*"

The beam suddenly crashed against a large purplish barrier. Tasi opened his eyes to see Divi standing in front of them, driven back slightly by the magnitude of Tiiamite's beam. Tasi had never seen a shield spell so large. Another beam connected with the first, which absorbed its added power. Divi tried her best to hold the shield as every few seconds another beam joined the attack. Her arms began to shake almost violently.

Tasi said softly, "Please, Divi. Be strong."

Divi's legs felt weak as the seventh beam added more force against her shield. She didn't know how much longer she could hold it. She'd only been successful this long because she was pulling the nearby life particles to strengthen it. When those ran out . . . Two more beams, maybe. Sweating profusely, Divi closed her eyes and tried to concentrate harder. Her body kept moving backwards. She ground her teeth.

The last beam connected with her shield, filling her with unbearable pain. She unleashed a blood-curdling

285

scream. This is how it was to end? How could it be? They were so close!

Levus appeared in her mind. *No, I can't give up and let this dragon win now. This is not how my journey is going to end! I have to save Levus.*

Before trying something she wasn't even sure was going to work, Divi said, "This is for you, Levus!"

Tasi's eyes opened when he heard something strange. He could have sworn Divi chanted another spell, yet if she did, how was the barrier still going? When he saw what was happening, his jaw dropped as far as it would go. Amid Divi's barrier, a large fireball began to form above her. How? She was . . . casting two spells at the same time!

The life particles were doing something he never saw before. They absorbed the energy from Tiiamite's attack, and Divi somehow separated those particles to form a fireball independent of the shield spell. Even though he was staring at it, he still couldn't believe he was witnessing it.

Even Amber stared in amazement at the sight. Divi didn't even appear to struggle anymore, despite the dragon's beams continuing to pound on her shield. The fireball grew to a gargantuan size.

Tasi could only image how befuddled Tiiamite must feel, having to cast his ultimate technique for this long. He had to know something wasn't right. That things were different.

Divi yelled, "*Goientii Sholuttoda Hierramon Gianta!*"

The fireball was unleashed toward Tiiamite. The middle head stopped emitting its beam as the reflection in its eyes of the large ball of light got bigger. The King of Dragons didn't like this. He took flight, using every evasive maneuver he knew. The fireball, though, followed his every movement. If he went high, so did it. When Tiiamite did a sharp turn, it would follow suit.

286

It had been ages since he had to fly like he was now. Feeling his wings tiring, he tried to rise up in a last-ditch effort. Maybe if the fireball entered the upper reaches of the atmosphere, that would freeze it. The spell was too strong for that to happen.

Within seconds, the ball connected with Tiiamite. For the first time in his life, he felt real pain. Divi dropped to the ground, shielding her face from the blinding light. They all shielded their eyes as it seemed brighter than the sun. After a few seconds, it began to dim until there was nothing.

Divi looked up for a brief second to see what had transpired. Out of the corner of her eye, a large object was in free fall toward he ground. It had to be Tiiamite. She covered her eyes, foreseeing the impact. As he struck the earth, dust and mud flew up around him. When everything was quiet again, Divi lifted her head.

She couldn't see anything through the dust, but she surely could hear the heavy breathing of a large creature. Divi tried to stand up, but her legs wouldn't respond. Her body must have still been in shock from what she just did. She didn't even know completely how she did it. She last remembered thinking about Levus when a strange feeling overcame her. Could it be that her love for him allowed her to do something no mage had done before?

A loud snort filled the area. There would be time later to think about this. At least she was able to move her arms, and she dragged herself to the edge of the city gates. Her eyes opened wide to see Tiiamite lying on the ground, badly wounded.

With staff in hand, she crawled over the ruined gate, her body slammed against the ground. Tiiamite's fireball caused enough damage that it created a short drop. She lost her breath, but she recovered and continued toward Tiiamite. Ten feet from the middle head, Divi put her staff into the ground and tried to pull herself up. It was a difficult task without the full function of her legs, but she did it eventually.

A tear came to her eye when she saw that Tiiamite, the King of Dragons, was weeping from the impact of her spell. Pity entered her soul the more she looked at the injured beast. She had to do something.

Tasi and Amber looked around in disbelief. They did it! They won! There was something more important on Amber's mind, though, even more so than the victory. She ran as fast as her tired body allowed her.

Tasi didn't understand until he saw the body of Gerritonnee lying amongst the fallen trees. He quickly followed. When he reached her, he heard something that he never thought that he would hear: Amber crying.

She gently petted the white dragon's snout as she wiped the tears from her eyes.

"What were you thinking, Gerritonnee? Why were you so foolish?"

Tasi joined Amber to examine the damage to Gerritonnee. He cringed when he saw the two tree trucks that had pierced Gerritonnee on her side. Blood pumped steadily from those wounds. Her dragon friend didn't speak, perhaps too weak to.

Tasi said, "I'll try to heal her, but I need you to have her lift herself up enough to remove the trunks, otherwise my spell won't work regardless."

Amber nodded and brought herself closer to the white dragon's ear. "Gerritonnee, I know you are hurting more than I can imagine, but I need you to be strong for a little longer. We can't heal you with the trunks still penetrating you. Do you hear me?"

Her dragon grunted, acknowledging her friend's request. She used what strength she could to push her body up. Amber heard the trunks as they slowly began to exit her body. Tasi was ready to telekinetically help her take them out. Gerritonnee struggled, but eventually lifted herself enough. Tasi quickly moved the trunks to the side, grateful for his speed as Gerritonnee dropped seconds after they were out of harm's way. He rolled so that the wound faced the sky.

He placed his palms on Gerritonnee's side. The dragon jerked slightly, but didn't have the strength for a sustained reaction. Tasi wasn't sure if this would work. He had never healed anything this large before. No mage had ever had the opportunity to heal a dragon. His spell might not work. That, and he was certain it would put him at his limit. He'd have to rest the whole week after this. Tasi closed his eyes and concentrated. A blue light formed around his palms.

"*Heamii totarra.*"

The light emitted from his hands until it surrounded Gerritonnee's entire body. Tasi glanced over at her. The wounds glowed a bright blue, which was a good sign. Once the spell ended, Tasi looked to see the results. Unfortunately, despite the blue glow, the dragon's injuries appeared no different than before. The bleeding had stopped, but it had already slowed when they took the tree trunks out. Gerritonnee rolling so the wound paced up might have helped too. Tasi sighed in frustration as he walked over to Amber. She wiped the tears from her eyes and turned to him to hear what he had to say.

"My spell had no effect on her. I'm so sorry."

Amber placed her head on Gerritonnee's scales. Tasi could see the great friendship between this half-mage and dragon. Both were willing to sacrifice themselves for each other's well-being. For Gerritonnee, though, her dedication to the friendship may have been fatal.

Tasi could see some of Gerritonnee in himself. What had he been doing with Divi his entire life, especially these past few weeks?

As Amber continued to pet Gerritonnee, a roar of pain resounded in the distance. She looked in the direction of Tiiamite, nearly motionless on the ground. A fire of hatred burned in her eyes. It was because of him that Gerritonnee might die. For that, Amber was going to ensure that Tiiamite would suffer the same fate. She unsheathed her sword and stormed toward the injured king. Tasi tried his best to catch up.

Divi slowly placed her hand on Tiiamite's snout. The dragon allowed her to without even flinching. She almost thought she felt a comfort within him as she touched him, bringing a small smile to her lips. Another tear fell from Tiiamite's eye. From the corner of her own, she could see something approaching them. Whoever it was made the dragon uneasy. Divi turned to face Amber, who limped as fast as she could with sword poised to attack. When she was close enough, she raised her sword and prepared to stab one of the heads. In one quick motion, Divi stopped Amber and pushed with her telekinetic powers until she was against a stone pillar. Amber struggled, but to no avail.

"Let me kill him! You have nothing to do with this, mage! This is personal! Let me go!"

Tasi finally arrived. "Divi, are you okay? What's going on?"

"I'm fine. Can you hold Amber back? There's something I need to do."

Tasi was hesitant, but he agreed. Whatever Divi planned had him worried, especially with her being so close to Tiiamite. Tasi held Amber while Divi placed her hand on Tiiamite.

She chanted quietly. A purple glow emitted from her hand.

Tasi stared at her in disbelief. She couldn't be doing what he thought she was doing. "Divi!"

Amber asked, "What's happening?"

"She's . . . reviving him."

Amber couldn't believe what she just heard. "Is she insane? We have to finish him now while he's wounded!"

"Wasn't it you who told me we are not to kill the dragons, just defeat them?" Divi asked.

Her retort took Amber aback. She never thought that one of the ideals she said she'd follow when she arrived here would come back on her like this.

"Well . . . I . . . This is an excepti . . . yes."

Divi nodded and said, "He is defeated. Let him be."

Amber hated to admit Divi was right. She wanted nothing more but to plunge the Holy Light into each of Tiiamite's ten heads for what he did to Gerritonnee. Yet, she herself had stopped Divi from slaying the Fafcul. It was only fair that she did the same for her in this situation.

The purple glow grew to cover the entire dragon. Tasi wasn't even sure if her magic would have any effect on dragons, though Divi has surprised him greatly these past few days. Plus, she was a sacred-blood. Perhaps she did have a spell capable of such a feat. The spell finished in a few seconds. She backed away, still using her staff as a crutch. Tiiamite slowly lifted its ten heads before raising its entire body. Tasi let Amber go in case the dragon king tried to attack.

Tiiamite roared before saying, "*You spared my life, even though I would not have spared yours. Perhaps I was wrong. Perhaps you are worthy of using the Wind Stone. Be wary, little one. Your cause may be valiant, but it may cost you your life. Until then, have a safe journey.*"

The dragon lifted his body up with his wings. The middle head grunted and bowed to Divi before turning southeast to the Temple of Elements. She smiled as it disappeared in the horizon.

"Congratulations."

All three turned their heads to a familiar figure walking toward them. He was clapping his hands, and the noise seemed to echo throughout whatever remained of the ruined city. Amber and Divi stared at the man in disbelief.

Divi asked, "Minat? How long have you been here?"

Minat stopped and examined them.

291

Amber confirmed, "You're the one who found me when I snuck on the continent."

"That is correct. I have been here the entire time keeping watch of your . . . progress."

"Our progress?" asked Divi

Chuckling, Minat walked to a stone, where he sat down and faced the group. The rolling of his r's still made him difficult to understand at times.

"It was my duty to ensure that if the stones were to be recovered from their Guardians, it was done properly. Amber, when you came alone, I enjoyed your spirit. Yet it would not have been enough. On your own, you would have failed. When Divi and Tasi arrived, I thought that perhaps it was the moment when the gates to the Isle of Time would be opened again."

"Wait a minute," Amber said. "What do you mean by the stones being recovered properly?"

"Why, by defeating all the dragons."

Tasi was beginning to understand what Minat was getting at.

"Then it was you . . ."

Minat explained, "I do apologize for helping Tiiamite find you, but understand, you had to defeat *all* the dragons before I could let you leave. With that completed, you have permission to continue your quest toward the Isle of Time. To the east, you will find a boat. The crew will nurse your wounds to the best of their abilities before they drop you off at the Isle. You have no need to return to your camps. The other stones and your supplies have been transferred accordingly."

Amber walked up to Minat. She was a little offended that he had gone into her private camps, but she had another concern she needed to ask him about.

"What about Gerritonnee?"

"Gerritonnee is a strong dragon, though young. Her wounds will heal. She will sustain far deeper ones than that

292

in her lifetime. This was the first time she faced Tiiamite in combat and he taught her a valuable lesson. I can assure you she will make a full recovery. I will help tend to her when we are finished."

Amber was eased by his news. Minat finally stood up and went to Divi.

He said, "It is time for you to leave. If you stay together, I have complete confidence you will succeed. And Divi, I have taken to heart our previous discussion. Perhaps even I have underestimated the power of love."

Divi smiled at his comment. Minat put his hand on her shoulder and looked into her eyes.

"Have a safe journey," he wished her.

He walked past Divi, out of the city, heading in the direction of Gerritonnee. Divi watched him until he disappeared into the forest by the fault scarp. She turned to her two friends, whose eyes were on her. Her quest to save Levus was coming to an end, and that thought excited and encouraged her.

Divi said, "Amber, why don't you get that final stone? He is right. It's time to leave."

CHAPTER 14
The Isle of Time

Thamalos sat silently on top of the southern part of the first wall, overjoyed to have some time alone at last. After joining his elven brethren to celebrate their god, he had spent all day in meetings with the other races. He was convinced that someone wanted these meetings held up. He didn't know exactly why someone would want to do that, but it concerned him.

Eraddor wanted to also spend some time in seclusion, yet Thamalos highly doubted that would happen. General Seth had been talking to Eraddor privately nearly everyday. He believed that the King of Cordca had something to do with that. In that sense, He pitied his friend. He could hardly imagine being in his position. Eraddor was a good man, perhaps the purest to Thamalos' knowledge. How could they be so blind to the obvious? As an elf, he probably would never understand why the human race decided to be this way.

"The day hides behind the white shadows."

Thamalos turned around to see Thetalis smoking his usual pipe. Thetalis had to be the quietest of all the council members. He usually only gave his opinion when asked and he never spoke out of turn. Being half-human, though, Thetalis also shared many of their weaknesses. Thamalos, like all the elves, felt pity for their half-blood race. Yet at some point in their lives, they must have seen something in the human spirit that countered all the advantages of being a pureblood elf. Whatever its attraction, Thamalos could not see it, even with his strong elf sight. He continued to stare into the dense fog surrounding Fort Za as Thetalis sat next to him.

"Do you think it a premonition?"

Thetalis took a puff of his pipe before answering, "Fog is fog. Everyone can interpret it a different way.

294

Perception is what makes us all different . . . and often disagreeing."

"And you see it as a shadow?"

"A white shadow. One that hides the truth, yet it can be seen. This fog comes on this day when I believe something formerly hidden will be uncovered. We will see the light."

Thamalos chuckled slightly at him.

"I am glad you still have your elf sense about nature and her signs. Most half-elves lose that part of their identity."

"Well, remember I'm a first-generation half-elf, so my abilities are still strong. My father fell in love with a human. Our elf senses may diminish in time through our children, but the blood of my race will never forget where half of it came from. We never lose our identity. We are just making our own."

Although Thetalis looked ahead, absorbed in his own surmises and seeing nothing, Thamalos finally unveiled what concealed itself behind the 'white shadow.' He stared toward the southwest, hoping that what he saw was only a mirage and would go away. No such luck . . . not on this day.

Thetalis didn't notice his strange reaction until he finished putting the tobacco in his pipe. "What is the matter?"

The half-elf followed Thamalos' gaze to find what kept the elf's attention, but he saw nothing but fog.

Thamalos squinted. How could he deny what he thought he saw? How far away was it? He concentrated harder, using his elf senses to the fullest. Suddenly his eyes opened wide and he stood up.

"By the gods!"

Thetalis asked, "What do you see?"

"Get the council together now!"

Thamalos ran down the stone stairs to the lawn behind the wall, leaving Thetalis perplexed by his order. He gazed once more where the elf leader had looked, but he only saw fog. Although not often, there were times he wished he hadn't lost that elven sight. He knew, though, that Thamalos wouldn't create a stir unless it was dire. Thetalis put his pipe away and ran after his friend into Fort Za.

"You saw what?"

General Seth Medkar stared at Thamalos, who stood in the middle of the council room. Many had been angry that he dragged them back in here, but after he told them the news he brought, they all changed their tune.

Thamalos continued, "I saw a *Dracleii*-class ship in the distance. It is heading for Fort Za."

Servion stood and asked, "For all of us who are not quite aware of that, including myself, what is this class of ship?"

"The *Dracleii*-class used to be our escape ships. We made seven of them, enough to carry our entire population at the time in case the Eratuu became too much. As you all know, my family's clan and the Wood Elves were the only ones to fully escape. To prevent the Ettui from using them for war, we tried destroying the remaining ships. We sunk five of them, but as the enemy drew closer, one ship we could only damage. I think they've repaired it and are leading an attack, starting with this fort."

Everyone started to discuss the matter among themselves. Seth didn't like the sound of this. If the Ettui had gained the ability to repair and sail ships, this threatened the entire world.

He asked, "Now, you say that these ships had the capability to transport the entire elf population. Exactly, how many can fit in one of them?"

Thamalos answered, "It depends on if you load any equipment. Full capacity though . . . can be about 250,000 a ship, if not more."

Herippi exclaimed, "Two hundred fifty thousand Ettui are on their way here!"

As the entire council expressed their concern, the room grew the loudest it had been since they first met. Seth was losing control of this meeting. He stood and slammed the hilt of his sword against his armrest. In time, the room fell silent once again.

"There will be order here as long as I reside as head of this council!" He sat back down and dropped his sheathed sword by his side. "Now, Thamalos brings some disturbing news to this council. For weeks, we have been quarreling over minor things. Now we are forced to action, which we must perform as quickly as possible. Any questions for Thamalos, ask now, and we then shall decide our course of action."

Nodding, Thamalos looked around. Hirroniise of Garlock stood, and Thamalos signaled for him to speak.

"How far is this ship?"

Thamalos explained, "It is nearly a day away. By this time tomorrow, the ship will have come down upon the shores of this island."

Panic appeared on everyone's faces. General Seth Medkar and Eraddor seemed to be the only ones refraining from the madness.

Cyp stood up and approached Thamalos. "We must begin plans for evacuation!"

Though Lascedis seemed as offended by the comment as Thamalos, he remained silent.

"Evacuation? How can this be an option?" Thamalos asked. "By agreement this fort's function is to protect the threat of invasion by any Ettui force. *Any* Ettui force."

Seth intervened. "My brave Thamalos, with this threat before us, we must keep any option open."

Thamalos' disgust at Seth's answer slowly dissipated. He shouldn't feel angry at this man. He just wanted to hear what everyone had to say. But in the end, there truly was only one option.

At this moment, Sydis and Bironn both stood up. Sydis hit the ground with his staff to gain the council's attention.

"I must say that I agree with the representative of Rudann. This fort must be cleared. What are we to do if we stay? Fight them? Thirty-what thousand against two hundred fifty thousand? That is not madness . . . that is lunacy."

Eraddor stood up and walked to Thamalos' side. "Such words from a mage. Your spells can take down more than our arrows or swords. Thamalos speaks not only with emotion, but with truth. Deserting this fort would be a disaster and against the treaty that enabled man to settle here on this island in the first place. Besides, how do we know they carry a full load? Perhaps this is a distraction or a decoy. How will we appear leaving our stronghold when the threat is smaller than we believed?"

Hirroniise stood up and added, "Staying with the elves has poisoned your mind, Eraddor. They are philosophers of nature and not of war. Part of war is knowing when you should stand your ground and fight . . . or retreat and fight another day."

"You speak of the elves like they are our enemy!" Servion shouted. "Yet you are quick to side with a mage! The same race that tried to invade Dyyros long ago. The same race that has left our people to die because of their own hatred for us!"

That comment spurred everyone to begin yelling. General Seth Medkar rubbed his head. The centuries of hatred between the races finally reared their ugly heads. He had hoped to avoid this conflict during the meetings. He finally rose and received a spear from one of the guards.

Seth yelled, "Silence! All of you!"

The room became very quiet. This was the angriest Thamalos had ever seen Seth. Observing everything back in order, the general sat down and rested his head on his arm.

He finally said, "Both sides present valid points, but I ask you, Thamalos: if we stay, do we stand a chance to win? Speak honestly."

Thamalos replied, "Yes, we do. The Ettui tend to retreat when their strength in numbers decreases. If we can kill their leader, they will retreat that much faster."

Sydis stood up once more and pleaded, "I will say this once more. You must leave this place or death will befall all of you."

"These walls have never fallen in over a thousand years of fighting," Eraddor disagreed. "They have proven they can stand against any enemy that tries to pierce them, and they will stand this time as well."

Sydis said, "Walls can fall and they will have fallen by this time tomorrow. The mage race will have no part in a massacre."

All eyes shifted toward Seth. He hadn't moved since he sat in his throne-like chair. He didn't need to remind himself the importance of this decision. Either way he chose, he would lose. Staying would keep him in good faith with the elves, but the mages and humans would be displeased. Plus, if they stayed, could they win against an army eight times their size? Seth wiped his brow as he stood with his decision.

He stated, "In this fort's existence, she has seen many great armies try to overtake her, most during the Ettui Island Wars. None, though, can compare to the threat that arrives in less than a day. By that fact alone, I should order this fort evacuated. I have commanded this fort for nearly forty years and not once have I turned away from an enemy. As Eraddor said, these walls have never fallen. I seem to agree with him. Thus, my decision is that we will stay here and drive this Ettui army back to the wastelands they call home! Any race that wishes to leave may, but as for me, I will defend this fort to my last breath."

Thamalos and Eraddor smiled. Thetalis clapped at Seth's speech, as did the members from Rudann.

Shaking his head in disappointment, Sydis whispered to Bironn, "Such fools. By tomorrow, this fort will become a cemetery."

Bironn stared at Sydis, worried. How would he know that? Maybe they did have a chance to win this battle. Their magic could help them. Why would Sydis just dismiss the idea? He knew how much Sydis hated humans, but was this a time to bring that issue up?

Sydis suddenly stood up and left the room without even acknowledging Bironn. Bironn, quickly stood up and followed him. He believed Sydis to be concealing something, and he wanted to find out what.

* * * * *

"There it is!"

Divi and Tasi looked ahead at the Isle of Time. Amber's amazement at how quickly the men on the ship patched her wounds, leaving only scars, meant she barely noticed it at first. At the mages' shouts of surprise, she finally looked up at the scene ahead of them. A large mountain seemed to grow from the waters. The sky loomed a dark blue, as if darkened by an approaching storm, and the waters crashed around the rocks. Amber looked back at the Dragonian ship, still anchored in the open waters, before returning her gaze forward.

She commented, "I think we should've stayed on the larger boat to do this. This one is going to be destroyed in those waters."

Divi didn't think so, but she could understand her concern. The Dragonians said that they needed to do this on their own and put them on the vessel's escape boat. The

300

waters were much rougher than she envisioned when Levus described this place to her. The winds grew heavier the closer they got. And despite those heaviy winds, it appeared as though the storm never broke.

Amber asked, "Well, now what?"

Divi covered her head with the hood of her cloak at the sight of the impending rain. A few drips hit the wooden hull as she spoke. "Not sure. Just make sure to secure the stones. We don't want them going overboard."

Amber tied the bags carrying the stones tightly to the planks that formed seats in the boat. As waves rocked them, she prepared to be on the receiving end of some very dangerous waters. Divi hoped she would be able to solve the puzzle of the stones. She tried to remember what saying Levus had told her, but she couldn't envision the words.

The first heavy winds rocked the boat and Amber and Tasi covered their face with their hoods. The waves were getting more violent and the rain became heavier as they inched their way closer to the mountain walls.

Amber yelled as a wave soaked them, "Divi! If you have any ideas, I suggest you try them now!"

Divi tried thinking as another wave slammed inside the boat. Tasi used an empty leather pouch to bail out some of the water so they wouldn't begin to sink. She looked toward the mountain, searching for any odd features or crevices to place the stones, but there were no such formations. There had to be a way.

Amber held on tight as waves reached the heights of small hills they had to climb. She was thankful they hadn't put the sail up; otherwise they would have capsized for sure with the winds. The closer they got to the mountain, the more dangerous the storm became. Amber tried convincing the two mages to turn back, but they either didn't hear her or ignored her completely because they kept pushing forward.

Ahead of them, Amber saw a very large wave approaching. She tapped Divi on the arm twice.

"I'm usually not a demanding woman, but Divi, think of something fast!"

As Divi finally stared forward, Levus' voice came into her head saying, "Only those who hoist the elements may prove themselves worthy of entering the gates of time."

She looked toward the end of the boat, at the bags with the stones. That was it! The answer to the riddle! She crawled to the bags and searched through them.

"What are you doing?" asked Amber.

Divi asked, "Where's the Water stone?"

Amber glanced at the next approaching wave before answering, "It's in the far bag!"

Divi grabbed the stone from the bag. The rain didn't seem to affect it. She looked at the increasingly violent waters before facing Amber and Tasi.

"Hold my legs!"

They weren't sure what she would do, but with a large wave bearing down on them they followed her order. It was difficult to hold on to her as her hanging weight made the boat veer in unexpected ways, but they kept her steady within arms length of the water.

Divi, grasping the stone with both hands, doused it in the water. The jewel inside emitted a light. Within seconds, the calamitous ocean calmed, although the heavy winds remained. The threatening wave, or what remained of it, splashed on them, but did nothing more.

Divi crawled up with the stone in hand. The jewel remained lit.

Tasi realized what she was doing and said, "Water."

Divi gave a smile as she opened the bag to her right and pulled out the wind stone.

Tasi said, "Wind."

She hoisted the stone in the air allowing the heavy winds to touch it. The jewel in the stone lit up a bright green. As the light glowed brightly, the gale winds fell to a barely felt breeze.

Amber had caught on, already taking out the stone in the bag closest to her. She tossed it to Divi, who caught it after placing the wind stone down. When she recognized the Earth stone by its jewel color, she and Tasi paddled with their hands until their boat came up to the mountain.

Tasi said, "Earth."

Divi slammed the Earth stone against the mountain. The brown jewel in the middle lit up. The world around them shook as large pieces of the mountain fell into the sea. After a few minutes, a waterway revealed itself to their right. Divi placed the Earth stone in the boat and pulled out the final stone.

Tasi finally said, "Fire."

A haunting silence fell upon the boat. All three searched the area. Nothing but open sea. Even the Dragonian ship had left at some point with none of them noticing. Amber pushed back the hood of her cloak and looked around.

"Umm . . . how are we supposed to get fire?" she asked.

Coming up with an idea, Tasi extended his hand. A small ball of fire appeared above his palm. Divi smiled as she placed the stone above the flame. To their surprise, the jewel inside failed to illuminate. She held it near the flame for a few more seconds before Tasi closed his palm, negating the spell.

"Perhaps it only reacts to naturally made elements," Amber suggested. "Mages' magic uses life particles, so maybe it considers them more artificial. Kind of wish we had an elf with us."

Divi tried to think. What could they use to make a fire? It would've been most unfortunate if they traveled all this way only to have to go back for a torch. She leaned farther on her hip until a sharp pain suddenly struck her left thigh.

Tasi noticed her wince as she scavenged for the cause of it. "Are you okay?"

Divi didn't answer, pulling her pouch from underneath her. This was the obvious cause of her discomfort, but what did she put in there? She opened her pouch and looked inside. Her eyes lit up with hope. Divi reached in and grabbed a stone with a gray and reddish tint. A big smile grew on her face.

Amber said, "Divi, a rock won't help us make fire."

"This one will."

Amber looked at Tasi, just as puzzled by Divi's statement.

Divi raised her eyes from the stone and ordered, "Break off a piece of the boat. I need the wood."

Amber said, "I think you have lost it, Divi. If you haven't noticed, there isn't much boat to break off. I'm surprised this thing hasn't sunk yet."

"Just do it. Trust me."

Amber followed Divi's demand very skeptically. Using her sword, she chopped a piece off quite easily. That didn't sit too well with her, as their vessel's condition already made her uncomfortable. She handed Divi the wood and they watched as she rubbed it with the edge of the stone.

Divi hoped she was doing this right. She had only watched Levus do it in the seaside caves on Dyyros. She also hoped the stone didn't lose its potency when wet, because the waves drenched everything. Amber showed less confidence with every failed strike. Divi raised her arm high and gave it one last hit.

A small flame suddenly ignited on the wood. Divi did her best to cover it from the little wind that lingered after she used the Air stone. The flame grew larger until half the board was covered in fire. She handed the board to Tasi and grabbed the Fire stone. She took a heavy breath as she held the stone over the flame.

Divi said, "Fire."

304

After a few seconds, the jewel in the Fire stone glowed brightly. Amber tapped Divi on the shoulder and pointed toward the passageway.

"Look!"

Tasi threw the fire-laden board into the sea, extinguishing it. They stared as a floating flame appeared to come from the mountain. It seemed like a phantom, as not even the wind affected it.

Tasi cleared his throat. "Well, what are we waiting for?"

Divi agreed. The way to the Isle of Time was open, waiting for them to reach it. Though she didn't exactly know what would happen when they landed. Did they have to complete another task? Would they meet someone who would help them travel back in time? Divi knew her adventure had only just begun.

She and Tasi went to either side of the boat near the back. Using a simple spell, they made the boat move quickly as it would with a constant, favorable wind. Amber stayed on one knee as they approached the entrance of the waterway. As they neared the first flame, it extinguished while another one spewed from the mountain, burning ahead of them. Tasi and Divi reduced the power of their spells so the boat wouldn't travel too fast. They followed the flames until the path split into three. Divi thought she heard the echo of a waterfall, but she wasn't too sure about that.

"There it is," pointed Amber.

The flame sprouted just inside the wall of the far-left waterway. Divi now saw the importance of obtaining the Fire stone. It would lead them through the labyrinth, whose wrong paths probably lead to death. Without the stone, one would have to be very lucky. Even with the flames guiding them, they traveled under tension. Whether from fear or excitement about what would transpire next, the uneasiness wouldn't go away until they were back on dry land.

The waterway had at least seven forks by Divi's counting. Sighs of relief escaped their lips when they saw a long, straight path after all the turning. This time, though, two flames appeared, parallel to each other on each side of the wall. They had to be close now. Divi's excitement caused her to unconsciously increase the power in her spell to get there faster. Tasi had no choice but to follow her lead or they would have rammed into one of the mountain walls.

Divi finally slowed down when the crevice between the mountains narrowed to three feet. Their boat barely made it through. Amber even had to pull her elbows in to avoid scraping them against the rocks. The closer they got to the end of the path, the louder the waterfalls sounded. After clearing the tight entrance, Tasi stopped the boat. All three stood up.

Amber commented, "My gods!"

In front of them lay an island surrounded by waterfalls. The land itself sprouted with many unfamiliar tropical plants. A flock of birds flew out of the trees toward them, with one landing on their boat. Divi had never seen one like it. Its back was colored like the rainbow. As it moved, the colors seemed to change. Divi tried to get close, but it returned to its flock as she did.

Despite the many watefalls, the water around them didn't even seem to move, like they floated in a large pool.

"This place is magical," Tasi said admiringly. "We might be the first to ever lay eyes on this beauty."

Divi added, "A world not touched by man of any race. Could the world have looked like this before civilization? If so, what have we done to it?"

Amber found their conversation interesting, but her attention was drawn to a flashing light coming from the land.

"Over there! Some light . . . some type of signal."

Divi and Tasi focused their attention on the strange light, too. It seemed to flash every few seconds. The two mages looked at each other.

"Well, let's see what it is," Divi said.

They powered the boat until they neared the land. When they drew close, Amber jumped in the shallow water, holding the rope attached at the bow. She tied it to the first sturdy object she could find, that being a large rock. Divi and Tasi both stepped on the small, sandy beach.

The beach appeared perfect, with no footprints or garbage. This would be an image any painter would love to feast their eyes on. Divi hated to leave it. Amber seemingly didn't care about that, as she walked across the beach toward the forest and the shiny object. To Divi's amazement, with every step Amber took, the sand filled in her foot's impression until it appeared no one had ever stepped there. Both mages slowly followed until they met her near the base of a small hill. Hanging on the closest tree was a flat piece piece of armor. Its crude design told her that it must have come from an older time period.

Amber commented, "Its some kind of shield. The wind was blowing it. Perhaps we weren't the first ones here after all."

Divi looked down. Perhaps they weren't. The beach had the ability to cover any traces of anyone treading upon it. She remembered Levus telling her that his father tried to reach the Isle of Time. Maybe he did make it! How excited would he be if she found out the truth? Levus . . . she was so close to saving him now. If only . . .

Her train of thought was halted at a shocking discovery. Her eyes went up to the top of the hill.

Amber asked, "What do you see?"

Divi said, "It's a path. Someone does live here."

Tasi gulped as Amber unsheathed her sword. Although this place showed no real danger, if someone else did live here she didn't want to take a chance.

The path was winding. Shields, like the one they saw from the boat, hung on trees and posts throughout their ascent. All of them had different shapes, sizes, and designs.

The pathway kept twisting until it led to an area of brush covered with vines.

Divi tried to pull the plants apart, but their tight growth made it difficult. "I can't break them."

"Let me handle this."

Amber brought her sword up. A flame suddenly surrounded her blade as she hacked unmercifully at the tough brush. Whatever her blade did not cut, the fire around it singed. It took a few minutes, but she finally cleared a path to walk through. Amber breathed heavily, surprised at how much work was involved, as she sheathed her sword once again. Divi and Tasi stepped through the passage she'd opened, then stood still in amazement.

An extravagant entrance into a cavern connected to the rock face of a cliff. The arch was made of some white stone. Numerous designs of men, women, and creatures covered it, but Divi didn't know what any of them meant. The largest carving depicted a man with a beard who seemed able to look out over the mountains surrounding them. Although just stone, the figure sent a chill down her spine. Even Amber, who had the tendency to rush into things, proceeded with caution.

The first room of the cavern was small, containing no more than a stairway and pieces of armor. A hole in the ceiling provided the only light.

Amber seemed very interested in the armor and shields. "This armor . . . it looks like its hundreds of years old. I remember seeing designs like this in books in Tydos."

Tasi commented, "I hope this isn't a trophy room of others who have sought the power of Time."

Divi wasn't interested in any of those things. Her journey was leading her to whatever resided at the summit of these stairs, and nothing would stop now. At the top, Divi stopped. The room was gigantic! Torchlight replaced the natural light that had come through the door of the previous room. Along the walls, bench-like objects had elegant cushions covering them. Ahead of her in a spacious area stood a pedestal elevated on a small platform. Twenty feet in front to that, closer to the entrance, a smaller plinth sat with the top covered by a cloth. It looked like an open book rested on the farther pedestal. The wall behind it, a little unclear from the distance, appeared very strange, as if numerous objects sprouted from it.

Amber said, "So, this is why we had to risk our lives, defeat four dragons, and solve an elemental puzzle . . . so we could find an empty sanctuary?"

Divi could feel they weren't alone. Someone was here . . . or something. Without a doubt someone had taken up residence here. Perhaps they had gone out and hadn't returned yet. Divi proceeded slowly toward the pedestal.

"I can assure you that this place is not empty."

Amber pointed her sword toward a dark area of the room to their right, from which a man's voice had spoken. "Who is there? Show yourself!" Divi and Tasi readied their magic just in case.

For a few seconds, the only noise came from water dripping on the stony floor. Divi tried to use her powers to see the man in the shadows, but she couldn't.

He said, "I can assure that your lives are in no danger. Please sheathe your weapons."

"Forgive me if I don't oblige," Amber replied. "I don't take orders from voices."

Divi, to a point, agreed with Amber, yet she wanted to see the figure who spoke to them and perhaps was the reason they came here in the first place. For that, she'd be willing to risk facing this person defenseless.

"Amber, put away your sword."

Divi watched until Amber fulfilled her request before facing the shadow again. "All right. Now, who are you?"

A man with a long white beard and wearing a white robe slowly stepped out of the darkness. He carried a long staff that Divi could've mistaken for a mage's staff.

The man answered, "My apologies. I have no name. You may refer to me as the Time Sage, keeper and protector of the flow of this Time, and I welcome you to my home."

Suddenly, candles and torches that had lain dormant danced with life. The entire area was illuminated and not one corner covered by shadow. The walls which had seemed odd to Divi were not walls at all, but bookshelves, and every shelf filled to the brim, though some candles occupied spaces between the books. Even Amber, not an avid reader, stood in awe by the sight. Despite the amazing scene, Divi's eyes grew attracted to the large book on the pedestal.

"I know you have questions, Divi," the Time Sage said. "Like you, I have been awaiting the day we finally met."

Divi asked, "You knew I was coming?"

The Time Sage came to stand between her and the large book. "I know who you are and why you are here. But you cannot expect to succeed after your weary journey on adrenaline alone. Rest for a few hours. We will begin near nightfall."

Divi hadn't noticed, but she was tired now that he mentioned it. Hard to believe that earlier in the day they were getting the Fire stone and then fighting Tiiamite. The Dragonians must have known a shortcut because she and her companions had rested on the boat for just a few minutes, it seemed, after sailing off. When they awoke, they found themselves on the Northern Ocean, only a hundred miles from the Isle of Time. She knew shortcuts existed, but only the elves knew how to use them to the best of her knowledge.

The more she thought about it, perhaps it would be wise to follow the Time Sage's suggestion of rest. She didn't know all the effects that the spell she cast on Tiiamite would have on her. Temporary paralysis of the legs was the immediate effect, being why she had to crawl toward Tiiamite after their battle. She felt so helpless needing her staff to even pull herself up just to stand. There have been other instances where mages collapsed hours later after casting a powerful spell. She certainly couldn't have that . . . not now. She finally nodded her head in agreement.

The Time Sage extended his hand toward the stone benches. "You may rest on those cushions. You will find them most comfortable. You shall be awakened at the proper time."

Amber and Tasi both proceeded cautiously. Unlike them, Divi lay down on her side facing the wall. Her muscles, which had been tense, suddenly relaxed on the strange material. Her eyes felt heavy. She felt some magical property emitting from the cushion, but she succumbed to sleep before she could think about it.

* * * * *

The sun began to set through the window of Levus' room. The elf guard who stood watch inside took a break from his constant pacing to look at it. Such an extremely beautiful sight! The colors of the clouds went from their normal white to an orange-red. The brim of day's sky showed a light purple and blue as the night crept over it. He couldn't believe that this might be the last sun they saw set over Fort Za. Even though he was willing to give his life to defend this fort, the odds made him doubt that it would be a success. Were the mages right? Maybe, but thinking about the Ettui being so close to Lozela made him forget his doubts. If the fort fell, their people would be under constant threat of invasion, reliving the horrors of the four Ettui-Elf Wars fought on Barbata thousands of years ago. They had to win.

He turned around when the door suddenly opened. One of the human guards outside the room stepped in, with another seen through the doorway. The human stopped by Levus to check on him.

"How is he?"

The elf left the window to join his human companion. "He is the same. Breathing is normal, but no reaction to the outside world."

"I hope he rejuvenates before the battle. We can use all the help we can get, even if the sword he uses contains dark powers."

The human walked to the window, where the elf soon went again, too. The sun was nearly covered by a cloud that passed in front of it.

The elf guard said, "Thus enters the night sky full of hate and shadow. Tomorrow the sky will resemble the night, and this red sky we had today will become the blood of our friends on the earth."

The human was a little confused by the elf's jargon, but the point couldn't be made clearer. He pounded his fist against the stone windowsill before turning around.

"Then let us hope that the gods favor us, for we will need it."

As the guards left the room, behind a crate on the outer wall of the fort, an Ettui assassin peeked his head out. He looked toward the window. A dark smile grew on his face.

The assassin whispered, "Levus."

The Ettui ducked back into hiding. The time was near for him to complete his mission, but it would have to wait until dark. Then, the first phase of the attack would be accomplished, with the second phase beginning tomorrow. For the Ettuii, this would be a great day, remembered as the Day the Elves Fell. The assassin growled in anticipation.

*   *   *   *   *

"Levus . . . no!"

Divi's once-comfortable sleep had ceased to be pleasant. She wasn't awake, but conscious enough to know she wasn't dreaming.

"Forget me."

That female voice. Why could she hear these things? She felt herself tossing and turning on the rustling cushion.

"Please . . . don't leave me!"

That was Levus! Was he calling to her? She wanted to call back, but she couldn't determine fact from fantasy at the moment.

Divi murmured, "Levus."

A dark cloud seemed to enter her head. She could hear and almost feel the lightning emitting from it. This had to be a nightmare . . .

"His soul . . . is Time's!"

No . . . Ulcinar's unforgettable voice spoke as if he was already victorious. She couldn't let him be, though. She would save Levus. Divi felt herself sweating and breathing heavily. She couldn't take it anymore. She had to wake up!

Divi quickly opened her eyes, relieved to see the Time Sage's domain. Anything had to be better than what she had just experienced. She looked to her right and left. Where were Amber and Tasi? She knew that neither one would leave her alone. Her gaze went to the pedestal, where the Time Sage now stood. Did he do something to them? She didn't think so, but she didn't want to underestimate his power. She slowly stood up and just as carefully walked toward the Time Sage. She couldn't really see what he was doing, so she thought it best to approach cautiously.

"You are awake early."

Divi asked, "Where are my friends?"

She tried to move closer, curious as to what the Time Sage did with that massive book. He didn't try to block her view, but she did notice him looking at her from the corner of his eye.

"They are running a short errand for me on my island. It needed to be done before we could begin. They will return shortly."

Divi sighed in relief to hear they were okay. She did wonder, though, what type of important errand they needed to complete that both would leave her with this stranger. Divi took another few steps toward the pedestal. What made this book so special that it sat always separated from the rest? She finally saw that the Time Sage was writing in it.

"What are you doing?"

The Time Sage gave a chuckle that seemed uneasy. "My job . . . recording Time. This book is the official history of this Time. These other books are the stories left behind by all those that have passed on and who continue to live. I need only write in this when an event of great historical significance is taking place or about to take place."

Divi asked, "Is there a book on Levus in here?"

"Somewhere. There is also one for you. Both are continuing sagas, as you both live. They will remain on these shelves when you live no longer. Time never forgets those who inhabited her. It is people that chose to forget. And before you ask, I know the answer to your next question. You may not look in any of the individual books. Even the slightest contact can change the way the person lived or is living. Only I can touch them."

Divi didn't hide how his answer upset her. She hoped that by looking in Levus' book she would see if the way she planned to save him was the correct one. Then again, she would not risk doing something bad to Levus' life just because she touched his book.

"How long have you been a Time Sage?" she asked.

He stopped writing and turned to face her. It seemed obvious that no one had asked him that question before.

He replied, "I have been a prisoner of Time for longer than some of the oldest trees that exist on your world. I know not how long. In this cave, time is frozen. One will not age while in these walls."

When the Time Sage turned his head, Divi noticed something strange. She wanted to make sure that she wasn't seeing things, especially in this dim cave.

Divi said, "Hold it! Turn your face in the light."

He did as she told him until his entire face became illuminated. Divi gasped from her discovery, backing a couple steps. The Time Sage's eyes were exactly like Levus' eyes! Was there a connection? Did this prove her theory that Levus could be the fabled Unifier of the Lands?

The Time Sage asked, "What is it? What do you see that shocks you?"

Divi wanted to answer carefully. Perhaps this man wasn't supposed to know that he and Levus shared that attribute. She still wasn't sure she completely trusted the Time Sage yet, although he had done nothing to prove otherwise. She had to say something to him, though, because he saw it in her expression.

Divi answered, "Your eyes . . . they are strange. Why is that?"

The Time Sage, instead of answering, asked, "Why? Do you know another like me?"

Some of the candles in the room burned higher when he asked the question. Divi backed away slightly.

The Time Sage asked, "What do you know, my mage? What is it you try to hide from me?"

Divi didn't want to answer him. She turned her back and returned to the bench where she slept. The Time Sage, seeing that he wouldn't get an answer, began writing in the book again.

As he wrote, he said, "Do not worry. I will find out what secret you hide. But now, the time is near. When your friends return, we shall begin."

Divi asked, "Begin what?"

"What you came here for . . . to go back in time and save your friend."

* * * * *

Night had fallen on Fort Za faster than normal
because of the increasing clouds. Although the security
around the fort had been increased outside, many of the
troops stood in front of Levus' room. Since Thamalos' "bad
feeling'" had proven correct before, General Seth Medkar
made no objection to his suggestion that they double the
guards around Levus' quarters. They kept the doors closed
tightly so no one would be able to enter if someone did get
by them.

Inside Levus' room a deathly silence loomed. They
lit a few candles every night in case he awakened. Thus far,
they haven't been so fortunate. The shadows cast by the
lights would be enough to scare anyone, man or child. This
reason alone made the elves close the door every night. Plus,
with the room being atop the highest tower of the fort, what
did they have to worry about someone sneaking in?

Another cloud suddenly covered a large portion of the
brightest moon. A sheet of darkness fell upon the fort the like
of which had never fallen before.

In Levus' room, the blotting of the moon seemed to
make the candlelight stronger. All was mute, even as a dark
hand grasped the windowsill from the outside. The quiet
ended as a small growl filled the air of the room, causing fear
even among the candle flames, which danced in the door's
direction, trying to escape.

As he climbed through the window, he examined the
area. Not a soul about, except for the incapacitated Levus.
The Ettui assassin slowly walked toward the door. He could
hear the voices of the elven guardians outside. He looked
down to make a pleasurable discovery. A key to the room
lay on the floor. A foolish guard must have dropped it in
haste. He grabbed it and slowly locked the door from the
inside. Now he could start his one mission: to retrieve the
Moonsaber. He had also been given orders to kill the boy,

316

but not until he had the sword in his possession. The assassin knew that if he couldn't find the sword here, the boy might be his only link to finding it. He suspected it wouldn't be far from Levus. Until then, his desire to feast on the boy's heart would have to wait.

Just the thought made the assassin search the cluttered room faster.

* * * * *

The time was nearly upon them. With every second it drew closer, Divi grew more nervous. The moment she fought so hard to reach lay within her grasp. Yet doubts entered her mind once again. Was her theory going to work? Would she make it to Levus in time? What if, no matter what she did, Levus fell in this coma and never saw the light of day again? These thoughts provoked Divi's greatest fear.

Tasi stood beside her. She knew he could feel her tensions. He and Amber returned nearly twenty minutes after Divi's talk with the Time Sage. From what they explained, he had them put the elemental stones on four pedestals across the island. As long as these stones remained on those pedestals, the elements that guarded the Isle of Time would remain locked. This was essential, especially when they had to leave. She could only imagine Amber's thoughts about this because that meant the stones had to stay here. Other than their personal testimony, how could Amber give proof of her success short of bringing the mage council here? Even that, Divi would never endorse. Mages, like any other race, didn't need to know this place existed.

The Time Sage remained on the elevated platform with the large book. He never looked back at them the whole time they stood behind him. Divi didn't know exactly what he was doing, though in a way, she would continue being comfortable not knowing. This man seemed nice, but his

317

intentions not as innocent. It would be something to think about later, however. She had a more immediate task to keep her mind on.

Finally, after minutes of silence, the Time Sage turned around to face them. The shadows across his face seemed ominous as he lowered the candles' light. Tasi stepped back to stand next to Amber, who never took her eyes off the Time Sage.

He explained, "Divi, you are about to do what few have been able to. I will be sending your soul into your past self, so all the actions done in the past will be your own. Before I send you back into time, there are a few things I must tell you. One, you are being sent for a single purpose. Do not pass your bounds. Sending you back like this means every little thing you do can effect Time in larger ways than you think."

Divi nodded. Seeing she understood the first rule, the Time Sage continued.

"Second, it is not recommended you use knowledge you possess now that you did not have then. For instance, in your case, your magic. If you do so, the Ettui might retain this knowledge and use it against you in the future. Nor do you want to cast magic because, at that time, you technically don't know how to. It would cause a mental imbalance that might drive you mad upon your return. Plus, it may jeopardize this meeting from ever happening."

Divi again nodded. The Time Sage again acknowledged her acceptance and continued with his final term.

"Lastly, realize that you only have one chance to return to a specific moment in time. If you fail, you and the rest of Time must live with the consequences."

Divi gave a third nod, though not as confident as the previous two. The Time Sage could see the difference, but he continued knowing she accepted the responsibility no matter how hesitant her response. He turned around and gazed toward the book. As he did, a stone slab surrounded by the bookshelves slid to the right, startling all three of his visitors. When the stone stopped moving, it had revealed a small room chiseled from the rock. It didn't look very big inside, enough to hold maybe four people. Divi could feel a cold wind coming from within. She swallowed deeply.

The Time Sage ordered, "Step inside. When you do, close your eyes and only think of the task at hand. Forget everything but your goals."

Divi slowly walked toward the room. The Time Sage turned to face Tasi and Amber when she neared the entrance.

"Tasi, if you would please lie down on one of the cushions. As you are involved in the moment Divi is entering, if she does something rash, you might be affected. This is for your own safety."

Tasi hesitated to comply with his request. Amber walked over to the mage and put her hand on his shoulder.

"Don't worry. If he tries something funny, he will taste my blade."

Her words convinced Tasi. She was serious about protecting him and especially Divi. If the Time Sage did something to harm either one of them, Amber would have her vengeance.

Divi finally reached the entrance. She peeked inside to see nothing but an empty, cave-like room. Yet a cold wind still emitted from it. Divi slowly walked in, her footsteps echoing. The deeper she went inside, the stranger a feeling grew within her. Images of people she never knew randomly flashed through her head. *What is going on?* Divi turned around as she heard a loud noise behind her. The stone slab shut before she could move, leaving her in complete darkness. Her breathing became heavier. With the biting cold, she was certain she'd see her breath if only there were any light. The voices filled her head again. Despite the frigidness of the room, Divi felt drips of sweat on her forehead. This couldn't be a good sign. She tried to remember what the Time Sage told her to do.

She reminded herself, "Focus, Divi. Focus on the moment. Just like your training. Complete and utter focus."

Divi stood in the middle of the room. Despite having no outlets for light, a soft white glow started to encompass it. She closed her eyes and concentrated. She could still hear the voices and images in her head. She figured they had to be a test. She had to clear her mind until images of Levus were all that she could see. She tried focusing her thoughts.

From outside the room, Amber stood watch over the Time Sage as he prepared. He surprised her by saying, "You may watch, Amber, from the crystal. Uncover it."

Amber realized exactly what he directed her toward. She had wondered what lay underneath that cloth when they first entered, but she didn't have time to check because the Time Sage had her running around all day. Amber removed the elegant silk material to reveal a large crystal. It was glowing and from the inside, smoke appeared. Despite that, she almost thought she could see an image within the crystal.

Back inside in the room, Divi continued to focus on the goal. The more she did, the fewer images appeared and the fewer voices she heard. The room got eerily silent. After a few minutes, it became entirely mute. The temperature seemed to rise and she felt conscious of something strange happening to her, but she never flinched. She remained with her eyes closed, concentrating.

Outside, the Time Sage opened his arms and chanted quietly in some strange language. As he did, a strong wind out from nowhere circulated around the room. Amber glanced up to see what was going on. The wind blew the pages of the massive book back. The feather pen, surrounded by a blue light, hovered over the page the wind stopped on. Amber didn't see it, but as the pen floated, a section of the writing began to disappear. Nearly a quarter page went missing before the pen moved again. Amber looked once more at the crystal. *What is that?* A clear image was projected inside.

Divi, meanwhile, continued to concentrate despite the distractions occurring. She didn't want anything to ruin her focus. The strange feeling lessened slightly. She eased her body.

"Divi!"

Divi looked around in perplexment. She thought she'd heard Tasi's voice. How could that be? He was outside of the room.

"This is quite the mess we are in," he commented.

Divi opened her eyes as Tasi shot a fireball at two incoming Ettui soldiers. *It's happening!* She was back at the Barbatan palace as they tried rescuing Levus! The fireball connected with the two Ettui, blasting them to the ground. Divi looked at Tasi, trying to remember what she had told him so that time would not change too much.

She asked, "What now?"

"Just go get Levus!" Tasi yelled. "I can hold them!"

She nodded and ran for the stairway.

"Hurry! Go!"

She ran as fast as she could. She had to get to Levus as quickly as possible. Every second counted if her theory was correct. Divi reached the stone steps and dashed up them. Halfway up, an Ettui warrior jumped out of nowhere. She had forgotten about that. Divi grabbed her staff, ready to cast a spell.

She suddenly remembered what the Time Sage told her. It upset her she couldn't use her spells. They would have made this much simpler, but she just had to do it the old-fashioned way. Divi charged the Ettui and quickly disabled it with her staff.

Two more Ettui came from hiding to attack her. She prepared her staff as both ran with blades ready to stab. Using her telekinetic powers, she knocked one of them back. It couldn't regain its balance and tumbled down the stairs past her. Divi used her staff to take care of the remaining Ettui. If she remembered right, that should have been the last one that separated her from Levus. She sprinted up the remaining stairs. She wished she could have an idea of how she was doing. Her only indication would be when she got to the top.

Arriving, Divi examined the situation in front of her. She wasn't too late, but she didn't get there much earlier either. When she looked to her left, Leeta already lay there dead. Levus fell to his knees while Kile and Ulcinar watched him. The glowing light started emitting from Levus. *This is it.* Divi's theory on how to save him was going to be tested with no margin for error.

The light began to radiate toward her. As it got closer, Divi seemed to burn. It had to be from the light. She must not have felt it last time because her soul from the future knew magic, so even in her body from back then, she could feel its immense power. The two Ettui she had disabled returned, and she heard their footsteps from behind her. Walking through that light would cause her great pain, but it had to be done. Divi took a deep breath before sprinting into the light.

The moment she entered it, she tumbled to the floor and screamed in pain. Her entire body felt aflame. Divi looked up to see Levus still on his knees. He didn't seem affected by this light. She had to get to him. She stood up and limped a few steps before falling again. The light kept getting brighter, and so did Divi's pain become greater. Time was running out.

She got up and again limped toward Levus.

"Levus! Please stop!"

It didn't do any good, as she once again fell to the ground. She didn't know how much more of this she could physically take. Her body was weakening. Her skin felt worse than when she miscued on her first fire spell. She lay only twenty feet from Levus. She couldn't give up now.

Divi yelled, "Please! Stop!"

She couldn't stand up anymore, so she crawled toward Levus. The light's burning was so agonizing that she could barely remain conscious. She had no choice. She had to use the rest of her strength to plunge herself at Levus. Divi lifted herself and made a last effort to reach him.

She got a grip on Levus' armor and pulled herself close so she hugged him. Levus' eyes opened but stared at nothing. She no longer felt the burning, being past the light. She embraced him harder, pressing him against her.

"It's all right, Levus. You're not alone. I'm here for you. I've always been here for you."

She lifted her head from Levus' shoulder. The light kept growing stronger. Her plan wasn't working. She started to panic, lightly shaking him.

"Please, Levus! Don't do this! I would travel to the ends of the land for you. Please!"

Tears rolled down her cheeks. Why didn't this work? She thought that telling Levus he wasn't alone in his darkest hour would be enough. Divi squeezed him hard. She couldn't fail. She had never felt this strongly for a person before. Her tears began to trickle onto Levus' armor.

Divi finally cried, "Please. You can't do this, Levus. I love you!"

She rested her head on his shoulder. A single tear rolled down Levus' cheek as he closed his eyes. She continued to weep as the light grew bright and engulfed them both. Her scream was the last thing she remembered before blacking out.

* * * * *

A tear rolled down Levus' cheek as he slowly woke up from his long slumber. His heart raced, and his body sweat profusely. Where was he? Leeta had been killed on Barbata. He didn't remember much after that, and it took

323

him a long time before he could see past the light to realize he wasn't alone. Divi came for him. She even admitted her feelings for him.

He wondered where she was. He wanted to see her again.

A loud growl disrupted his thoughts. Levus turned his head to his left. In the shadows of a strange room, an Ettui assassin stood, growling angrily in his direction. It realized he had awakened from his long slumber. He needed a weapon and fast. Where was his Moonsaber?

The assassin charged him. He quickly tossed the blanket over the Ettui as he jumped out of the bed. That slowed it down, but not long enough for Levus to locate his sword. The two circled each other. The assassin finally made a move, deking to its right before aiming its attack to the front. Levus grabbed the small table near him to use for defense, letting the candlesticks that had been on it clatter to the floor.

The guards outside the room must have heard the ruckus, finally, since they pounded on the door telling him to open it. The small table nearly cracked from the impact of the Ettui running into it. Levus had to do something to buy some time. One of the table legs snapped off and fell near his feet. He looked down to happily see it had a sharp end to it.

In one quick motion, Levus let go of the table and rolled to his left. The assassin ran the table into the wall, thus destroying it completely. Levus, before standing up, grabbed the sharpened table leg and waited for it to charge him. When it did, he drove the leg into the assassin's exposed shoulder. The Ettui backed up to the window, trying to pull out his desperate weapon. Levus knew that was exactly what he needed . . . a *real* weapon.

"*Kiilantaa saleetee a.*"

That familiar voice filled his head. He turned to the bed that he originally found himself in, where something stuck out from underneath the mattress. *There it is.* Levus chuckled, realizing it had been underneath him the entire time.

The Ettui made another charge. When it tried to tackle him, Levus rolled out of the way, toward the bed. As he got up, Levus grabbed the Moonsaber and faced his opponent. They slowly paced in a circle, never taking eyes off each other.

The elves still tried their best to pry open the door, Eraddor's voice joining theirs.

The assassin growled at Levus, neither one making a move yet. What could Levus do to finish this? It had to be inventive, something his enemy wouldn't expect. The jewel in the sword began to glow brightly. That was it! A dark smile grew on Levus' face. The Ettui also took notice of the glowing jewel and prepared to strike.

Suddenly, Levus became blurred, while numerous transparent copies of himself formed to both sides of him. The Ettui stared, confused, until all his thoughts ended as a sword pierced through his back and out his chest. He gave a short cry as the shadow of Levus disappeared.

The real Levus, standing behind the Ettui, pulled the Moonsaber out as it fell dead. He stared at his work with a smile. That showed it. He wasn't going to let anything separate him from the sword . . . or anybody.

Levus snapped out of his trance as the door was finally forced open. Eraddor, Thamalos, and the elf guards stormed into the room. The guards secured the perimeter, while Eraddor and Thamalos showed more concern about Levus as he stood over the lifeless Ettui, holding the Moonsaber. How did he find it? Thamalos originally resisted hiding it in his room, but the fort's doctor was fearful of what other physical changes it would do to him if they took the sword away like last time. They determined the best place to conceal it was ironically the closest to the boy. In the end, their logic failed.

"What kept you guys?" he asked.

As the human boy helped clean the area, Thamalos looked at Eraddor. Both could read in the other's eyes that they thought the same thing. They needed to have a talk with Levus tonight to determine how he woke up. If it had been from the sword's calling, there would be cause for concern.

Eraddor sheathed his sword and started assisting the guards.

Thamalos continued to watch uneasily. He didn't like this. First, a large Ettui ship, and now this single Ettui, an assassin no less, identified by the scars on its cheek, tried to kill Levus . . . or steal the sword. Besides its evil potential, what great importance could this sword have that the Ettuii wanted it? It would be something to discuss with Eraddor and Levus when they finished cleaning the remains of the attack. It could wait no longer. Time before the battle was running short.

CHAPTER 15
Dark Morning

"Umph . . ."

Divi's head hurt, pounding like a drum. She tried to collect her bearings, wondering where she would wake up. Was she in Fort Za, still in the past, or in the Time Sage's domain with her friends?

"Divi."

She tried to open her eyes. Everything was still blurry, but she believed a familiar face hovered above her. She saw a distorted smile on it before closing her eyes again. She rubbed her forehead gently. She couldn't believe how much her head hurt.

"I'm glad you are back with us."

Divi wiped her eyes before opening them again. "Did I succeed?"

She tried to lift herself up, but her muscles refused to cooperate, still too physically weak from the time travelling. Tasi and Amber both helped her sit upright. Her eyesight returned to full strength.

"You did well, my young mage."

The Time Sage walked into Divi's view. He handed her a cup and beckoned for her to drink its contents. She didn't know what he had given her, but her throat was so dry she didn't really care. As she took a sip, the refreshing effect it had was a pleasant surprise. Her aching head seemed instantly cured. The Time Sage returned with a cloth and handed it to Divi before kneeling next to her.

She said, "I thought I failed. Nothing I said seem to faze him. The light still engulfed us."

The Time Sage assured Divi, "Levus, regardless of what you did, was destined to become comatose. What you did is give him the memory he needed to go on living. You

327

still seek me after Levus falls in the coma. Time has been repaired for the moment."

A gleam of hope entered her eyes as she asked, "Then Levus is awake?"

"Yes, but your adventure does not end here."

Divi twisted her body so her legs dangled over the side of the cushioned bench. The Time Sage stood up and walked toward the large book.

He explained, "A great battle is about to take place. A battle whose impact on Time will be greater than what Divi accomplished. Your intervention will determine the battle's fate. Its success lies in your hands. I think you know where it is going to take place."

Divi didn't want to say it, but she knew the answer. "Fort Za."

Tasi looked over at her with an expression of horror. "That is where Eraddor and the others are!"

The Time Sage continued, "You will be outnumbered and hope will have seemingly forsaken you, but the truth remains. It is you, Divi, who will decide the fate of Fort Za. And let me add, it is a battle which must be won . . . no matter what the costs may be."

Divi uneasily nodded. What did he mean by *whatever* costs? Did he foresee a point where she'd need to ensure the success of the battle by sacrificing her friends? Was he referring to Levus? She hated these vague premonitions the Time Sage offered.

"The journey is long, so I will send you down a special path out of here. It is a 'time hole,' which I must warn will feel a little strange when you exit it. However, it will take you to an island about two hundred miles north of Fort Za. Your map will be marked. I would get you closer, but . . . forces are not allowing me to, so you will have to make it the rest of the way."

He spoke the truth, too. He had planned on sending them to a small set of islands just twenty miles north of the fort. All his attempts to set up the time hole there were stymied, though. Only two beings could do such a thing; one he was sure didn't do it because it would be in her greatest interest that Divi succeed. Was the magnitude of this event so great that it risked involving . . . *him,* the one he'd been told never to speak of? The Time Sage certainly hoped not.

Could he, the Time Sage, help them kill Ulcinar? Of course he could, as that was supposed to be part of his job. But could he help them defeat the dark equivalent of Mother Time? He seriously doubted it. The Dark One's involvement obviously meant to delay their arrival, with the hope the two mages and half-mage wouldn't make it in time. Two hundred miles would be pushing it, but they should make it . . . if Divi's friends were as good as she had told him they were.

What had the Time Sage more worried was that his premonitions were now becoming reality: Gyyerlith was going to be the battleground for this Time's survival. He always knew this situation could happen during his period of service in the position. But to now be in the middle of this had him . . . scared.

Amber cleared her throat. "Well, you said this battle is going to take place soon. There's only one thing left to do."

Tasi and Divi looked at her and nodded. Amber spoke the truth. Divi didn't know what the future held in this battle, but this was seemingly the destination of the odyssey she had chosen. Whatever happened from this point on would be because of her. Any choices that she made she would have to accept.

Divi finally said, "It's time to leave."

*   *   *   *   *

"We need any man who has the ability to fight to please volunteer! Anyone who can bear arms please come with me to the armory!"

The human guard nodded as a couple of middle-aged men walked past him and through the doorway. General Medkar ordered the families stay in the main storage room located underground beneath the barracks. It was only accessible via the Administration Building and through a complex series of passageways. Should the battle above ground go sour, at least the civilians would be safe. Women and children huddled together amidst the confusion. Why did the soldiers ask them to take up arms? They were here to visit their loved ones stationed at this fort and nothing more. The ship to return home to Cordca was supposed to come back tomorrow morning.

A couple of teenage boys made their way past the guard. Their mother rushed over to try and stop them, but they turned her away. The guard, seeing her grief at her sons' action, tried to console her.

"Listen, I will make sure they are kept out of harm's way. They will serve deep in the fort."

"What is going on?" the mother asked. "Why are you making us fight?"

"We have a situation. General Seth Medkar is doing this strictly as a precaution. You and the rest of the families will be safe."

She wasn't very comforted by his response, but she backed away to a corner as she continued to weep. The human joined an elf guard, who watched another four men walk slowly through the doorway. After a few minutes, the human guard leaned over to the elf.

"I think that is all the help we will get. We cannot force them to help."

"How many have volunteered?" asked the elven guard.

"Nearly a hundred. Not bad out of the four hundred that had come. So many woman and children are here."

The elf guard sighed silently. "Although their assistance is appreciated, it might not be much help. Many seem never to have wielded a weapon in their life. I hope we need not rely on them."

The human guard added, "I hope this threat that Thamalos has seen is nothing more than a false alarm. We should lock the door now. Guards will be down this hallway, with a few inside the room. They have keys outside and in here."

The elf guard nodded as he left. The human guard looked once more toward the crowd of families and cleared his throat.

"Everyone! We are locking the doors for the time being! You will be well protected and no harm will come to you! We will acknowledge to the supervising guard when everything is clear and it is safe to come out!"

The guard waited to see the response. The people only answered with cries of fear. Seeing that, the guard took a deep breath as he slammed the door in front him and locked it.

* * * * *

On the main wall of the fort, Thamalos and Eraddor looked out toward the sea. Thamalos' elf sight had once again served its purpose. He made out the silhouette of a large ship through the morning fog. A heavy wind blew toward the fort. Thamalos knew it would be at most an hour before the fog lifted and the ship would be fully visible. In less than two hours, the ship would crash against Fort Za's shores and then the true test of courage would begin.

A human soldier ran up to Eraddor and whispered something into his ear. He replied in the same low tone before the guard bowed and ran back to the ground level of the fort. Thamalos gazed at Eraddor with much curiosity.

Eraddor stated, "There were not many who volunteered. I knew there wouldn't be."

Thamalos looked toward the ship again. As it came closer, he could hear the roars of the Ettui. The wind seemed an ally to the Ettui, as it carried the sound on its wings to strike fear in the soldiers long before they arrived.

Eraddor continued, "Sydis and the mages have already readied their boats. They will leave shortly."

His comment almost made Thamalos sick. "In the time we have been here, the mages have been slow to decision and reluctant to agreement. Now they leave like cowards."

Eraddor couldn't deny it. Sydis seemed to be the only opposition while everyone else was in agreement. Indeed, it seemed that he only wanted to create turmoil when none existed. Yet, when the choice to leave because of the Ettuii arose, no one was quicker to depart.

Eraddor finally said, "I'm going to have one last talk with Sydis. See if I can convince him to stay."

He walked down the uneven stairway toward the fort. Thamalos knew that Eraddor's attempt would be fruitless. Especially now, since Sydis could sense the great dangers that would land on this shore very soon. Thamalos couldn't bring himself to tell Eraddor. If he mentioned it, would they all have left? Elves weren't supposed to feel guilt, though hanging around Eraddor had given him a keener sense of the human emotion. He quickly shunted these thoughts. The walls would hold, he assured himself. No army of any size had ever passed through these gates. Things would not change now . . . he hoped.

* * * * *

Divi, Tasi, and Amber were struck by a strong breeze as they exited the cave. The cool wind certainly felt good; sad that they wouldn't have time to enjoy it. According to the Time Sage, the battle would happen within hours. They would have left earlier, but the Time Sage insisted on the importance of eating before they left.

Divi was more excited at the prospect of seeing Levus again. It had been over a month since she last had, not counting the journey back in time. Ever since she held him in midst of the light, she thought of nothing but holding him again. If they succeeded today, her desires would come true. The reason she fought for this whole time was within her grasp.

Divi and Tasi sat in the back of the boat while Amber readied it for their journey. As they allowed the current to bring them out into the ocean, Amber prepared the sail, fitting the wooden pole in the middle and spreading the cloth out.

"Yeah, not that I want to lower anyone's spirits, but how are we supposed to get there within a few hours? The Time Sage's mark on the map shows where we need to go and I don't think it's possible. The winds are strong, but not that strong."

Divi and Tasi faced each other and smiled.

Tasi said, "Have you forgotten, Amber? This is a mage-powered boat."

Both mages lowered their hands in the water, chanting a spell silently as Amber continued to work on the sail. Balls of light suddenly formed in Divi and Tasi's hands. The peaceful waters rippled at the power of their spells. The boat moved slightly faster, but not enough for Amber to notice.

Tasi said, "Hold on tight!"

The balls in the mages' hands grew much larger. The boat made a violent jerk. Amber, still fixing the sail, fell to the back. The vessel moved at an incredible speed. Amber was shocked at the waves being left in its wake. It almost seemed that they glided over the water. Divi and Tasi smiled as Amber sat up, slightly dazed, before Divi looked forward confidently. Her quest was nearing its climax. She only hoped that they would not be too late. She had already given up so much to see her Levus again. She wanted badly to tell him not to worry, but they were still hundreds of miles apart. Keeping her eyes focused on the ocean ahead, she quieted her mind.

"Levus, be strong. I'm coming."

* * * * *

Eraddor and Sydis' eyes never left each other as the five mage boats departed Fort Za's island, heading into the fog that was only apparent in the south. All the mages, including Sydis, had covered their heads with the hoods of their robes. Dark clouds crept toward Fort Za. A few drops fell from them, though nothing heavy yet. Eraddor didn't try to hide his anger at Sydis' decision to desert them in this time of need. If they happened to survive this incident, this act of cowardice would not be forgotten.

Then Levus shouted, "Eraddor! Come quickly!"

Eraddor gave Sydis one more dark look before turning to walk up the stairs. Sydis also gazed to the west. He shook his head as the mage boats were swallowed by the fog.

At the top of the main wall, Thamalos, Levus, and Seth stood speechless, watching the west. What approached them was nothing that could be expected.

Seth commented, "Perhaps we didn't make a wise decision."

Eraddor finally made it to the top of the long staircase and stood next to his friends. His eyes opened wide.

334

Thamalos had been wrong. There wasn't just one huge ship, but eight of them!

Seth did the math in his head and the answer terrified him. "There are so many. There must be millions of them."

Eraddor didn't know how to reply. He could see a chance against two hundred-fifty thousand Ettui, but to face nearly two million of them? The ships would land in less than an hour. That would not be enough time to organize an escape. Not now. As much as Eraddor hated to admit it, they were trapped here, surrounded by water. Was this Sydis' plan all along? Did he know about the size this army and not tell anyone? Although Eraddor trusted Thamalos' elf sight, he did realize that a mage's power wasn't as clouded as an elf's by evil auras, possibly allowing them to feel things more accurately.

Levus asked, "What are we going to do? There are far too many of them for us to fight. Without the mages, we don't stand a chance."

"Regardless, we will stay and fight," Eraddor replied. "We made the choice and now we must live through it. Levus, I want you inside. If this attack is to retrieve that sword you carry, I want them to have to work for it. Thamalos, you and I will maintain the front wall and the first line of archers. General Seth, the rest is in your hands."

Eraddor and Thamalos went to the entrance of the fort in the southwest. Levus walked down the stairs and headed inside to the courtyard. Seth stared for a few minutes more at the situation in front of him. The lead ship would crash into the shore any minute now. The first wave of two hundred-fifty thousand Ettui would soon be knocking at his gates. He needed a miracle to win.

As he put his helmet on, General Seth said, "May the gods be with the men, woman, children, and elves of this fort," Then he stopped and shook his head. "What am I saying? To send this army to us means you have forsaken us. I shall see you in hell."

335

CHAPTER 16
The First Wall

The first of the large craft landed on the shore of the island. The Ettui on the decks roared. This generation had never sailed on the open sea before. The Ettui Island Wars cost their race much in terms of lives lost. Some thought they'd never take to the open waters again. Thanks to the prowess of their great leader, Darca, and the influence of his ally, Ulcinar, the ocean became a renewed reality, as did vengeance against their age-old enemy. It would repay the many deaths at Mount Hrithgorn so many years ago at the end of that war.

From his cabin, Kile stepped out to join the mass of Ettui soldiers. All moved out of his way as he walked to the bow of the ship. Kile smiled at the situation before them. Just as Ulcinar predicted, they stayed to defend Fort Za. It wouldn't matter, as Kile had nearly two million under his command. The more inside the fort, the better.

"Lower the anchors."

One of the commanding Ettui repeated Kile's order at a shout. Five Ettui deckhands ran over to the four anchors and turned the locks. The rattling chains of the anchors could be heard even over the army's roars. As they splashed in the water, two more ships landed to the right of Kile's. He waited until the fourth ship joined them before continuing his orders.

"Open the gates! Line up the troops and prepare the projectiles!"

The commander again shouted to the others. From the side of the ship, five Ettui held a black flag and faced it toward the other ship. The other ship acknowledged the message and did the same until the other two ships also received it. On Kile's ship, two large doors opened like a drawbridge. Mud kicked up as they slammed into the ground. Doors on the other three ships followed their lead.

Slowly, Ettui marched out of Kile's ship. After every three regiments exited, a small group would push out a large catapult. Each already had a large spear-like weapon loaded, and a wagon followed containing more spears.

* * * * *

On the first wall, Eraddor and Thamalos watched. Elf and human forces stared in fear at the challenge before them. About a half-mile away, the Ettui army gathered into well-established formations. Thamalos knew the attack would only start this way, becoming chaotic and unorganized as the battle progressed.

He observed, "They are going to rush the wall."

Eraddor replied, "It is good that we reinforced it with iron blocks. They shouldn't be able to come in that way. If we can hold this wall and take out the archers, we might be able to win."

Before Thamalos could reply, both men were distracted by a crying sound. They turned their heads to see a boy who could be no more than fourteen, holding a sword almost as large as him and wearing armor too big for his size. Eraddor walked over to the child, who didn't notice him until Eraddor's hand touched his shoulder. The boy jumped slightly, but seeing who it was, returned his gaze to the sea of black monsters before them. His uncontrollable shaking made the loose armor rattle.

Eraddor asked, "Afraid?"

"I have never known it until now."

"What is your name?"

"Tefferis," replied the boy.

"Tefferis, that is a wonderful name. Why do you fight instead of being in sanctuary with your family?"

337

Tefferis didn't reply at first. Perhaps he was too afraid to speak the truth. Boys his age were expected to take on larger roles in life, whether as a farmer or an aristocrat. Eraddor himself was already a drifter by then, so he never had those expectations. He did know, though, why the boy had to fight. He only hoped it wouldn't be a regrettable decision by the time the sun set.

Tefferis finally replied, "I have heard what the Ettui do to prisoners. I will not allow them to take me easily. If I am to die this day, I will take some of them with me."

Eraddor admired the courage the young man showed, even though fear dominated any other emotion in him. He was certain everyone here felt the same. Not a word had been said by any of the men since the discovery that more than one ship barreled down at them. The elves seemed composed, but Eraddor believed that after today even this supposedly fearless race would no longer be known as such.

Eraddor patted Tefferis on the shoulder. "Show strength then, my friend. I guarantee you we shall be victorious. The gods will be on our side."

Eraddor wished he had the full confidence that his words projected. He couldn't promise them victory, as much as he would have liked. His oath, though, did seem to comfort Tefferis enough to lessen his fearful quivering. Eraddor stood up and rejoined Thamalos, who continued to look ajead, not even acknowledging him.

Eraddor said, "We better get in position. The Ettui forces are nearly in formation. Seth is ready at the tower."

Thamalos adjusted his bow and ran toward the north end of the wall without saying a word. Eraddor suspected the elf prince felt guilty for not telling everyone at the meeting that he had seen more than one ship. He had made an apology to General Seth, but Eraddor could understand why Thamalos kept quiet. If he mentioned that more than one ship was on its way, everyone most certainly would have deserted Fort Za. If they had, the Ettui would have had a stronghold within striking distance of anywhere on the mainland. For the Elves, this was perhaps the setup for a pincer attack with the Ettui force they saw in Sardon. For everyone else, it allowed the the enemy to attack anywhere from Myyril to Cordca with no warning. Even if it meant their annihilation, Thamalos thought it important to hurt the enemy as much as possible here to delay such invasions. The elves would find out soon enough. Was it worth all the life that might be lost here today? Time would tell.

* * * * *

On the lead boat, the commanding Ettui standing next to Kile watched his hornblowers until they waved their instruments, then turned to Kile. Ulcinar's second hand man never took his eyes from Fort Za. Somewhere on that doomed island was Levus. He did hope that he would be the one to slay him. Not one of these Ettui pawns would be worthy of such an opponent. His strict role, unfortunately, per Ulcinar, had him remaining on the ship until the fort fell. Ettui tended not to take prisoners. Kile could do the math.

He finally deigned to order the commanding Ettui, "Prepare the troops."

The Ettui nodded and shouted something in the forbidden language. The Ettui hornblowers acknowledged it by blowing twice. The troops responded quickly. The entire army, even those still inside the ship, roared in unison. The roars became rhythmic, and everyone in Fort Za could feel the power those voices carried.

* * * * *

"Truly frightening!"

Bironn knew his reaction must be shared by every single mage as they watched from a rock that jetted from the sea. They docked at least five miles away from the island, but it sounded like the Ettui were five feet away. The longer he listened to their war cry, the more he trembled, and he wasn't even involved in the battle.

"And you wanted to stay and fight. Now you see how foolish they are."

Bironn faced Sydis, who had made the decision to stop here before heading back to Myyril. What was the logic of such a move? To prove to the other mages that he was right? He would not be so cruel as to watch the fort fall . . . at least Bironn didn't think he would.

Bironn said, "I still think we should have stayed. Whether the fort falls or not, once it is discovered we left, we will feel the wraith of the other races."

Sydis replied, looking almost offended, "You speak of illogical fears. You see the army they will fight. They have no chance of victory. I have just saved the lives of fifty mages, and this is the thanks I receive? If you wish to join the rest of them at the fort and die, so be it. Take a boat and sail back. You will not be remembered as martyrs, but as fools."

The other mages remained silent, none of them stepping forward to volunteer. It was difficult enough to think over the continuous war cry of the Ettui. Sydis gave a small smile.

"Wise decision. Come now and let us leave this place. I do not wish to see a massacre. The election of a steward for Myyril is only days away and I will not be absent being a candidate. Plus my apprentice, Cyprinus, is probably missing me."

The mages headed toward the boats and followed Sydis as he embarked. Bironn took one more look at Fort Za. The Ettui were louder than ever and the attack would begin soon. Part of him wanted to return to the island and defend the fort, but what could he, a lone mage, do that would make a difference? He placed his hand before his eyes and bowed his head slightly.

"May you be safe and the gods watch over you."

He quickly turned around and made his way to one of the boats before Sydis saw his prayer.

*   *   *   *   *

"Archers! Ready your fire!"

The men and elves on the first wall followed Eraddor's order without hesitation. The Ettuii chanting had quickened its pace, which could only mean their imminent charge. The forces on the first wall stood five rows deep, making it a little difficult to move around. Eraddor figured, though, that by the time the Ettui made it to the wall, there would be some room. He glanced toward Thamalos, who also prepared the troops to fire. Eraddor had to give credit to the elves. He didn't care if it was their nature to show no emotion. Facing this army would bring fear into anyone's heart, yet they remained calm.

On the large tower connected to the second wall, General Seth Medkar had an even better view of the enemy. They filled the landscape so thoroughly that he couldn't even see the shoreline.

His second-in-command, Tyrrarin, reported the current situation. "Sir, the main attack force is nearly ready to charge. The fifth ship to the left has yet to disembark their troops despite their ramp being partially down. There are still at least three ships heading to the north of the island: two on the west side and one on the east. We believe they will be trying to flank us from the back and both sides."

Seth sighed. "Surrounding us. Is there a chance that those ships will be too large to enter in the shallow waters?"

"It is possible. The elves docked their ship like these farther north of here."

"We can't afford to defend the northern section of the fort. With no real coastline, they can't land there. They haven't shown their strategy for breaking through our wall, so let us focus on this main group. If we can hold them and stop the ships from going to flank us, we might be able to send a small ship to destroy their leader."

"I will give the order to our troops."

Seth nodded and Tyrrarin climbed down the tower. That did give him some hope. He always believed the shallow waters around Fort Za as a natural defense against invading forces, but they never had a ship large enough to test it. It was probably the reason the elves hadn't landed here in the first place. If this worked, that would disable part of the Ettui attack. He'd also need to keep an eye on that fifth ship. Maybe they had a problem that prevented them from landing and getting their troops out, leaving a quarter million Ettui idle and unavailable. He had to look for any luck he could, given their circumstances.

Seth turned to the archers on the second wall and ordered, "Second line! Ready your volley!"

* * * * *

Kile unsheathed his sword and smiled. The time had come for his great victory. He lacked an Ettuiis senses, but he could almost taste the fear of those on Fort Za. He scanned the Ettui forces on the boat, all staring impatiently at him. They, too, couldn't wait to for the attack to commence. They had a thirst for blood, that of the occupants in the stronghold. Many of them were salivating, some enough to form small puddles at their feet.

Kile pointed the Marasam to the sky. The Ettui on deck grew excited, cheering and banging their armor. He lowered his sword so it was directed at Fort Za. The hornblower gave the signal, and the horns on the neighboring ships followed his lead. The army gave a roar of approval as they charged.

* * * * *

The men and elves on the first wall watched in horror as the swarm of Ettui came at them. Eraddor nocked his arrow and lined up his shot.

"Ready your aim! On my command, fire! The time to show fear has passed! Let us show them who needs to be afraid!"

The men followed his order, though many still showed the fear that Eraddor hoped would subside. Within seconds, everyone on the first wall was prepared to fire. All they could do was wait for the enemy to get within range.

General Seth Medkar, seeing the Ettui coming fast, shouted, "Prepare for second wave! Aim high!"

All of the archers on the second wall did as he ordered. Seth raised his sword in the air and waited for Eraddor and Thamalos' command. He knew how important keeping up a steady stream of arrows would be in cementing victory. He wished they had maintained the cannons that used to don the first wall after the Ettui Island Wars. But through neglect, almost all of them were useless.

Eraddor tried to maintain focus, but he found that increasingly difficult as the mass of Ettui reached the halfway point between the sea and the fort. Dust and mud rose, making it difficult to see the army behind the incoming first wave. The rumble of the charge caused the fort's old stones to vibrate. Pebbles clattered loose on some of them.

Eraddor yelled, "Wait for it!"

The Ettui army had come within a hundred yards of the first wall. He would have normally fired already, but the second wall division of archers was to fire directly after the first. If they did it now, every arrow would have hit nothing, and they needed every strike possible. The enemy army was nearly in range.

Thamalos picked his target area as he heard Eraddor's command, "Iilatta." (*Wait.*)

The Ettui forces were fifty yards from the wall. Sweat covered Eraddor and he was certain everyone else felt the same. He did his best to block out the noise of battle and closed his eyes briefly. He silenced his mind, trying to concentrate on the situation. Time for the defense of Fort Za to start. He wasn't even sure how he received the role of leading the forces on the first wall. He had no prior experience at the head of an army, with the exception of the failed Barbata campaign.

Eraddor slowly opened his eyes, the advancing Ettui now only twenty-five yards away. He took a deep breath and exhaled.

"Fire!"

Thamalos, hearing Eraddor's command, repeated in Elvish, "Firatelii!"

The first wave of arrows were unleashed upon the army. Nearly every one connected with its target.

Seth lowered his arm as the front wall reloaded.

"Second wall, fire!"

The three rows of men fired their arrows with a higher arc. They sailed above the front wall and into the incoming wave. By this time, the front set of archers was ready to fire again. Eraddor and Thamalos both gave their commands and as before, every arrow hit its mark. Indeed, with so many targets, it was hard to miss for even the poorest of shots.

So far, their progress pleased Eraddor. The Ettui would inevitably reach the wall, but the steady stream of arrows depleted their front lines. It could slow or even completely prevent them from getting organized or assembling their own archers.

Seth yelled to the men on the ground, "They are near the wall! Begin your attack!"

The commander below acknowledged his order and rushed to a single row of archers lined in front of the wall, shouting, "Remove the plugs!"

344

The archers removed two-footlong wooden plugs from the wall, revealing the battlefield through the slits left behind. The archers readied their arrows, the tips partially inside the slits. They could see the Ettui only ten feet from the other side.

Theie commander yelled, "Fire!"

The archers unleashed their arrows, hitting their unsuspecting targets with haunting accuracy. Despite all the best efforts of the combined human and elf forces, though, the surviving Ettui were about to reach the wall.

Eraddor, seeing their advancement, yelled, "Brace yourself!"

As the Ettui tsunami hit the wall, it rumbled slightly. Eraddor sighed in relief, however, that it held much stronger than it appeared. For the time being, the Ettui were stopped with no place to go.

Eraddor commanded, "Keep firing! Kill any archers first!"

The soldiers on the first wall and just behind it resumed their efforts. Seth, seeing the wall survived the initial impact, sighed with relief. He raised his arm and lowered it again as the second wall's forces shot another volley of arrows past the first wall, who were preparing to fire the next surge.

Suddenly, a small wave of arrows emerged from the Ettui sea. Only a couple found their mark, but any casualties they could little afford. Both fallen men dropped into the Ettui horde. Eraddor didn't want to imagine what future lay ahead for them, however short.

He ordered, "Find the archers!"

He asked the impossible. There were too many Ettui bunched together to differentiate archers from anyone else.

Thamalos saw more approaching and shouted, "Shields!"

The soldiers on the first wall quickly grabbed their shields as the Ettui arrows arrived. One elf was injured, but no more than that. More importantly, they identified the positions of the archers. Eraddor whistled for his troops. "Archers forty feet into the mass! Take them out quickly!"

The first wall's forces aimed and fired into the vicinity of where the arrows had come from. With the archers out of the way and so long as the wall held, they would be shooting at easy targets all day.

* * * * *

On the ship, Kile and the head Ettui watched the progress of the battle. It seemed like forever since their forces advanced on the island. The head Ettui growled.

"Our army has been unable to penetrate the walls. They are stronger than we have anticipated."

Kile laughed ominously. "Then we destroy it and walk over its remains. Order the catapults to begin their onslaught and have the troops prepare the bridges."

The Ettui bowed and grabbed the horn around his neck. He blew a rhythmic tone and the hornblowers on the other ships followed suit. The ground forces understood the orders given to them. The Ettui who controlled the catapults, indicated by their helmets with antlers on them, each grabbed hold of a large lever. Showing much strength, they pulled the lever down. The spear-like projectiles lifted into the air toward Fort Za.

* * * * *

"What is that?"

Eraddor could swear he heard something as well, despite all the noise the Ettui were making. To him, it sounded like a large arrow whizzing through the air, coming closer. Yet, he was not able to see anything yet.

Seconds later, Eraddor spotted the source. It was made of dark wood exactly like that of the ships, so it blended in against them, only seen when it went against the sky.

Eraddor yelled, "Prepare for impact!"

The men on the first wall had very little time to react, though. As soon as Eraddor spoke, the spear-like missile drove itself through the wall. The soldiers not fast enough to move were crushed by the force of the missle and falling rocks. He didn't want to think how many had died, but there was nothing he could do about it. Although thankfully the hole it left behind was too high for the enemy ground troops to use, their new strategy caused Eraddor great concern.

"More on the way!"

Eraddor didn't have any time to react before three missiles reached the wall. The first one fell short into the enemy army. The second one hit closer to the bottom of the wall, but it didn't penetrate. The third one went through the top taking a larger chunk off than the previous one. The soldiers on the ground moved out of the way as the blade portion crashed to the earth.

Tyrrarin rushed to Seth's side and said, "Sir, we have to reinforce the wall. Their strategy of attack presents a danger."

Seth couldn't agree more. "Prepare the bricklayers. Have them patch any sections that appear weak. The first wall must not fall!"

Tyrrarin nodded and blew a horn. After two short hoots, the second wall's gates opened a crack and about thirty men came out carrying buckets and tools. The ground troops between the first two walls backed up to the second. The workers patched the lower holes with pre-made bricks. Seth was curious how this group would do, since he first ordered it formed up it a year ago. He introduced it because of a near-fatal accident where a section of the far east wall crumbled on a group of training soldiers. The bricklayers worked well in practice with mock attacks, but Seth knew that the face of real combat sometimes changed men and how they acted.

Separated into teams of six, four people applied the mortar while two men handed them the bricks to various parts of the wall. Although the damage was minimal and too high for the enemy to break through, they seemed to work better once the first layer blocked their view of the enemy masses on the other side.

Eraddor and Thamalos continued their attack from atop the first wall, but it seemed like they got nowhere. For every Ettui that fell, another filled its spot just as quickly. Most of the archers had started running short on arrows. Seth's runners tried resupplying the forces, but the Ettui noticed this as they stood out against their stationary attackers. Wanting to keep their enemy's quivers empty, they focused on the runners. The barrage from the archers on the second wall lessened as many of them shared their arrows to keep the front wall's attack strong.

"Look out!"

Eraddor heard the scream and turned to see a giant spear connect with the very top of the wall. It knocked off at least twenty soldiers injuring or killing most of them.

Thamalos heard a crash of another sort from his right. One of the Ettui ships advanced toward shore. By the large splash that it made, though, Thamalos suspected that the shallow water was stopping their advancement as the boat's hull scraped on the ocean floor. It even began listing to starboard before resting to a halt. For a change, something had gone their way.

The bricklayers were doing an adequate job securing the holes created by the large spears. It became tougher as the battle continued and the Ettui became more accurate . . .

* * * * *

The Ettui continued their ravaging assault, unleashing the projectiles as quickly as they could load them. Some of their ground forces tried to scale the wall but failed as they had nothing to grasp on to. Kile's displeasure that the first wall hadn't fallen yet showed on his face. At the same time, he did admire Fort Za's resilience, and remained confident that despite it, it would only be a matter of time before the wall fell.

The Ettui commander, who was returning after correcting a flag signal mistake, leapt in front of Kile. "The ships are nearly in position. One of them on the left appears immobilized."

Kile replied, "When the other ships are in position, begin the next phase. Have the small boats ready to move. The sight of that first wall still standing sickens me!"

The Ettui nodded and returned to his place on the bow. Kile folded his arms, disgusted. He would have preferred the extra bodies from the now-grounded ship. Because of the angle of list, that ship couldn't commence its attack on the western facilities, which housed the war room among other things. Plus, the fifth ship that was supposed to land just southeast of them had missed their landing point, so its ramp could not open onto of the higher coastline. Such a bother!

Yet all those little inconveniences in the end wouldn't matter. He just had to adjust the plan slightly. Kile uncrossed his arms, looking once more at Fort Za ready to deliver his next order.

* * * * *

"Bricklayers! Return to the second wall!"

Most of them heard Seth's order, but others had been deafened by the howl of flying projectiles, the thunder of them crashing against the stone walls, and the screams of injured and dying men. He was pleased with their effort, but it ultimately did little. The enemy caused more damage to the wall than the bricklayers could repair. They also started running short on materials. Had the enemy forces been smaller, this group of rebuilders probably would've been their savior. The force they now faced, though, was anything but small.

Seth had to yell his order again before all of them returned safely behind the second wall. As he examined the area in front of him, he shed phantom tears. Many elf and human men lay dead from Ettui arrows or from falling off the wall. Through the remaining holes he could see glimpses of the army that wished to annihilate every last person in this fort. He gave all the brave soldiers on the first wall credit for staring into the odds before them and still having the courage and strength to fight in this time of need. If he stood in their boots, his reaction would be different . . . and one he was quite ashamed to think of.

"We need more arrows!"

Eraddor barely turned around when one of the runners provided him with a full quiver. He quickly exchanged it for his depleted quiver and continued his attack. Every few minutes he scanned the battlefield for their leader, but with little success and much displeasure. Normally, the Ettui leader would be in the middle regiment when they formed for battle. The more he thought about it, though, with the size of this force and the uncommon intricacies of communication they were using with the horns and flags, the head commander didn't need to leave the ship.

"Eraddor!"

Thamalos weaved toward him. The elf stopped to help a human who had nearly slipped from the wall before reaching Eraddor.

"What is the matter?"

Thamalos said, "The Ettui are up to something. Have you noticed that their archers have slowly travelled out of range?"

Honestly, Eraddor hadn't. He wasn't sure how one could in that discolored mass. The only way they knew about the archers was when they started firing at them.

"What do you suggest we do?" he asked Thamalos.

"Keep an eye on the ships. I feel the next attack will come from there."

Eraddor could hardly believe his suggestion. What could the docked ships possibly do? No known cannon could fire from that far away; the catapults had to cross half the battlefield to be in range of the fort. He didn't even see the mouths of any cannons on the deck or from the small portholes near the top. The elf had been right, though, about many things which Eraddor thought impossible.

"I will."

Thamalos nodded and sprinted back to his side of the wall. Eraddor stared out at the ships. The elf prince did have a point. Even the barrage of large spears decimating this wall had lessened. He might be right, but what could they possibly fire from the ship that would come near to penetrating the wall?

*   *   *   *   *

"Kile, the cannons are in position."

At last! It had seemed to take forever, but they were ready for what should be the attack that took the first wall for good. If he wanted, he could've continued shooting projectiles at the wall until it fell, but what was the fun in that? Not only did he want to break that wall, he wanted to break the wills of every individual in that fort.

Kile walked up to the bow of the ship alongside the Ettui leader. He smiled deeply, barely able to wait to deliver the order. He wanted to be sure he could clearly see the great wall of Fort Za crumble.

351

Finally, Kile raised the Marasam and ordered, "Fire the bridges and begin the final phases of Operation Surround."

The Ettui bowed. "Yes, noblest of Ulcinar's followers!"

He licked his lips with a deformed tongue before blowing the signal from his horn. The other hornblowers, hearing the order, repeated it so all the battlefield could hear. The ones bearing flags waved red and black colors.

On the twentieth floors of the twenty-three-level ships, groups of Ettui soldiers surrounded four cannon-like machines, complex with numerous blinking lights. Behind them stretched out miles of mangled rope and wood. At the stern of the ships, very heavily armored Ettui awaited. They wore so much armor that they had to stand to their full extent, making them nearly as tall as humans. Two Ettui near the cannons grabbed large hooks, with the rope contraptions connected at their back ends. After loading the guns, they stood back and waited. One Ettui behind each cannon had a torch so they could clearly see the panel in the darkened innards of ships, and all of them drooled as they eagerly awaited the order.

After what seemed like hours, the hornblowers delivered Kile's order and the Ettui on the twentieth decks ignited the cannons by pressing the button on top. The insides of the artillery pieces began to spin and glow. The distance was already pre-entered on the device, a gracious gift from the Dark Lord, Ulcinar. He had told them these instruments of war came from one of his travels, but the Ettui had been nearly everywhere and none recalled ever seeing some this . . . new. Ulcinar called them thrust cannons. Although they looked out of place on the older ships, the soldiers operating them knew of their potential after training on them these past weeks. The enemy hiding behind the walls would never expect it.

The cannons, nearly ready to fire, grew louder and louder.

* * * * *

Eraddor and the others on the first wall rested, wondering what would happen next. The enemy archers had ceased firing for the moment, as had the Ettui launching the large spikes. Even the Ettui army below had stopped its advance and filled the landscape with a bone-chilling chant. Despite the loud calls, the silence from the lack of fighting noises disturbed Eraddor. Like a volcano, the enemy had saved up something and it was near to erupting.

Thamalos had started caring for one of the injured elves when numerous booming sounds came from the distance. He had never heard anything like them before. They resembled cannons, but quieter. There wasn't any smoke as from a fired cannon. Due to his exceptional elf hearing, he listened beyond the Ettuiis chanting and what mere human ears could grasp. He wasn't the only elf to hear the strange sounds as many looked in the ships' direction. Something was coming their way, but no one could identify it.

"Eraddor! Eyes forward!" shouted Thamalos.

He barely heard the elf prince's suggestion over the chanting. Nothing out of the ordinary, from what he could see. A couple of the men curiously gazed in the direction Eraddor stared at.

After a few seconds, he did see something hurtling toward them.

Eraddor yelled, "Look out!"

The soldiers nearest to him tried locating what alarmed their commanding officer, but couldn't see anything. Eraddor pointed in the direction of the incoming objects, but to no avail. Like the large spears, they blended in with the ships behind them.

Tefferis, the boy he'd spoken to earlier, froze in fear. Eraddor noticed this and rushed toward him. The object reached the wall just as Eraddor snatched Teffaris away. The men surrounding them were jolted off. Eraddor protected the boy as more of those objects crashed past. After a few seconds, the barrage stopped.

"I want you to go behind the second wall. Help them with the fortifications."

"Yes, Mister Eraddor."

The young man ran as fast as he could. Eraddor made sure that Tefferis got safely behind the second wall before he looked at what the enemy had shot at them. They looked like . . . large grappling hooks? Much different from those used for climbing; these were attached to a complex series of ropes and wooden planks.

Some of the men nearby examined the hooks, an examination which stopped after more of them collided with the second wall.

"What type of madness is this?" asked Eraddor.

Seth tried to decipher the enemy's new strategy. He had never seen such a thing before in his life.

Tyrrarin suggested, "I think they are trying to bring down the wall from the inside. That is the only explanation for these hooks."

"I don't think so. It would take more than what they have fired to do such a task. Even if that was their plan, it would surely be faster to continue firing those large projectiles and blast their way through instead."

Shortly after Seth said this, the hooks began dragging on the ground back toward the ships. Eraddor and the others could hear a loud humming from the enemy vessels. The Ettui on the ground softened their chants in preparation for the next phase of the attack. Eraddor had a sick feeling in his gut that this would be the last stand on the first wall. Whatever the enemy had planned, if it succeeded, then the wall would come down. May the gods help them all should that happen.

* * * * *

Behind the second wall, Levus stood among the rest of the army. They didn't know the situation on the first wall, but from what the lieutenants preached, the longer the first wall stood, the more likely they were to win. Somehow, Levus doubted that. They could hear the Ettuii war cries and the orders of General Seth Medkar, who stood on the highest tower of the second wall. If victory sounded like this, he didn't want to know what defeat was like.

"Restock the archers on the first wall! Every arrow you can spare!" yelled Seth.

It had been a while since he'd given that order. Something was happening. Except they could not see it. They could only follow the battle with their ears. Levus tightened his grip on the Moonsaber again. The enemy would soon be coming to him.

Isiiarra....

Not now, voice! The battle would be coming not only to him, but for his sword. He wasn't going to let them take it from him. It was his!

Suummanta friac....

Levus quickly loosened his grip on the sword's handle. Both men next to him moved slightly away. Did they hear the voice as well? Did he maybe whisper the words? Why was this happening now? He checked his neck for the amulet the Great Tree gave him, but couldn't find it. Whatever protection he had against the voice would not be there. Maybe it was for the best.

"Second wall archers! Focus on the bridges!"

That definitely didn't sound good . . . and what bridges? Levus adjusted the ill-fitting helmet they gave him and stared uneasily at the right-hand gate of the second wall.

Harrtuann eestarra ....

If the Ettui broke through the first wall, there was no way that this second one would stop them. Once they found their way past that, all hope of victory would be lost. He closed his eyes, trying to focus on what he could do to help win this battle.

As he did, the jewel on the Moonsaber glowed ever so dimly.

* * * * *

Eraddor could not believe his eyes. As the hooks secured themselves at the top of the wall, each ship sprouted four bridges, made of the rope connected to them. He had never seen ropes this thick, impossible to snap with arrows. Being short on those, he didn't even want to suggest that. A strange metal wrapped around the ropes all the way up to the hooks, which extended at least five feet over the front of the wall. The bridge decks were tightly formed boards of wood.

The Ettui on the ground banged their armor with their weapons. If there was any consolation, it was that the ground forces had been unable to break through. As they'd hoped, the first wall held.

Yet the enemy apparently had a backup plan. They no longer planned on smashing though it. They decided to go over it.

The bridges swayed slightly from the wind until they were pulled taut.

"They come."

Eraddor didn't have Thamalos' elf sight, but he could tell when the enemy started making their move. The bridges now vibrated as the Ettui moved across them. Soon Eraddor could vaguely see the oncoming forces. They wore much heavier armor than the rest of the army below and even stood upright, rather than slouched over like their brethren.

Thamalos said, "They are mutants. They can run like men instead of normal Ettui."

Eraddor figured they had five minutes before the first wave of armored Ettui would reach them. They didn't have a choice. They needed to destroy the bridges. To do that required a very dangerous, but also unavoidable attempt. Eraddor grabbed a short knife from his belt and raised it in the air.

"Anyone with a knife! Cut the bridges!"

Eraddor charged first to jump on the bridge above the Ettui masses, heading to where the rope emerged from the metal casing, left exposed. Others followed on all the bridges. The rope proved very tough, but Eraddor sliced at it, fraying the area he worked on. The other soldier helping him on the other side had more difficulty, mainly because his attention stayed on the Ettui crossing the bridge.

Thamalos watched the ground forces for archers who might shoot anyone attempting to cut the ropes. Whether because they didn't see Eraddor and the others, or because all their archers had retreated out of range temporarily, the only danger seemed to be the enemy on the bridges.

After what seemed like an eternity of cutting, Eraddor weakened the rope on his side, causing the bridge to shudder. That impeded the Ettuii progress slightly, but they recovered. Eraddor assisted the other soldier.

The Ettui on the bridge had come very close to them now. Taking an arrow, Thamalos fired at the leader, hitting it in the neck. It did slow the rest of the line as they had to climb over the dead body. He wished he hadn't used his sacred quiver so much during the Barbatan campaign. Like all objects maintained by Juiiladdor, prized elf smith and the guardian of the elves' sacred items, after heavy use it needed a long time to recharge. Although it had helped immensely against the shadow dragon in the Thorii Palace, an unlimited quiver giving him the ability to take out three to four enemies at a time would have been invaluable now.

Thamalos yelled, "Archers, cover the cutters! Don't fire unless necessary"

Although he realized they would be using much-needed arrows, it would at least give them more time to take out the bridges before the Ettui could reach the wall. He kept grabbing arrows out of his quiver to slow their progress.

Seth, who saw what Thamalos tried, realized they could use some relief.

"Archers, fire at the leaders!"

The archers on the second row aimed carefully before firing their volley toward the bridges. Many arrows were blocked by the Ettui shields, but most found their mark.

After what seemed like forever, Eraddor and the other soldier finally frayed the rope on the other side, causing the bridge to shake violently. All the Ettui on the bridges dropped to their knees. It was time.

"Eraddor! Get off! Archers! Aim for the ropes!"

He and the other soldier left the bridge as quickly as possible. The Ettui attempted to move forward, but the bridge was unstable due to the weakened rope losing its taut, and thus made it difficult to support their weight. Five elf archers readied their bows.

Thamalos yelled, "Firatelii!"

The archers fired and hit the ropes with impressive accuracy. Eraddor smiled as the bridge and the near mile-long line of Ettui on it fell onto the ground forces.

He went to work organizing the remaining troops on the first wall. "Everyone! Join the others!"

He tried not to think about all the dead bodies he leapt over to reach the next closest bridge. Eleven more bridges remained . . . a seemingly insurmountable number. He was thankful the ship on the far west hadn't fired any of theirs. Fort Za's defenders needed to try, though. If they could take out even seven of them, Eraddor figured they had a realistic chance to succeed. On the bridges, the Ettui were bottled up and contained.

Another bridge crashed to the ground.

* * * * *

The Ettui commander turned to Kile, slightly concerned. The enemy had found a way to counter their attack. Kile, however, watched without a flinch.

Fort Za's recent success was valiant, but useless. Their defeat was inevitable, and Kile knew it. The Ettui forces had gone three-quarters of the way down most of the bridges. The elves and humans had no possible way to destroy them all in time . . . especially without the mages.

Kile finally noticed the concerned Ettui leader. "Why stare at me so? Continue focusing all the cannons on one spot of the wall."

* * * * *

One more bridge crashed to the ground, silencing the enemies it landed on. Eraddor began to feel the exhaustion as the third one fell. The muscles in his right arm ached from the constant slicing with his knife. All around him, other soldiers labored as well. If only Sydis and the mages hadn't abandoned them, they could have just used their magic to destroy the bridges easily.

Eraddor stepped away as another soldier replaced him. He needed rest, if even for a few seconds. The Ettui were nearing the wall on every remaining bridge. His hope of cutting all of them had fallen apart.

Eraddor ordered, "Stop cutting! Take up your spears and swords and prepare for close combat!"

Thamalos ran to him, clearly dismayed by Eraddor's decision. "What are you thinking? We can do this!"

Eraddor replied, "We can't cut the remaining bridges before the Ettui forces reach us! There are far too many of them and we haven't enough arrows to hold them back. This is the best chance we have at deterring the enemy. You must see this, old friend!"

He truthfully could not. Yes, the Ettui drew closer with every second, but they already had taken down three bridges. A few more and they could focus all their fighting forces on the remaining ones. Despite his belief that they should stick to the plan, he didn't want to undermine Eraddor's authority. The humans here had started respecting him, maybe even more than Seth Medkar. To argue with Eraddor, a man he himself gave this command to, would be counterproductive in encouraging the humans to fight. Hesitantly, Thamalos ordered the remaining elf fighters to prepare to engage the enemy. He looked toward Eraddor once more.

"It is decisions like these that make people heroes or fools. I hope this turns out to be the former."

Eraddor realized those words meant a lot, especially coming from an elf, but he felt it the right thing to do. The remaining forces on the first wall readied their spears and pointed them at the incoming Ettui, who were no farther than thirty feet away.

Eraddor, manning a spear as well, yelled, "Brace yourself!"

The soldiers tightened their grips on their weapons. Eraddor suddenly rushed at one of the bridges and stabbed the lead Ettui, killing him and the one behind him too. Leaving his spear impaled in their bodies, he retreated behind the remaining spear-bearers, the Ettui less than ten feet from them.

Unsheathing his sword, Eraddor yelled, "Show them no mercy!"

Soon, all that could be heard was spears crashing against Ettui armor. Nearly every spear broke, but not without taking an enemy soldier with it. Despite that small victory, the Ettui on the bridges continued to move forward.

Eraddor yelled, "Take up swords! Charge!"

As the lead Ettui set foot on the wall, Eraddor's blade greeted it. On the other bridges, the rest made their first steps into bared steel. Now the real battle was beginning.

*　*　*　*　*

"I'm scared!"

In the secret room of Fort Za, the women, children, and elders sat shivering. Despite being underground and near the back of the island, they could hear the Ettui outside. The soldiers inside, meant to help keep morale up, even found themselves doubting. They had been down here for hours and all they could hear were the enemy's chants and the power of their footsteps. They wondered if the invaders had won and that it was only a matter of time before they discovered this hideaway. Everyone knew the difficulty of hiding from an Ettui nose.

A slight knock came from the other side of the door. The soldiers inside sighed in relief that at least the enemy hadn't taken over the fort. From the news expressed in code by the series of knocks, it appeared that the first wall, although laboring, still held strong. The closest soldier to the door told the comrade-at-arms next to him to inform the people.

The next series of knocks described the number of the enemy left. This the soldier did not report.

*　*　*　*　*

Kile stared at the scene, disappointed. Nearly twenty minutes had passed since the bridge attack started and the first wall had not yet fallen. He could see why the Ettui had such difficulty in defeating the elves. Even with the gracious help of Lord Ulcinar, they still failed.

One of the hornblowing Ettui ran to Kile and reported, "The catapults are almost positioned as requested."

361

He didn't wait around to see Kile's reaction. *At least they can follow orders well*, he figured. He hadn't thought he would have to resort to this, but he wanted to get this attack to the next step. Time for that damn wall to be destroyed.

Even though no Ettui stood near him, he knew his order was still heard. "When they are in position, fire them all in unison."

* * * * *

"Strengthen the right side!"

Eraddor shouted the order as an Ettui soldier killed another one of the elves. He dispatched it as the reinforcements arrived. Although he could only speak for himself, Eraddor thought the first wall's forces had done extremely well against this attack. They lost more men by the minute, yet more enemy soldiers fell than human and elves. If they could sustain this, perhaps they had a chance to survive this latest attack. He was beginning to hope that Seth would call the troops behind the second wall to fill in for lost reserves, but he would make do with what he had.

Behind Eraddor, several Ettui cried out. He turned around and quickly swiped his sword down three times on the first one, then kicked its body over the side of the wall into the Ettui hordes. The second one had a spear and tried to impale him. Eraddor moved out of the way and grabbed the weapon. Using his weight, he forced the Ettui down into the reserve soldiers, who finished it off.

Thamalos had his own success. Not one of the Ettui had made it more than ten feet from the bridge. Elves were commonly known more for their archery than hand-to-hand combat, but Thamalos proved otherwise. Using two weapons which looked like short swords or long knives, he killed the more heavily armored, but slower Ettui soldiers in seconds.

Eraddor helped kill two more before a loud noise carried through the air. Those damn hornblowers! This meant only one thing—they were changing or adding to the attack. There was something different about their position, but he couldn't quite place it.

"Thamalos! Look out!"

He heard the whistle of the large spears, but it wasn't until they'd come close that he could see them.

Thamalos screamed, "Move!"

Every one of the catapults now aimed at one section of the first wall. No one had noticed them move into this position, as all focus had been on the Ettui on the bridge. If all the spears connected . . .

Thamalos got most of the soldiers out of the way, but for some it was too late. One projectile fell just short of the wall, but four hit directly, while another smashed into the base. Stone and debris flew everywhere as a whole section of the wall collapsed. Thamalos stared shocked as it fell on the enemy armies below, and several of his soldiers fell with it.

Seth and the others on the second wall stared at the disastrous development. They could hear the Ettuii cheer in celebration. They'd finally succeeded where no army ever had—they penetrated the first wall. It was only time now . . . only time.

Eraddor tried to bring focus back to the troops on the first wall as, throughout all of this, the Ettui on the bridges kept coming. Even though they were not defeated yet, there would be no more reinforcements for the first wall's forces.

As Eraddor and Thamalos composed themselves and the troops, the first wave of Ettui ran through the destroyed section of wall. Fort Za's ground forces, who had been mainly served to reinforce the soldiers on the first wall, got into a phalanx formation and waited for the enemy to crash against their shields. It didn't take long. The soldiers did their best to hold back the Ettui while striking at them with their spears.

As most of the ground forces concentrated on the first wave, a smaller second wave ran across the wall and began climbing the steps toward the troops atop it, attempting to flank the phalanx and break it apart. Seth spotted this.

"Eraddor! Watch from below!"

Seth had to shout several more times before Eraddor heard him. By then, the first Ettui had made it to the top of the stairs. This was going from bad to worse.

"Men! Careful behind you!"

Eraddor ran to the nearest stairway, killing the lead enemy soldier. Using the dead Ettui as a shield, he pushed the others following it back down, causing the whole line to fall. He killed a heavily-armored Ettui from the bridges who tried to sneak up on him and threw its body in the direction of the stairs, hopefully taking out any stragglers.

Seth scanned the ground forces once again. They'd successfully halted the first small wave, but at heavy losses. He realized that most of them were not his soldiers, but mainly volunteers, men who shouldn't even be in this fort. As the healthy men dragged the injured behind the second wall, Medkar's advisors watched in concern.

Firress, the advisor to his right, said, "General?"

What to do? He knew that in a minute or less, more Ettui would come through the wall. The remaining ground forces would not last long, as most of the experienced soldiers defended the top. Those soldiers were strong willed, still putting up a fight, but the odds they faced would be overwhelming with the enemy coming from above and below.

"General Seth!"

He heaved a deep sigh and closed his eyes. He had no choice. "Blow the horns. Get the troops behind the second wall."

The advisor followed his order. The ground and wall forces each looked back as they heard the bellows. Eraddor met Seth's eyes.

Seth yelled, "Eraddor! Get your men out of there! The first wall is lost!"

Eraddor hated to believe that. Looking down at the ground forces, though, he could understand why Seth did. Many had already retreated behind the second wall, and the remaining ones limped as fast as they could. Underneath the countless Ettui bodies on the crumbled wall, he could make out fallen humans and elves. They stared emptily into the dark sky. Perhaps Seth was right ...

Eraddor finally yelled, "Men! Take shelter behind the second wall! Move!"

Thamalos repeated the order, which was difficult to hear over the sound of the nearest staircase collapsing. Eraddor fought his way through some lingering Ettui on the stairs. By the time he made it down, the next wave rushed through the first wall. With the ground forces receding, they needed to buy time to get everyone behind the wall safely.

"Men! Take them out! They mustn't get through to the second wall!"

Many of the men joined Eraddor as he rushed to engage the incoming Ettui. Some of the enemy split off and ran directly for the second wall gates. With two gates leading to the inner courtyard it would be difficult to defend, but he felt they could do it. They weren't fighting alone for long. From the north, Thamalos and his forces attacked the Ettui flank. As the next wave fell back, more troops took cover behind the next wall.

Seth, seeing nearly all the troops from the first wall had made it in, grabbed his helmet and put it on.

"When Eraddor and Thamalos get in, close the gates. Prepare the troops behind the second wall. We will hold them there!"

Eraddor and Thamalos stayed at one gate to help any other soldiers who filtered in, many of them delayed by wounds they had received. Thamalos used the few arrows he had left in his quiver to hold back the heavily armored Ettui while Eraddor hurried a man with a deep cut on his arm. A familiar voice from the tower gained his attention.

"Get inside! We're closing the gates!"

Eraddor turned around. "There are still men out there!"

Seth replied, "I know. But the enemy is drawing closer! If we don't close these gates now, we risk losing everything! Get in now!"

Eraddor looked at Thamalos, who nodded in agreement. Eraddor dragged the injured man with him as he ran through the gate. Thamalos killed two more armored Ettui before it shut. Seconds later, it shuddered, reverberating as Ettui projectiles hammered it. Still, they were safe for now.

Most of them. In the distance, Eraddor heard the screams of at least two men . . . may the gods have their souls.

* * * * *

"There it is! Fort Za!"

Amber held tightly to the mast, though she wasn't sure if she should be so excited about the scene. A large ship at anchor dominated her view, with several bridges spreading from its top deck. Chilling Ettui cries could be heard clearly even from their position. At least they came in from the correct direction. The dock meant they were on the backside of the island.

Tasi said, "The attack has already started. I hope we are not too late."

"We aren't," Divi replied. "I can still feel Levus. We must hurry though."

"Guys, we might have a little company."

Tasi looked in Amber's direction. She pointed to a flotilla of about fifty rowboats containing about ten Ettui

366

each. Some had already landed at the dock, but many were still heading to it.

"We're gonna have to take care of these guys if we want to get past them."

"Divi, take care of the boat," Tasi said. "I've got the Ettui."

Divi nodded as she moved her spell directly behind the boat. It kept them moving along at some speed, but not nearly fast enough that one needed to hold on to anything. Tasi went to the bow and extended his hands.

As their little vessel approached, the Ettui close by took notice.

Tasi said, "*Seiinana wavora!*"

He brought his hands forward and dropped them into the water. As he did, the sea ahead of them formed giant waves that hurled themselves at the Ettui rowboats. They had no chance to move before they were taken out. Amber and Divi cheered as they made their way past the large Ettui ship.

CHAPTER 17
The Second Wall

"Divi?"

Levus almost thought that he could feel her near. No, she couldn't be. He didn't know where she currently was, but she couldn't be near. He hoped she wasn't, at least. Not long ago, the forces from the first wall had taken refuge behind the second. Every soldier felt the sting at their loss. It seemed hard to believe. The truth was, though, that the enemy was banging on the doors of the second wall and would probably break through any minute. Sydis had been right.

Kiulann reiulann...

The slaughter here would most likely claim all their lives. Levus prayed to the gods that Divi was nowhere near this place of death.

"I need everyone to reinforce these doors now!"

Seth yelled his order, but there wasn't much else that they could use. They resorted to furniture from inside the fort, but Levus saw little point in wasting the energy to save a few measly seconds.

Eraddor and Thamalos returned to Seth, at the front of the army. He acknowledged his two temporary lieutenants, though Eraddor still looked bitter for leaving some men out there to die.

Seth asked, "Are all the wounded taken care off?"

"The wounded who can still fight are mended enough," Thamalos answered. "Those who cannot are inside. The doctors will try to save as many as they can."

"Good. Be sure to have those injured stay in the back. It might be their only chance for rest."

General Medkar started to walk away, but suddenly stopped. He could almost feel Eraddor's eyes piercing him like daggers. Those weapons not even his chainmail could

368

deflect or avoid. He felt his pain, but now Medkar was practicing one of the most important things he had learned. He would have to accept and understand that.

"You may think I'm a cold person, Eraddor. We cannot save everyone, though, as much as we would like to."

Eraddor could hear the sincerity in his statement. He shouldn't judge Seth's decision too harshly. He'd done what he felt best for the people in this fort.

A loud sound and echo on the other side of the wall caught everyone's attention. One of Seth's advisors, who had stayed on the tower to report their progress, ran down the stone steps. Seth, Thamalos, and Eraddor met up with him.

"Ease down. What is going on there?" Seth asked him.

The advisor reported, "They are taking pieces from the first wall and building a stairway to the top of the tower."

Seth said quietly, "Resourceful little monsters."

He nodded to his advisor and went to face the troops, who waited eagerly for the general's orders.

"The enemy is trying to come from above again, as well as through the gates! I need all archers to aim at the tower and at the doors! If we can keep the enemy bottled up, we can win. Their numbers will count for nothing when their dead clog up the entrance! If by some chance this is our last stand, I am honored, then, to die by your sides. If this day is our last, let it be that when the Ettui leader reports to Darca on Barbata, he must proclaim this victory came at a heavy loss. Let it be that on this day, we show those Ettui we are not afraid! Let's show them what humans and elves are made of!"

Though still uneasy, the soldiers cheered. They were afraid, yet they appeared fearless. Levus admired Seth's ability to bring out the best of his soldiers even in the face of imminent doom.

What was that? Levus could have sworn he heard something behind them. He examined the Administration

Building closely. Nothing. Perhaps he imagined it. Levus returned his gaze to rest of the army.

* * * * *

Divi, Tasi, and Amber couldn't believe their eyes. There were so many Ettui! The mages could see no signs of resistance by the Fort Za defenders, and that couldn't be a good thing. Ettui warriors poured out of the ships. Divi wondered what she could do to determine the fate of this battle.

They slowed the boat so that it wouldn't be so noticeable, not that it would have mattered as every Ettui on the island seemed focused on attacking the fort.

Amber finally asked, "So, what's the plan?"

Good question, Divi thought. For the whole trip she hadn't even thought about devising a strategy. And she could never have imagined that there would be so many Ettui involved.

Taking Divi's silence as meaning they had none, Amber continued, "Well, from what I know about the Ettui, once their leader is defeated, they usually retreat. Where is the leader?"

Divi searched the battlefield, but quickly gave up, seeing how many of them there were. It would have been impossible to find him if he was out among them. She then turned her attention to the ships. Perhaps the leader stayed on board so that, if they tried to reach him, they needed to get past the whole army first. Her scanning eyes stopped suddenly on the second closest wester n ship.

"Oh my gosh!"

Tasi asked, "You see him?"

She pointed at the second ship, "It's Kile."

"So, he's the leader of this whole attack then, huh?" Amber asked.

370

Tasi said, "Unless Ulcinar is here, but I doubt that. He's Lord Ulcinar's right hand, from what Divi tells me."

The boat went silent for a while until Amber casually said, "Drop me off at that boat. I'll sever his right hand so we only have to worry about his left."

Tasi and Divi glanced at each other and then at Amber. Was she serious?

Amber picked up on their doubt. "What? You take care of what needs to be done to save the survivors. I'll get the leader. Besides, he doesn't look so tough."

"Don't take him lightly, Amber," Divi warned. "He's the greatest swordsman on Dyyros, and even my Levus had a difficult time against him."

"Well, it's a big world and there are others better than him. I'm the best swordsperson in Tydos. We'll see who the better is between us. I'll be okay, really!"

Though still hesitant, Divi and Tasi steered the boat to the ship where Kile was stationed. A series of ropes hung over the side, once used to hold rowboats. The mages stopped their boat under the closest rope, and Amber tested it to make sure it could hold her weight. Quite the dangerous climb, as it was a very large ship, but a more reasonable option then fighting through an Ettui army inside the hold. Satisfied, she pulled herself out of the boat.

"I don't know what you are going to do, but I hope you have one hell of a spell to knock out those soldiers," she told Divi, then started climbing.

Divi stopped her, "Wait! Be careful of Kile's sword technique. He mainly uses it when he gets distance from his opponent. It paralyzes you before it kills you. Try to stay close."

Amber nodded, and with that, she started her long ascent to the deck. As she moved, she commented to herself, "Man, me and my bright ideas."

Divi thought about Amber's words. No spells that a normal mage could do would be able to take out this many

Ettui. Her spells, though, went beyond normal. If her father's spirit spoke truly, then she knew . . .

Divi said, "I have an idea. Find an empty spot along the coast."

The men in the courtyard behind the second wall stood silent, waiting. They could hear the enemy on the other side getting closer and closer. Nearly every soldier that could nocked an arrow in his bow, ready to unleash against the first wave of Ettui warriors. Eraddor, Seth, and Thamalos stood in the front, although Seth was the only one without a bow and arrow.

Levus stood near the back, with many of the wounded from the first wall. Eraddor seemed insistent that he stay as far away from them as possible, probably because of his sword.

Levus still couldn't understand what made the others worry about this sword. Sure, he sometimes felt weird and he knew the sword gave him a strange power, but how could a blade possibly cause his mood swings?

Juoppanan . . .

That damn noise again! Levus once again turned around, expecting to see something this time. Once again, nothing in his visual range. Was something playing games with him? It hadn't been that eerie voice that seemed to talk to him sometimes . . .

Levus' train of thought was interrupted as the pounding on the south door got louder. The wooden gate weakened with every violent hit. Pieces started splintering. Seth and the archers turned their attention toward it, as the north one still held strong.

Seth yelled, "Wait until you can see them!"

Anxiety grew among the soldiers. Many had to adjust their grips on their arrows as sweat made them slippery, shaken with fear. The wounded behind Levus, however, acted no more nervously. They had already faced death and seemed ready to face it again laughing.

Another loud crack overshadowed any other noise as the Ettuii pounding on the south door got more ambitious. Levus felt something whiz past his ear. Had he not seen an arrow lodged in the back of the soldier in front of him, he'd have no idea what happened. Levus turned around to finally see what he had probably heard the past few minutes. The Ettui had somehow found a way to sneak up around them.

Levus yelled, "From behind! They're attacking from behind!"

Seth, Eraddor, and Thamalos turned around to see about forty Ettui archers firing down on the rear guard. Is that where the vanishing archers had gone, or were these from one of the other ships? In any event, this battle truly went from bad to worse.

Thamalos yelled, "Provide them with cover!"

He and nearly all the others fired their arrows at the newly revealed enemy. Levus couldn't tell how many arrows connected, as the Ettui hid after they fired, but he thought they took down quite a few. Eraddor loosed one more arrow before turning back to the south door. The Ettui warriors had nearly broken through now. A few more solid hits and the door would crumble.

Eraddor readied another arrow and yelled, "Aim at the southern door! They're almost through!"

Many did as he said, but the archers' attack from behind kept the others preoccupied. Seth tightened the grip on his sword. Was this how the enemy planned it all along, or just sour luck that they outflanked Fort Za's defenders when they did? This seemed much too organized for a strictly Ettui-led campaign. They were getting help, but from whom?

He didn't have any time to think of an answer, as the hole in the door became wide enough for an Ettui arm to pass through it. Thamalos aimed carefully as the arm flailed, presumedly searching for whatever kept the door locked. At just the right moment, Thamalos fired the arrow through the hole in the door, killing its owner instantly. It seemed fruitless, though, as another arm quickly replaced it.

The soldiers in the back grabbed shields to help defend against the Ettui archers' arrows. Levus was pretty certain that the rear attack wouldn't last long. He assumed they arrived by rowboats of some kind, and they could only have so many Ettui on board even with the size of ships they brought. The doors just needed to hold for a little bit longer . . .

Crack!

Wishful thinking, Levus thought as the southern door finally gave in under the mighty weight of the Ettui. The first wave pushed their way through.

Seth yelled, "Let's send these creatures back to hell! Fire!"

All the archers shot at them, not one missing his mark. They quickly reloaded and waited for the next group to enter, which didn't take long. Eraddor could see that at this rate the enemy would overrun them. There simply weren't enough arrows to stop this opponent. He could tell Seth thought the same.

The general ordered, "Men! Ready yourselves!"

Eraddor admired his fighting spirit. Seth was no longer a young man, yet he showed more determination than anyone else in this fort. He would protect Fort Za, even if it cost his own life. Eraddor knew too well what it meant to fight for something . . . or someone you love. He would give everything to live beyond this day so he could feel Cordela's sweet lips against his. That was what he fought for, yet like Seth, he was willing to give his last breath if it meant she would be safe.

"Eraddor!" Thamalos called. "Heaven to earth! Heaven to earth!"

He knew exactly what that meant: Thorii elvish jargon for an attack from higher ground. He looked up at the tower to see that the Ettui finally completed their makeshift stairs on the conquered south side and were now coming from there as well. The elf forces unleashed their arrows at the Ettui on top of the tower, while the humans fired at the ones trickling through the door into the courtyard.

The soldiers around Seth dropped their bows and unsheathed their swords. The Ettui had taken the first wall and they may be taking the second wall, but Seth would be damned if they took this courtyard.

He yelled at the incoming wave, "You want this place? Pry it from my dead fingers!"

"Lord Kile! We have just taken the second wall!"

Kile could not help but smile at this report. The time of victory was quite near. It did make him a little sad that he could no longer see the fight, with the walls of Fort Za blocking his view. Disappointing, but an easy win where he didn't even need to dirty his hands didn't come often. He would take some pleasure walking over to see the handy work of his Ettui forces when the battle ended. He wondered if he should order them to keep some prisoners alive so he could have some fun, but shook the notion off. No, let the Ettui enjoy this moment. Their anger had been suppressed for thousands of years. Let them feast on this opportunity.

Kile said to the Ettui messenger, "Report to me when we have recovered the sword. Our taking this fort means nothing if we do not retrieve it."

The Ettui nodded and retreated back into the ship. Kile had spoken only the truth. Lord Ulcinar expected to have the metal back by the end of this battle. Even though he didn't say it, Kile's master implied that not winning the sword would be considered a failure. He was confident now they would get the Moonsaber. He only wondered whether they would need to get through Levus to take it. That foolish boy had no idea the power he had at his fingertips. Yet, he was a good fighter. Kile hoped that the Ettui that killed his rival would survive the battle so he could hear, in excruciating detail, how Levus finally perished.

Amber had rest about halfway up the rope to the deck. Why did they have to make these ships so damn big? She forced herself to take breaks so she would be in good enough shape to fight the leader, Kile. She almost hoped that one of the Ettui soldiers would notice the ropes had remained down and pull it, and her, up. That wasn't going to happen, though. She went the hard way for so long, why should it stop now? No different than climbing the cliff to get to Dragonia.

She did hope that Divi and Tasi were having an easier time of it. She had no clue where they went after leaving her to do this, but felt that they were safe. Divi had gone through too much for this to end now.

After another minute, Amber continued advancing. Suddenly, the gun port to her left opened and an Ettui soldier stuck his head out to spit. Not a very pleasant sight, for sure. And before he could, he noticed Amber out of the corner of his eye.

Amber muttered, "Uh-oh."

The Ettui stared at her, obviously getting ready to call in reinforcements. She couldn't have that now. Amber swung herself and scissor-kicked it, dragging it out of the porthole and into the water below. As Amber swung back, the cannon hatch on her right opened. She used her momentum to kick the soldier there back inside. Her feet crashed against the wooden hull of the ship as she tried to stop herself. Both ports opened once more.

"Great."

These two came better prepared. The one to her left had a sword and the one to her right had a bow and arrow. The Ettui with the sword prepared to attack as Amber swung in that direction. As he slashed at her legs, Amber lifted both up, doing the splits. The swordsman successfully cut the rope from her knees down, though. No turning back now, she figured.

Her momentum had her swinging to her right. The Ettui archer aimed at her very carefully. She needed to be quick. She watched his hand holding the arrow. As he let it go, Amber twisted the rope so that her back scraped the hull of the ship and made herself as flat as possible. The arrow barely missed her, but it hit the swordsman. As her momentum carried her to the left, she grabbed the sword hilt between her ankles. The nearly lifeless Ettui let go of it without a fight before limping into the ship.

The archer tried to ready another arrow. Amber spun her body as the rope swung her back. When she was close enough, she lifted her legs and the sword grasped in them, stabbing the stunned Ettui in the chest. Before she could swing back, she lifted her legs higher and brought them down on the cannon hatch, hitting the archer over the head and sending him plummeting to the sea below.

Amber held herself in place and waited. She let out a sigh of relief as the portholes remained closed. She pulled herself up a bit higher so she could once again use her feet to climb. Although she wanted a breather after that little skirmish, she knew it would be best to move forward. She was quite certain one of the Ettui that attacked her remained alive if unconscious, and she didn't want to be by those hatches when he woke. Amber glanced up. Half a climb done, one more half to go.

*   *   *   *   *

"We could use a little help back here!"

Levus yelled, not even certain if anyone heard. The courtyard had become very crowded, mainly with Ettui forces. He was actually impressed how well Fort Za's forces had fought up to this point. For every man or elf that fell, at least a hundred Ettui did. Those odds, though, would get slimmer the more men they lost. If only he could use the sword's abilities! With the way things were at the moment, he would be killing Ettui, humans, and elves. Of course, he only knew a couple of techniques. More existed, but how to find them?

Killuu mon....

That was a good point, voice. Perhaps he needed to wait until the right emotion presented itself; then they would come as easily as the Circle of Fate ability did. Yeah, that had to be it. Just be patient. Levus gave a dark smirk as he killed another two Ettui with one swipe of the Moonsaber. The blade cut through the strong armor as if the Ettui wearing it were naked. Nothing could keep the sword from its bloodlust. The glowing jewel on its hilt gleamed with its approval. *Feed, my little friend. Feed on that ripe flesh just waiting to be scourged.*

When the Ettui fell, Levus looked around to see how the others faired. He still wasn't getting the help he requested. Seth fought with an unexpected energy. Any Ettui that stood within arm's reach of him found nothing but his blade. Surprise that he had so much energy, being that old, moved Levus. Though when compared to the likes of Kile, he was nothing special, if the Ettui could fight half as well as he, this fort would have fallen long ago.

Eraddor, too, fought with great passion, but Levus sensed his hope dwindling. Fatigue set in as his blows lost their luster. Even with all of his effort, he was only human. Surviving the ordeal on the first wall took unsurmountable courage, but now he had to fight through a seemingly endless

378

supply of Ettui. Could whatever drove him be enough? Levus doubted it, but who was he to judge?

....suugu giopfromon da.

Thamalos tried to do his part. By no means as effective with a sword as with his bow and arrow, he at least had better hand-to-hand prowess than the rest of his brethren. The other elves looked clumsy holding their short-bladed weapons and fell faster than the humans did. Maybe that was why the elves couldn't defeat the Ettui. They were too weak to do it on their own and needed men's help. Very interesting, how the races used each other for their personal gains.

Another three Ettui ran toward Levus. Finally! He'd started to think the enemy forgot about him. He easily killed the lead one, letting the other two pass him. They quickly turned around and charged. Levus waited until they got close before he ducked and sliced at their legs. Both fell to the ground, crying in pain. How pathetic! Levus finished the job so he wouldn't have to hear them cry anymore.

Huiiman yl evaan un kuippa nu.

Levus cackled with laughter. That's right, voice! What a great feeling! He felt unstoppable. The jewel in the Moonsaber glowed bright. Maybe he should just use his technique. These men would probably die anyway, so what difference existed if it was by his hand or the Ettui? After all, nothing was going to....

Levus snapped out of his trance when an Ettui fighting a soldier behind him knocked into his body. It sent the Moonsaber out of his hands. What had just come over him?

He realized then that he had been unarmed . . . his sword! Levus saw it, flying toward the main door of the Administration Building. As though it moved in slow motion, he watched it land in the arms of an Ettui soldier who tried to enter the main offices of the fort. It looked puzzled at first until it realized what it held. It gave the closest thing to a smile that an Ettui could do and held the sword up victoriously.

"Hiiava suuaddi! Hiiava suuaddi! Hiiava . . ." I have the sword! I have the sword! I have . . .

The Ettui couldn't finish its announcement as two large blades decapitated it. Levus knew those swords well. Out of the shadows came Cerrapies with the Twin Vipers. Levus had never been happier to see him! What was he doing here at the fort? Though, that explained why the Moonsaber looked different. He should have recognized Cerrapies' work when Eraddor told him an unknown smithy melted the emblem that used to be on his breastplate and added it to the blade.

As the Ettui's body fell limp, Cerrapies grabbed the sword, resting one of his own against his body, and said, "I'll take that!" He then looked at Levus and smiled. "I believe this is yours! Take better care of it!"

Cerrapies tossed him the Moonsaber and he grabbed it. At least he didn't get that strange feeling when he touched the sword this time. He turned around to face the enemy. What luck! A straight path with no humans or elves! Levus brought the sword back, causing the weapon to glow orange.

"Circle of Fate!"

Levus performed the technique flawlessly and smoothly, killing every Ettui that stood in his path from one end of the courtyard to the other.

Cerrapies smiled and drew his other sword again. Two Ettui came from his right, snarling and bearing their sharp teeth. The blacksmith raised his massive weapons and voiced a scream so bone-chilling that the two retreated in fear. He wasn't going to let them get away that easily, though. He chased after them, taking out two to three other Ettui with each swing. The two soldiers ran, terrified, back toward the first wall. Cerrapies laughed heartily.

"Why couldn't things like this happen when I was younger? Hey, get over here!"

Seth gave a silent chuckle as more of the enemy cried out, fleeing in terror from the arrogant blacksmith. He had a talent for hearing the battle around him as well as the one in front of him. He thought it was why others considered him a good soldier, especially in his younger years. He'd fought quite a few campaigns against the Ettui in his teens and recieved generalship at twenty for his valor. Though after twenty-something years, he supposed he could have become a little rusty at his craft.

As much as Seth hated to admit it, grew tired. Age had started catching up to him, although his heart wouldn't consider it.

Seth ducked underneath an incoming Ettui blade, striking at the trailing enemy soldier. He had to dispatch this one quickly before the other recovered. In this fight, he couldn't trust that someone else would help him. It took him a few more thursts and blocked attacks, but he finally stabbed the Ettui and pushed him away. He turned around to see the previous one who'd missed him ready to go, holding a long, curved blade.

The two parried each other's blows for a short time before they locked swords, turning it into a test of strength. Their eyes met and stared coldly, full of hatred. Seth, despite being older, was winning the one-on-one battle. Another Ettui noticed this and charged at him.

Eraddor, keeping an eye on the situation, yelled, "General! Look out!"

Seth saw the attacker out of the corner of his eye. In this position, any direct hit could be fatal. He sharply kneed the Ettui he was fighting and punched it down. The other one arrived just as Seth turned around. He ducked and threw it off his back, onto the ground. With the Ettui stunned, he spun and plunged his sword into it.

As he straightened up, he felt a sharp pain on his left arm. He didn't need to see the fresh wound spewing blood to know very well what had happened. On Seth's left, the Ettui with the curved blade smiled at his accomplishment. Seth tightened his grip on his sword, suppressing the pain.

It stared unmercifully into his eyes until it felt a tapping on its shoulder. It turned to see Eraddor, who flashed a smile before bringing a long knife across its throat.

As the Ettui fell dead, Seth acknowledged, "Much obliged."

Eraddor said, "You're wounded. Go inside to get it tended to."

"No. I have had worse. We need every man who can still fight out here. I will not leave my soldiers, not now."

Seth walked toward the central fountain, now black with more Ettui blood than water. A short break in the enemy waves allowed him to wipe the sweat off his brow—a much-needed rest. Yet, it wouldn't last long.

Eraddor looked at the wounded. Not one man here would come out of this unscathed. Their numbers dwindled. One or two more Ettui waves would be all they could probably handle before the bodies and spirits of these brave men and elves completely broke. As much as he hated to believe it, they would need a miracle if they were going to win this battle.

CHAPTER 18
The Deck and the Tower

"Over there!"

It took a while, but Divi and Tasi finally found a small cove on the northwestern part of the island near the first wall. The challenge forced them to travel slowly. They didn't want to attract attention now of all times.

Tasi fastened the boat to a rock and joined Divi in hiding. "So, what's your plan?"

He would think she was crazy once he heard her idea, but she knew this might be the only way, despite the risks.

"Well, you see that tower? We need to get on top of it."

Tasi exclaimed, "Oh, that's going to be easy! Only about three hundred thousand Ettui lie between the tower and us."

Divi didn't really appreciate the sarcasm, but she could see why he'd think that. Even though they were probably less than fifty yards from the tower, the entire area was clustered with Ettui, with even more coming out of the ships.

"Regardless," she said, "that is the highest point, and I need height for what I plan to do. Besides, we may not need to fight our way up there if my theory is right."

Tasi took a few seconds to suppress his disbelief before asking, "What theory? I wish you would tell me these things beforehand!"

She didn't answer because she knew what his reply would be. Ever since they escaped the capital of Barbata, she couldn't get over that piece of fabric they'd found. Did it really come from a mage? Or was Ulcinar trying to frame the mages so that the frail truce between them and humans would be snapped? Divi figured there was only way to find out. Even though she'd hoped to be wrong about a mage involving themselves with Ulcinar, for their purposes now, she hoped her suspicions was right.

Divi said, "Tell me when you see an important Ettui."

Tasi, more confused than ever now, wondered how he could know what an important Ettui looked like. And why? The more her plan took effect, the more worried he got.

Divi didn't know what determined an Ettui's importance either. Maybe their armor. Generals and other higher ranks usually wore different armor then the common soldiers. After she and Tasi scanned the battlefield, luck fell on their side, as an Ettui whose armor was more elaborate than the others walked into their view. He wore a helmet of antlers and his pauldrons bore sharp spikes.

Divi said, "Okay, just follow my lead and be ready. If I'm wrong, we're going to need to leave quickly."

"That's very reassuring."

Divi stood up from her hiding place and started waving her arms. The Ettui officer took immediate notice to this action. What was she doing? She grabbed Tasi's arm and brought him to her side.

Divi yelled, "Hiiollo! Magiianwe oddoruum kuippala humaii y elvii scullampa! Needala usnii tuwwa immediiatalii!" *Hello! We are mages ordered to finish off the human and elf scum! We need to get to the tower immediately!*

The Ettui seemed to be analyzing Divi and Tasi, probably wondering if they had brought any mages along with them. She tried to appear as confident as she could so it would not suspect her deceit. The Ettui stopped a passing group of his warriors and whispered an order Divi couldn't hear. She also hoped they understood her. Although she spoke pretty good Elvish, she knew the Ettui used a different dialect.

"Be ready to make for the boat," She whispered to Tasi.

384

The Ettui finished speaking and stared at the two mages. At once, he signaled for them to come forward. It worked! Divi took up her staff and signaled for Tasi to follow her. There was no doubt in her mind now that a mage traitor existed, and she had a very good idea of the culprit.

As they got close, the colonel barked orders to the surrounding Ettui. Although she couldn't understand most of them, she did pick up on the words "protect" and "tower."

However great Divi's excitement in her plan's progress, Tasi's nervousness equaled it. He knew she felt more confident since learning magic, but the carelessness of this made for a very dangerous situation. If they had to escape, they couldn't.

"Divi, what did you say to him? Divi!"

The Ettui hordes began leading them to the hole made in the first wall of the fort. Divi really didn't want to explain to Tasi . . . not right now, at least.

She replied, "Later. If any of them give you strange looks, just say 'Kuippa elvii, kuippa humaii.'"

"Okay, what does that mean?"

"Death to elves, death to humans."

Tasi repeated, "Death to elves, death to. . . What? Why do I need to say that?"

He glanced to his left to see a couple Ettui warriors staring at him. They couldn't understand what he said and didn't suspect anything of him, but his own fear suggested differently.

He chanted over and over, "Kuippa elvii, kuippa humaii."

The nearby Ettui, approving of Tasi's war cry, repeated his every word. From now on, he needed Divi to tell him of these suicide plots beforehand. He would have never gone along with this if he had known.

Divi was more concerned about her surroundings. To see the after effects of the Ettui attack disheartened her. Many human and elf bodies dangled off the side of the wall.

Although it still looked stable, many sections of the once-proud structure bore heavy blemishes. The collapsed rubble they were being led to made a sad reminder that this used to be the wall no army ever penetrated, a reputation it could no longer claim.

A couple of Ettui archers helped both Divi and Tasi up the fallen portion of the first wall. To her right, she could see the large spears that must have been the cause of this damage. She also recognized the many bridges that seemed connected to the ships. She'd wondered what those were when they sailed past them. No one traversed them now, but she imagined endless Ettui making their way across to take the wall from above. The more she saw of the aftermath, the happier she was not to be here at the start.

As they headed for a hastily made staircase on the southwest side of the tower, Divi spotted even more bodies of fallen Ettui, humans, and elves. One thing troubled her. She didn't see any mage bodies. She knew that there wouldn't be many, but the mages were supposed to be here the day she left for Dragonia. Had the meetings ended before the attack occurred, and they left? It would be something to ask when the battle concluded.

The Ettui rushed them both to the staircase. Divi's nerves rekindled as she started to ascend it, feeling it shift under her feet with each step. The Ettui were much lighter than a human or a mage, and much more agile. Climbing these stairs would not be any trouble at all for them. Divi secured her for fear of dropping it, though with her telekinetic powers, it was a small fear.

Near the top, Divi heard the battle still raging behind the second wall. A couple of Ettui stood on the tower watching it. They too wore decorated armor, so they must have been lesser commanders or colonels as well. The Ettui warriors trailing Divi and Tasi shouted at the two on top as they helped the mages up.

386

As Divi made it up first, she was the first to witness the horrible scene around her. To the northeast, the remaining human and elf forces made a last stand against the Ettui. To the west, an uncountable number of Ettui soldiers marched from the great ships still at dock. Even though the battle furiously continued, were they too late?

Tasi soon had the same view as she did and the same reaction. This was absolute madness! Literally thousands of Ettui still crowded the island, and who knew how many remained on the ships? What could they do as two mages to make a difference?

Divi focused on the northeast side of the wall. She had to know that Levus was alive. She saw Cerrapies at once as his giant weapons took out numerous Ettui with each swing . . . that and his vulgar taunting carried to her ears. Eraddor and Thamalos fought close to each other, so she noticed them next. Both held their own, but even she could feel the pain of their fatigue and injuries. General Seth fought near Cerrapies in the center of the courtyard, taking a long time to dispatch his opponents. It wasn't until she looked in the southeast corner of the courtyard that she saw him. He was alive . . . and awake! She succeeded! She did save him just as the Time Sage said! Despite that fact, she was not certain if she could trust their time-controlling "friend" completely. Their last conversation stuck with her.

"Divi?" Tasi had a worried look on his face. "I don't know if you really care, but if you have a plan, we'd better start it now. Our guides up here are getting rather restless."

Two Ettui officers and the other two still on the steps shouted at them to begin the carnage. Divi had honestly forgot about them as she was so focused on finding Levus. With that done, she could now turn to the task at hand . . . her idea. As most Ettui couldn't understand the common tongue, she felt comfortable explaining her plan to her friend.

Divi faced the battle and said, "We'll begin to do our basic fireball spells, aimed at the armies, but then take out the

Ettui on this tower. I'll need you to take out the stairs behind us."

Tasi nodded. "All right. Can do that easy enough. What about the rest of them?"

"When we're isolated, I need you to protect me. I'm going to cast 'The Destroyer of Cities' spell. I have to concentrate a long time to pull it off. I need you to stop any arrows or Ettui from getting to me."

"Forbidden magic was your plan? Divi, you realize how dangerous those spells are! No mage alive has any idea of the effects it will have on you! It could very well kill you as well as everyone in this fort! The magic of the gods was not meant to show any favorites."

"I know, but there is no choice! I either do it or everyone here dies and the Ettui win! I will try and aim toward the ships so that the fort won't feel the full brunt of the blast."

Tasi remained silent for a short while. Now he could see why Divi had refused to tell him anything. What she planned was absurd and extremely dangerous. He only hoped she really knew the consequences of her actions. As she said, they didn't have another choice, especially at this moment. Her decisions since they arrived forced this situation upon them. What effects this would have, though, only time would tell.

The Ettui officers' impatience with the mages became evident. One of them even readied his weapons. Divi nodded at Tasi and both raised their arms in unison. The Ettui backed away slightly, seeing the mages finally complying.

After they said the words of the spell, above their opened hands small fireball formed. The turned their attention to the battlefield, hoping to get a first-hand view of the damage their mage friends would do.

Divi figured she shouldn't disappoint them.

"You ready?" asked Divi.

Tasi replied, "As ready as I can be."

She scanned the positions of the Ettui one more time. The officers were on her left, while the others stood to the right behind them.

"You take the ones behind us," she said. "I'll get the ones in front."

She glanced once more at Levus, who still had not noticed her. This was for him.

She yelled, "Now!"

Divi separated her fireball and took out the two officers, who fell, dead, down to the courtyard. Thamalos and Eraddor were the only ones of the lieutenants who noticed that something changed, and only the elf didn't doubt what his eyes saw.

"Divi."

Tasi took out all three remaining Ettui with one fireball since they were bunched together. He formed another fireball in his hand and fired it at the stairs on the west side of the tower. The poorly made stairway crumbled even under the low-powered spell. His pleasure at the damage it did was negated when he observed the Ettui on the first wall witness their "betrayal" and signaled to their friends on the other side. Horns blew from the horizon.

"Uh-oh. Divi! Get moving on that spell! We're gonna have company!"

Divi nodded and outstretched her arm. She didn't know how long it would take to cast this. She wasn't even sure of the proper way to do it, as there was no precedent for casting forbidden magic. It had never been used in any current mage's lifetime. For the sake of everyone here, she hoped it'd be rapid. She quieted her mind, as she needed all her concentration into this spell. Please, let Tasi succeed in protecting her. She would be completely defenseless while casting. Please . . .

* * * * *

389

Kile stood on the flagship, expressionless. Something wasn't right. After some glowing objects appeared near the tower, he heard the hornblowers requesting archers. Too far to see who was on the tower to decipher the threat—what could be so dangerous that they needed archers? Could it be some of them . . . no, he promised Kile that all would cooperate.

His concern soon diminished. It wouldn't matter even if some had betrayed him. They would fall like the others. It would only be a minor inconvenience and the archers would soon eliminate this threat.

Kile's thoughts were interrupted when an Ettui screamed behind him. When he turned around, he discovered a most intriguing sight before him. Walking toward him was a woman wearing upper body armor and leg guards that went to her knee-length skirt. A few of the other Ettui on board started running to attack their new foe.

Kile ordered, "Halt! It will be my pleasure to take care of this one."

Amber smiled as she heard this. Kile was obviously overconfident, probably even judging her because of her sex. It would just make his defeat more enjoyable.

"And what is your name, foolish yet brave woman?"

"My name is Amber, Kile."

"So, my reputation proceeds me . . . Who did you hear of me from?"

Amber unsheathed her sword and replied, "There is nothing more to be said. You're going to die here, so why waste any more valuable breath answering your silly inquiries?"

She definitely had a feisty side, showing no fear against the best swordsman in the world. But for the disrespect she just showed him, she needed to be punished. Whether he would kill her would depend on how willing she would be to beg for forgiveness. Kile unsheathed the Marasam and impacted the indestructible weapon against the deck of the ship.

"I have no quarrels with you, Amber. I don't even know how you know me, nor do I care. But no one is going to stand in the way of my victory. I am the best swordsman in the world and I fear no one!"

Amber only commented, "And I am the best woman with a sword in the world and I've beaten tougher men than you. Bring your worst."

"My worst you shall have, then!"

He charged at Amber, making the first attack. She blocked it with relative ease and a firmness that Kile had never experienced in an opponent. Maybe his initial assumptions of her were premature. She seemed well-trained and strong, despite being a woman. No matter, though. His X-Slice technique showed no favors to men or women.

The Ettui on the deck watched with anticipation and hunger as Amber and Kile exchanged blows. They wanted to participate in this fight as well, but would not go against their master's wishes unless in dire need.

Kile attempted a killing blow at her neck, but she ducked and countered by sliding her boot hard into his right shin, sending him to one knee. As she stood, swiped her blade at his throat. Kile rolled to his left, barely missing the tip of her blade. He returned to his feet.

She was fast! This definitely wouldn't be an easy fight. He normally fought against heavily-armored men with very little combat experience. He also didn't fight women, normally, as they mainly flocked to him instead.

Amber became the aggressor, her movements short and quick. She tried to keep Divi's advice in mind. She didn't know what a sword technique did, but she didn't care to find out. As long as she made sure the fighting remained close, Kile's techniques would be useless.

Kile needed to stop her charge before he hit the railing at the ship's bow. He supposed he could have ordered the Ettui on deck to do his dirty work, but he had his pride on the line. Calling Ulcinar for help wasn't an option either. Kile could understand if she was someone like Ardeeza, his former biggest rival for the Dark Lord's attention, but she seemed to be just a normal human woman. How much faith would Ulcinar lose in him if he requested help against a common girl? Kile didn't want to find out. He'd be on his own for this fight.

Kile quickly moved to his left, but Amber followed to match him. Anticipating a counterattack, she put her sword up defensively. Her gamble proved correct as Kile swiped at her side, an attempt she harmlessly blocked.

He had never seen such instincts in a fighter. It would be a waste to kill an adversary with this skill. She would make a better captain of the Dyyros forces than Corweig—but he got ahead of himself. He needed to subdue her first, then perhaps Lord Ulcinar would decide her fate.

After a few minutes of parrying, Kile felt he had to begin his assault. He charged at Amber hard, making her back pedal. Although she had no trouble blocking Kile's fierce attacks, it would be difficult to keep it up. As Kile brought his sword up to strike, Amber rolled to her right, sweeping her arm guard against his shin, similar to the blow she'd struck before. He felt the sting even through his leather boots, and her momentum knocked his feet from under him, sending him to the deck on his stomach. It left him temporarily out of breath. Although a successful attack, it left Amber with her back facing Kile.

Both sensing their vulnerable positions, they stood up in defensive stances.

Kile commented, "You are good, so don't make me kill you."

"You, kill me? What fight are you in that makes you feel you're winning?"

Amber really started to get on his nerves. Her confidence in her abilities made her very arrogant . . . just like himself at times. This woman seemed to not show any of the weakness common in humans. Perhaps she was something more than human. Meanwhile, if Divi had not carried her staff, he would have mistaken her for a regular human instead of a mage.

Amber circled slowly, trying to figure out Kile's next move. By now his surprise at her skill had passed. He knew he was not dealing with an amateur. That didn't bother her, though, as she had plenty more to show him. That's when things would be fun.

Kile charged and the two warriors once again prepared to exchange a flurry of attacks.

"Help cover the mages!"

Thamalos did his best to order the troops, but it was near to impossible in the mayhem. The funnel of Ettui forces grew larger every moment as the hole they created in the door widened. The odds kept falling in the enemy's favor. Now every soldier faced two of them, and the longer the battle went on, the worse those odds would get. He had to get to Divi and Tasi. Thamalos felt they could turn the tide.

The elf prince sprinted toward the tower, accidentally bumping into Levus on the way. Assuming an enemy, Levus turned with the Moonsaber ready to strike. No Ettui soldier stood there, but he did spot Thamalos dodging an enemy attack as he attempted to reach the tower. What was so important that he risked such a move? Levus raised his eyes and his mouth dropped open.

"Divi? Divi!"

She was alive! She was here. He hadn't seen her in so long except in his dreams. That long, horrific dream. Had he not remembered Divi admitting her feelings for him, who knows if he would still have been surrounded by the overwhelming sadness that made him never want to wake again? She came for him, and that was all that mattered.

The tragedy of his thoughts then struck Levus. Why did he think it was great to have her here? They were making their last stand. This outnumbered, they couldn't defeat the Ettui. Tasi's spells seemed to make an instant impact, but he couldn't keep it up. As Divi had told Levus once before: Even mages have their limitations. He had to get to her somehow . . . and tell her to leave as fast as she could.

"Divi!"

She remained still. He hoped she was okay. She faced down with her arms stretched forward. Despite all the spells being cast and arrows whizzing by her, she stood unwavering. Was she in some sort of trance? Maybe she attempted to use her telekinetic powers to move something huge, requiring her full concentration, though, he couldn't imagine anything short of a mountain or one of the moons that would take such effort for her.

Levus' focus broke when two Ettui warriors with pikes faced him. Though the fewest of the enemy troops, the pikemen were the easiest. As they jabbed, he moved out of the way, slicing pieces of their weapon poles off with each move. Within seconds, both pikemen lay dead on the ground. Levus wanted to move ahead, closer to his Divi, but the Ettui kept coming after him. Why didn't they do this with Thamalos? What made him so different?

Huuontii . . .

Levus heard that voice again as he attacked the Ettui in front of him. He'd heard it frequently since he awoke from his long slumber. He couldn't allow it to take control of him. Not here . . . not now. He used whatever willpower he had to keep the voice from distracting him.

Despite his attempt, the voice's power grew stronger. The area around him became muffled. Even though he could see men screaming in pain, he could not hear them. Only the clashing of swords and the voice. He had to be strong. This voice thought it could control him anytime it wanted. He had to fight it.

Three more Ettui fell before the voice stopped trying to reach him. The sounds of warriors in battle once again returned.

Levus regained his focus long enough to see a large group of axe-wielding Ettui moving his way. This would not do. Levus brought his sword back. Seconds later, the charging Ettui disappeared in the wake of his technique.

Tasi shot a fireball in the direction of the archers, but he had no idea whether it hit its target. He was not sure how much longer he could maintain this pace. He had never used his magic this rapidly, switching between attack and defense. Not even during their battle with Tiiamite did he have to do this. For Tasi, though, the importance of holding out long enough never felt greater. Someone he cared about deeply would die if he failed. Failure was not an option. She had protected Amber and himself against Tiiamite. His time to return the favor.

As soon as Tasi finished with his short fireball spurts, he used his powers to create a magic barrier that blocked incoming arrows. The soldiers behind the second wall enabled Tasi to focus his strength toward the south. The conditions for his best defense of Divi were not going to get better than this.

Tasi blocked one more wave of arrows before dropping the barrier and firing at the archers again. He hoped Divi would hurry up with this spell. Even though he was doing well, at this rate he would be physically drained within twenty minutes . . . if even that long. No one was sure how long it would take to cast this spell except the gods themselves. He could only imagine how they would feel when Divi finally unleashed that great power.

Tasi prepared to fire one more barrage of fireballs when he felt an arrow whiz near his head. He glanced down to see what happened. Some of the archers had moved within range, firing from the ground. Not good. He also noticed the Ettui had almost finished repairing their makeshift stairway up to the tower. Tasi had been so focused on the archers he almost forgot about the rest of them.

Tasi aimed one more fireball straight down the middle of their work, crushing the new steps. Any Ettui on them fell to their deaths, smashing hard on the bloodstained ground. A small victory for sure, but one he couldn't enjoy. He had to get that shield back up . . .

Tasi's concentration rattled when a thrown pike drew blood from his arm. He screamed in pain, but knew little could be done to dress the wound. He had to get the barrier up before any of those weapons got to Divi. The pikemen and the archers fired their volleys at the same time. Tasi put all his focus into the spell, casting it just in time for the projectiles to crash against it harmlessly. As they did, though, he felt the blood flow from his wound. He swore quietly. Even an injury as minor as this would drain his energy that much faster.

After another pike broke under his shield, Tasi quickly lowered the spell and unleashed a fireball at the group of pikemen below. It was a direct hit, killing at least three of them and one of the archers. The Ettui near the blast area backed away to make sure they didn't suffer a similar fate.

Tasi scanned the situation, feeling tired and weak. Even though that spell gave him a personal sense of revenge, it didn't help in the long run. The archers who had made their way onto the first wall aimed their volleys. He didn't bother hiding his worry. As he got weaker, his shields would too. That meant more of the projectiles would get though.

He stepped in front of Divi. If any of them did, he had to make sure none of them reached her . . . even if it meant his own death. Tasi raised his magical barrier in front of him; it flickered because of his diminishing strength.

Suddenly, all four of the archers fell dead before they could fire. The other archers lowered their bows to find their new attacker. Had another mage stayed and finally decided to help? When another archer fell dead on the wall with an arrow directly through his heart, Tasi concluded his ally was an elf.

"Concentrate on your shield! I will cover you!" ordered Thamalos.

Tasi was more than happy to obey. With Thamalos helping, some of the focus would be taken off him, allowing him to replenish his strength a little. Then again, now he had two bodies to protect instead of one. Maybe Thamalos created more work for him than he needed at this point. No way he could defend both. He hoped the elf would be able to take care of himself.

Three arrows crashed against his weakened shield. Thamalos quickly dispatched of the two archers for Tasi before returning his aim to the pikemen below. He was quick! The tenacity of the elves went greatly underappreciated. The elf prince thrived, showing no signs of struggle. Good for him, too. Tasi could once again focus on the most important person of all, the one who had to survive if they wanted to survive: Divi.

Amber and Kile had reached a stalemate. Kile, as good a fighter he was, could feel himself tiring. Never had he encountered a fighter with such endurance. Amber, even seemed to be getting stronger. He questioned again whether his opponent was not a normal human.

Unlike Kile, Amber was having a little fun. Now that she knew she could fight head-on with the world's *supposed* best swordsman, the time drew near to put this fight in her favor for good. She just needed the right positioning . . .

The Ettui on board, watching, were getting restless. They wanted to participate badly. Amber believed she could even hear the rumble in their stomachs from aching hunger for this fight. She wasn't worried, though. Their time would come soon. She wanted to see how their thirst for battle would be after she finally finished Kile off. She didn't know too much about the Ettui, but they didn't look like the kind of warriors who would stay once their master was slain. First things first.

Kile tried his hardest to regain some of his momentum from earlier in the fight, but it got much harder than he thought it would be. For every move he made, she had a counter. If only he could get enough space between them so he could perform his technique. It would be a cheap way to end such a battle as this, but any victory would be just that—a victory. He really didn't care beyond that at this point.

Amber evaded a couple swipes from his sword as he attempted to gain some distance. She could see him growing desperate to put space between them. She assumed it was to get some rest, but then again, he might be preparing to use his technique. Neither was an option she could afford to give him. She knew he grew tired. She felt it in his blocks and parries. Had it not been for the dragon fights, though, she might be in the same situation. The battles in the Paladin Trials *had* actually proven helpful, disproving her prior belief that the mages made them simply to be impossible. Despite that, she knew the time was right to finish the battle. Time for some fun.

Amber waited until Kile slashed toward her. As their blades clashed, Amber's glowed a light blue. The Marasam suddenly became coated with ice.

Kile's eyes grew wide as he concentrated hard, causing his sword to glow purple. After a second, the ice around his blade broke, leaving the weapon unscathed. What in the world happened? Was she a mage? Impossible. Mages didn't believe in using swords. Most refused to even carry a knife. Swords were inventions of humans and elves and they didn't want any part of them.

Amber raised her sword. As she did, the blade burst into flames. Did she have a piece of the sky metal that the Marasam and Moonsaber were made of too? She couldn't have. She used powers that a mage or an elf commanded, yet she was neither. He suddenly found himself on the defensive as she attacked aggressively with the blazing sword. As their weapons locked, the fire on Amber's shot toward Kile. The cloth mantle over his armor started to burn. He quickly stepped back, padding out the flames.

With a smile, Amber rushed at him. As he continued trying to extinguish his ignited garment, she shot off an ice blast that landed behind Kile. A small patch of ice formed as she charged. He had just put the fire out when Amber reached him.

Kile sloppily tried to defend himself, but his position wouldn't allow it. He had no choice but to retreat. After his first couple steps, he suddenly lost his footing and fell hard on the deck. He knew she'd had him off balance, but not enough for him to take such a tumble. He then saw the ice that had been under his feet. This woman must be a demon! One thing he knew for certain: this whole time she had held back her true potential. She played with his confidence until she saw fit to use it against him. That wretched wench! Just wait until he got some space between them. It would be the most satisfying X-Slice he ever performed.

Kile barely managed to dodge a water spell Amber sent his way, which left a dent of cracked wood in the ship's deck. That should have been his leg, she thought. It wouldn't be the only chance she got. He had no defense against her magic. She just needed the right opening. Amber charged after him as Kile attempted to run toward the captain's cabin on the ship's aft, which happened to be closer to the Ettui forces.

He stopped near a corner of the bridge's lower level, hoping to maneuver Amber into it. Unlike most ships he knew where the bridge was on a quaterdeck, behind the mainmast, on these elvish ships it was located on the middle deck. It looked like a letter 'T' that was squashed, making a corner on both sides of it near the stern end of the bridge. A couple boxes labeled as food was also in the corners.

He would not be able to defend against her magical attacks for long, so trickery had to be his ticket to victory. Amber met him with an earth magic spell, surrounding the Holy Light's blade with stones, making her swings land even stronger. Kile couldn't parry them efficiently. He waited until she swung high, then ducked underneath her blade.

Now the roles reversed and Amber became the one left with very little space. Clever. Kile aimed the Marasam aimed at her stomach. Amber quickly turned toward the corner. She hadn't tried this move in a while, but it was her only chance at regaining the advantage. As she neared the corner, she jumped on one of the food boxes nearby before leaping at the wall. Kile's stab missed and Amber pushed off the right wall and then the left wall before swirling to kick him in the face. He fell to the deck as Amber regained her balance.

Kile rolled away. Amber's move had taken him completely by surprise. He wiped away some of the red liquid that seeped from his mouth. It had been a long time since he'd seen his own blood, not since the takeover of Dynis years ago. One of his teeth even felt loose. This woman would pay for that! He turned to see Amber coming toward him. Time to summon some assistance.

Kile yelled, "Ettui! Get her!"

Though more than halfway across the ship, by the bow, the Ettui who understood the common tongue heard his order clearly. They lost many elf traits when they took on the hideous forms they wore now, but their strong hearing stayed.

The first Ettui neared Amber, who shook her head in disappointment. She nonchalantly activated a lightning spell on her sword. As the Ettui got in range, she swung the Holy Light. Not only did she connect, but the lightning effect sent him into the air and clear off the side of the ship. The Ettui's screams faded as he dropped out of view. The other Ettui, seeing what happened to their brother, backed away fearfully.

Amber smiled as they returned to hiding. So much for that. She returned her attention to Kile, who had gained some distance, but still bled from her kick. He probably had hoped the Ettui would give him more time so he could use his technique, killing her and the Ettui she was engaged in battle with. Too bad for him that she figured out the weakness of his allies. She wouldn't have to worry about the Ettui anymore, at least until she got through with Kile.

He glanced over to check on the Ettui progress. Much to his dismay, they'd gone into hiding near the bow of the ship and Amber, very much alive, walked comfortably toward him. Those filthy cowards! Lord Ulcinar would most certainly hear of this cravenness. No, he would not even trouble the Dark Lord with this. For their sake, they had better jump off the boat now, because once he finished off Amber, Kile would kill them himself.

Amber readied her sword again, lightning bolts crackling around the blade. With the Ettui no longer an option, the responsibility fell back to Kile to dispose of this enemy once and for all. Their blades clashed once more, sparks flying everywhere from her spell.

* * * * *

Divi wondered how much longer it would take. She'd shut herself off from the world, focusing as much as she could. She could feel the powers inside her growing with every life particle she absorbed—many had escaped from the fallen warriors on both sides. Such an incredible feeling! Her body tingled in every inch of flesh. This is what it felt like to summon the power of the gods?

Something whizzed by her ear, followed by shouting. That had been the toughest part of this. Although muffled, she could hear everything that happened around her. Despite being in the middle of a battle zone, she had to maintain her concentration. Her father told her that to cast a spell of the gods, she first had to get to their level of being. Only then could she plead with them to use the spell. That always confused her. What did he mean by plead?

More voices surrounded her. How much she wanted to help, especially when she heard Levus call her name. It was the one of the few she could identify while in this state. She wanted to reach him and fight by his side, but she knew this had to be done. She only hoped that Tasi was wrong about what this spell might do to her.

She knew she took a terrible risk by doing this. Her father had told her the rumored power of these spells. Only a sacred-blood could cast them, but she had never suspected that her father was one. What she feared the most, Tasi had stated earlier. She didn't know how much strength it would drain from her. If it reached beyond her limit, it would possibly kill her. Even though she was much stronger since her father's spirit passed his powers to her, she had no idea how far she could go. Just because she could cast the spells, didn't mean she could survive them. If she went this far to save Levus only not to live herself, the disappointment of her last momements would hurt more than any spear or sword.

"Divi."

Whose voice said that? How did they know her name? It wasn't the same voice as the Great Tree's in Lozela, and it certainly didn't belong to the one that she feared. Then who?

"Divi. Daughter of Neeza. You have awakened terrible spirits. Blackest of black. You wish to cast the forbidden magic. Why do you violate the truce that your father kept so clear? Why do you rebel against his teachings?"

No . . . it couldn't be. Was this really one of the— Myyrilian gods?

"Stop now, daughter of Neeza. Powers like this were never meant to be in your hands. Stop now. You are not ready."

Divi replied in her mind, "I will not stop. My friends will die if I do."

"Stop now. Violations awaken us from our slumber. Your kind living was your punishment. Stop now so we may sleep again. Stop now, for for strength you lack."

Divi, despite the orders given, remained focused. What did they mean by "violations" and that "her kind living was punishment"?

"You fight for fools. Betrayals you will find. Blackest of black truths. You know not what you do. Powers like this are not meant for your hands. Stop now. Fighting you do not know why."

Divi replied, "But I do know. I know why I fight. I fight because I love my friends . . . and I love Levus. I fight because I will not watch them die when I have the power to save them. I fight . . . because I would rather die myself than see the only man I've ever truly loved die in front of my eyes."

Divi waited for a response, but the gods remained silent. Suddenly, the tingling of power went away. She felt . . . different. As if her whole body pulsated with energy, so great that she could barely contain it. It was ready: one of the most powerful spells, spells that only a god had the right to control, ready to be cast by her hands.

A sudden fear entered her mind. This could be the last thing she ever did if this spell actually killed her. She had to make the most of it.

"Everyone! Get down!"

Divi felt her words as she spoke them telepathically to every surviving human and elf soldier that remained in Fort Za. Even though she couldn't see them, she knew they followed her order. She even thought she could hear Tasi relaying it, but she couldn't tell for certain as all sounds were muffled.

She quieted her mind. If this would be the last moment of her life on this world, she would end it with a good memory. Levus' face entered her mind, smiling at her as if she was the only thing that mattered. She knew what she was fighting for.

"Levus, this is for you!"

* * * * * *

"By the gods!"

"Levus! Get down now!"

Levus dropped as flat as he could. There was no concern that the enemy would attack them. Since the purple sphere formed before Divi, none of the Ettui cared about them. Even though the army had just been ready to finish them off, they showed fear. Levus couldn't blame them.

He looked at Divi, unable to believe his eyes. In the time he was unconscious, did she learn magic? The answer seemed obvious, but what had made her change her mind?

The sphere grew larger above Divi's hands as she chanted, her voice echoing, "*Heeronom firragga, nunnaman siago . . .*"

Atop the tower, Thamalos kept an eye out for more archers, but he didn't need to. The Ettui on the wall had all lowered their weapons, staring in horror. Tasi was more scared than the entire Ettui army. He knew the consequences this spell could have on Divi. She might not survive this. And worse than anything, she was doing it for a human. If Divi died, could he forgive Levus? It would be, after all, his fault.

In the same breath, though, curiosity and wonder captured him. This was a once in a lifetime experience. Never had anyone seen the spells of the gods since the destruction of their home continent, Kilbarra. That happened nearly five thousand years ago, as the stories went. Stories that old had become not history, but legends. He only hoped that Divi's strength would be enough to survive it.

"Giomat firanna, sull atta treevis . . ."

Divi's words got stronger and echoed louder. Her body now glowed purple like the spell above her. Tasi believed everyone and everything for miles could hear her voice. No longer did the Ettui army chant confidently. Their current silence spoke louder than anything they could have yelled. The sphere in Divi's hands grew gargantuan as it rose, soon hovering above her head.

Tasi wondered if she could sense any of this. Did she know what she was doing? Could she see the horrors of the Ettui army? He would have to ask her about what went on, in detail, when she recovered. He no longer wanted to think of the possibility of her not making it. She'd find a way. She was just as stubborn as her father, though she would never, ever admit it.

"Guiopp senntennta, biromie wuparra . . ."

The spell neared its completion. Even the human forces watching from the ground could feel the climactic finish coming. The ball above Divi's head grew to ten times her size, pulsating light.

Eraddor, who crawled next to Levus, tried to get the best view possible, as if that would convince him this was truly happening. This was not the same Divi who left Fort Za a month ago. Then again, he also knew what she fought for, and he could relate. Love could provoke one to things they would not otherwise do. The man he lay next to now was her love, and she would not stop until he was safe.

"Firramon citiia, destroian evanta!"

Those behind the wall could only speculate what happened as Divi's hands unleashed the sphere light. Tasi, however, had the pleasure and horror of witnessing it. Divi's spell landed about halfway between the fort and the ships. Hundreds of thousands of Ettui were blasted in the air. The bridges connecting the first wall to the ships remained stationary, only because of the strength of the strange cannons the enemy used. The impact covered a quarter mile, sending all within it to their doom. The ground shook violently as if the very earth itself trembled in fear.

Tasi wedged his staff into a gap between the flagstones paving the tower and held on as the spell pulsated strange waves of energy, first purple, then blinding white. More than half of the first wall ended up reduced to rubble, sent flying toward the second one. Against the spell's poweful blast, Tasi even doubted he'd stay on the tower. Though afraid to look, he had to keep watching.

The vast sphere of the spell rested in the crater where it had touched down. From the purple border of the spell, seven rings projected. Their heights varied, though none reached high enough for Tasi or Thamalos to worry about . . . he hoped. The rings themselves never touched the ground, instead, following the bumps and grooves of the ground as they expanded, almost reaching the first wall. When each ring passed through an Ettui, the enemy suddenly stopped moving. The blast that followed showed him why. The rings cut through anything in their path, while the secondary energy behind them finished the job. Ettui parts splattered against the first wall remnants. That was why she ordered them lie down.

"Stay on the ground!"

Even if no one could hear him, Tasi yelled the warning just in case. As the rings passed through the remnants of the first wall, they turned any stone they touched to pebbles. The trailing blast decimated most of the remains, with the only parts surviving being the ones attached to bridges from the Ettui ships. Not one Ettui standing on the wall remained there after the spell hit. The rings continued, killing any Ettui soldiers on the ground as they neared the second wall and the tower.

Tasi glanced at Divi, who seemed not at all concerned by anything going on with the spell. He tried to grab her before the rings hit the second wall, but he was too slow. The tower shook violently as the rings passed though it. The blast must have gotten weaker, as only the top half of the wall surrounding the tower was pushed into the courtyard. Tasi had a hard time holding on to his staff as the tower shortened from its original height by a good fifteen feet, no longer able to see over the still standing piece of the first wall. They were fortunate that it didn't topple, the thick, well-made stones their salvation being able to withstand the blast. Thank the gods whoever built this fort did so well enough to withstand an apocalyptic event! Thamalos, using wind and earth abilities, was able to maintain his balance through it all.

"Stay flat!"

Nearly all the remaining men were too afraid to move, much less stand up, so Eraddor had little worries his command wouldn't be followed. A small few ran when the stone from the top of the second wall fell in the courtyard. Yelling at them was all he could do as he witnessed the rings passed through the second wall like a warm knife through butter. He also witnessed what they did to the Ettui and the few men who stood, who watched in frozen fright. The rings cut through them, leaving only an orange mark where they passed. Eraddor suddenly noticed Levus lifting himself. What was he doing?

"*Shuarra jupona*"

Why did it beckon him now? Couldn't it see he was trying to survive? It called on him at the most inopportune moments, that voice. That mysterious voice which spoke to him.

"Levus! Get down!"

Eraddor used his right arm to force Levus flat just as the rings reached them. Levus watched as they passed not even a centimeter above his nose. Eraddor didn't move his arm from Levus' chest. It would have cost him the limb if he did. Too close.

Eraddor looked to the northeast, where the rings continued expanding. The Ettui and the human soldiers who stood up in the wake of their light each dropped in four to five pieces.

Tasi struggled to maintain his balance. After the rings passed, the wind became very strong, almost too strong for Thamalos keep his stance. With the exception of the spell, which still roared in the crater it created, the island had gone deathly silent.

As, across the battlefield, the rings reached the boats, Tasi came to another harsh realization. Amber was still on the flagship. She had to be fighting Kile still. He hoped she got Divi's message before the rings crashed through the hulls of the five landed vessels . . .

* * * * * *

"Wha . . ."

That was all Kile could utter at the time of the explosion, and also his last voiced opinion on the matter as

Amber continued her relentless assault even as the sphere's attack occurred. He could only assume that most of his army had died. In the bright light of the explosion, he'd seen an uncountable amount of his Ettui soldiers thrown in the air like dolls. What could have caused it? Did the elves, in a final effort for victory, combine their powers to form this catastrophic incendiary? Even if a mage stayed on the island, one person could not use that much magic and survive it.

Amber, no matter her curiosity about the results of Divi's spell, knew there was still an important task at hand. Even as the first effects struck and rocked the ship, she had to focus on defeating Kile. She slashed at him more aggressively, changing her sword's elemental status between ice, fire, and lightning with every swing. It got harder to fight effectively as the ship began to crumble under the weight of its wound left by those ring-like beams.

Kile staggered between Amber's blows and the ship's instability. The Ettui that remained on the deck had started to jump off the edge, hastening their inevitable doom. They didn't want to wait for the vessel to finally give way, so why was he? He had never before failed at something this significant. His thoughts went to Ulcinar. How would he respond to this? Would it perhaps be better to jump and end it now himself? Ulcinar would not care that Kile defeated a lone warrior when the larger plan at hand ended in a loss because he couldn't take Fort Za. Ulcinar would kill him. No, that was not how Kile wanted to be remembered. He'd rather fall here and now by a warrior's sword than by Ulcinar's . . . magic.

After dodging a few more swings from Amber, Kile regained enough composure to block her next blow. Their swords locked.

This was a duel of remaining strength. It was strength Amber knew she had more of. Both tried to gain the advantage, metal sliding against metal. This would be it. Whoever won this would most likely get the final blow.

Although both fighters wanted it to end fairly, it was the ship that decided who would win and who would lose. The port side of the stern started to collapse, sending Kile to fall back toward the edge. Amber, farther toward the bow, maintained her balance. *Time to end this.* As Kile tried to keep from falling off the ship, Amber bent to one knee. Her sword grew bright before she fired her Steelbreaker projectile toward Kile.

It hit him in his left shoulder. He had little time to be troubled by the pain because the momentum of Amber's attack sent him off the edge. As he fell toward the waters, Kile saw what had struck him. It looked like a piece of her sword. Probably some of that strange magic she knew. *This is not over,* he vowed to himself. Her only success was in angering him. He would have his revenge . . . one day.

Amber wasn't able to witness Kile's landing in the water, but she could only assume that between the blow she delivered and the nearly two-hundred-foot fall, he was unlikely to survive. With Kile out of the way, now she had only one thought: her own survival. She felt certain that the bow would suffer the same fate as the stern soon, as the ring attack had hit the entire ship. She ran to the bow to find a manner of escape. She couldn't go the way she came because her rope had been located near the stern and was probably already making friends with Kile in the ocean's depths. Plus, that one Ettui had cut it off halfway. She wasn't jumping into the water with all the splintered wood that must be down there.

As she peered over the edge, the answer sat only twenty feet away from her: the bridges! The Ettui had long abandoned this phase of the attack, yet one of the three remaining bridges miraculously remained in place after Divi's spell. She could still hear humming underneath her and probably what was keeping the bridge taut. The spell itself had diminished to a haze, dimming the land and sea as if at twilight.

The ship shook violently once more. Now or never. She only hoped the bridges could support her.

She leapt and landed as softly as she could, though she could feel the boards she landed on snap partially. The bridge's stability impressed her, as did the fact that it led all the way to Fort Za, even with the first wall in apparent shambles. No wonder the Ettui could walk across these with little fear of falling, as if walking on a road in the air.

The bow of the ship slumped, pulling the bridge with it. Amber raced toward the fort and over the battlefield. If she could make it to the first wall, she would be safe. She didn't believe, though, that she had that kind of time, as the creaks and moans of the ship's disintegration grew louder. Amber made it halfway before the collapse became complete. Amber fell forward, holding on to a board of the bridge with everything she could. She closed her eyes as she couldn't watch the earth come closer. This would most likely hurt.

She felt a violent jolt from the bridge and then nothing. Silence. She didn't hit the ground, so that was good. She slowly opened her eyes.

Shock overtook her when she saw a sword pointed just inches from her forehead. She quickly drew the Holy Light and fired her Steelbreaker ability at the head of the Ettui holding it. It pierced the creature's helmet, penetrating its skull easily. Luckily for it, though, it was already dead.

Amber breathed heavily as she stood up.

"Good god!"

It looked more like a cemetery than a battlefield. Parts of Ettui bodies cluttered the landscape. Only the top half had remained of the one Amber used her Steelbreaker on. Who knew where the bottom half landed.

Did Divi do this? Such a frightful power she gained when she learned magic. Maybe Amber would have to apologize again to Divi for her angered words on the Dragon Continent. Not a wise move to get on Divi's wrong side.

Amber navigated the corpse-strewn field, making her way to the first wall.

Tasi and Thamalos relaxed as the wind died down and everything went silent. Tasi normally didn't like it being this quiet, but after what he just witnessed, it was welcome. He struggled to stand on the tower that had become unstable from Divi's attack. Perhaps the recent events just made him paranoid. No one could blame him, though. Not after what he seen and the destruction it caused. He was now well aware why the gods had forbidden these spells, only allowing a select few to know them. It was for everyone's safety. Imagine what one with evil intentions could do with the power of gods in their arsenal. Thankfully they'd be safe in Divi's good hands . . . Divi.

She had brought her arms back to her sides, but Tasi could feel a coldness to her. Her legs looked weak, barely holding her up. He'd seen her like this before, after she cast that spell on Tiiamite, but the coldness . . . it even chilled his bones.

Divi allowed one word to escape her lips: "Levus."

She suddenly collapsed. She thought Tasi's voice called her name, but that was all she could hear before everything went silent.

CHAPTER 19
The Aftermath

General Seth Medkar stood on the remnants of the first wall, continuing his survey not only of the damage done to the fort, but also on the damage to the enemy. *Amazing*, he thought. Just yesterday, he stood on this very wall wondering if he or anyone in this fort would see daylight again. The enemy they faced seemed unbeatable. Yet, here he was, still standing while the enemy had fallen. The magnificent ships that landed on the shore yesterday lay broken, ghosts of themselves. He imagined that those ruins would stay there. He had no way of moving them and to destroy them completely would take a long time, even for a mage or elf. He almost wanted them to remain, a lasting reminder of what happened here for all to see, even though he believed those who survived that day would never forget.

The condition of his fort faired no better. The entire first wall was nearly gone. The second still stood, but with many places susceptible to falling. The tower nearly collapsed under itself late last night, but somehow remained upright. The barracks, which were over the storage room where the families had stayed, were destroyed, but didn't cause any damage below. The building known as "The Lair" which housed the war room, guest beds, and mess halls, appeared in good shape do to part of it being reinforced with metal beams. Overall, better than it could have been.

Seth's thoughts were interrupted by one of the soldiers, named Fuharra if memory served. He put him in charge of finding any surviving Ettui and bringing them back for questioning. He wanted to know why they attacked the fort unprovoked and with such a large force.

Fuharra saluted before saying, "General Seth Medkar, I am here to report on our findings so far."

413

Seth nodded with approval and Fuharra relaxed. "The two ships to the north that didn't land are completely sunk. Anyone on board would have drowned by now. On the landed ships, we have thus far found no survivors, though we know that there are many Ettui still trapped in the lower decks. We can hear them banging on the wood with metal from their armor."

"Can we get them out?" asked Medkar.

Fuharra shook his head. "I don't think so. At least not before they starve to death. Although the ships' collapses have settled securely more than halfway down, removing the necessary planks to reach them quickly would cause greater collapse and risk our men as well. We'd have to start from the top and work our way down. That could take months, especially after losing so many men, sir. The elves mostly seem content to leave them there."

Seth nodded. He didn't want them to die that way, even though they were the enemy. Plus, he demanded answers. Yet he would not risk the lives of the surviving men, less than half of what their numbers had been yesterday, just to gather this information. These men had experienced fear to last them thirty lifetimes. He wasn't prepared to add more to that.

He then asked, "What about their leader, Kile? From the report Amber gave me late last night, she wasn't sure of his fate."

"As of now we have found nothing," Fuharra said. "We have searched all around the ship where you told us they fought, but found nothing. In my opinion, though, he could not have survived. Sharp pieces of wood blasted from the ships have wedged themselves in the coral everywhere under the water. If he fell there like you were told, then he must be dead. There is a slight chance, though, the tide could have taken him back toward Barbata. If it did, Darca would probably kill him for losing so many of his soldiers."

He had a point. Darca would not be pleased at the loss of two million Ettui. If Kile had survived, Barbata was no longer a haven for him. Landing there, he'd be as good as dead.

Seth nodded to Fuharra again. "Thank you. Continue your search for a couple more hours, then bring your team in for food and rest."

Fuharra saluted and headed back to the boats via the bridge still anchored to the first wall. Such a bleak report, thought Seth. He hoped that something good would come out of it. A clue of some kind that would help them decipher why this happened in the first place. It seemed from every report so far, though, that the answer would remain a mystery.

"How goes the search?"

Seth turned with a smile to see Eraddor, with Cerrapies by his side. He was so glad to see these two right now. Their contributions aided immensely in the defense of the fort. He doubted it would have gone half as well without them. Seth walked down a plank from the top of the wall to meet them on the ground.

"Nothing much to report, really. There are still Ettui trapped on the ships that we can't reach and Kile's body has gone missing. How about your mission?"

Eraddor replied, "The soldiers' families are safe. Divi's spell harmlessly passed over them. With only the barracks built over the storage room, they were the safest in the entire fort. It will be hard explaining to many of them that their loved ones perished in the battle."

"It is always the hardest part. They should be told, though, that their loved ones died earning the greatest victory ever recorded and their memory will forever be blazoned in history. How about your mission, brave blacksmith?"

Cerrapies cleared his throat and winced a little from a wound on his arm. He fascinated Seth because although they matched in age, the blacksmith had so much more energy than himself.

"All injured soldiers are being tended to by Thetalis and the remaining half-elves. We found none between what's left of the first and second walls. The Ettui had control of that area for too long, I'm afraid, before Divi arrived."

Seth nodded, further saddened at the bleak news, but understood how lucky they were to have won. Cerrapies was also right in saying that Divi's intervention changed the tide, if it was not the only reason for theur victory.

He asked, "How is Divi doing?"

"She is very exhausted, but she'll live," Cerrapies answered. "Tasi said he could feel her . . . lifeforce or something like that, so I guess that means she is recovering."

Seth heaved a sigh of relief. He remembered how Divi looked as they carried her from the tower right after the battle. He believed ghosts were less pale. She barely moved, making them fear they had lost her. Her eyes rolled to the back of her head. He had been in a few battles and seen many horrible things, but nothing compared to the blank gaze on Divi's face. He hoped to never see its like again.

"Someone must tell me when she regains her strength," he said. "She deserves our gratitude for what she did. We would not have succeeded without her."

Eraddor added, "We are most fortunate that she knew how to cast magic at all. Wherever she went, she seemed to grow up. This was not the same Divi that left this fort just a month ago."

"General Seth! General Seth!"

They all turned to see Tasi rushing up, almost out of breath. Something on his mind, though, made him forget his exhaustion.

"Tasi, my thanks again for your and Divi's arrival. We are forever in your debt. What can I do for you?"

"General, I have gone through every crevice of this fort, from the enemy ships to the south, up until the docks behind me to the north. Something is troubling. Where are the mages? I found no survivors and I can find no bodies. There had to be at least twenty-five if not fifty who arrived here a month ago."

The humans looked at each other, almost embarrassed. Seth, though, being the leader of the establishment, gave a deep sigh before telling Tasi the truth.

"The mages never participated in the battle. When we learned the Ettui were on their way, Sydis absolutely refused to stay here. They left yesterday morning, just moments before the Ettui ships landed."

If Eraddor had not agreed with Seth, the baffled Tasi might not have believed him.

"Thamalos told me that he had reported only one ship when he first announced their presence," the mage said. "Did they leave before or after the other ships became known?"

Eraddor answered, "They prepared the night before, and it wasn't until the morning they left that we saw more than one ship. In my opinion, the meetings shouldn't have lasted as long as they did. At times we made tremendous strides, but Sydis always seemed to disperse whatever hope was revived."

Tasi didn't want to believe his suspicions. Was it possible they knew about the odds and didn't inform the rest? His thoughts went to Sydis. Surely no other mage was capable of such a deviant act. Tasi knew that Sydis opposed Neeza on many decisions. Although he never voiced his disagreement in public, one could read his eyes easily enough. Yet what could he have possibly gained by intentionally dragging the meetings out?

Tasi considered. If Sydis did this on purpose, he almost certainly would be aware of the consequences. The backlash, especially from the humans, would be very strong.

417

As he thought further, though, how could anyone report his treachery if everyone on the fort island had been killed?

There had to be more to this. Mage hatred for the humans was great, but not so strong as to send thousands to their deaths. Sydis had nothing to fear about his actions from the mage end, however, because without a leader . . .

A look of horror crossed Tasi's face as he asked, "What day is it?"

Though confused, Seth said, "It is the fourth and last week of the summer moon."

He didn't know if he answered the mage's question or not because mages followed a different calendar. Mainland humans referred to the phases of the larger mother moon rather than any specific days. Yet, from the urgency on Tasi's face, he assumed the mage understood him.

"How quickly can we get a ship? It doesn't have to be a large one. Just one that will take us to Myyril at the quickest speed. Divi and I must leave."

His request perplexed the three humans.

Eraddor asked, "What is on you mind, young mage?"

Tasi sighed, a little frustrated. He didn't have time to answer such complicated questions. They wouldn't understand if he told them anyway.

Seth could see his impatience and said, "The waters around Fort Za are still cluttered with wood and metal that would prove hazardous for any ship. The soonest I could get something would probably be a couple days. Would it be wise to move Divi, especially after☐"

"She will have time to rest on the journey, Tasi replied. "It is of the most importance that we reach Myyril in five days' time."

Seth wondered what made it so important. Did Divi, now that she knew magic, have to receive something in Myyril in that time? Whatever the answers were, he would not get them from Tasi at this moment.

"I will speak to Thamalos before tonight. Perhaps the elves can spare a small ship from Lozela to transport Divi and yourself. They are better navigators and could get you there in the shortest amount of time." Seeing his answer appeased Tasi, he continued, "On that same note, though, at nightfall, we would like you to help us in purifying the land of the Ettui blood. Though Divi will not be able to participate, the men have requested your help, because of your significance in our victory."

Tasi nodded. "If that is what you desire, I will be there. Do you know where Levus went?"

Cerrapies said, "Last I saw him he said he wanted to spend some time alone. I still think this latest battle took a little out of him. Levus is no warrior. He's a hunter from a small village. I'm proud that he has lasted, but the burden he has taken on is great."

Tasi only replied, "Good. He should be alone."

Cerrapies had a hard time reading his tone, but the comment offended him a little. Tasi was the one who deserved to be alone, he thought, and not Levus. Levus helped Divi when no one else would after discovering her identity as a mage on Dyyros. It was Levus who had protected her since this journey started. Tasi obviously had some bitter feelings toward him, and it seemed that Divi stood in the middle of it, whether she knew it or not.

Tasi didn't think any further of his words as he went off to the Administration Building. The three men waited until he was out of view before they spoke again.

"He is a strange one," Seth mused. "I am grateful for his help, but there are times when I feel I can call him friend, and other times his demeanor can make it seem like we are enemies. Like he is trying to play both sides. That is a dangerous action."

Eraddor replied, "From what I know about Tasi, his major flaw is that he is overprotective of Divi. I am not certain if that is normal between teacher and student, but he, like Levus, would kill anything . . . or anyone who threatened Divi. I hate to say that we must keep our weary eyes on them both, despite their being our friends."

Seth nodded and Cerrapies remained quiet. He obviously had a different opinion on the matter, but there would be another time to quarrel over something so trivial.

Eraddor concluded, "If you will excuse me, gentleman. I will talk to Thamalos about this ship for Divi and Tasi and when the debris will be cleared."

He headed toward the docks, where Thamalos currently sat meditating on how to maintain the clearest communication possible with the elf-folk back in Lozela. Seth and Cerrapies strolled to the large eastern field, which was still cluttered and stained with various Ettui parts.

Seth said, "I only wish to know why. Why did the Ettui send such a force? We have done nothing to them. And why here? They could have easily sailed by us and headed straight for Lozela Minor. Even taking Mount Hrithgorn would have made more strategic sense as it would put them within two hundred miles of the Wood Elves without having to face an army. They'd have been far from any elf forces' interception. I don't believe Arionn's people could have driven such a mighty foe from their lands alone."

Cerrapies answered, "I think it is because the situation is much larger than you know. Tell me, as I was not present at all of the meetings this past month, nor did I have the right to be in many of them—what do you know about Lord Ulcinar?"

Seth replied truthfully, "Very little. His name was mentioned only sparingly and only in connection with Levus."

He didn't think that Seth would have known much, being stuck here on this fort. Ulcinar and his evil deeds might be considered ghost stories. He was no ghost, though, and Seth should understand exactly what they were dealing with.

Cerrapies said, "I know tonight is not the time, as tonight we mourn. Perhaps not tomorrow either, but before we leave, we must discuss Lord Ulcinar. The being practically took an entire city by himself when he invaded Tartus a few years back using his strange abilities. Scary thing was, he was obviously holding back. I barely survived two battles with him. What Divi did yesterday, he is possibly capable of more. If what this Amber says is true, and she fought Kile on the boats, then that is solid proof that Ulcinar and the Ettui are allies.

"I wish I could tell you exactly what they are up to. I know one thing for certain, though. It has something to do with that metal. The one that Levus' Moonsaber is made from. At first, I hated the idea of Levus carrying it, but now I think he is the only one who can and should."

Cerrapies talked about this Ulcinar as if he would be the destroyer of the world. If he was that serious of a threat, Seth thought for sure he would have at least heard something from the elf soldiers stationed here. Even though he didn't believe in all their talk, that didn't stop him from listening to them.

"You may have a point, Cerrapies. I saw Levus fight with it near the end of the battle. He seemed to gain powers that I have seen no man possess. I can see why this Ulcinar person would want to acquire as much of the metal as possible. If he is as powerful as you say, then it would give him powers to go unmatched."

Seth shivered at the thought, chilled to the bone. This Ulcinar sounded very much like the last dictator of Cordca, before the kings took over. He had used fear to gain power and tried to locate barbaric religious artifacts to attain more. That ended up being his downfall as the relics didn't provide the ancient protection that their stories had claimed. Yet such greedy acquisition seemed to be happening again, this time on Dyyros, the cradle of humanity. What possessed humans to do this? And why only humans? Were they, as a

421

race, doomed by fate to be this way? He truly didn't want to believe it. There were good people in the world, you just had to find them, and never let go of them.

Seth said, "Very well. In five days time, I will gather everyone and we can discuss this matter of Ulcinar. But as you said, tonight we mourn."

* * * * * *

Nightfall had fallen quickly over the remains of Fort Za. The area became near pitch black without the torchlight once scattered around the southern part of the island. Yet Seth, like everyone else, knew that the darkness tonight would only be temporary. A flame would soon burn here that would possibly be visible from Barbata.

He made sure that everyone finished their missions for the day early so they could participate. Most had come here. The half-elves were excused as they had to tend to the injured. Thetalis, though, was kind enough to represent his race. Seth had also excused Divi, for obvious reasons, and Amber, who kept guard outside her room. Levus joined the list of the excused as he found himself rather shaken by the whole ordeal and preferred to spend some time alone. Cerrapies and Eraddor stood on either side of Seth, Eraddor holding his bow at the ready. Thamalos led the elves near the southeastern remnants of the wall. Each had a cauldron of fire beside them. Only one person Seth could think of remained absent. Where was Tasi? The mage had said that he just needed to check something fast. What could it possibly be?

Tasi strode through the shattered hallways of the second floor, quite impressed about how well the western part of the fort known as "The Lair" looked compared to the

422

others. Perhaps it was newer and built better. He didn't really care about the reason, except that its condition had been the reason Seth offered it as the place where Divi could rest. With the exception of the storage room where the soldiers' families stayed during the battle, and which still housed the civilians and survivors, this area ended up being the safest to keep her without fear of further collapse.

He didn't want to obsessively check on Divi. Since he could feel her lifeforce, he knew she'd be okay. What got him concerned was Levus. When he spoke to Seth a few moments ago, the general explained how Levus found him and asked to be excused, a request which he granted. Tasi had to make sure that the boy wasn't anywhere near Divi. She would be very weak still and if he wanted, Levus could easily take advantage of her, something Tasi would never allow to happen.

He finally saw Amber, standing diligently in front of the door. Her legs looked tired as she leaned on the wall for support, but she would never let her guard down completely for one second so long as she had eyes. She knew Tasi approached even before he saw her.

"Aren't you supposed to be at the cleansing thing they are doing?"

"I had to check to make sure everything was okay," he said.

Amber laughed and asked, "Do you not trust me enough yet? Even after all we've been through? Nothing will get in here while I'm here."

Tasi nodded. He agreed that no enemy or assassin would get past her, but his worry was about a friend rather than a foe.

"Has Levus came by here lately? I haven't seen him all day and wanted to check on him too. You know, to make sure he's okay as well."

Amber sighed silently. So, his true reason for coming here became clear.

She said, "You are jealous of him."

"Just answer my question!"

"Yeah, he came by about an hour ago. Wanted to know how Divi was doing. I told him she was fine and sent him on his way. Probably going to the docks again. Mentioned how he was there all day."

Tasi nodded, eased a little by her report. Maybe she had him pegged. He was being a little selfish. With how many times she saved his life on Dragonia, why should he ever distrust her? He gave her a small smile and walked down the uneven floor.

Before he turned the corner, he stopped and turned around. "Thank you, Amber."

"No problem!"

It took a while, but she felt him finally beginning to trust her. Shame, really. For after tonight, if he found out, he might never trust her again. Amber smiled silently to herself. She would give them another half hour before it was time to send him back to his room.

General Seth started almost as soon as Tasi got there. He felt bad making everyone wait, but they didn't seem to mind. The elves were the only ones who appeared the slightest bit annoyed that he arrived late. Tasi didn't really care about their opinion. Elves were different in so many ways that he deemed it impossible to please them. He commended Eraddor and Divi for having something not many people had: the ability to put up with them. Besides, checking on Levus was the most important thing he'd needed to do tonight. With that accomplished and Amber on watch, he could now commence with this little business.

Seth started speaking. "Tonight, we come here to purify our lands. Ettui blood has flown freely this past day, and so as not to spoil the earth like the Ettui have spoiled theirs, let us bless the ground in fire. From its ashes, may the grass grow green again, and the glory return to this fort. To our soldiers whose remains we were unable to recover, your bones will not mingle with the enemy's and you shall see heaven while the Ettui will return to hell."

Seth's silence was the only signal that he had finished speaking. The elven archers dipped their arrows in the fires, setting them alight. Tasi, raised his hands, making a fireball. He personally thought this tradition silly. The elves had always taught that when Ettui blood touched the ground, unless purified it would be lost forever as useable land. There had never been any physical proof of this other than the Barbatan continent, and in his opinion, it was a poor example because it probably took years for such degradation to happen. Still, people are quick to do something if they think it protects their way of life.

On Eraddor and Thamalos' orders, the archers released their arrows. Tasi, in turn, unleashed the fireball from his hand. As they struck the ground, it burst into flames.

Seth certainly hoped that they had used sufficient fish oil to complete the task. All day he'd had many men catching the Opponion fish, whose oils were flammable despite being wet, and although they had caught many, he only prayed it enough to cover the entire southern portion of the island. At least they had enough fish meat to last them a solid month.

The archers fired their second wave of flame-laced arrows while Tasi released a third fireball. He couldn't hide his amazement at how quickly the fire spread across the landscape. If it continued at this pace, everything past the first wall except the Ettui vessels would be engulfed in flame in a couple minutes. They opted to leave the ships intact, per Seth's request. It met heavy opposition from the elves, but they eventually gave in under the agreement that they would revisit the decision in a years' time. Darca or any Ettui on

Barbata would be able to see it, even from so far away. Perhaps that was another reason Seth did this: to let the enemy know that they had failed. To Tasi, Seth didn't seem like the religious type who would believe in superstitions and such.

Tasi turned his head as almost everyone recited a chant of some kind. He wasn't sure if these words were universal, as the elves sounded like they were saying something completely different than the humans. They seemed to be praying to whatever gods they believed in. Seth and Cerrapies appeared to be the only two not saying anything, instead keeping their heads down in silence. Although Tasi knew about Cerrapies only because of Divi and Levus, he could tell that he had the soul of a warrior. After having to kill so many, Tasi imagined that these men had forsaken their gods, wondering whether a heaven existed or not.

His thoughts once again returned to one human: Levus. The boy from Dyyros who had stolen his Divi's heart was still not accounted for. Although others had seen him, he continued to be a mist to Tasi. He didn't think he'd be at the docks. What could he do there? After this ended, he would not rest until he discovered where the boy hid. Then he could sleep easy.

By now the entire island beyond the first wall burned, the flames' illumination eliminating any darkness that once presided there. With the second wall still mostly intact, little reason existed to worry the fire might spread to the innards of the fort. It would be allowed to burn until it could burn no more.

The end of the ceremony drew near. Tasi had to wait until Seth officially called it to a close before he could begin his last mission of the night before retiring: to find Levus.

* * * * * *

426

"I will have to go soon."

Levus ruffled the sheets, making a half-hearted effort to get up, but the desire was just not there. In fact, his desire was somewhere very different. He wished he could stay here all night. But he knew, at least for tonight, that would be impossible. Amber had bought them some time, but it needed to come to an end.

Levus' thoughts were interrupted as Divi's bare feet played with his. She looked so lovely in the bed. Moonlight reflected off the silver silk sheets, casting a soft bluish glow inside the room.

Divi said, "Stay for a few more minutes. Please."

She and Levus cuddled in each other's arms and kissed gently and often. Although she was still extremely tired, being with Levus gave her an extra vigor she didn't know she had. Her quick recovery after casting such a powerful spell surprised even her. She couldn't hide the joy that she did, though. Throughout this entire journey, she wanted to feel Levus' touch. That need had been satisfied for the past couple hours.

Levus lightly asked, "How mad do you think Tasi is going to be when he finds out about this?"

Divi had never really thought about Tasi until Levus brought him up just now. In her opinion, Tasi had nothing to say in this matter. She had made her choice. Tasi, as her teacher, had fulfilled most of his duty to her, though she knew he had some more to teach her along the way. Now that she knew magic, Tasi's role had him bound to her in a special way. Not one, however, in Divi's eyes, that would give him the power to tell her who she could and could not love. Yet she was dealing with age-old customs that she'd have to fulfill. Her life was about to change so much. She had not even considered this aspect when she asked Tasi to train her. There would be time to sort that out. Tonight would not be it.

"He will not find out," she said to Levus. "Amber has told me she will keep this secret from him. I know Tasi will go berserk if he discovered it. We don't need that now. This adventure is not over yet."

She could not have been more right, Levus thought. Many questions remained unanswered. What was Ulcinar up to? Had Kile survived the fall from the ship during his fight with Amber? Were these Dragonians that Divi was telling him about really friends willing to help them? What would the Ettui do to respond to this catastrophic failure?

A soft series of knocks came at the door. Both knew this as the signal. The purifying ceremony was almost finished, meaning time for Levus to get going. He didn't want to. He'd spent so long in an involuntary slumber, not even realizing that in his heart, the only thing he ever desired was Divi. Now that he had her in his arms again, he didn't want to let go. He knew, though, that he couldn't stay with her until Ulcinar's defeat. How close they were to achieving that, though, he wasn't certain.

Levus faced Divi and said, "I'm going to have to leave."

"I can't wait until we can do this without hiding," replied Divi.

"That day will come soon. I promise."

Levus and Divi exchanged one last long embrace. She knew that Levus meant what he said. Once Ulcinar was defeated, they could live together in peace. That alone would give her enough inspiration to defeat the dictator. She no longer feared that creature. Let him try and stop her now.

They ended their embrace as the moon continued to gshed heavenly light on the secret lovers.

About the Author

TOM ROGAL

Born and raised in northern Illinois. Graduated with Honors from Northern Illinois University in Communications in the Media Studies and English. History has always been a large interest as one can always learn from the mistakes and successes of the past. Primary areas of interest are Alexander the Great, The Greek and Roman Empires, Medieval times, and WWII.

A big sports fan and is very active athletically. Loves running, doing at least ten races a year. Also, an avid movie lover and can be found often in a theater.

The Saga Continues in . . .

BRINKS IN TIME:

SHROUDS OF DARKNESS

Book 3 of the Ulcinaric Conflict
Book four of the Brinks in Time series

Coming soon

For more information on the *Brinks in Time*
series, check out the website.
www.brinksintime.com

Be sure to check out and Like the Facebook page
at https://www.facebook.com/BrinksInTime for
updates.

APPENDIX A

PRONUNCIATIONS

Characters

- **Amber** -- am-bər
- **Bironn** – bir-rän
- **Cerrapies** -- sə-ˈrap-ēz
- **Corweig Vallance** -- kòr-wēg va-ləns
- **Cyp** -- kip
- **Cyprinus** – sī-prin-əs
- **Dakarius** – dak-kär-ē-əs
- **Darca** – där-kä
- **Diera** – dē-er-rä
- **Dinermar** -- di-nər-mär
- **Divi** -- dē-vē
- **Eraddor** – ir-rad-dòr
- **Firress** – fir-res
- **Firtarr** – fir-tär
- **Frey Sintar** – frā sin-tär
- **Fuharra** – fü-här-rä
- **Gelvia Sudin** – gel-vē-ə sü-din
- **Gionti** – jē-òn-tē
- **Girjinii** – jir-jē-nē
- **Herippi** – her-rip-pī
- **Hideon** – hid-ē-ən
- **Hiiminta** – hē-mēn-tä
- **Hirronisse** – hir-rōn-nēs

- **Jared Sintar** – jer-red sin-tär
- **Jarek Vullner** – jer-rek vəl-nər
- **Kazcum-hi** – käz-cüm hī
- **Kile Craslin** -- kī(ə)l kras-lin
- **Kremmos** – krem-mȯs
- **Lascedis** – las-cid-dis
- **Leeta** – lē-tä
- **Levus Sintar** – Lev-əs sin-tär
- **Marrva Triola** -- mär-vä trē-ō-lə
- **Merrah** – mir-rä
- **Mierena** – mir-rē-nə
- **Minat** – mī-nät
- **Neeza** -- nē-zah
- **Servion** -- sərv-ē-ən
- **Seth Medkar** – seth med-kär
- **Sydis** – sī-dis
- **Tasi** -- täsē
- **Tefferis** – tef-er-is
- **Tetoliis** – tet-ō-lis
- **Thamalos** -- tham-ä-lȯs
- **Thetalis** -- thet-ä-lis
- **Time Sage** – tīm sāj
- **Tyrrarin** – tī-rer-in
- **Ulcinar** -- əl-sin-är

Locations, Rivers, and Landmarks
- **Al'Huriman** – al' hər-ē-män
- **Barbata** – bär-bät-ä

432

- **Black Plains of Arltraii** -- blăk plānz of ahl-trā
- **Cordca** -- kȯrd-kä
- **Dragonia** – drag-ōnē-ə
- **Dyyros** – dī-rȯs
- **Fort Za** -- fȯrt zä
- **Garlock** – gär-läk
- **Ghrove** -- grōv
- **Gunimai Volcano** – gün-ä-mī väl-kä-nō
- **Gyyerlith** – jī-ər-lith
- **Isle of Time** – ī(-ə) of tīm
- **Lozela** – Lō-zel-ä
- **Mount Hrithgorn** -- mau̇nt rith-gȯrn
- **Myyril** – mī-ril
- **Porsita** -- pȯr-sit-ä
- **Rudann** – rüd-ȯn
- **Sardon** – Sär-dän
- **Sjvernii Bay** -- sɪv-ûrn-ī bā
- **Temple of Elements** – tem-pəl of e-lə-mənts
- **Tydos** – Tī-dȯs
- **Water Temple** -- wȯ-tər tem-pəl

Races
- **Elves** -- elvz
- **Ettui** – et-tü-ī
- **Dragonians** -- drag-ōnē-ins
- **Half-elves** – haf elvz
- **Half-mages** – haf māj
- **Humans** -- hyü-məns
- **Mages** -- māj

433

Dragons and Beasts

- **Borrifrit** -- bȯr- i̦ frēt
- **Fafcul** – fäf- kül
- **Fenrise** – fen-rēs
- **Fryyup** – frē-əps
- **Gerritonnee** – jer-rit-tōn-ā
- **Gillantis deet** – gil-ant-iss dēt
- **Graysclah** -- greɪ-sklɑ
- **Leviadon** – lev-ī-ä-dän
- **Nitklarii** – nit-klär-ī
- **Oliser** – al-is-ər
- **Suikan** -- su-ē-kĭn
- **Tiiamite** – tī-ä-mīte
- **Titarin** – tī-ter-in
- **Ulkitmores** -- əlk-ət-mȯrs
- **Verritiss** – veh-ree-tis
- **Zazzarat** – zä-zer-rät

APPENDIX B

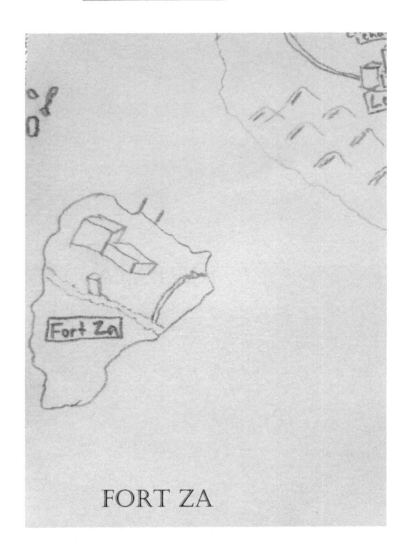

FORT ZA

BARBATA

EASTERN BARBATA, FOUR FORKS TO THE WEST

DRAGONIA:

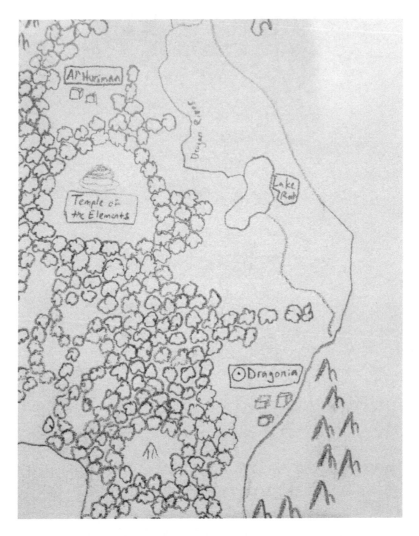

DRAGONIA AND TEMPLE OF ELEMENTS (TIIAMITE'S LAIR)

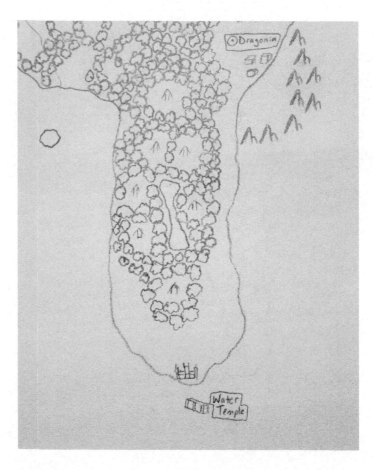

AMBER'S CAMPS AND WATER TEMPLE
(LEVIADON'S LAIR)

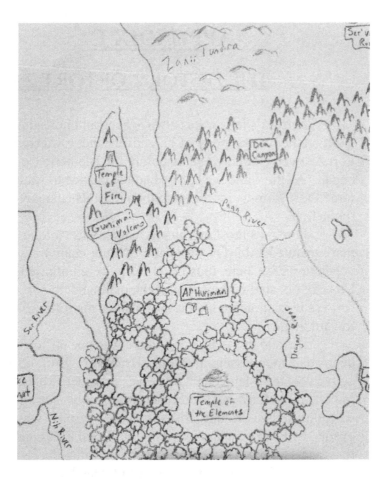

NORTHERN MOUNTAINS,
GUNIMAI VOLCANO (FAFCUL'S LAIR),
AND AL'HURIMAN

APPENDIX C

THE HISTORY OF FORT ZA

Fort Za's legacy has always been an interesting one. Built on the highest point of Farzellii Island, it was renamed Fort Za twelve hundred years before the Ulcinaric Conflict began. As the Time Sage, I've had the chance to watch this famed fort from its inception to the fall of its enamored reputation.

Fort Za's most prominent feature was its long wall that separated a third of the island. As not many trees or vegetation grew here, most food stuffs were imported from Lozela. Located within sight of the mainland, this island fortress held strategic importance against any Ettui assault toward them.

Despite this distinction, there was one elf fortification deemed as more essential: Mount Hrithgorn. Built on an active volcano island chain, the elves considered it an impenetrable fortress. Protected with the most current weapons to date, Mount Hrithgorn's sole purpose was to evade any Ettui attack planned on the Wood Elves and their only accessible coast directly east from Hrithgorn.

Fort Za, at the time of the Ettui Island Wars, only had elves stationed there. As the conflict continued and became bloodier, the elves allowed humans to help in its defense. During the conflict, Fort Za repeled numerous attacks, most unable to reach the famed first wall. With nearly eighty percent of its defenders being archers, it left invading ground troops at a disadvantage. It also had seven old, but serviceable, cannons to be used against projectile weapons or assault vehicles.

Fort Za, along with numerous other islands, were supposed to provide a ring of protection against the Ettui,

440

who themselves were also trying to take over islands in the ocean separating the mainland from Dragonia.

The Battle of Mount Hrithgorn was effectively the final battle of the war, with the Ettui losing most of their high-valued capital ships due to the volcanic eruption. Although the victory won the elves the war, it lost them what they thought could never be infiltrated.

After the Ettui Island Wars ended, Mount Hrithgorn was in shambles. The elves thought about rebuilding it (indeed, repairs had commenced for years after the war), but the emergence of the Garchai persuaded the elves to abandon the once proud facilities at Hrithgorn.

With that, Fort Za became the newest impenetrable fortress. The defenses planned for a rebuilt Mount Hrithgorn went to Za instead. New, more powerful cannons, developed later in the war that helped make elf warships formidable, replaced the old cannons. They raised the total from seven to forty-three, creating an effective kill zone against any enemy artillery vehicles, which didn't allow them to get within range of the first wall. This meant an enemy needed to break the wall with ground troops, a nigh impossible task with the magnitude of archers available.

The walls were strengthed, making it harder to be penetrated with even the newest invention of the time, called bombs. They upgraded the dock so that more modern warships could port there instead of the shallower ones both armies used. Keeping a ship docked at all times, it forced the enemy to use a smaller craft if they decided to attack from behind.

Because of the great help the humans provided, they made a deal with Cordca's leadership about stationing men there permanently. Although, this would not take place for another hundred years, this nearly doubled the troops living here year-round.

For the first hundred and twenty years after the Ettui Island Wars, Fort Za lived up to its reputation. One stray

441

Ettui ship lost during the war, attacked with two thousand soldiers and three siege towers. The towers never made it within two hundred yards (the edge of the kill zone) and the Ettui troops lost more than half their numbers before they reached the first wall.

News of the dominant defensive success spread quickly throughout the mainland. Fort Za was gloated as having a wall no army would ever break through. Defense of the elf lands were no longer a concern by sea. The elves even allowed the commandante to be a human.

Some say the fort's fall happened on 1 AU. In reality, it happened two hundred years after the Ettui Island Wars.

When enemy attacks were so small and spread out, the elves became convinced the Ettui could never threaten the mainland again. Financial support began to dwindle. The prized cannons that enemy armies feared began to rust due to a lack of maintenance. Many broke as they continued to use them for training and war exercises. During tha Battle of Fort Za in the Ulcinaric Conflict, only three of the cannons could still fire. Although most of the commandantes requested to repair the equipment, as the elves were the only financial backers of Fort Za, they fell on deaf ears. The elves saw little purpose in making these fixes, believing their archer units could repel whatever enemy approached them.

The silence of the cannons was heard by the enemy as well. Darca continually sent scouts to many of the remaining elf forts, with the hopes of one day striking back at their enemy. Although he didn't have the men or ships to do so after the war, he always kept Fort Za on his radar. Unlike the rest of Gyyerlith, Darca knew the true state Fort Za was in.

Since the fort was barely being used militarily, it began to take on other responsibilities, keeping its name and its reputation relevant.

Because of Fort Za's past as being unbreakable, it decided that every five years, representatives of the races would meet in what became known as the Summit of the Six. It involved the Elves of Lozela, the Mages of Myyril, the half-elves of Desris, and the three human kingdoms (Cordca, Rudann, and Garlock). Designed as a neutral spot for the races to try and hash out squabbles, they rarely did anything to solve them. Some were done in days. The longest was a month. Despite its ineffectiveness over the years, it continues to this day.

As time went on, the humans posted here began missing their families as their term of service was a minimum of ten years, though most would be there for twenty to thirty. To the long living elves, this wasn't a problem. Also, since they were so close to home, it was never an issue. The commandante, to allow himself more say in matters concering the fort, changed his title to general. He convinced the elves to allow families the option to visit every three years. Another tradition that to this day continues.

During the Elf Games of 125 BU, the second event took place at the fort, the one and only time Fort Za hosted an event for the prestigious games.

It became the staging point for the invasion of Barbata in 53 BU after the Night of Long Arrows the year prior, which led to the disastrous Battle of the Four Forks. The military blunder of the campaign led to at least the mages seeing the extent the fort had fallen from the fabled stories. Neeza voiced his concerns, which resulted in restrictions of any foreign dignitaries touring the fort, even during the Summit of the Six. The human general, Clavis Mertore, didn't want word to get out of its disarray, moreso because he knew it would be blamed on him.

It wasn't until 40 BU that Seth Medkar, a veteran of the Battle of the Four Forks and stationed at the fort for a few years prior, was appointed the generalship at the age of 28. His promotion was significant not only for what he would end up doing in the future, but in also finding ways to keep

Fort Za's deteriorating morale become as strong as a sturdy castle.

Although they couldn't get the funds to repair artillery for defense, he used other ways to make the fort's defenses last. He created a bricklayer division being as he received a full company of soldiers who were not good with weapons, formerly architects and builders. This played with little success during the Battle of Fort Za, but in principle, given they didn't need to have any of the materials imported, it allowed them to have a decent repair unit for the famed wall.

He disallowed the soldiers from using the nearby coral reef to buy things from the merchant boat that came once a month. Apart from keeping the area around the fort beautiful, the hard coral acted like jagged stones against wooden ships. It was an unpopular decision, but one that played a huge role on the attack during the Ulcinaric Conflict.

He restored having set routines instead of letting the soldiers go sometimes full weeks without drills. He tried making catapults since the elves wouldn't give him the materials to fix the cannons, using the wood that was supposed to be designated for arrows. Once the elves discovered why he was requesting the extra wood, they halted shipments until Seth went back to using them for their intended purpose.

He commissioned a fountain to be placed in the courtyard, with two flagpoles: One for Cordca and one for Lozela. He hoped this would reinstill some national pride by both nations. He increased the soldier capacity from twenty-three thousand to thirty thousand, which would be the troops available at Fort Za the day of the battle. He also improved the barracks, making newer ones for increased troops and improving the previous ones. When Cordcan ships came with the families, he had them bring food stuffs from home, a nice change from the almost entirely elvish diet. This arrangement was possible by his friendship with the Aldaran line of kings.

All these changes were improving morale and quality of life for all those stationed there. And little did they know, they were going to need it soon.

On Barbata, Ulcinar and Darca discussed potential targets. They were looking at military value and the impact taking that target would mean. The primary objective, however, was choosing a location that would draw the elves to retake it or for them to mobilize coastal defenses closest to the taken island. They narrowed it down to three: Hiierland, Mount Hrithgorn, and Fort Za.

Hiierland was a tiny island, its location unknown to the Ettui. It served as a place the elf leadership could go to if Lozela was ever compromised. Militarily, it had only five hundred elvish troops, making it the lightest guarded fortress. The problems here were many. For starters, they didn't know exactly of its location, only that it existed. The castle's location at the top of the highest point meant the army would have to attack uphill the entire way, with only one way up through a narrow path. By using boulders to roll down the path and arrows, the five hundred soldiers would make it feel like fifty thousand. Plus, estimated to be eight hundred miles from the Lozela coast, the loss of the island wouldn't bring the elven response they were looking for.

Mount Hrithgorn, militarily, was still an important set of islands. It was the only islands within striking distance of the Wood Elves. An assault here would definitely draw a response from the elves. If they took the islands, the fortifications alone would keep any elf forces at bay for a long time. This location presented its own set of unique problems, however. The Garchai, even though losing many when Neeza and Orznaii both penetrated the base for Valendri's Relic, still had a strong grasp. Ulcinar certainly had the means to stop the Garchai, but the normal Ettui soldier wouldn't stand a chance against them. Orznaii and his group were specially trained. They were prepared. They would need to clear the islands of the Garchai, which would cost many of their troops. Plus, it would not be killing elves to get it. To Darca, clearing the Garchai would almost be a gift to the elves, who had to desert the fortess because of them.

In the end, Fort Za was chosen, especially after hearing a final report. On the negative side, it had the most volume of troops, meaning it would result in a heavy toll of life. The first wall was indeed strong and would need massive artillery to destroy it. On the plus side, however, the famed fort's strength had deteriorated more than anyone imagined. With almost all their cannons broken and nothing to replace them, it meant they could get artillery within striking distance of the first wall. Taking Fort Za would put them within view of the mainland, which would certainly result in the elves mobilizing forces at Lozela Minor to defend against an invasion. More importantly, the loss of Fort Za would be a psychological blow felt throughout the entire mainland. Za was the new impenetrable fortress touted heavily by the elves. If occupied, the morale of the humans, elves, and mages would take a massive hit.

To ensure the island fell, Ulcinar convinced Darca to send seventy percent of his forces on Barbata, nearly one and a half million soldiers. The Dark Lord would also provide some unique cannons he acquired from one of the other Times he once visited. Finally, he would place in charge of the operation his most trusted general, Kile Craslin. Darca, putting his trust in Ulcinar, approved the plan and began repairs on the eight ships that would be used in the assault. These ships were built thanks to Ulcinar providing detailed plans and by using slaves and political enemies from Dyyros, who were subsequently killed after the ships' completion.

With the target now selected and the troops being trained and assembled, all Ulcinar needed was the right time to order the attack.

After the failed attack by the allies in the Thorii Palace invasion, which eventually led to Divi and her friends seeking me, Ulcinar realized that the cards were being laid out perfectly. The Summit of the Six was meeting days after the retreat, thus representatives from all the races would be assembled in the same location. Not only that, but it fell on the approximate time frame that the human families would be visiting the fort. These events coinciding happened only once every fifteen years. They could maximize the loss of life for the allies in this strike. Thankfully for Ulcinar's cause, Darca's efficiency enabled them to have the assault army ready at a moment's notice. The only delay would be the final repairs to the ships, which would take at least three weeks to complete. That was acceptable. He had an inside man that could drag things out if he needed.

After analyzing the battle, I was impressed how Ulcinar planned the attack. He organized it so there was, in my opinion, only one possible way the Ettui could have lost: Divi. And I am certain that not even the Dark Lord took into account what she was capable of.

Fortune smiled on Gyyerlith that day. Divi, just before she came to see me, didn't even know magic. Back home, nearly all ridiculed her for it. She learned only because of love. Had it not been for that connection, Fort Za might not exist now. Even more importantly still, Myyril would have been very different. Funny how things change, and how one discovers the true strength of a person when they previously thought them weak.

That is why no one should ever completely distance themself from people they know who are good. I have seen far too often anger cause immeasurable rifts. Like Divi, you never know when that person will become important in your life. That is the beauty and sometimes horror of being a Time Sage. I get to watch it happen repeatedly throughout history, frustrating no matter when I see it. People don't realize that what vexes them means little in totality. There is no such thing as perfection in life, only our idea of what perfection is to be. Everyone makes mistakes, even the good people. Time Sages can, on rare occasion, make them. I have made some in my time, not too long ago, actually. . . well, that is for another time.

This concludes my history of Fort Za, as well as what we can all learn from it. Although continuing to be an active military installation, the destruction caused hindered its usefulness. Three of the Ettui ships still stand, phantoms of their former glory. Their bridges stayed connected to original sections of the remaining first wall. Divi's role in the defense is now legendary, the only time in current history where the magic of the Myyrilian gods was used. The challenge is, will others listen to what history says and wants us to remember? I know for certain I don't forget. Will you? Time will tell.

APPENDIX D

The brief history behind *Memories of Merrah*

This tells the sad last story of Merrah, the wife of Firtarr, the half-mage who led the first and only rebellion against the mages to this point. Being his wife, she attained a status of high respect even though her involvement was minimal, serving as a doctor to the wounded early on.

Half-mages have always been considered inferior by pureblood mages once humans and mages started breeding with each other around 1000 BU, not long after trading began between the two races. It angered their gods and so the mages, led by the Kittara, secluded them to an island far away on the other side of Dyyros, on what would become Tydos.

The rebellion started in 798 BU. He recruited half-mages who had yet to be named and registered, thus making them ghosts in the system. After many initial and shocking victories, they grew bolder. Their numbers also increased dramatically, allowing Firtarr to take greater risks. After the abduction and slaying of a mage councilman, Myyril finally took notice as them being a threat.

The difficulty for the mages was they couldn't send a large force to subdue the growing threat. They only had one ship, so reinforcements couldn't be supplied for at least a week after the initial troops landed. Plus, their military training didn't prepare them for guerilla warfare, which was the rebel's mode of attacking. Unlike human armies, half-mages knew exactly where to hit a mage to get a quick kill.

Merrah eventually tried to stop her husband as she had a horrible feeling the mages would one day punish them, but he was becoming a legendary figure with the half-mages for his courage to go against their oppressors. The rebellion tore families and friends apart. Merrah herself was left nearly alone as many people she loved became hardcore rebels.

She finally convinced her husband to pass the reins when she told him she was pregnant with their first child. Firtarr decided to get the members of the rebellion together at a secluded abandoned cottage in a large area known as the Ghrove to share his intent. Unfortunately, a spy in his ranks overheard the location, which was also the perfect spot for an ambush.

Firtarr never got the chance to tell his troops as the attack started prior to the meeting's start.

In 794 BU, in what became known as the Battle of the Ghrove, the rebellion was crushed by the mages and everyone who was at the cottage was executed in the famous garden the Ghrove was known for. Three hundred half-mages fell that day, nearly two hundred to executions. The mages buried them in unmarked graves, not even leaving markers to act as tombstones. Incredibly, florets of flowers grew only in the spots where the dead were buried, a phenomenon unexplained to this day.

Many feared to come here afterwards as the Tydosians knew the mages were watching this place, but not Merrah. She came everyday, at the same time her husband was executed to sit in the garden and mourn. Merrah, after coming day after day, praying for her fallen husband and the rest that gave their lives for their freedom, disappeared never to be seen again. They say she fell into such grief, questioning whether it was worth losing people she cared about because of the conflict. It led to her losing friends, family, and the ones she loved the most. They were gone, and yet she was still alive.

Many believe she committed suicide, while others say she left Tydos to live among the humans, far away from the crushing memories of her homeland. No one knows the fate of her child either as she was eight months pregnant when she disappeared.

SONGS COMMEMMORATING MERRAH

This was one of two songs written for Merrah. The other categorized her role as the strong wife supporting her legendary husband. It goes on to say that "her fire as fueling Firtarr's courage". This one is more light-hearted, never once touching on the rebellion except near the end. Memories of Merrah, on the other hand, focuses on the sad fate of Merrah and the rebels after the ambush.

Memories of Merrah is interpreted in many ways by the Tydosians.

1. The pacifists say it is to remind themselves that actions have consequences and that sometimes, there are casualties, many of them innocent. Although they are not 100% opposed to one day being free, they prefer to do so in a way that would cost the minimal of Tydosian lives

2. The militant factions and Paladinship candidates see Merrah and all the men and women who died during the ambush as martyrs. They use it to show that one day their suffering will end and that no matter how many will fall, that their freedom is worth it.

3. The general populace interpreted it as a lesson that one shouldn't hold on to the past as that only reminds one of the pain and sorrow, opting for forgiveness instead of anger because life is better not being angry or hating someone.

APPENDIX E

The Battle of Fort Za: Course of Battle

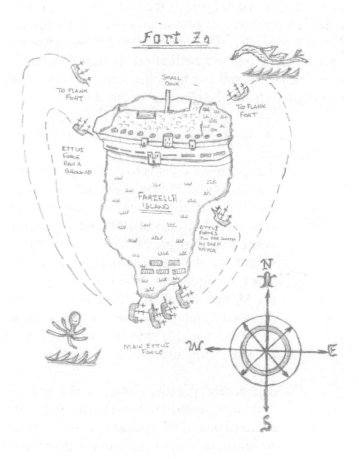

Start of the attack (Main Gate)

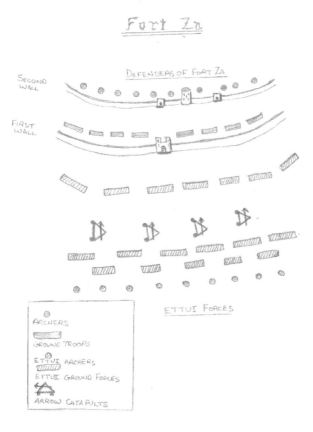

Ettui bridge attack/retreat of Fort Za defenders

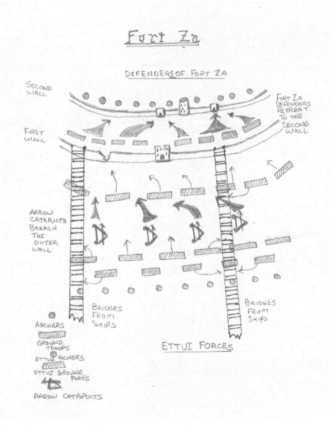

Fort Za

DEFENDERS OF FORT ZA

SECOND WALL

FORT ZA DEFENDERS RETREAT TO THE SECOND WALL

FIRST WALL

ARROW CATAPULTS BREACH THE OUTER WALL

BRIDGES FROM SHIPS

BRIDGES FROM SHIPS

ARCHERS

GROUND TROOPS

ETTUI ARCHERS

ETTUI GROUND FORES

ARROW CATAPULTS

ETTUI FORCES

Even in your darkest hours, as long as you have one good friend, then you are never alone.

Made in the USA
Monee, IL
14 August 2021

74927032R00252